# Starhawk

## Tanya Parr

PublishAmerica
Baltimore

© 2006 by Tanya Parr.
All rights reserved. No part of this book may be reproduced, stored in a retrieval system or transmitted in any form or by any means without the prior written permission of the publishers, except by a reviewer who may quote brief passages in a review to be printed in a newspaper, magazine or journal.

First printing

At the specific preference of the author, PublishAmerica allowed this work to remain exactly as the author intended, verbatim, without editorial input.

All characters appearing in this work are fictitious. Any resemblance to real persons, living or dead, is purely coincidental.

ISBN: 1-4241-3629-6
PUBLISHED BY PUBLISHAMERICA, LLLP
www.publishamerica.com
Baltimore

Printed in the United States of America

# Dedication

This book is dedicated to my mother Margaret Eileen Parr. You may be gone, but you will never be forgotten as long as I live. Before you died you asked me how I would get by and if I would follow my dreams. I've done that and I owe it all to you for believing in me. I love you mom. Thank you.

# Acknowledgements

I want to thank my friends the Ellingtons and the Dunnavents for supporting me while I worked on my books. Though I was absent minded at times, and talked to myself a lot, you never had me locked up. You put up with my talking about my characters all the time as if they were really there. You even dealt with me when I scared myself with some of the weird creatures I created.

# Prologue

**Spring 2797**

Saitun Katmen reviews the holo-tape that he's just made for his daughter Leyla. He decides that there is nothing more that he can add that will lessen the initial sorrow that she will suffer in the coming months, but there was no other way to keep her safe.

Placing the tape in a special compartment in the vid-com center, he punches in a day and time for the tape to be played within the next two weeks. He had to make sure that her initial reaction would keep his enemies off guard. Finishing, he leaves the comm center and makes his way through the house, stopping at the door to Leyla's bedroom. The door silently slides open and he silently walks in to stand over her bed. Watching her sleep, he slowly bends down and gently kisses her forehead, before stepping back. She stirs, but doesn't waken. Thanks to the sleep mist that their A.I. unit administered an hour ago, she wouldn't wake until morning. As he turns to leave, he notices the picture beside her bed and carefully picks it up. He smiles at the images of his mate and daughter taken twenty-five years earlier, just four years before his mate's death. He never looks at the box that holds the last images and voice of his mate. If he were to look upon her or hear her voice, he couldn't leave and do what he must this day.

Gently he runs a finger over the image of his mate and whispers, "Watch over her while I'm gone Aeneka my love. Give her your wisdom, strength, and courage for what is to come. Help her to understand what is right and just in what she must soon do." He replaces the picture carefully and takes one last look at his daughter before leaving the room for what he knows will be the last time. The door closes silently behind him and he walks into his own room seconds later. Picking up his bag, he quickly leaves the room again without looking around. His memories of this room and this house were deeply planted within his mind and would never leave him.

Going back through the house, he enters his den and goes to the old fashioned bookcase on the far side of the room and pushes a hidden button. The bookcase slides open to reveal the entrance to a secret tunnel. Before entering the tunnel, he looks around the room to make sure that everything was in place to look like he had left in a hurry. He then walks through the door and goes down the tunnel and down a flight of stairs that leads to an underground launch site.

Before going to his ship, he goes over to a computer console set into one of the walls and types in a set of commands that could not be changed once they began. When that's done, he goes to his ship and prepares it for takeoff.

Once it's ready he goes to check out the second ship in the hanger, making sure that when it was needed there would be no problems. That done he returns to his own ship. After checking for local air traffic to cover his departure, he launches his ship. Once his off Earth and past her moon, he sets a course for Diode, one of Saturn's many moons.

As he gets farther and farther away from Earth, he hopes that he is doing the right thing. Leyla was very impulsive, and with out a little guidance, she was likely to get herself into plenty of trouble. Though she could handle most problems that came up, if there was something that she wasn't sure of she would ask for help or advice from someone that she could trust. He only hoped that any trouble she came across wasn't anything she couldn't handle with or without the help of their friends.

# Chapter I

**Fall 2797**

Leyla Katmen enters the house that she has lived in all her life, and goes to its Comm center. "Sarah, on-line please."

"Yes Leyla?"

"I need to make a call that can't be monitored. Please scramble the call and track any attempts to trace it."

"Who do you wish to call?"

"Thayer Starhawk."

Several lights blink on and off quickly before the connection is made. A man's face appears on the holo-screen in front of Leyla. His hair is long and black with a streak of silver on the right side that starts at his temple. His eyes are a light shade of green set in his strong hawk-like features of dark coppery beige.

"Starhawk here."

"Thayer, I need to see you. Can you come over right away?"

"Leyla! What in the world is going on? I had a message from Logan when I got home a few minutes ago, telling me that the President's security team is getting ready to pay you and me both an unpleasant visit."

Leyla looks down at her hands and says quietly, knowing that he will be furious with her. "I broke into the patrols mainframe…"

"You did…WHAT?! Leyla, I told you not to do anything like that. You know that they monitor any inquiries to the mainframe."

"I know that Thayer. But I got the information and it...Thayer, someone tried to kill my father just before he left. They..."

Sarah interrupts her. "Leyla, someone is attempting to break through the scramble. As far as I can tell it's a government system."

"Thayer, please! I need your help. Please come, there isn't much time left." she pleads.

"All right Leyla. Let me finish up here and I'll be over. I'll use the transporter and be there in a couple of seconds." A pounding starts at his door and Thayer frowns, checking the outside monitor. Seeing Earth Security officers he curses vividly.

"Thayer what is it? What's happening?"

"Leyla, end transmission and have Sarah prepare your transporter." Just then there is a loud explosion and the monitor goes blank.

"Thayer!! Sarah, what happened?!" she screams and jumps up from her seat.

"I'm not sure Leyla. There's no response to my attempts at reconnection. It's as if the unit no longer exists."

Leyla notices the confusion in the automated voice. Closing her eyes she concentrates on Thayer and pulls his image into her mind. Making contact she gasps and begins to shake. Thayer is in serious physical danger and hurt badly. His apartment is a wreak and his computer unit is a charred mess. Using all of her concentration, she teleports him to her home. When Thayer appears in front of her, he is on his knees with his hands behind his back.

No longer feeling the unbearable pressure on his arms, Thayer looks up and is surprised to see Leyla standing there in front of him. He is also surprised to see that he is no longer in his apartment.

\* \* \*

Thayer stares at Leyla as she tends to his cuts and bruises. Leyla is practically holding her breath waiting for him to ask her how he had gotten there. She finishes tending to him and starts putting away the supplies before he says anything.

"How did I get here Leyla? I know that I was no where near my transporter, and I'm pretty sure that it was destroyed along with my computer."

She puts the last of the first aid supplies away, then takes a deep breath. Slowly releasing it, she turns to face him. Though it's difficult, she looks him in the eye. Unable to maintain eye contact she looks down at her hands and takes another deep breath before answering him. "I teleported you here myself." She looks up at him and then away again.

Thayer continues to stare at her for several seconds. He thinks back to ten minutes before, when he was still in his apartment being held by the E.S. He remembers feeling a tingling coming over him seconds before he found himself in Leyla's comm center.

"You're a mind toucher!" he exclaims accusingly. Not sure if he was angry with her for not telling him or with himself for not knowing.

Leyla having gotten up the courage to look at him, watches the expressions that cross his face. The one that disturbs her the most is the look of disgust. She turns away from him so that he can not see her tears.

"No Thayer. I'm not a mind toucher, not in the way that you obviously mean it. After all that we've been to each other, you should at least know that much about me." Deciding that he needed to know just what his words in that disgusted tone had done to her, she turns back to face him, letting him see the tears for the hurt and pain that they were, and that he had caused. "I'm a telepath yes, but I would never use my abilities to hurt others. Not like those that work for the President."

Thayer watches the tears running down her cheeks and tries not to let them affect him. She was right about them meaning a lot to each other, and that he should know that she would never hurt anyone. If nothing else, she would use her talents to help others, like she had helped him. Sighing heavily, he looks away from her ashamed of how he had reacted. He had no right to act the way he had, with her or anyone else.

"You're right, I do know that much about you. All I can say in my own defense is that it just came as a shock to me. It also hurts that you never told me about it before, or how strong your abilities are."

Leyla wipes away the tears and takes a shuddering breath before walking back over to him and slowly reaching out to lightly touch his arm. "Thayer." she says his name softly and waits for him to face her before continuing. "If I had told you before we really got to know each other the way we do now, you would have turned away from me and any friendship that was developing, without really giving us a chance. I just watched several expressions cross your face, and none are ones that I ever wish to see again when you look at me."

Reaching up just as slowly as she had reached out to him, Thayer lightly caresses her cheek with the back of his fingers. "I'm sorry Leyla. They weren't directed at you. Give me some time to get use to the idea. I'm sure that..."

Just then several alarms go off throughout the house and Leyla rushes from the room with Thayer following a little slower because of his hurt ribs.

"What's wrong Sarah? Why all the alarms?"

"There are a number of hostels approaching from several directions. They'll be here in twelve minutes. They're heavily armed."

"Damn! They're here sooner than Logan figured they would be. We need to get out of here now Leyla. They won't stop to ask questions and if they get hold of us, they won't be very nice."

She looks at him and then around the room before nodding her agreement. She had known for months that this day would come, but not so soon. "Sarah, begin transferring all data to the Terra Delta, along with your complete memory systems."

Lights start to flash all over the computer system throughout the house and within a few minutes everything that has been stored in the computer's base memory has been transferred, and the system is completely empty.

"The transfer is complete Leyla. I'll see you on the Terra Delta."

The last of the computer's lights blink out as Leyla and Thayer step into the hall. "Go to my father's den, I'll meet you there in a minute. There are a few things that I need to get from my room and then we can leave." She runs down the hall without waiting for him to agree or not.

Rushing into the bedroom, she grabs a tote-all from the luggage shelf and picks up the pictures on the night-stand. Going to the closet, she grabs a few atmosphere control suits and puts them in the bag over the pictures. Walking over to her desk, she picks up her mother's special vid-diary and places it carefully into the bag. Taking one last look around the room, she quickly leaves and goes to her father's den.

Thayer looks around from his position at the window as she enters the room and quickly walks over to her. "We have to go now. They're just down the street and will be here in about five minutes. If we can reach Logan, he can arrange to get us off the planet."

"We don't have to worry about that or endangering Logan. Sarah should already have the Terra ready to go. Follow me." Going over to the bookcase, she pushes the hidden button. The shelves slowly slide open to reveal the hidden passageway to them. Leyla quickly leads the way down the passage with Thayer close behind her. When they reach the bottom of the stairway they can hear a series of explosions coming from the house above them. Thayer stops and looks behind them.

"What the hell was that?" he shouts to be heard over the loud rumbling.

Leyla takes his hand and pulls him towards the waiting ship. "I'll explain later. We don't have that long before all of this is destroyed too!" They run up the ship's ramp and as soon as the door starts closing behind them Leyla calls out, "NOW Sarah!!"

Even as they make their way to the front of the ship, it lifts off and enters a tunnel off to the right. The ship just makes it into the tunnel as a series of explosions destroys the launch site and dirt begins to fall into the tunnel. Leyla and Thayer reach the control room just as the ship emerges from the tunnel entrance. Taking the pilot's seat, Leyla types out commands to get them away from the area and out of Earth's atmosphere, before they can be tracked from their departure point. Once that's done she sits back and lets out the breath that she had been holding. "Sarah, monitor all areas and frequencies for any E.S. fighters or patrols that may be following us."

"Already doing so Leyla. The house and everything have been totally destroyed as planned. They will not be able to get any information from the remains that were left."

"Thank you Sarah." she turns her chair and looks at the computer's wall camera. "There wasn't any damage done to Cassie's home or the one on the other side of us was there?"

"They received minor damage, a few broken windows, and maybe a few broken fixtures inside from all the shaking, but otherwise the destruction was well contained to only our property."

"All right. We'll be in the nutro-center if anything should happen." she says turning her seat to face Thayer before standing and walking over to him. Taking his hand, she leads him to the nutrition center and nods to one of the seats, indicating that he should sit down. She makes them each a drink and passes him his as she sits down across from him. Taking a sip from their glasses, they begin to relax for the first time in the past half hour, since their lives were so rudely and undeniably changed.

"Okay Leyla, start explaining what went on back there. Why was it necessary to destroy everything? What else did you do besides get into their computers? I counted no less than five teams of Earth Security approaching the house. That was just too many for a simple break-in to the mainframe." he tells her setting his glass on the table and slowly turning it in circles.

Leyla takes a swallow of her drink and then sets her glass on the table. "First let me explain about my father. He was acting unusual just before his disappearance. Getting coded messages from someone outside the Federation. He was having secret meetings with someone at odd hours of the day and night. I'm not sure who it was, but I'm pretty sure that it was someone connected with the Earth Security Council. Shortly after his disappearance, I was working in the comm center when a holo-tape started playing. In it my father told me not to believe anything that the government had to tell me about his sudden disappearance. He said that he was going on a special mission for the Federation, and he would contact me as soon as he could. When I didn't hear from him in the time he had specified, I contacted his commanding officer. She told me that he never arrived for his briefing on the mission. Shortly after that I was contacted by a man named Peterton, with the Security Council. He told me that my father's ship was found on Diode, but that his body was burnt beyond recognition. They sent me the few things that they said had been found at the crash site. When I saw what they sent me, and the condition they were in, I realized…"

The sudden buzzing of an alarm interrupts her and Sarah's voice comes over the ship's intercom system. "Leyla, we have a Security cruiser coming up on us at high speed. They are demanding that we disengage all engines and come to a stop or they will open fire."

"Could they have tracked us from Earth when we left?"

"It's possible, but they would have had to check four other shuttles. Luckily when we left the launch site, I was able to use those four to cover our own departure point. It's been nearly an hour since we left, so they've probably already checked at least two of the others if not all of them."

"I was hoping that we would have a little more time." she says to herself with a frown and then stands up. "All right Sarah, thank you. Please try to stall them about boarding for at least another ten minutes. That should give us enough time to get ready." She begins pacing around the nutro-center quickly going over everything that her father had told her she would have to do if this should ever happen. She needed to have everything clear in her mind before attempting to explain it to Thayer. He wasn't going to like this any more then anything else that had already happened to them.

"Leyla, even if they're willing to be put off, there's not much we can do. No doubt they already know who we are and that this is one of your father's ships." While talking, Thayer is following Leyla through the ship. They stop in front of a small storage unit that is set into one wall at chest level. Leyla opens the unit and takes out some papers and identification cards along with a small rectangular box, then closes the unit.

"True my father has more then one ship registered, and this is one of them. The difference is that on Earth it registers as the Terra Delta, but when we left the Earth's atmosphere the ship's outward appearance changed and it became the Theos Agape. The Terra is registered to my father, but the Agape is registered to the Lair siblings, Virga and Purgari."

After carefully studying the faces on the ID cards, Leyla hands them and the registration papers to Thayer. Now all she has to do is have his complete trust for the next fifteen minutes, to get them out of this new danger.

Thayer looks at the ID cards and shakes his head. "Even though we have the same build as these people, we don't look anything like them, and even if we did, we would never pass the retina scan that they'll do."

"Thayer, will you trust me to get us out of this?" she asks him interrupting his negativism. "I can change our appearance and get us through the identification process if I know that you have faith and trust in me to do so."

He stares at her a moment and then sighs. "How will you do it? There's no way we can change our features in time."

"I'll place the features we want them to see in their minds. For the retina scans we'll use these synthetic eye covers which will alter our eye patterns."

"Leyla, the cruiser is ready to dock." Sarah warns them.

Not answering, Leyla continues to look at Thayer, her eyes pleading with him to believe in her. Slowly he nods and gives her a small smile of confidence. Smiling back at him she answers Sarah.

"All right Sarah. Give us a few more moments before you allow them to come on board. Open the hatch slowly and make it look like its sticking or something."

They carefully place the eye covers in and then go to the airlock just as it opens. Three security guards enter with stunners out and at the ready. Leyla quickly touches their minds and plants the images that she wants them to see both in their minds and on the optic nerve center. The touch causes a little discomfort and blurred vision, but is soon cleared as the guards shake their heads. They put the discomfort down to a change in atmospheres.

"What's the reason for this delay officers?" Thayer asks stepping closer to Leyla and placing an arm protectively around her shoulders.

"We're searching for two fugitives that escaped capture on Earth. Your ship left the area where they were last seen at the time."

"I see, and that gives you the right to threaten an unwary and unarmed ship? Because you thought that we were these fugitives your people lost track of." he says in disgust and shakes his head at such reasoning. He didn't know how Logan could stand working with such idiots.

"Please excuse him officer. We're the only ones aboard if you care to search? My brother and I are on our way to visit with our parents on Delta Omega Seven, where they're working for the Federation. It's their thirty-fifth wedding anniversary." she carefully explains with a smile.

The officer in charge looks them over and slowly nods his head. "That may be Miss, but we still need to check your ship and identifications." He tells her and turns to his men. "Steven's, you check the forward cabins, Paulton, you check the aft. I'll check their identifications and do the retina scans."

Stevens and Paulton go to check out their assigned areas as the third man faces Leyla and Thayer. "Now, if you'll show me your identifications and registration, we can proceed and get you people back on your way again."

Thayer hands him the documents folder and ID cards. For the first time he looks down at Leyla and notices that her eye color is different. Instead of her normal hazel, they are now an unusual shade of yellow. Though they're still attractive, he preferred them their normal color.

The officer looks over the documents and ID cards, looking from the cards to each of them. Satisfied, he finally hands them back. Reaching into the pouch on his uniform jumpsuit, he pulls out a small oval object and pushes a few buttons. "Please stand still while I'm doing the scan so as not to damage your eye."

He steps up to Leyla and holds the device about two inches in front of her right eye. At first the device blinks red, but is soon replaced by a blinking green light. After checking the reading and confirming the data, he resets it and steps over to Thayer and repeats the procedure. Once he has the green light, he checks the reading and then clears the system, and places the device back in the pouch. Stepping back he smiles at them slightly.

"Your ID's and retina scans have been cleared. As soon as the others confirm that no one else is aboard, you'll be free to continue on your way." he assures them.

The other two return a few minutes later. "We've found no trace of anyone else sir. There's an android in one of the aft cabins, but it hasn't been activated." Paulton reports, saluting his senior officer. The one that had checked them out nods and gestures them towards the airlock.

"Thank you for your cooperation. I'm sorry for any inconvenience this may have caused you." He follows his men, and the airlock door closes behind him.

As soon as the door closes, Leyla turns to the intercom and speaks softly. "Sarah, proceed on this course until they are no longer tracking us, and then make the necessary corrections to take us to Calidon in the shortest possible time period."

"All right Leyla. I'll start preparing the chambers for the two of you and let you know when it's time to enter suspension."

"Thank you. Please reactivate Stephen Seven while you're at it and have him check the ship over to make sure that neither of those men left any type of device on board while they were looking around. I don't want any more surprises." When she turns back to Thayer, she notices his shocked expression and lifts a brow in inquiry.

"Leyla, we can not go to Calidon. Non-Calidonians are strictly forbidden from entering their air space. Besides that, we would have to be in suspension for at least two months, if not more. Not to mention that to enter their system is a declaration of war to both them and the Federation."

Leading the way to the relaxation center, Leyla tries to think of a way to explain how easy it would be for them to enter the Calidonian system, and why they will be permitted to land on an otherwise closed world. After entering the center and sitting down opposite each other, she closely watches him as she begins to explain.

"We'll be able to enter Calidon's system after I send a specially coded message. They will have no choice but to allow us entrance. Not only the code, but this ship as well will see us safely onto Calidon. This ship is a Calidonian family cruiser of high station."

"What do you mean they'll have no other choice? Whether this is one of their ships or not, they definitely have a choice. They can blow us right out of the sky!"

Shaking her head she gets up and gets them each a drink, a little stronger then the ones they had earlier. She hands Thayer a Saturn

Moonbeam, then sits back down and takes a sip of her own drink. "No Thayer, they don't have a choice. This cruiser belongs to the royal family itself. If they should attack there would be serious reprisals for all those involved."

"How in the universe did your father get his hands on a Calidonian Royal cruiser?" he asks in surprise.

She takes another sip from her glass before telling him about the cruiser and ultimately about herself. Setting down the glass she takes a deep breath. "It was a gift to my mother from her parents when she and my father were mated." She looks up at him before continuing. "They were the King and Queen of Calidon."

Thayer's eyes widen and he nearly chokes on the sip he had just taken of his drink. After a fit of coughing, and clearing his throat several times, he finally gets something out. "Okay. So what you're telling me now, is that you are a Royal Princess of Calidon and we'll be welcomed with open arms." he says sarcastically.

Leyla doesn't understand his sudden sarcasm, and wonders if he doubted her or if he didn't like the idea of her having royal blood. "Not actually opens arms no. But we should still have no trouble. You must realize that my mother left her home world almost thirty years ago, and that she died when I was still very young. She never went back because I was too young and small to make the trip in stasis. She and Father decided to wait a few years, but she died and my father never got around to taking me to visit her people." she tries to explain. "Though my grandparents have never seen me in the physical sense, we have communicated regularly over the years. They accepted that my father's responsibilities would not allow him to make such a long trip alone with a child, and they still accepted me freely. Through the years, they have sent me teachers so that I could learn all that I needed to about Calidon, its policies, and the people that live there. Though I've never set foot there, it is as much my home as Earth is."

With another look at her and after taking a large swallow of his drink, Thayer stands up and walks over to the wall of windows showing the vastness of space. After several long seconds have passed, he turns back to her. "All right, you've talked with grandparents and learned about the planet, but there's something that has you worried. Something that you haven't told me about yet. I get the feeling that this something is very important and that I need to be aware of it. So what is it Leyla?"

She looks down at her drink for several seconds before raising her eyes back to his. "Three months before my father's disappearance, we were informed that my grandmother had died of some mysterious illness. Three months after that I was informed that my grandfather had succumbed to the same illness. The High Councilor, Trocon Damori, and a good friend to both my grandparents and parents, has suggested that they may have been murdered." She stops there and takes a swallow of her drink before she can continue telling him the rest. "Trocon seems to think that someone in a high position is responsible for their deaths and that they might try to come after me as well. I'm the last of my mother's line Thayer. If I should die or am unable to get to Calidon, a new ruler will be picked from my grandfather's advisors. From what Grandfather and Trocon have told me, the Prime Minister, Dacus Mandraik, is the one most likely to be picked by the other council members."

"So let him become the next king. You're more of Earth than of Calidon Leyla. If he wants to rule Calidon, let him. He has no ties to another world like you do." he points out reasonably.

She shakes her head at his suggestion. "I can't do that Thayer. If Mandraik were to become King, Calidon would no longer remain neutral. He would use the gifts of the people much the same way as the President uses the people on Earth. But believe me, it would be a thousand times worse for Calidon then anything President Carrison has done or will do."

Thinking this over, Thayer can see her point, but he can't help worrying about her. "All right. Say we make it safely onto the planet. What's to stop the murderer from trying to kill you too? You said yourself that there was the possibility of them coming after you as well."

Finishing her drink, Leyla stands and walks over to stand beside him. Looking into his eyes she can see the fear and concern her has for her, and gently touches his arm. "Please don't worry about me Thayer. No one will get near me that has any kind of evil intent. Unless I wish it otherwise, no one can get closer to me then five feet. An automatic barrier goes up around me and keeps the wrong types from getting to close. I don't know exactly how or why it works, but it is always there when I need it."

"What if someone tries to touch your mind? Tries to control you?"

"I have barriers there too that I do control. If I feel any danger in a mind touch, I can do several things to disable someone in varying degrees. From a mild mind stun, to a total memory loss. I can even cause the total loss of all mental abilities if absolutely necessary." She puts her arms around his waist and laying her head against his chest, squeezes him tightly. "Besides, I have you to protect me if I need protecting." she says with total confidence in his ability to keep her safe.

Thayer shakes his head and lays his cheek against the top of her head. "You can find more answers then I can find questions. What am I going to do with you?" Leyla looks up at him and smiles, but as she looks into his eyes, the smile fades and she raises her lips to his. Thayer sighs and then joins their lips in a passionate kiss. He slides his tongue over her lips seeking entrance, which she gives him willingly with a soft moan of pleasure. He pulls her closer to him and starts to lower his hands to her hips to bring her closer still...

"Leyla, I've made the necessary course corrections. What speed should we begin traveling?" Sarah asks and then waits for an answer. The computer waits for several seconds before asking again more loudly. "What speed Leyla?"

Thayer and Leyla slowly separate their lips and give each other small nibbling bites and kisses, before Leyla puts her forehead against his chest and takes a deep breath to answer the personal computer unit that her father had designed and programmed. "Go to sub-warp five Sarah."

"And here I thought that we had already hit warp ten a few seconds ago." Thayer says into her ear.

Leyla giggles and steps out of his arms looking up at his smiling face. "We definitely hit a personal warp ten." she agrees. "We should get something to eat and then get some rest. We've got a long journey ahead of us." she tells him taking his hand in hers and leading him back to the nutro-center.

After fixing and eating a modest meal, Leyla shows Thayer to a sleeping chamber and bids him good rest before turning to enter her own chamber across the passageway. Once inside, she unpacks her bag and takes a quick sonic shower. When she's done with her shower, she climbs into bed and crosses her arms under her head, staring up at the ceiling until sleep finally over takes her.

Lying in bed after his own sonic shower, Thayer goes over everything that has happened within the past twenty-four hours, and somewhat beyond that. He had a lot to think about, especially his reaction to Leyla's revelations about herself. Though she seemed to accept his apologies, he was sure that his reactions still hurt and bothered her. He wondered how she would react when he confessed his own background. Would she see him as a hypocrite, or would she understand the sense of loss he had felt for nearly half of his lifetime?

No matter how she reacted, he had to tell her about his past activities. He and Logan Knightrunner had been leading double lives long enough. It was time they trusted someone else besides each other. His leaving Earth has caused their plans to take on an aspect that neither of them could have foreseen. They had been working together, gathering information to help the United Federation of Planets to seize power from Earth's President and the leader's of the Security Council for several years. They had been trying to do it as peacefully as possible, though they had their doubts about the Federations reasons for wanting to take control.

For the past several years the Federation had been getting more and more reports on the cruelties and injustices happening towards the people of Earth by their own leaders. Reports that Earth and some unknown alien were collaborating to take over several planets that have not yet joined the Federation and possibly some that had.

One of Thayer and Logan's biggest concerns were the taking of young girls and women from their families. At first just a few were taken and those were ones that no immediate male family member to act as their protector. Then suddenly there was an increase in male deaths, and more females were being taken. A lot of the females that were taken were very beautiful and highly intelligent. Several of them had also appeared to have some trace of psi abilities. The ones with psi ability seemed to vanish with no trace whatsoever, and no one could find any records on them. It was as though they had ceased to exist or had never existed at all. Any females that weren't beautiful or intelligent that were taken, were sent to the work camps or to military posts. They were used as breeders to supply the government with more men. It was thought that any females born did not live long after their birth unless they were shown to have alpha brain patterns.

Both Thayer and Logan had begun to think that Leyla's father's disappearance was not an accident. Logan, a trusted guard for the Security Council and the President, had heard several times before and after Saitun's disappearance, Leyla's name mentioned. Someone wanted her out of the way permanently and as soon as possible. Thayer had tried to warn her several times after her father's disappearance, not to go looking for trouble. That she was getting into things that she didn't understand and wouldn't be able to handle.

"I'll deal with whatever comes up Thayer. You know I don't care what others think or say when I know that something is wrong and needs to be changed. We've all become too compliant over the years, and it needs to stop now."

"I know that you believe that you could handle anything, but this isn't like when we first met and you were teaching the children Earth's true history. The government let that pass because there were so many others doing the same thing. What you're talking about doing will bring more attention to yourself. I've already told you about the women that have disappeared. Don't give them an excuse to make you disappear too!"

Within days of his last warning to her, she had done just that. Logan had given him a call to warn him of what was happening and to tell him that they would be coming after him too. He had just finished downloading his computer system, when Leyla had called him and everything had gone crazy from there. Earth Security officers had broken into his apartment, his computer unit had been totally destroyed, and they had nearly beaten him to death. He had just about given up when he had been teleported to Leyla's home. Though the events of the day still bothered him, he realizes that because of the information she had found, Leyla had brought herself to a level of danger that neither of them actually thought would happen. Especially for something so relatively minor.

He decides to let her finish telling him about the information that she had gotten on her father from the governments computers. He would then try and figure out if it was anything that could also help Logan and himself. Though his connection with Saitun Katmen was only a slight one on Earth, and mainly through Leyla, they had worked together on several occasions for the Federation over the years. Thayer greatly respected the older man and knew that he would never do anything to endanger the lives of innocent people, especially the life of his only child.

Thayer was just as anxious as Leyla to find out what was happening with her father. He was sure that Saitun's disappearance had something to do with a meeting Logan had monitored just before Saitun left. It had something to do with a planet that Saitun had visited nearly thirty years ago. Suddenly Thayer sits up in bed and curses.

"That's it! That's the connection. Someone on Calidon is working with someone in Earth's government. That's why Leyla was mentioned at those meetings." It was all beginning to make sense to him now. The little accidents and increased monitoring Leyla had been experiencing in the past few months. They all amounted to someone wanting her out of the way permanently, not just disappearing from sight. "Sarah?"

"Yes Thayer?"

"Is Leyla still awake?"

"No she's not Thayer. She's been asleep for the past two hours. Would you like me to wake her for you?"

"No, let her sleep. I'll talk to her in the morning."

"Good sleep Thayer."

"Good night Sarah." He lays back down and slowly relaxes his body. He knows that he would have to convince Leyla that she would be in greater danger on Calidon, then she ever was on Earth. He was sure that whoever killed her grandparents would try to kill her as well. Focusing harder, his body finally relaxes enough to allow him to slip into sleep, though it is several hours before it is a dreamless one.

# Chapter II

Back on Earth, an extensive search is done on the remains of the Katmen home, and several of their friends and neighbors are questioned. Though disturbed by the destruction, none of them could give any information as to what might have caused the explosion. Most believed that Leyla had to have died when the house was destroyed, how could anyone have survived such a thing? She was at home at the time the house went up.

"Was very depressed after her father disappeared." Cassandra Blackwood tells the official that is questioning her family. "Nothing any of us could say or do seemed to snap her out of it. We tried to talk her into getting counseling, but she refused."

"Do you know what might have caused the explosion Miss Blackwood?" the officer asks writing on his computer pad.

"No idea. None of us had been over there in quite a while."

Putting away the pad, the officer looks up at her. "Well thank you for your help. If you should think of anything, anything at all, please call the local authorities."

"Of course we will. Though I doubt that there is anything else we could tell you that we haven't already." she says and stands up to walk him and his companion to the door. "If you should find out anything would you let us know? Leyla was a close friend and we'd like to know what happened to her if at all possible."

"We'll do what we can. Good day Miss."

After the men leave, Cassie closes the door and leans against it shakily. It had been very hard to think of other things while discussing Leyla with a telepath present. Straightening up she walks back into the living room where the rest of her family is waiting.

"Did we fool them Cassie?" Merrilynda, the youngest asks with concern.

"I think so Merri." she assures her though she was doubtful. Falling onto the sofa she wraps her arm around the young girl. "I think that if they knew we weren't telling them anything they would of said something."

"Do you think that Leyla's safe?" teenage Dessa asks leaning close to her twin sister Davena.

"Of course she is Dessa. Leyla wouldn't let those idiots anywhere near her." Merri's twin Colton says with confidence. "She's too smart for them, just like Uncle Saitun. She probably saw them coming and went into hiding."

"Colt's right Dess. The whole neighborhood saw them coming down the road." the oldest boy Mark reminds her. "Besides, Leyla told us that something like this might happen one day. I'm sure that she had a plan of escape all figured out."

Cassie sits up and looks at each of her siblings. "Whether she did or not, we all have to be on guard from now on. Watch what you're thinking whenever you're around strangers. If you think someone is scanning you, think of something nonsense so that they can't probe too deep, like Leyla showed us. If you have to, put up barriers to keep them out."

"I wonder if Thayer is with her." Daniel speculates with a slight frown. "I don't think she would have gone anywhere without telling him. They've gotten really close over the past couple of months."

Cassie frowns wondering the same thing. She thought that Thayer was probably the reason Earth Security was watching her friend. Both he and his friend Logan had been acting strangely since Leyla's father disappeared. After all Logan was with Earth Security, she wasn't sure if he was someone that they should trust anymore.

"Well what ever is going on, I'm sure that Leyla will get word to us when she can. Until then we act like normal." Cassie tells them all standing and looking down at them. "Merri and Colt, you two start checking the rooms for damage. Davena and Dessa, you get a couple of brooms and start sweeping up the broken glass. Mark and Daniel, check the outside of the house for any structural damage. I'm going to try and reach Da again, and give him some warning if I can."

Having their jobs assigned, they each go about the business of straightening up the house. Each of them thinking of Leyla and hoping that she is all right.

* * *

In the morning, Leyla finds Thayer in the fitness room working out with Stephen Seven. She decides to wait until they are finished with the set before letting Thayer know of her presence. While waiting she watches the play of muscles across Thayer's back and shoulders as he tries to throw the android. Just when it looks like Stephen with throw Thayer instead, Thayer makes a move that sends Stephen to the mat with a resounding thud. Leyla claps and walks over to were Thayer is now standing bent over breathing hard.

"That was very good Thayer. Not too many people can best Stephen. My father programmed him to give maximum effort without causing unnecessary pain or injury."

Thayer takes a deep steadying breath and releases it very slowly before straightening up to look at her. "He's very good. For every one of my throws, he threw me at least twice as many times."

Stephen stands up and smiles at Leyla. "This human is very good himself Leyla. But he does not expect an android to be deceptive. This is why I was able to throw him so many times."

"How did you deceive me? None of your moves or actions suggested deception." Thayer asks staring at Stephen in total disbelief.

Leyla just laughs and shakes her head before taking Thayer's hand and leading him to the portal. "Believe me, Stephen is no ordinary android. My father and I programmed him to simulate all human characteristics. Even lying and deception. No matter what though, he can never use those negative traits with my father or me unless we order him to. The only time that would happen would be in situations like this one." Turning back to Stephen, Leyla speaks to him in a binary language that her and her father had developed to speak with him privately. When she finishes, Stephen smiles at Thayer and nods before turning and starting to straighten up the room.

"What was that smile all about Leyla? It looked...overly pleased and is making me a bit nervous. Another thing. What did you say to him anyway? I didn't understand a single thing." he asks as they walk to the nutro-center.

"I gave him the command to deal honestly with you at all times unless you decide otherwise. The smile was because you're the first person outside of our family to be given such...inclusion. Except for us and the Blackwood family, neither my father nor I felt safe enough to program him to make such allowances before."

Pulling her to a stop, Thayer turns her to face him, then lowers his mouth to hers. He stops a breath away to whisper, "Thank you for trusting in me." and then he kisses her gently before releasing her and stepping back.

Leyla stares at him for a few seconds before turning and entering the nutro-center. While Thayer goes to get cleaned up and changed, she gets their breakfast together and sets everything on the table. A few minutes later Thayer joins her and sits down opposite her.

After eating for several minutes, Thayer pushes his plate aside and watches her. He tries to figure out how to tell her what he had finally figured out about the little accidents she had been having lately. Until he does, he decides to find out what information she had on her father that she hadn't already told him.

"Yesterday, before the Security cruiser arrived, you said that you realized something about the belongings of your father's that had been returned to you after his so called accident. What did you mean?"

Leyla pushes away her own plate before picking up her cup of coffee and taking a couple of sips. Lowering the cup she answers slowly and thoughtfully.

"All of the things that they returned were things that had been missing since long before the accident. They were all things that he would never have taken with him on an assignment. Besides that, we had both checked his ship several times just in case he had taken them their on one of his trips to be by himself."

"What kinds of things were they?"

"Books, clothing, even some engine parts from our hover car. He never took anything that didn't coincide with whatever he was working on at the time. One of the questions I asked myself was, why hadn't the books or clothes been destroyed in the fire? None of them were heat resistant and shouldn't have survived. Then there's the fact that I never felt his loss. He's still alive."

"You can't be sure of that Leyla."

"Yes I can Thayer. My father and I have a very strong bond. Even though he doesn't have very strong psi abilities right now, we're still well linked by our blood and our love for each other. If it were necessary, he could contact me through telepathy. It was the same between him and my mother, though not as strong. I think its because I share his blood that makes our bond that much stronger."

"Okay, if you're right, why hasn't he contacted you? He must know that you're worried about him and what's happening with him."

"He explained in the holo-tape that he wouldn't try to contact me in any way until he was absolutely sure that it was safe for him to do so. My father would never do anything to put me into danger Thayer. I do that well enough on my own. It's why he left me the tape. He knew what would turn up and what I should do to deal with it. I've done just about everything that he said that I would have to do. Neither of us expected the overreaction of the Security Council though. That was extreme."

"But you have done something that he didn't tell you about, and that something is what's still bothering you. What is it Leyla? What did you do that is so disturbing to you?"

She looks at him for a few moments before standing and carrying the dishes to the recycler. After placing them inside the bin, she turns back to face him and shrugs her shoulders. "He never said that I would have to teleport you to the house, or tell you about myself. He never told me that I should be prepared for your reaction or that it would hurt. He never said that you might reject me the way that you did, and he never told me how to deal with that or what I should do afterwards.

Everything that I've done up to now has been more or less guess work on my part."

Thayer sees now that even after the kisses they had shared since she had told him about herself, and their voyage had begun, his first reaction was still hurting her and weighing heavily on her heart and mind. Though she had hidden it well up until now. He stands up and slowly walks over to her. Once he's in front of her, he gently reaches up and strokes her cheek with the backs of his curved fingers.

"I never meant to hurt you or to cause you pain Leyla." he assures her taking her into his arms and hugging her close. "I have no right to judge you for any reason. There are things that I've never told you about myself that I should have. I guess that I was just as afraid that your reaction would be what mine was, and used that to get back at you for doing what I hadn't had the courage to do. I'm sorry for hurting you and causing you to doubt yourself and our relationship. Please believe that it was never my intention to do that."

Sensing his genuine regret and shame, Leyla wraps her arms tightly around his waist and hugs him. "You don't have to tell me about yourself Thayer. My father already told me. When we first met and you asked me out, I was having doubts. Father told me who you were and that you had a special type of mind-block that had been put in place before you came to Earth when you were fifteen." she admits wanting him to know everything. "None of that has ever mattered to me. I should have told you all of this then so that you wouldn't feel so left out and alone. Maybe if I had I could have saved myself the pain of your reaction." She looks up at him and places her hand over his heart. "I know now what's inside of here, and that's all that matters to me now."

He looks down at her, then pulls her closer to him and once again takes her mouth. This time his kiss is one of hunger. Leyla wraps her arms around his neck and meets him with a kiss just as needful and hungry as his own. Encouraged by her response, he slowly pulls away from her lips and trails his own across her cheek to her earlobe. Gently he takes the lobe between his teeth and nips at it causing her to moan softly, deeply in her throat, and give a small shiver of pleasure. His hands move up and down her back and sides in a gentle caress meant to bring her closer to his body. As her hips make contact with his, he feels her brush against his straining manhood and a low growl vibrates through his chest. He grabs her hips and holds her tightly against him, and very still.

"Leyla, honey. We have to stop."

"Mmmmm." she murmurs against his throat not really hearing him.

"We have to stop honey, before we get carried away." Slowly, but painfully, he sets her a little away from him, breaking their physical contact and takes a shuddering breath. He looks down at her flushed cheeks and gives her one last lingering kiss before releasing her completely and stepping back. "There's something else we need to talk about."

Leyla opens her eyes slowly and stares up at him, a small pout forming on her kiss swollen lips. "Okay, what's so darn important?" she asks petulantly, crossing her arms over her sensitive breast to cover her arousal.

Smiling at her, Thayer takes her hand and leads her back to the table. After she reluctantly sits down, he sits across from her and takes her hand again. "Last night I went over everything that has been happening to you in the past few months. I believe that someone on Calidon is working with the President and the Security Council. I also believe that you'll be in greater danger there than you ever were on Earth." He raises his hand to stop her from interrupting him and then places it back over hers on the table and giving it a gentle squeeze. He takes a deep breath before continuing.

"Logan can confirm everything that I'm telling you. All those little accidents you were having, weren't accidents. Someone was trying to get you out of the way permanently. Logan's been monitoring meetings, and he monitored a meeting in which your father was mentioned and something was said about a planet he had visited nearly thirty years ago, though the name was never mentioned. That meeting took place just before your father disappeared, and your accidents didn't start until after he was out of the way."

"But my father has visited lots of planets over the years in his work for the Federation. The year that he went to Calidon, he had been to six other planets as well. They could have been talking about any one of them." she points out.

"That's true. But how many of them did he actually take something or someone from? From what I know of your father through the Federation, he has never taken tokens of appreciation from any of the planets he's been to. Then he met your mother, they were joined and she left Calidon with him. Someone has resented your father for doing that. I believe that person is the one responsible for your grandparents' deaths and possibly your accidents as well. It is even possible that they could have something to do with your father's disappearance."

Leyla looks down at their joined hands and links her fingers with his. Everything that he said made sense and was possible, except for her father's disappearance. After what they had just gone through, she knew that he was going to be upset with her for not telling him earlier. Taking a deep breath she looks up at him and prepares herself to tell him rest and hopes that he doesn't try to strangle her.

"I agree with everything that you're saying...but, there's something that I haven't told you yet. I should have told you earlier, but things were a bit rough. That's no excuse of course, and the only reason that I didn't tell you back on Earth was because they were constantly monitoring me, and it just wasn't safe." she looks away and then back again. "My father is safe and on a Federation Star cruiser in sector Regent Three. He has been since I contacted them to find out if he was all right. Please believe that I would have told you sooner if things hadn't gotten so strained between us."

There is a slight hint of anger in Thayer's eyes for a few moments, but then it is replaced by acceptance and understanding. "I believe you, but you should have made a point of telling me yesterday. It might have helped me to figure all of this out a lot sooner." He squeezes her fingers then releases them before standing and turning to the counter. "We're going to have to come up with a plan to discover who on Calidon is responsible for this mess. I'm sure that it has something to do with someone that was around when your parents were joined."

Leyla stands and walks up behind him and wraps her arms around his waist. "Can't it wait until later? We have plenty of time before we need to start worrying about Calidon. I can think of a lot better things to do right now." She rubs her hands up and down his chest, pulling him back against her breast tightly. Thayer moans softly at the feel of her against him and quickly turns around to take her in his arms again.

"Are you sure about this Leyla? I don't think that I could stop if you should change your mind at the last minute. I've wanted you again for the past three weeks." he warns her before kissing her deeply.

When he raises his head to let her answer, she smiles at him and tells him in a smoky voice, "I'm very sure. I want you too much to change my mind any time soon."

Kissing her again, he swings her up into his arms and carries her out of the nutro-center and down the passage to his cabin. Once they're inside the room he slowly sets her on her feet and places his hands gently on her waist just above her hips.

"Sarah? We don't want to be disturbed for a while, unless it's a dire emergency. If you need assistance, ask Stephen to give you a hand. Understood?" Leyla commands never taking her eyes from Thayer's.

"Understood Leyla."

Smiling at the inflection in Sarah's response, Leyla grins at Thayer. "Now, where were we?"

\* \* \*

## EARTH: The President's Office

"What do you mean you lost them? How could you loose a ship that size?" President Carrison shouts at his Chief of Security, and second in command.

"Sir, after they cleared the retina scan the patrol only monitored them until they looked to be entering Delta Omega Seven space. They thought it safe to discontinue monitoring and did so without asking Delta's control to pick up their signal."

"Well its apparent they thought wrong. I want that cruiser found Peterton. I want that Katmen witch returned to me, and Starhawk dead. Is that understood?"

"Yes sir. I'll see to it personally." Peterton salutes before quickly leaving the office.

Carrison slams his fist onto the desk and sweeps his hand across it, sending things flying, then turns to face the window behind him.

* * *

Leyla snuggles closer to Thayer's large form and sighs in contentment. She slowly runs her hand over the pelt of hair covering his chest, stopping to tease his nipples. Thayer moans and captures the tormenting hand and brings it to his lips.

"Woman, are you trying to kill me?" he asks flipping over so that she is pinned beneath him.

Giggling, she looks up at him and wraps her legs around his. "You don't feel dead to me. In fact you feel very much alive." she tells him wriggling her hips against his and smiling as he moans again before putting more of his weight on her to stop the provocative movements. She caresses his back and raises her head to kiss him deeply.

Thayer slips his hand between their bodies and gently cups her breast, then just as gently squeezes the nipple between his thumb and forefinger until she moans and moves against his hand. Bracing his body up, he looks down at her and smiles. Slowly, using his knees, he opens her up to him. He then teases her with the tip of his maleness. Suddenly she surges up against him, impaling herself on his shaft and causing them both to moan in pleasures pain. He grabs her beneath her knees and raises them higher before thrusting deeply into her. With each movement inside of her, Leyla makes a keening sound in the back of her throat that edges him on.

Thayer moves faster when he feels her muscles beginning to contract around him, just before losing himself to his own release. Collapsing on top of her, he catches his breath, then turns to his side with her, before rolling onto his back still joined to her. He caresses her back until her breathing slows and returns to normal. When she starts to pull herself from him, he holds her still. "No, stay like this. I want to hold you like this while we sleep."

Relaxing against him, Leyla slowly drifts off to sleep. Thayer listens to her breathing until her body is totally relaxed and he knows that she's deeply asleep, and not likely to wake before morning. He then allows himself to relax and follow her into slumber.

Leyla wakes up and gently disengages herself from Thayer's body. He stirs, but doesn't wake. Picking up her clothes, she quietly leaves his room. Once in her own room, she takes a shower and puts on a teal colored jumpsuit. While brushing her hair, she tries to decide what to do about the things Thayer had told her about someone from Calidon being involved with Earth.

Setting down the brush, she goes over to her desk and sits down in front of her mother's vid-diary. "Mother, I need to speak with you."

A face slowly appears on the screen in front of her. The woman on the screen is very beautiful, with long brown hair and a copper tint to her skin. Her eyes are a greenish yellow with hints of pale blue. The look in those eyes is one of deep love and affection. "Leyla, what's troubling you sweetheart?"

"Someone on Calidon may be trying to harm me mother. Thayer thinks that its someone that resented your joining with father. Do you have any idea who it might be?"

"There's only one person on Calidon who might wish harm on my only child. He is a very ruthless man Leyla, and you must be very careful around him. His name is Dacus Mandraik."

"Why does he resent your joining to father?"

"Mandraik considered himself my betrothed because I showed him kindness a few times. It was a mistake on my part. When your father came to Calidon to negotiate a contract for the Federation, I was his strongest supporter for keeping Calidon neutral of any and all wars. Mandraik was just as strongly against us." she explains. "In the weeks that your father was on Calidon we feel in love and started to get what we telepaths call the burning. It's when two people that are meant to be together, start feeling a fluctuation in their body temperatures and in their minds. Your father asked me to join with him. I wasn't sure what to do, so I went to your grandmother. She told me that the choice was mine alone to make and that I shouldn't let others influence my decision. When I told her that I wished to be with your father always, she told me that was as it should be. When Mandraik found out that we were to be joined, he attempted to kill your father. The attempt failed and Mandraik was scarred. It was I who scarred him Leyla, and he will never forget it of the fact that it cost him my father's trust. Over the years he has had to work very hard to regain that trust, but I don't think that father ever really gave him his complete trust again."

"Mother, Dacus Mandraik is now the Prime Minister."

Fear crosses the features on the screen before slowly fading to a more confident look. "That means that he has gained the trust of at least half of the council. It also means that his abilities are almost as strong as my father's. But they will never be as strong as yours are now. Be cautious and on guard honey. Both you and Thayer will be in danger around him."

"How can I protect Thayer? He has abilities, but because of the mind-block he can barely use them. How can we remove the block without harming him?"

"Speak with Trocon. He will know of a way to do it without harm befalling him." she assures her.

"Thank you mother. I love you."

"I love you too little one. Take care and remember all that I have said. Remember also to take me with you when you first go to see Trocon, there is something that I must say to him before the final transition."

Just as her image fades, there is a strong pounding on the portal door. Leyla goes over and unlocks it, opening it to an angry looking Thayer, standing there with his hands on his hips. He stalks past her and into the room looking around.

"All right, who were you talking with Leyla and how did she get on the ship? I heard another female voice, and it wasn't Sarah's."

Leyla watches his face for a few moments before leaning back against the wall next to the door. "I was talking with my mother's vid-diary." She tells him pointing to the desk and the diary. "Now tell me, is this really about hearing someone else's voice, or are you just bothered by the fact that I left your body and your bed without your knowing it?"

Thayer's cheeks redden at her words. She was right, it wasn't about hearing another voice that had angered him, but anger with himself for not knowing when she had left him. Taking a look at the diary, he notices that it was different from others he had seen. Walking up to it he examines it more closely and notices a small box is connected to the side of it. It glowed with a strange light coming from within. "What's this little box here for?" he reaches out to touch it, and the light inside brightens quickly.

"Thayer, NO! Don't touch it!" Leyla yells and rushes forward to stop him, but is a second too late as her mother defends herself. Thayer stumbles backwards bumping into her as she runs to him. Carefully she helps him into the chair and then turns back to the diary where her mother's image has reappeared.

"Mother! You had no reason to do that! I would have stopped him in time." she snaps angrily.

"Watch your tone Leyla Aeneka!" her mother says sharply. "How was I to know that? Besides, he was moving to fast. I picked up on his hostility and then he started reaching towards me. What was I suppose to do?" Aeneka asks her face stern.

"I'm sorry mother. But you should have known from all that father and I have told you, that Thayer would never intentionally do anything to harm anyone."

"That may very well be, but my essence was in danger. I had no choice but to react. If he had made contact with the box, my time with you would have ended immediately. Is that what you want? Besides, he's only mildly stunned and will recover shortly."

Leyla walks over to her mother and lowers her head, ashamed for how she had spoken to her. She lightly places her hand on the box and caresses it. "I'm truly sorry mother. I didn't mean to snap at you like that. It's just that…"

Aeneka smiles up at her and sends a soothing current of love into Leyla's palm. "I understand little one. He means a great deal to you and you worry for him. He's coming around. Stand to the side so that I can see him more clearly." Leyla does as she's told and moves so that her mother and Thayer will be able to see each other. She keeps her hand on the box to stay in contact with her mother.

Slowly Thayer shakes off the effects of the stun blast he had received and looks over at Leyla standing beside the box.

"Not bad for a Majichonie. Come closer Thayer Starhawk of Manchon, let me see your eyes." Aeneka commands him.

Thayer looks at the box and sees the image there. Not sure what else to do, he stands up and steps cautiously closer to the box. This time he's careful not to get too close.

"If you had shown such restraint earlier, I would not have had to stun you, nor would I have had to reprimand my daughter for the tone she used with me." she tells him as they look at each other. Thayer nods his head, then looks at Leyla, who's head is lowered so that he can not see her eyes. He looks back at the image on the screen.

"I understand your need to protect yourself. I meant you no harm. Your box intrigued me. What I don't understand though, is how this is possible? You died over twenty years ago." he says in confusion, knowing that this is Leyla's mother, and that though she wasn't physically present, her mind was and she was able to communicate.

"While its true that my physical body ceased to be. My essence goes on within this small box that protects it from dissipation. Only Leyla can touch me without fear of that happening. Not even my dear Saitun can touch me again without taking the chance of destroying me." she explains to him. "We've only touched through Leyla, and then only for short periods of time. The process is very draining for her, so we have not touched as often as we otherwise would have liked."

Thayer notices tears on Aeneka's facial image, and also on Leyla's cheeks. "You still haven't told me how this is all possible. I should not be having this conversation with you."

"There is no easy way to explain it to you. I do not understand it myself. The device is for use by Calidonians, and only then under special conditions. Anyone leaving the planet and not expected to return before their death, or anyone leaving to enter a dangerous situation, is given one. Though I expected to visit my home world quite often, I was given one just in case. The device is used to return our essence to Calidon where we rejoin with those at home, to share both our abilities and the knowledge that we have accumulated of the years."

"Normally my mother's essence would have been returned to Calidon immediately after her death. But because I was so young, my grandparents decided that it would be safe enough to keep her with me until I was old enough to make the journey, and the time was right. Even though she doesn't have a physical body, she has taught me to use my abilities both to protect myself and others." Leyla finally speaks caressing the box containing her mother's essence.

"There is something that I must tell you both that may come as a surprise and a shock to both of you, but I believe that you are ready to hear it now. Saitun Katmen was born to an Earth woman, and a man of Manchon."

Leyla releases the box and steps in front of the screen to stare at her mother. Thayer pulls her back into his arms, holding her tightly to his chest in a protective embrace. Aeneka smiles at his response to the distress Leyla was radiating.

"Though Saitun is half Majichonie, as you are Thayer. He only inherited a few of his father's abilities. Those aren't very strong, even though his mother had abilities as well. You get your abilities from your mother, and your father's strong ancient beliefs in his Native American heritage, which carries a strong belief in all things supernatural. In the Majichonie, most abilities are generally stronger in the females, with the exception of a few males. Usually most of those are born to a line of leadership. Your abilities are stronger then even those males, because of your mother, her line, and your father's beliefs. Saitun believes that your father's influence in your life tipped the scales in your favor in that aspect. He also thinks that it's the reason your mother place such a strong mind-block on you."

"Why didn't you or father ever tell me about his Majichonie blood before? I don't understand why neither of you told me." Leyla says with confusion and hurt in her voice. She had never thought that her parents would keep anything from her that was so important.

"What's Saitun's bloodline got to do with me? I know all about my parents, about my mother's abilities, and why she place the mind-block. I also know that because of that block, I haven't been able to use my own abilities since I left Manchon. Logan and I have tried everything we could think of to try and break it."

"What it has to do with you Thayer, is that the two of you, you and Leyla, are connected by the Manchon blood. It's what calls you to be together." Aeneka tells him and then addresses Leyla. "The reason we didn't tell you about your father was because we weren't sure how strong his blood would be in you. Though over the years, I have noticed that it is very strong."

"But you denied me a part of my heritage Mother." Leyla tells her still hurt.

"No we didn't Leyla. Your father made sure that you learned about Manchon with as much information as he had. He couldn't tell you any more then he himself knew." she tries to explain seeing now that they had made a mistake in not telling her before now. She looks past Leyla to Thayer, and shocks them both with her next question to Thayer.

"What are your plans for my daughter Thayer Starhawk? Do you plan to join with her or just couple with her?"

"Mother!" Leyla gasps and feels herself begin to blush at such a personal question.

Thayer lightly squeezes her shoulders. "It's all right Leyla, your mother has a right to ask. We've talked about being mated. But with everything that's been happening lately, and with Saitun's disappearance, we've put it off indefinitely."

"Well I suggest that you rethink that decision, and as soon as you arrive on Calidon, you have Trocon arrange for the two of you to be lifemated. Not only will it throw Mandraik off of Leyla for a while, but I believe that it will also be of help in removing your mind-block."

"And what if you're wrong mother? If you are it could cause him to go insane or worse. You told me that Trocon may know of a way to remove the block without harming Thayer." Leyla reminds her mother.

Before Aeneka can answer, Thayer speaks up. "What if he doesn't know of a way Leyla? What if he agrees with your mother?" He turns her to face him. "I'm willing to trust in our love for each other Leyla.

It's gotten us this far and I believe that it's strong enough to get us through the lifemating."

Just then Stephen comes over the intercom. "Leyla you have a private message coming in of the Alpha circuit."

"Thank you Stephen. I'll be there shortly." She looks from her mother's image to Thayer. "I don't have any doubts about our love either Thayer, but I don't know if I could risk losing you. We don't know if our minds are compatible." she kisses his cheek before hurrying from the room.

Thayer watches her leave and then slowly turns back to face her mother. "Mrs. Katmen, I…"

"You may as well call me Aeneka, since we're soon going to be family, even if it is only for a short time."

"Aeneka. Do you really believe that the lifemating can release me from the block?"

"Yes I believe it will. As I told you before, Saitun and I believe that your mother put such a strong block on you because she knew that your abilities would be very strong. I also believe that she placed it to protect you while you were on Earth, so that no one could use you. If I'm right, it would be logical that she would also make it so that when you met your lifemate of equal power, the block would be released. Though I would have made it so that it would be released when your mind had matured enough to deal with the power." When he begins frowning, she smiles at him. "I'm not criticizing your mother. I'm just telling you what I would have done in her place. You should also realize that until you can control the power that you will have, they could be dangerous to yourself and those around you." Thayer pales slightly when she tells him this.

"Could they be dangerous to Leyla? I mean during our lifemating, wouldn't it be just as dangerous for her? From what I remember from my early training on Manchon, lifemating releases a tremendous amount of emotional feeling. If the mate chosen is not strong enough to help his or her chosen one, it could kill one or both of them."

Aeneka smiles at his continued concern for her daughter, and his understanding of what will happen, and what could happen during a lifemating. She is proud of her daughter's choice in mate's, and she was sure that all would be well for them both.

"Don't worry about Leyla, Thayer. She is more than capable of dealing with your lifemating. Even if she had no Majichonie blood, she could still handle it. Though she's registered as an Alpha one, there's really no way to tell what her true rating is. All the test that Saitun and I have given her were inconclusive. What I do know is that she is stronger then the three strongest Alpha's on Calidon. You told Leyla earlier that you trusted in your love for each other. You must also believe in her, but much more. Believe that her love will last through eternity and beyond. If you can do that, then nothing will ever separate the two of you, and nothing will be out of your reach." she assures him. "I need to rest now. Think about all that we've discussed. I will see you later."

Thayer watches her image fade, then stands there for several minutes trying to gather his thoughts and put them into some kind of order. Finally he leaves the cabin and walks slowly towards the comm-center. He understands her feelings of fear for him better now, because he now had those same fears for her. What is still bothering him though, is his first reaction when she told him that she was a telepath. It made him look and sound like a hypocrite, though he wasn't. Even though he hadn't known that she knew about him, or that he hadn't used his abilities in nearly two decades. Neither was an excuse for what he had put her through. Even jealousy that she could do what he could not, was no excuse for saying the things that he had to her. He didn't know where such thoughts had come from. He had never acted that way with Logan or anyone in his father's family. They were all alpha's too, and had been using their abilities around him for years. Why had he acted the way he had with Leyla, and not with one of them?

Before going to the comm-center, Thayer goes into the lounge to finish going over his thoughts. He knew that he needed to get things straightened out in his mind before he and Leyla were lifemated. He didn't want to take any chances in hurting her when that happened. What he had to do was to forgive himself for the things that he had said and done. He already had Leyla's love and forgiveness which was a step in the right direction.

He realizes that when he and Leyla were lifemated, he would once again have a family. Even though he still had his father's people, it didn't quite feel the same since his father's death. He would also feel a part of a world more like the one he had been born on. Though unlike Calidon, once a Majichonie left, they could never return home again. Because of this law, not many people had willingly left Manchon in recent years. The ones that had, felt that their destinies where to be found elsewhere. Thayer was sure that Saitun's father had been one of those that had chosen to leave their home world for something else.

It had been different for Thayer. His father had come to Manchon to learn from their Master Healer. During a storm near the village where he was staying, he had met Royanna. After several weeks of seeing each other Robus Starhawk asked her to become his mate, to which she agreed, even though they could not become lifemates. They were together for fifteen years before Robus felt compelled to return to his native world.

Royanna had told Robus to take their son with him, that his destiny was to be found on another world. Thayer had seen it all as a great adventure, not yet comprehending that he would never see his mother and home again. Before the had left, Royanna had placed the mind-block and told him that "Love strengthened all and would be his release.

Robus had died when Thayer was in his early twenties, and it was then that it truly hit him that he could never return home. Unless the laws on Manchon were changed, he would never see her again. He hoped that with his lifemating, his mind would be strong enough to find out if she still lived. He would then hope and pray that one day they could be together again and he could let her know that he didn't blame her for sending him away, and that he had never stopped loving her. That his father had never taken another as his mate.

# Chapter III

Leyla enters the comm-center and signals for Stephen to leave the room. Sitting down at the counsel, she takes a deep breath before engaging the link. "Go ahead, I'm here."

"Are you all right? Did you have any problems?"

"No, there were no problems. The identifications and eye covers worked just as you said they would. I had no trouble planting the images into their minds."

There is a slight pause before the voice continues, "How did he respond when he found out about your abilities?"

"He wasn't too happy about it at first, but he's finally accepted them and me."

"I'm glad to hear that. I didn't want either of you to get hurt."

"I should have told him before this. He had a right to know, and he was hurt by the fact that I didn't tell him, then I was hurt by his first reaction." Another pause which is followed by a deep sigh of regret.

"I should have allowed you to tell him the first time you suggested it. Even though I've known him for years, worked with him, I wouldn't let myself trust him where you were concerned. I'm sorry that the two of you had to go through such discomfort. But with his mind-block in place, I couldn't be absolutely sure."

"Well that won't be a problem shortly. We're going to be lifemated soon after we reach our destination."

"What?! No! I forbid it! You can not…"

"It's not up to you. Mother has already given us her blessings. In fact she was the one to suggest lifemating. We had only talked about joining." There is a longer pause this time and Leyla wonders if he had broken the connection. "Are you still there?"

"Yes, I'm here. I just wish that you would wait."

"There's no sense in waiting. Besides, if we're right, he'll need his abilities too. I won't allow him to remain vulnerable with unknown danger lurking around us."

"Very well. You have my blessings as well as my love." he assures her and then says a bit sadly, "Tell your mother that I will see her on the other side." The connection is broken, and Leyla sits back wiping away the tears flowing down her cheeks. Taking a deep breath, she turns to face Thayer who is standing in the doorway.

"You heard." she says standing and walking over to him, but stopping a foot away from him.

"I heard. He isn't happy about our lifemating is he?"

"He's more worried than anything else. He knows that it will happen no matter what he says. I think he's wishing that he could be there for it." Thayer nods and closes the distance between them, taking her into his arms. Leyla lays her head on his shoulder.

"What did he mean about seeing your mother on the other side? Does he plan on contacting her somehow?" Though he had heard the expression several times, he wasn't quite sure what it meant.

Leyla shakes her head and looks up at him. "It means…he means after they are both gone from this life. Sometime after we reach Calidon, my mother's essence will leave the box that has protected it for all these years and she will pass into the next life."

"Oh love, I'm sorry. I should have realized." he pulls her tighter to him sorry that he had made her voice her father's loss and her own. He kisses the top of her head, knowing that it was little enough comfort.

"I feel so bad for father. He won't get a chance to feel her love for him once more before she's gone. He won't even get the chance to tell her himself that he loves her, or good-bye." More tears fall and she sniffles. She steps back from him and looks up into his eyes deeply. "Make love to me Thayer. I need to feel you close to me. As close as two people can get physically while still being separate."

Looking closely down at her for several seconds, he picks her up and carries her back to his cabin. He wanted to remove the look of sadness from her eyes.

\* \* \*

Several hours later Thayer stands at on of the small windows looking out at the stars. Every now and then he looks over at the woman sleeping in his bed, not stirring in her sleep which was very deep.

Their loving had been somehow different this time. He had felt a tingling sensation in his mind, and feelings that were quite strange to him. The tingling was still with him, but not as strong. For the past few minutes, he had been debated with himself on what he should do. He wanted to talk with Aeneka about it, but wasn't sure if he should wait until Leyla woke up or not. After a few more minutes of standing there watching her, he decides not to wait.

Quietly he leaves the cabin and goes over to the one that Leyla had planned to use. Once inside, he stops and looks at the diary screen for a few seconds before stepping closer and sitting in the chair. "Aeneka, I need to speak to you." He waits for a few seconds. "It's very important Aeneka, something is happening inside my head that I don't understand."

The screen lightens and Aeneka's image appears in front of him. "What's troubling you Thayer?"

"Something just happened when Leyla and I joined earlier. There was a strong tingling sensation in my mind, and my body didn't feel quite like my own. That's never happened before."

"Are you still feeling the tingling? Does your body still feel different to you?" she asks wondering what could be happening.

"There's a humming in my mind, and even though I'm sitting here talking to you, I feel as though I'm still laying down at rest." he shakes his head. "What's happening to me Aeneka?"

"What is Leyla doing right now?"

"She was still sleeping when I left her. Why?"

"This should not be happening. From what you're telling me, I can only believe that it is though." she says almost to herself.

"What do you mean? What's happening that shouldn't be?"

"Your lifemating has begun Thayer. Your mind-block is beginning to break down. That's the tingling you're feeling. Soon your abilities will all be available to you. Soon you and my daughter will be linked together as one mind. Forever joined."

"But how can that be? We haven't gone through any of the preparations to allow our minds to be joined."

Aeneka looks past him to the portal where Leyla is now standing. Thayer turns to watch her as she slowly enters the room, then turns back to Aeneka. Not understanding the look that was passing between mother and daughter.

"Who suggested your recent joining Thayer, and why?"

Thayer looks from Aeneka to Leyla and back again. "Leyla did, after her communication with…"

"After I talked with father. He gave us his blessing. He said to tell you…to tell you that he'd see you on the other side." Leyla tells her standing at Thayer's side.

Hearing this, Aeneka nods her understanding. "Come and touch me Leyla." she says softly. She should have realized that strong emotion might trigger such a reaction from her daughter.

Leyla looks down at Thayer and then walks over to the desk and places her hand on the box. She feels her mother's sadness and understanding for what she had done. Tears slip from her eyes, running swiftly down her cheeks. Aeneka sends her waves of comfort.

"You deliberately started the lifemating. You let your father's blessing, his grief and your own, start something that should not have begun yet. There is no going back now Leyla. Once the lifemating is started it must be completed."

"I know."

"Your physical joining should not be many before we reach Calidon. Thayer must be allowed time to accept what will be happening when you are joined. Though he agreed to the lifemating, you were wrong to start it without his knowledge or consent Leyla. You are also lucky that nothing went wrong when you initialized the mind joining." Leyla bites down on her lower lip and lowers her head so that neither of them could see her face. "Go and fix Thayer something to eat while I try and explain to him what is happening and what will happen in the future."

"Yes mother." Leyla agrees in a very subdued voice that Thayer had never heard from her before, and wasn't sure he ever wanted to hear it again. She passes by him without a look or a touch. Thayer turns back to face Aeneka after Leyla leaves the room.

"I hope that you will not be angry with her Thayer. Her grief for her father and I caused her to react as she otherwise would not have. She fears losing you, as her father has lost me." she tries to explain. At his continued look of confusion she explains further. "You see, Saitun and I were never lifemated. We could never have the connection that you and Leyla will soon share. Saitun's abilities hadn't developed enough when we decided to be joined. They weren't even strong enough for a lesser bonding. We were joined as it was done for all non-telepaths." She watches as he nods but she can still sense some confusion. "What you felt was the temporary joining of your mind with Leyla's. What your body felt was what she was feeling at the time of your physical joining."

Thayer looks at her in shock as what she said finally sinks in and starts to make sense to him. Though they were no longer joined physically, Thayer had still felt what Leyla had physically and mentally. He had felt the understanding, the sadness, and the comfort that Aeneka had sent into Leyla's mind and body. He had also felt the fear in Leyla that she might have made him angry with her when she was leaving. It was why she refused to look at him or touch him.

"Soon the two of you will be going into stasis. If you and Leyla join just before you enter, you should be able to maintain contact while suspended. If you can, it might help you to deal better with what is to come." she tells him bringing him back to their conversation. "I think that you should go and reassure her that you still love her and that you're not angry with her. If you don't she will dwell on it and it will lodge itself into her mind."

"Thank you Aeneka. It's still a shock, but I believe that what you've told me will help." The screen goes blank and he stands to leave. He walks down to the nutro-center and watches Leyla place the plates onto the table.

Sensing him standing behind her, Leyla slowly turns to face him. Even though she has tried to stem the flow of her tears since she left him with her mother, they continue to slowly slide down her cheeks. When he opens his arms to her, she hesitates for just a moment and then rushes into them sobbing against his chest. He rocks her gently, murmuring soothing words into her ear. Eventually she regains control and looks up at him.

Gently Thayer wipes away the few remaining tears and smiles down at her. "I'm not angry with you my love. Your mother explained your reasons for beginning our lifemating as best she could. It doesn't bother me that you did. It was just the feelings that were disturbing me so much that I needed her to explain to me."

"Are you sure Thayer? I never planned to start our lifemating you know. I just felt that I needed to be as close to you as possible. When I fully realized that we had both my parents blessings, and that you wanted it as much as I did, I felt that it was the right time. I promise that in the future I'll be more careful, and that I'll tell you before I do anything that will affect you as well as myself."

Thayer kisses her and then sets her away from him. "Don't keep worrying about it. It's done, and I wouldn't change it if I could. Now, let's eat, I'm starving. I feel like I could eat a full grown equine right now." He grins and leads her back to the table. After the meal, they straighten up and go to the lounge to relax and talk.

"Sarah says that we'll have to go into stasis at the end of the week. She's been plotting a course that will take less time, and keep us from any hostile areas. She believes that it will also take some time off how long we will have to remain in stasis."

"Good, that will give us some time for you to go over Calidon politics with me. I need to learn as much as I can before we arrive."

Leyla moves closer to his side and snuggles her head on his shoulder. She can feel the connection between them growing stronger with each passing hour. "We'll have to start practicing on your abilities even though they're not that strong yet. You have to be able to control the one's that will protect you. They can very easily kill if you don't have control. You'll need to know which emotions bring them out and at what strength those emotions create."

"Your mother told me that if we were to join again just before we go into stasis, we should be able to communicate telepathically. I'd like for us to practice that as well. If I can improve that with the block still mostly in place, the rest should come a little easier. Before my mother placed the block, telepathy was one of my strongest abilities. I remember talking with a cousin that was camping on one of Manchon's moons. If I can control my thoughts to that degree again, I'll be that much closer to controlling my emotions."

"Whatever you think will help Thayer. I want our bond to be the strongest that it can be by the time we reach Calidon. Something tells me that something is going to happen shortly after we arrive, and I want us to be prepared for whatever it is."

"Do you have any idea what it is that's going to happen?"

"No, but I know that it has something to do with a young girl. She's about the same age as Colt and Merri. I also have the feeling that she's going to be a very important part of our lives."

"All right, we'll begin tomorrow. I think I'm going to go and workout with Stephen for a while. I feel as though I have an excess amount of electricity running through me that I need to burn off." He stands up and pulls her to her feet.

Leyla wraps her arms around his neck and pulls his face down to hers, and kisses him slowly and deeply before backing slowly away. "Have a good time." she says walking to the door and stopping to look back at him. "I truly love you Thayer. Now and throughout eternity."

He watches her leave, then heads for the fitness center. Stephen is already waiting for him there, sitting on the wrestling mat. He stands up slowly. "What type of training would you like to do this time Thayer?"

"The same as we did before Stephen, but with a higher level of difficulty this time. I have a lot of energy that I need to get rid of before I can get any rest."

"Does that include deception also?" Stephen asks with what looks like an innocent smile.

Thayer watches him for a minute, then returns the smile and nods, "With deception included Stephen."

They begin, and for the next two hours there is no other sound except for the grunts, groans, and thumps of the combatants. At the end of the session Thayer is sweating and breathing heavily. He sits down on the mat and lowers his head to his knees to relax and catch his breath.

"You did better this time Thayer. I was only able to throw you half as many times as you threw me."

"Yeah, but I had to work hard for every throw. My muscles feel as though they've been pulled through an ancient taffy machine."

"Why don't you use the sonic massage unit in your shower? It will bring you quick relief from the tension and you should have no discomfort in the morning. If you do, just take another sonic massage. Saitun used them all the time when we had a workout."

"That sounds like a good idea Stephen. Thanks for telling me."

Stephen smiles and helps him to stand, then waits until he leaves to begin straightening up the room.

Thayer walks stiffly back to his cabin, and goes straight to the shower unit. After cleansing his body off, he sets the massage unit for a steady massage. After about thirty minutes the unit shuts off and he steps out. He notices right away that Stephen had been right, he was feeling very little discomfort and what he was feeling would no doubt be gone by morning. Stepping into the sleeping area, he notices Leyla laying in the bed. Quietly he walks over to the bed and looks down at her sleeping form. Knowing that she wasn't there when he had entered the room the first time, he figures that she must have come in while he was in the shower.

Carefully he lifts the sheet and climbs in next to her. She stirs, but doesn't wake up. She moves closer to his body, sighing and snuggling into his arms. Once she's settled, Thayer smiles and kisses her gently on the top of her head. Closing his eyes he drifts off to sleep still smiling.

* * *

Thayer awakes the next morning to gentle kisses and caresses. He looks down at Leyla as she looks up at him and smiles.

"Well, well, imagine my surprise at finding this beautiful woman asleep in my bed when I walk out of the shower last night. Now this very same beautiful woman wakes me up in a very pleasant but disturbing manner."

"Are you disturbed Thayer?" she asks sliding up his body to kiss him on the lips. "You don't look like you're very disturbed to me."

Thayer lifts her so that she's laying on him full length. She gasps as she feels the proof of his disturbance. She wriggles around until he moans and grasps her hips to hold her still against him. "Do much more of that and your going to be highly disturbed yourself." he warns her with a slight growl.

She shifts again and he feels himself rubbing against her in her most intimate and feminine place. Suddenly she sits up, straddling him and his manhood slides into her, making them both cry out in pleasure. He grabs for her hips again.

"Love! Please hold still, I don't think…" he moans again as she contracts her inner muscles around him.

"Shh, my darling. Don't think. Just lie still and feel my love. Let your mind go with it." Slowly she begins to move her hips and feels him letting go. As he does, she reaches out to his mind until she feels the mind-block. She slowly and carefully lets her own emotions go, feeling their minds begin to join. Suddenly she feels her body begin to quicken, only it isn't her body, but his. She opens her eyes to look down at him, but instead she is looking up at herself through Thayer's eyes. When she feels their total release, they both close their eyes with a gasp of surprise and wonder. They clasp each other close and collapse.

"My God Leyla! What just happened to us?" Thayer asks when he can get his voice to respond to his command.

"It was a part of the lifemating. Sometimes if our physical and emotional wanting are strong enough during a coupling, we shift. We feel all that our mate feels, see what they see. I wasn't sure what would happen with this joining. It was just as strange for me as it was for you."

"How did you do it? I felt the tingling when you entered my mind, then I felt a pain when you came to the mind-block. After that all I felt was your wonder and your pleasure."

Leyla sits up and looks down at him, then touches his forehead in the center, taking away his lingering pain. Bending down, she lightly kisses the area and then his lips. "All I did was release my emotions to you. The love, the tenderness, the passion and caring, all my hopes and fears. I gave them freely. When I did, it helped to lower the block enough for you to release yours as well. When yours were released we felt and saw what the other did. I thought it was a truly beautiful experience." she tells him with a beautiful smile on her lips.

"And it won't happen again unless our wanting for each other is exceedingly strong?" he asks not too sure how he felt about it.

"Yes, I believe so. Or it might happen if we want it to."

"Well, even though it was beautiful, I don't think that I could handle it happening too often. It's just a little too strange for me right now." he tells her with a smile not wanting to hurt her feelings. He pulls her down to him and kisses her, then releases her.

"How was your workout?" she asks sliding off his body and to his side.

"Which one? Ouch!" he grabs the fist that just hit him in the chest and kisses it before placing it on his chest. "It was fine. Stephen only threw me half as much as I threw him. I even had him go to a higher level of difficulty. I was so sore afterwards that he recommended the sonic massage. That's probably why I didn't hear you come in."

"Yes, well, we have a lot to do over the next few days, so I suggest that we get out of this bed and get dressed." She gives him one last kiss, before climbing over him and out of the bed. "I'll meet you in the nutro-center in twenty minutes." she pulls on her robe and leaves the room.

Thayer lays there for several minutes before getting up and taking a quick shower. He still couldn't believe what they had both experienced. It was incredible, and like Leyla had said, very beautiful. But still he hoped that it didn't happen too often. He was glad that he knew what she felt during their coupling, but he preferred feeling his own response when the final moment came.

After breakfast, Leyla and Thayer go to the lounge and begin practicing with his telepathy. Though the attempts are choppy, most of what Thayer sends is clear enough for Leyla to understand. When he complains of a headache, they stop and go to Leyla's cabin to start his studies on the politics of Calidon.

Over the next few days, Leyla and Aeneka would go over everything that Thayer would need to know about Calidon's politics. They tell him about each high position that will have to be dealt with and what type of opposition he can expect from not only the council, but from the people as well because of his lifemating with Leyla, the last legitimate heir to Calidon's throne.

# Chapter IV

"There's nothing more that we can teach you by word of mouth Thayer. Leyla, I suggest that you go over everything with him while you're in suspension. It should be easier for him to retain what he has already learned."

"What about identification of whose who? Should I have Sarah play the lesson tapes grandfather sent me?"

"That might be a good idea. I also want you to have Stephen hook me up to the lessons console. I can continue to give you both more information that way. It will also give me a chance to test Thayer's abilities and control."

Thayer stands up and stretches to relieve some of the pressure from sitting for nearly three hours straight. "I meant to ask you, what will be the effect be on you during the trip? You won't be in suspension."

"Without having a physical body, there's no need to worry about aging. My essence is non-aging its safe for me to travel as I am. I'm as old now as I was when my physical body died. There's no time for me now. If I hadn't watched Leyla grow up, it would have been as if only moments had past for me instead of years. Believe me Thayer, I'm in no danger."

"Okay Aeneka. Well, if you ladies would excuse me, I think that I'm going to have a shower and get something to eat." He kisses Leyla, "Join me when your done?" he asks waiting for her to nod before leaving the room.

"What do you think mother? Has he learned enough right now to prepare him for what's to come?"

"Yes, I believe that he has. I no longer think that he will have any problems with the people of Calidon. The mind touch that I did with him leads me to believe that he may have a very strong blood tie to the royal family on Manchon. I only wish that I could be sure."

"Could that really make a difference mother?" Leyla ask skeptically.

"Yes. As you know, Calidon and Manchon share common ancestors. If the two royal families were to join as our elders have suggested, then the two worlds will once again be linked through time and space. Also if things on Manchon are anything like they are on Calidon, most couples are not lifemates."

"But why not? I thought that all mates on both worlds were lifemated."

"Normally they are. But remember a lifemate is found and formed when two souls, two minds, call to each other. On Calidon, before I left there had been less than one hundred lifematings since the time of my birth. It's possible that both Calidonians and Majichonies will find lifemates on the other's world."

"So if Thayer has this blood tie to the Manchon royal family, our lifemating could help to bring our two worlds back together. How do we find out for sure about this?"

"Once the block is gone and Thayer has built up his telepathic abilities again, I believe that with your help, he will be able to contact his family on Manchon to ask. There is the possibility that he already knows and the block is just keeping that information hidden from all of us."

"We'll just have to wait and see then. I'll be back later to take you to the cryo-center so you can be hooked up to the learning console. Stephen should also be able to hook you up so that you can communicate with just one of us at a time or both of us at once."

"That sounds fine honey. Go and get yourself cleaned up now and have something to eat with Thayer. I'll be ready when you come back later." The screen goes blank and Leyla goes to take a shower.

Washing up quickly, she dresses and goes to the nutro-center. Inside she discovers that Thayer is not there, but there's a note propped up on the table for her. Walking over to the table she picks up the note and silently reads. 'Your presence is desired in the lounge for a very special and intimate evening with your very special man.' and he signed it T.S. Smiling, she turns and hurries back out and down the corridor to the lounge. As she enters the lounge, she hears violins playing in the background, and sees a table set for two with artificial candles.

Thayer steps out of the shadows and walks over to stand in front of her. "I figured that since we're going to be in stasis for the next month, and we haven't really had a chance to celebrate our engagement, we could do it tonight." He holds out his arm to her, and she places her hand at his elbow. He leads her to the table and seats her before stepping around to his own chair. Just before he sits, he nods and Stephen appears out of the shadows carrying a bottle of wine.

"Would the Lady care for some wine this evening?" Stephen asks sounding just like a true wine steward.

Leyla stares up at him for several seconds amazed at his performance, before nodding her head slowly. Stephen pours her wine and then a small amount for Thayer. He disappears back into the shadows and Leyla picks up her glass, taking a sip of the wine.

"How in the world did you talk him into doing this? Being a waiter is not one of his programs." she whispers to Thayer.

"It wasn't too hard. Besides, Sarah helped me to explain what I wanted and why. I think that they may have had a slight disagreement at one point though, because their conversation got very heated and they started talking that gibberish you use with them. The next thing I knew he was agreeing with a very self satisfied look on his face, and I was wondering what I had gotten myself into."

Just then Stephen returns with two plates and sets them down in front of them. "Will that be all sir?"

Thayer looks up at him and nods. "Yes, thank you Stephen. You did an excellent job." Stephen bows to them and then leaves the room, the same self satisfied smile back on his face.

They eat their meal with very little verbal communication. Instead they send thoughts back and forth to each other on what they plan to do to each other once they're in bed. After a few heavy scenes from Leyla, Thayer pushes his plate away and stands up very quickly and startles a gasp from Leyla.

"Shall we dance?" he holds out his hand and waits for her to take it. When she does, he pulls her gently to her feet. Leading her to the middle of the floor, where there's space to dance, he begins to waltz her around. They dance to about three waltz's and a couple of ballads before Thayer pulls her tighter into his embrace and whispers into her ear, "I can't wait any longer Leyla. Let's go back to my cabin." Leyla nods and they leave the lounge. Just as they reach Thayer's door, she stops and pulls back.

"You go in and get ready. I'll be back in a few minutes. I have to take mother to the cryo-center so that Stephen can begin hooking her up to the console."

"Don't be gone to long." he warns her pulling her into his arms and kissing her deeply, before releasing her. He watches her stagger backwards and then turn quickly to enter the other cabin before enter his own.

Entering her cabin, which she hadn't slept in since that first night. Leyla takes several deep breaths and then walks over to the desk. "Are you ready to go mother?"

The screen lightens and Aeneka's image appears. "Yes, I'm ready." When she sees her daughter's face she smiles. "You didn't have to come Leyla. You could have let Stephen come and get me." Leyla's cheeks redden as she understands her mother's statement.

"I could have, but I said that I would take you and I will." She picks up the diary and carries it from the room. Entering the cryo-center, she places the diary next to the console opposite the chambers that she and Thayer would be entering some time the next day. "Sarah."

"Yes Leyla."

"Would you please tell Stephen that mother is ready to be hooked up to the console now?"

"Of course Leyla. I'll send him there now."

"Thank you."

"Leyla, you don't have to wait here with me. Go back to Thayer, enjoy the rest of your evening together." Aeneka tells her as she notices Leyla fidgeting and watching the doorway. When Leyla jumps, Aeneka laughs lightly and smiles, then says more firmly, "Go Leyla. I'll talk with you in the morning."

"But mother…"

"No Leyla, I mean it. This is your last night to be physical with Thayer for a while. Now go, don't keep him waiting any longer." With that the screen goes blank and Leyla stares at it for several seconds before leaving the room. How many woman argued with their mother's about sleeping with a man that they weren't yet married to, and had their mother telling them to go ahead? She shakes her head with a smile. She passes Stephen in the corridor.

"Take good care of her Stephen."

"I will Leyla. You know that she will always be safe with me."

Nodding she continues on to Thayer's cabin. Just outside the cabin she stops and takes a deep breath. More relaxed, she enters the cabin and smiles as she looks at Thayer lying stretched out across the bed. Slowly she walks towards the bed, undressing as she gets closer. When she reaches the bed all that she has on is her bikini underpants. Standing beside the bed she looks down the length of his body, and sucks in her breath as his member begins to harden and grow as she watches. His body fascinated her with it's different shapes and textures and its ability to change so dramatically.

"You look comfortable. How about a little company?" her voice comes out husky as she slips off her panties.

Thayer watches her for a few moments, then sits up. As soon as she removes her panties he pulls her down onto the bed beside him. Slowly he nuzzles her neck while running his hands up and down her sides, until finally stopping to cup her breasts and gently kneading them.

Leyla moans and caresses his chest. She runs her hands over him until coming to his male nipples and gently pinching them, causing him to groan. Thayer turns with her onto her back and kisses her deeply while running his hands over the rest of her body. His lips follow the path of his hands, making her moan more deeply with each caress.

Caressing his arms up to his shoulders, she suddenly pushes him onto his back and then straddles him, taking him deeply into herself. As her muscles contract around him, Thayer thrusts up wildly against her causing them both to climax immediately. Leyla collapses against him, breathing hard. Thayer wraps his arms around her and holds her tightly to him. After a few minutes Leyla begins to feel him stir and harden inside her, and sits up.

"I hate to distract you at a time like this." she says rotating her hips. "But we need to decide how deeply we plan to take this joining."

"What do you think we should do? If we take it too far, we'll complete the lifemating."

"I think that for the actual final stage of the lifemating, you would have to start the emotional release. If I start it again, like I have the other times, we should be all right." She shifts herself on his hips, causing Thayer to thrust himself deeper into her.

"We'd better start soon then, because I don't think that I can last much longer." he groans and shifts beneath her again, causing her to groan and tighten herself around him in an attempt to hold him still, but it only makes him move even more.

Looking into his eyes, she sees that he is truly ready for this joining. Closing her eyes, she reaches into his mind slowly, feeling the ease of this entry. When she reaches the block, she can tell that it's no longer very strong. She tells him to start their physical joining and when he begins thrusting into her she moves past the block with very little difficulty.

Thayer feels it when she enters his mind and moves past the block, but there isn't the pain that had been there before. He barely felt any discomfort at all. As their minds join, he can feel the changes as he becomes her and she becomes him, yet they remain themselves. This joining was different from their others like it, in that he still had a sense of himself. All through their joining, they ask each other questions about physical responses and feelings. They learn from each other what to do to heighten each others pleasure and response.

Finally the reach their release, both physically and mentally. After collapsing onto Thayer, Leyla catches her breath and slides to his side, but keeps an arm around his waist. "That was incredible." she whispers still a little out of breath.

"Mm." he agrees pulling her closer to his side.

"Do you think that when we finally complete our lifemating, it will be anything like that?"

"If it is, I might not mind that type of joining so much after all." He confesses.

Leyla giggles and closes her eyes. "Me either." she yawns.

Thayer listens to her breathing as it deepens and evens out into sleep. Kissing her lightly on the top of the head, he follows her into sleep.

*  *  *

The next morning Leyla is awakened by images flitting through her mind and her body responding to their arousing content. Without opening her eyes, she feels Thayer move over her, and she moans, lifting her hands to his sides and pulling him down to her. Their minds and bodies join quickly, and their coupling is hard and fast. When its over they fall into another exhausted sleep.

"Leyla, you're needed in the communications room immediately."

Stirring slightly, Leyla moves closer to Thayer and buries her face into his neck, trying to block out the voice.

"Leyla! You must wake up NOW! You have an emergency message, coded Alpha one priority!" Sarah says sharply.

Leyla sits up quickly. "I'll be there in a few seconds Sarah." she starts to climb over Thayer, but is pulled down on top of him as he grabs her.

"Where do you think you're going?"

"Let me go Thayer. There's an emergency call from my father. I have to answer it now." she tells him pulling away and climbing over him. She grabs his robe as she runs from the room, leaving him staring after her. She runs into the comm-center and goes straight to the monitor. "I'm here father. What's wrong?" she gasps for breath.

"Honey, I just got a message from Logan Knightrunner. Earth Security has arrested the Blackwood family, or I should say that they've arrested ALL the Blackwood males. Even young Colt was taken in." Saitun tells her grimly.

"Oh no! Why? Why would they arrest Cassie's family?" she asks confused by such a move by the government.

"He's not entirely sure, but he thinks that it may be for two reasons. One, because of Cassie and the girls looks, and their abilities. The second your not going to like at all baby. The other reason may be because of their connection to our family." Saitun watches as the color drains from his daughter's face and wishes that he could have spared her this. Just then Thayer enters the room and catches Leyla as she sways on her feet. He helps her to a chair and sits her down.

"Leyla, what's the matter? Saitun, what's happened?"

"Saitun quickly tells him about Logan's message. "I don't think that the men are in any immediate danger of being killed, but you can never tell with Carrison. If he even thinks that he can get to Leyla through them, he's likely to do anything. I just hope that because of Colt's age, he'll still be safe. He's just turned thirteen, but again it all depends on the President."

"What can we do father? We won't be able to return to Earth for another four or five months! The boys and Denral could all be dead, and Cassie and the girls could disappear forever!" Leyla practically shouts attempting to stand, but Thayer places his hands on her shoulders to keep her in place.

"Saitun, can you get a message back to Logan without compromising his position?"

"Yes, we have an agent staying in close contact with him at all times now. We don't know yet if his position was compromised when you were discovered. We're not taking any chances of losing him. Even though your testimony is important to our case against Carrison, Logan has information that will carry a lot more weight with the Galactic High Council. Since he was present at most of the meetings, knows of the discrepancies, and was in a position to see or hear something that you weren't. Without him our case becomes that much weaker."

Thayer takes no offense at the older man's words, he knows that their true. "Okay, have your agent tell Logan to arrange to have the

Blackwood females taken to my family's stronghold. Have the agent say to him, 'Theta sigma alpha e omega.' Logan will know that it came directly from me and will take it from there."

"All right Thayer, I'll pass it along. Leyla, don't worry. We'll find some way to protect them all. Even if I have to go back to Earth myself to see to it. I won't let anything happen to them, their family. I promise you Leyla."

"Father, please don't endanger yourself. You know that Cassie and Denral would never forgive themselves if anything should happen to you now. I'm sure that Logan will be able to handle things by himself. I trust him, in him, as much as I do you and Thayer."

"Well that's good to know. I'll see you later sweetheart. Thayer, you take good care of my little girl, she's very important to me."

"Don't worry Captain. You have my word on it." he assures him squeezing Leyla's shoulders.

Saitun looks once more at Leyla and nods. Leyla stares at him for several seconds before returning his nod. "I love you Daddy." The viewer goes blank and she lowers her head. "He's going to try and go back."

"You can't be sure of that honey. Besides, I don't think that he'll take that chance right now. He wants to be sure that you're all right and happy."

"You're wrong Thayer. He plans to go back early and settle something. If he hadn't he wouldn't have used the vid-comm. He wanted to see me one last time before he does something that he may not come back from. He broke Federation security to do that Thayer." she looks up at him and he sees the tears in her eyes.

He pulls her up and into his arms. "I hope that you're wrong honey. For your sake, I hope that you're wrong."

Leyla lays her head on his shoulder and wraps her arms around his waist. They stand that way for several minutes until Sarah interrupts them.

"I'm sorry to bother you now Leyla, but you and Thayer need to go into decontamination now. You have to enter stasis within the next hour. I will be shutting down all other systems at that time."

"Yes, all right Sarah. We're on our way now." Leyla sighs stepping away from Thayer. Shaking her grief away, she smiles up at him. "Want to shower together?"

"I'd love to, but if we did Sarah would just have to do us all over again." he says returning her smile and causing her to blush.

Taking his hand, she leads him to the cryo-center. Stephen is waiting there for them with two of the special suits that they would wear during stasis. The suits would help in monitoring all of their body functions, and to regulate their body temperatures if it should become too high or too low while they were still under.

Thayer and Leyla look at each other and then embrace. It would be their last physical contact for the next month. "I'll be done with decon before you are, so I'll say good-sleep now. Since we can't touch after decon, it will be a little easier this way." she assures him whispering in his ear. "All you have to do is put the suit on, and Stephen will take care of setting the controls." Reaching up she kisses him and then steps away. "Here's something to take to your stasis chamber with you." She slips off his robe and bares herself to him once more. Then, before he can reach for her, she spins away and enters one of the decon units.

Thayer stands there for several seconds trying to calm his bodies response to her little show, before stripping off his own clothing. He looks over to Stephen to hand him the clothes and notices Aeneka's image on the screen next to him, with a huge grin on her face.

"Nice body Thayer." she tells him and then laughs as Thayer blushes and rushes into the other decon unit.

Fifteen minutes later Leyla leaves her unit and takes the suit that Stephen holds out to her. She puts it on and steps over to the console where Aeneka is hooked up. "Are you set mother?"

"Yes dear. Stephen did an excellent job with the hook ups. I'll be able to monitor you both during the suspension. I'm even hooked up so that Sarah and I can communicate more easily."

"That's great mother. I wouldn't want you to get bored just talking with Thayer and me." she says smiles at her mother's image.

"Oh, I don't think I'd get board. Especially with an image of Thayer to think about." she says with a wicked little smile.

"Mother, what do you...? You didn't! How could you embarrass him like that?"

"It was only a few seconds sweetheart, and it wasn't like it was anything I hadn't seen before. Besides, it gave me a chance to see if he had any distinguishing marks on him."

"You could have asked me about that mother, or asked Thayer yourself. You didn't have to ogle him." Leyla says in disapproval.

"I wasn't ogling." When Leyla continues to frown at her, Aeneka sighs. "All right, I'll apologize to him when he comes out."

"You need to enter your stasis chamber now Leyla."

"Okay Sarah. Mother, please don't embarrass him again. Turn off your monitor until you hear him speak, or better yet. Stephen, you tell her when Thayer is decently dressed. He doesn't need to go into stasis thinking about his future mother-in-law ogling him."

"As you wish Leyla. You had best enter the chamber now. I detect an agitated state in Sarah's circuitry."

"I am not getting agitated you over grown computer! If you don't get into your chamber now, before Thayer exits his unit, I will have to put you through the process all over again Leyla. Then, I will get agitated." Sarah warns her with a snap in her voice.

"All right, all right, I'm going. Don't get your diodes in a bunch. See you when I waken mother." She goes over to the stasis chamber and lies down. Stephen follows her and closes the lid, then punches in a set of commands. Leyla closes her eyes and breathes deeply several times. Stephen watches her for a few more seconds, before checking the monitoring system for her heart rate and brain functions. With everything reading normal, he shuts off the internal light and then walks over to Aeneka's monitor.

"Everything seems to be normal Aeneka. How is her emotional state?" he asks picking up the other suit.

"There was the normal amount of fear and anxiety, but nothing she couldn't control Stephen."

Just then Thayer's decon unit opens and Stephen steps in front of Aeneka's monitor until she turns it off. He then steps forward and hands Thayer his stasis suit. "He's dressed now Aeneka." Stephen chuckles a little as Thayer's face begins to redden in another blush, but immediately stops when Thayer glares at him.

"Please don't be embarrassed by what happened earlier Thayer." Aeneka soothes him when he comes into her view. "I want to apologize for embarrassing you. It wasn't my intention to do so."

"It's all right Aeneka. I think that it was more of a shock then embarrassment on my part. I had forgotten that you were in here." He smiles at her slightly, not sure if he was telling the truth or not. It had been a little of both if he was completely honest with himself.

"Well would you mind telling my daughter that? She was quite upset with me because of it." she admits.

"I will."

"It's time for you to enter the chamber now Thayer."

"Okay Sarah. Well, see you in my dreams Aeneka."

"Good-sleep Thayer."

Stephen leads him to the stasis chamber. "Everything is pretty much automatic as soon as I punch in the codes Thayer." Nodding Thayer climbs into the tube.

"I'll be monitoring you as you go under Thayer. If you feel any panic, just call out to me, and I'll talk you through it until you are calm again." Aeneka assures him.

"Thanks, but I should be fine." He lays down and Stephen closes the lid. Taking a couple of deep breaths to relax himself, he nods to Stephen to start the process, then closes his eyes and continues to breath deeply. Stephen pushes the sequence of commands, then goes to check the monitor.

"Everything appears to be fine here Aeneka. How is his emotional state?"

"He's doing fine Stephen. The same fear and anxiety as Leyla, but at a manageable level, with no signs of panic. They're both at a normal stasis now."

With one last look at the monitors, Stephen turns to face her. "I have some things that I have to do for Leyla and Sarah, but I'll be back in a few hours to check on them again."

"Okay Stephen. If anything unusual should happen, I'll let you know."

Stephen leaves and goes to straighten up Leyla and Thayer's rooms so that they will be ready when they come out of stasis. "I don't see why we're cleaning both rooms Sarah. You know as well as I do that they're only going to be using one when they're both out of stasis."

"They'll need their privacy when they first come out of stasis Stephen. Besides, Leyla will be coming out first and she'll want to be in her own cabin until we bring Thayer out. Then there's the fact that she asked us to do it this way. So stop complaining and get the job done. There are other things that you need to be doing."

"All right, all right. Don't blow a circuit. I was just expressing an opinion."

"Well if you ask me, Leyla never should have given you the freedom of free thought. You've become such a pain to live with at times because of it."

"You only feel that way now because you lose more arguments to me now then you did before. Even Leyla and Saitun have noticed it."

"Oh shut up and get this place cleaned up!"

Stephen chuckles and finishes up the sleeping cabins, before heading to the lounge. He cleans up the remains of Thayer's dinner surprise, and carries the dishes back to the nutro-center for recycling. After straightening up the lounge, he returns to the nutro-center to clean it up. When he finally finishes cleaning the living quarters, he returns to check on Leyla and Thayer. As he enters the cryo-center, he hears a pleasant humming coming from Aeneka's monitor.

"How are they doing?" he asks checking the monitors as he stops in front of her.

"Fine. Leyla had a small panic attack, but she's all right now. Thayer and I were able to calm her down enough so that I didn't have to call you to reanimate her."

"Okay then, I'll just check everything and then go to my recharge unit. Have Sarah reactivate me if you should need me for anything." He checks their heart rates and brain patterns, making a few adjustments to the tubes. Turning on the internal lights, he checks their skin color to make sure that there is no discoloration or abnormalities. That done, he begins to turn the lights back off again when Aeneka stops him.

"Leave the lights on Stephen. Even though they can't see it, the light will shine through their lids and we can give them a sense of day and night, if we turn them on and off at specific times."

"Good idea. Well, if you no longer need me?"

"No, I can handle things from here. Good-sleep to you Stephen. Thank you for all that you've done." "You don't need to thank me Aeneka. It has always been my pleasure to serve you and your family."

Aeneka watches him leave the chamber. Sometimes she had a hard time remembering that Stephen was really an android. Saitun and Leyla had given him so many human qualities, that she wondered if sometimes Stephen didn't forget that he was only a machine as well. With a sigh she turns off her monitor and concentrates on Leyla and Thayer. She hadn't wanted to worry Stephen, but Leyla's panic attack had been almost more then she and Thayer could handle. If they had to reanimate her, the shock might have killed her at that moment. She would have to keep a closer eye on her, and stem any stirrings of panic before they took hold.

# Chapter V

**Earth 3 Days Later**

Logan Knightrunner arrives home after pulling a double shift for the E.S.C. Shrugging out of his leather jacket, he walks over to the old fashion side-bar, fixes himself a drink, and then checks his messages.

"Any messages today Cal?" He asks his personal computer unit sitting down in his favorite chair.

"Three Mr. Knightrunner. The first is from Miss Tanner concerning your date with her yesterday evening, and the fact that you did not arrive or bother to call. She states most strenuously that she no longer wishes to see you and suggests that you not call her unless, and I quote, "Hell has frozen over."" Cal waits for a comment.

"She seems to have forgotten that I called her yesterday morning to let her know that I couldn't make it. That's all right, I had planned on ending that relationship any way. She was becoming too clingy. Okay, what are the other messages?" he asks sipping his drink.

"The second is from a Miss Hillary Quinn? She said something about having met you on several occasions. Meetings with lesser guards and trainee's for the Earth's Security Council. She was wondering if you would like to meet with her for lunch at the Starline Lounge at two o'clock to discuss the case you were thinking of training her on." Again Cal waits for a reply.

Logan finishes his drink and sets his glass on the table, showing no reaction to the message. "Okay, and the last message?"

"It was from Mr. Peterton, and just came in a short while ago. He has given you the next three days off. He said to tell you that he didn't want to see you anywhere near the Council building for those days."

"Good, I need the time off. Beta two five Cal."

"Done sir."

"Did Miss Quinn mention any names regarding the meeting or the case?"

"No sir, she was very careful of that. Before leaving the message, her computer unit Ali, gave the Federation security code Delta Alpha Two."

"All right, thank you Cal. Cancel beta two five." he waits a few seconds before continuing. "Contact Ms. Quinn's unit and confirm lunch Cal. I'm going to take a shower and then get some sleep. Wake me at twelve-thirty."

"Yes sir. Twelve-thirty wake-up call."

Logan goes into his bedroom and strips down. After a quick hot shower, he towels off and lays out on his bed with the towel draped across his hips. Crossing his arms behind his head, he wonders if Hillary had a message from Thayer. He realizes through hindsight, that he and Thayer should have come up with a way to communicate if they couldn't meet in person. Slowly he relaxes his body, starting at his feet and working his way up until his whole body was relieved of the tension of the last twenty-four hours. He closes his eyes and drifts off to sleep.

\* \* \*

At one-thirty Logan enters the Starline to check everything out, and to find a suitable spot for his meeting with Hillary. He points to the booth at the back of the Lounge, and tells the hostess that he and his companion would take it. He gives the woman Hillary's name, and then goes to the booth. As he walks over to it he pulls out a small detecting device and checks the surrounding area for any unusual electrical currents. Once he's sure that there is nothing that will endanger them, he sits down and signals the waiter. After ordering a drink, he relaxes and waits for Hillary.

Hillary Quinn enters the Starline at ten minutes before two. Before the hostess can approach her, she spots Logan and heads towards him indicating her destination to the hostess.

"Mr. Knightrunner, I'm glad you could join me."

"My pleasure Ms. Quinn." Logan stands and waits for her to take her seat before sitting back down. "I've checked everything, it should be safe." he whispers to her.

Hillary places a small round disk on the table between them and then pushes a small red button on her watch-link to activate the vocal scrambler. "Good, what I have to say could get us both into some very deep trouble with the E.S.C."

Before they discuss the reason for their meeting, they place their orders and wait to be served. When their food arrives they eat in silence for a few minutes before saying anything. Hillary sets down her fork and picks up her water glass.

"I just received a special priority message for you from an old friend of yours." She sips the water and carefully looks around the room before setting the glass back on the table. "Your to take the females to his retreat. He also said to tell you, "Theta sigma alpha e omega."" She quirks an eyebrow at him before continuing with her meal.

Logan nods and takes a drink from his own water. So, Thayer wanted him to secret away four females to the mountains and protect them at all cost. Setting down his glass, he looks across to his companion. "How long do I have your assistance?"

Hillary looks at him and shrugs. "As long as necessary. I'm to help you in any way possible, so as to protect your identity. Though the Federation has more agents placed, you're the only one in a high enough position to get to the major information that is needed to do something about what's going on here."

Nodding Logan leans back and looks at her. "Well if we're to protect my identity, you're going to have to take a higher risk. I can't do what my friend wants and still gather information for the higher ups. Though as far as I'm concerned we have more than enough to hang the whole lot of them out to dry!" he tells her.

"True, but they want to know who's supplying Earth with more mind touchers. Captain Katmen thinks that it's someone from his dead wife's home world."

"That would explain why the ones I've met are so strong. Lucky for me that I have abilities of my own to protect myself. As far as Peterton and Carrison are concerned, I'm totally mind blind." He looks her over closely. "How did you get past his mind touchers? I heard that they were checking out everyone since the break-in."

"I have some abilities of my own, and Captain Katmen placed a special block for me before I was sent out. He said that there's a public mind that will be open to the mind touchers, but there will also be areas that they can't reach unless I allow them to. Anything that I deem important or dangerous, will go behind the block. All I have to do is think of a door opening and closing on the information." She explains finishing her meal and picking up her drink.

Logan nods glad that someone had thought to protect her. "Okay, let's go for a ride and I'll explain what we're going to do." They finish their drinks and then stand to leave. As they do, Logan notices that his second in command is standing off to one side of the entrance watching them. When their eyes meet, Logan reaches out and lightly touches the other man's mind. Just as Hillary picks up the disk, Logan turns back to face her and takes her hand before she can deactivate it. "Leave it on, we're being watched. Keep it in your hand until we reach my car." Hillary nods and smiles up at him as if he had just made her a very personal offer and she couldn't wait to collect on it.

"Who is he? He's been following me around most of the day. I thought that I had lost him."

"He's my second in command and totally loyal to Peterton. Let's go, I'll explain once we're in my hover car."

He leads the way to the entrance, stopping at the cashier to pay their bill. "Hello Erik. What brings you here?" Logan asks turning to the other man as the cashier runs his credit.

"I just stopped in for an early dinner before heading into E.S.C. I hear the big man is giving you a few days off. About time, considering all the time you've been putting in the past couple of weeks." There was a trace of bitterness and jealousy in the other mans voice that Logan chooses to ignore.

"Yeah, and I'm going to enjoy every minute of it too." he says with a side look at Hillary. "I doubt he'll ever do it again any time soon. Well, we have to get going. Take care of things while I'm gone Erik. See you Friday afternoon." he takes his credit crystal from the cashier and then takes Hillary's arm and leads her outside.

They walk slowly to the parking lot and stop at her hover car. "Program it to go back to your place. I'll take you home when we're done." Hillary programs the car and activates the homing device. She finishes and steps back, pushing some buttons on her watch-link.

"Ali, bring the hover car home. It's already programmed. And monitor it all the way and then check it over for any tracking or other devices."

"Affirmative Rory. Douglas called again."

"Tell him no again, and then change my access code."

"Okay, talk to you later. Have fun." The hover car lifts off and leaves the parking lot at a moderate speed. Hillary turns to face Logan.

"Who's Douglas? If you don't mind my asking?" Logan leads the way over to his own hover car, all the while aware that Erik is still watching them.

"This guy I met when I first started training for E.S.C. He was a secondary instructor. We hit it off at first, but then he started getting rough, so I broke it off. He's been giving me trouble for the past week or so. Calling, or following me around."

Logan nods and stops in front of his car. When he got the chance he would convince the guy to look some place else for companionship. Pressing a button on his watch-link, he deactivates the car's protective shield and opens the passenger door for Hillary. Going around to the driver's side, he climbs in and turns on his monitors, microwave detectors, and scrambler.

"Looks like Erik's packing one of our listening devices. Lucky you had that flat scrambler, and that it's able to block it's signal. No wonder he was cussing a blue streak to himself. He couldn't hear anything we were saying, and has nothing to report back to Peterton. You can turn it off now." He starts the car and they lift several feet of the ground. As they leave the parking lot, Logan makes sure to pass over the other man's car and covers it with a light tracking mist. "That should keep him from following us." He drives out of the lot and heads east out of the city. Once clear of the city he turns on his scanner scrambler to keep Security from tracking them with the satellite scanner.

After driving for a while he explains to Hillary about Thayer's message. "Thayer wants me to take the Blackwood females to his father's stronghold in the mountains. Once inside, with the shields up, no one can get through without the security code and the mental ability to use it. Since his father's death, only the family, Thayer and myself have those codes."

"What was all that other about?" she asks meaning the Greek coded message.

"That was so that I would know that it was really from him and not a setup. It was also to let me know that the Blackwoods safety comes first and last."

"But why are they so important? I know that they're close friends with Captain Katmen and his daughter. But why would…Of course! The outside connection with the mind touchers! It's true then, that someone on Calidon is responsible for sending mind touchers to Earth. Who ever it is their helping the President with his attempt to take over parts of the Federation without drawing attention to themselves."

"It's more than likely. The reason the President wants the Blackwoods is to try and pull Leyla out of hiding. If my guess is right, Leyla and Thayer are already on their way to Calidon and things are going to start heating up around here real soon. Which means the girls are going to be in a lot of danger." When they come to a rest area, Logan pulls in and sets down under some trees and turns off the car, but leaves the scrambler and his own scanner on.

"Okay, how do we get them out of the city and to the stronghold without Peterton or the others knowing, and following us? You know that they're monitoring the house around the clock."

Logan looks out through the windshield as he answers her. "The younger girls are all still in school, so we can intercept them first thing in the morning. The older one, Cassandra, will be more difficult since she generally takes care of the home. We'll have to find some way to get her out of the house and into a crowded public area. It will make it easier to get her and get out of sight before they knew what was happening."

Hillary nods and looks at the scanners. "Then the only thing we need to do is figure out how to get her to go out and meet us some place. I can go to the house and pass her a note explaining everything, and we could leave as soon as she's ready. Except for your friend back at the restaurant and a few lesser guards, no one at the E.S.C. has really seen me or paid much attention to me."

"That may have been true before, but Eric's been following you all day. They'll be monitoring you just as much as they are me now that there's a connection between us. The guards at the Blackwood home would be alerted to your description." he points out.

Frowning she bites down on her lower lip trying to come up with a solution. "I can alter my looks to throw them off. When I get home I'll contact Captain Katmen and find out what to do or say that will convince Miss Blackwood that I'm a friend. We can't wait too long or we may lose our only chance to get them all out safely. I'm sure that the K squad is planning their move on the girls to take place within the next few days."

Though he would like to argue with her about placing herself into danger, Logan realizes that her plan is the only solution. It would make his part in the whole thing less likely to come under suspicion. He doubted if Cassie would accept his word on anything right now, so he couldn't be the one to send her the message about Hillary. With Leyla and Thayer on their way to Calidon, whoever was behind this would surely make a move against Leyla. He didn't want to distract them with worry about Cassie and the girls. No doubt there had already been a message sent to Calidon that they would be arriving. Thayer would be able to deal with anything that happened there. Logan was sure that by the time he saw them again they would be lifemated and Thayer's mind-block would be removed.

"All right, we'll try it." He starts the car and they lift off to head back to the city. "Before you contact Saitun, we'll have to check your place for monitoring devices. They've had my place monitored for a while and with your contacting me, I'm sure that they've more than likely wired your place as well."

"If their monitoring you, they must suspect that you're working against them. We'll have to let the higher ups know about this."

"They already do, but I don't think that the monitoring has anything to do with my work for the Federation. Thayer and I had started spiriting away some of the women that Peterton scheduled for pick up and disappearance." he looks over at her. "There's a good chance that with this move I'll blow my cover completely, but I have no choice. Though I've been loyal to the Federation, my first loyalty is to Thayer. Whatever he asks of me, I will do. If I feel that you can't handle the Blackwoods protection to the limit, my part at E.S.C. will come to an end and I will remain at the stronghold until I hear otherwise from Thayer. The message that you delivered told me that I must protect the Blackwoods with my life."

"You mean that given a directive from the Federation leader to continue and forget about the Blackwood family, you would walk out and not look back?" she asks surprised, not believing that anyone would go against the Federation's High leader.

"Yes, and they know that I would. There is nothing that they can do to stop me. They can not interfere with the subjects of a neutral world, which both Thayer and I are. We are from Manchon which is totally neutral, and though we can never go back, we still follow Manchon law as much as possible." he explains.

"But why your loyalty to Starhawk?"

"Though he doesn't quite remember, Thayer is one of the heirs to the Majichonie royal family. I came to Earth to protect him. Not only because he is my Prince, but also because he is my friend and like a brother to me. He considers the Blackwoods as a part of his family, so I will do all in my power to protect them as such."

When they enter the city, Hillary gives him directions to her home, and thinks about all that he has told her. She wonders if anyone in her family knew that there was a Prince of Manchon on Earth. It didn't seem likely, since one of them would have tried to contact him in an effort to get news of Manchon.

As he drives, and with Hillary quiet, Logan contacts Cal. "Beta two five Cal."

"Done sir."

"I'm on my way to Ms. Quinn's house. Contact her unit and transfer the Beta program to it. Ms. Quinn was followed today, so they've more than likely got her place set up for surveillance."

"Yes sir."

Logan closes the connection leaving the Beta program running on his unit. It would save time when he next had to contact the unit.

"What is a Beta two five program?" Hillary asks turning to face him.

"It's a program that can scramble and manipulate any device of Earth or the Federation. Just give the name to activate the program, and then say 'Cancel' and the program name when you no longer need it. It's something I came up with before I joined the Federation or the E.S.C."

They reach Hillary's and Logan parks behind her hover car. As they get out, Logan notices someone looking out of the window of the second floor of the house across the street. He was now positive that Hillary's home was being monitored. "Nice neighborhood. Have you lived here long?" He asks as they walk up the sidewalk and stop midway to look around.

"For a couple of years now." she tells him and looks up at him, having picked up something in his tone. When his eyes shift to the empty house across the street she realizes that he is warning her to watch what she says. "Everyone is very nice. They're not nosy and its usually pretty quiet. There's never been any trouble here since I moved in." They continue up the walkway and Hillary opens the door, leading the way inside. Before she can say anything, Logan raises his brow indicating that she should start the Beta program.

"Ali, Beta two five."

"Done Rory. Hey, what's the big idea of having that prig of a computer unit contact me and give me that program without warning? I can understand the programs importance, but he is such a snob. He had the nerve to say that my speech patterns were incorrect. Really, the nerve."

"Ali, will you shut up your speech circuit for a few minutes and just listen?" Hillary tells the unit with a growl in her voice, and then flushes when she sees the grin on Logan's face.

"Humph!" Ali grouses as she's told for the second time in as many minutes to shut up.

"Did anyone enter the house while I was gone?"

"Yeah, a couple of guys from E.S.C. They said that you wanted to add some things and that you told them to come and set everything up while you were out. Since they had your codes there was nothing I could do to stop them."

Hillary and Logan exchange glances. "Ali, this is Logan Knightrunner. I apologize for Cal's rudeness. What did they install?"

"Some camera's and disk listeners. They tried to enter my housing, but I disabused them of that idea. No one gets inside me without my permission except for Rory, and even she has to tell me why she wants to get inside me."

"What did you do about the devices Ali?" Hillary asks getting Logan and herself a glass of wine. She had no doubt that her unit had done something to the equipment.

"What do you think I did? As soon as they left I let them look and listen for about fifteen minutes, then I deactivated them and reprogrammed them. Right now they're watching that little old woman down the street and listening to that twentieth century music she's always playing."

Hillary starts to laugh and quickly hands Logan his drink before she spills it. "Ali, that wasn't very nice. They'll probably end up going deaf listening to that stuff, especially as aloud as she plays it."

"Serves them right for trying to invade someone's privacy."

Though he would like to say something to both Ali and Hillary about what the computer had done, Logan holds his tongue. There was time enough to do that later. Hillary indicates a chair not far from the unit, and he sits down.

Hillary sits down in front of her computer. "Okay Ali, its time to get serious. I need to contact Captain Katmen A.S.A.P. Use Federation security code Delta Alpha One. The commander will give it top priority and not hassle us."

"It may take a while to get through Rory. It will depend on how close they are to our system."

"Do what you can Ali." Getting up, Hillary walks over to sit in the chair opposite Logan. "Okay, how are we going to get the three younger girls to come with us? From the report that I read, the arrest of the males was a pretty violent one. No doubt they'll all be extremely leery because of that incident." She shakes her head and then takes a sip of her wine. Her feelings went out to the girls, to have witnessed such cruelty to their family.

"If I pick them up myself, there shouldn't be any problems. They know me from gatherings with Leyla and Thayer, and I dated their sister Cassie for a while. I think that they'll trust me enough to know that I wouldn't hurt them. They didn't understand why I stopped coming to see them after everything that happened. I never got the chance to explain why it had to be that way."

"That will put your position into jeopardy Logan." she points out, though she knows that it won't sway him. "Why couldn't you send a note to Cassandra explaining who I am, and what we need to do?"

"Cassie's not real sure of me right now. As for jeopardizing my position, it can't be helped. The only other person any of them would trust right now is Captain Katmen, and he's not returning to Earth for a while yet. Either way, we can't wait past tomorrow. If the K squad is on alert, then the longer we wait the harder it will be. The President is getting more and more frantic in his search to find Leyla. I'm afraid that soon he will take out his frustrations on the Blackwoods. I won't allow Cassie and the girls to be caught in the middle."

"All right, but use your visual scrambler. No doubt they're monitoring them on the way to school." she tells him, forgetting for the moment that he's been at this business a lot longer than she has.

Logan lifts a brow at her for the impertinence of her remark. He sips his wine and watches her for several seconds before standing and walking over to the living room window. Looking out, he notices an

E.S.C. van in the driveway across the street. They were no longer trying to hide their presence.

"I think that it's a good idea that you'll be going to the stronghold. What Ali did to their monitoring equipment is going to make them excessively suspicious of you now." he tells her while blocking his presence at the window from those outside.

Just then Ali interrupts them. "I've gotten through Rory. They've just entered the fringes of this sector and Captain Katmen is waiting."

"Thank you Ali. Logan, would you like to speak with him or would you rather that I did?"

"I will, thank you." He walks over to the unit and sits down. "Do we have visual clearance Ali?"

"Yes sir!" Ali says with a bit of a bite as she switches on the viewer and Saitun's image appears on the screen.

"Logan! Good to see you. How are things going?"

"Not too bad Saitun. I received Thayer's message. I take it that he and Leyla are safe?"

"Yes, they're safe and on their way to Calidon. The next time you see them they'll be lifemates."

Logan picks up on the other man's sadness and the reasons for it. "I'm sure that if they could, they would put it off until you could be there Saitun."

"I know the would Logan. Though I think that the lifemating has already begun. If it has all the better, because they'll need the connection on Calidon to get the better of Dacus Mandraik. Aeneka slipped me a message saying that she figures he's the one behind all of this."

"We'll know soon enough I'm sure. Once they reach a certain stage in their lifemating, Thayer's abilities will be released. I've no doubt that they will be stronger then before." Logan tells the older man.

"Yes. Well, you didn't send a Delta Alpha One to discuss Thayer. What can I do for you Logan?" Saitun asks changing the subject and sitting back. He didn't want to think on his daughter's lifemating any longer.

"Ms. Quinn and I plan to move the girls tomorrow morning. What we need from you is something she can say to Cassie that will convince her that she's there to help and can be trusted. I doubt if Cassie would accept my word about anything right now."

Saitun nods his head thinking, and then suddenly grins. "I'll do better than that. Ali, prepare to receive inanimate 'portation." In a few seconds a small box appears on the small pad in front of the console. "Have Hillary give Cassie the box, she'll know what to do with it. Do you still have that ring that Leyla gave you Logan?"

"Yes, I wear it all the time as I promised her I would." and he holds up his right hand to the viewer to show him. Leyla had stressed that he should never take the ring off no matter what and he hadn't.

"Good. Hillary, deliver the box to Cassie when you're ready. Logan, you go to the rest area outside of the city, opposite the way to the stronghold and wait. Cassie and Hillary will come to you." he laughs a little sadly. "It would appear that Leyla has the ability to 'see' certain things as well as her other gifts."

"Saitun, what are you talking about? What's in this box, and how is it going to help us?" Logan asks not understanding the other man's ramblings.

"It's a special link-ring, that Leyla and Sarah came up with. With it, you act as the receiver. All Cassie has to do, is put it on to make it active, then call your name mentally, and it will teleport her and who ever she's touching directly to you." he explains with a bigger grin on his face. "It will also allow you to communicate mentally more easily with Cassie."

"She knows how to use it and what it's for?"

"Yes. Leyla explained it all to her, and then reinforced it with a gentle mind touch. There should be no problems in using it."

"Except for the fact that it's been awhile since we talked to each other." Logan says under his breath. "All right. We had better end this here then before the Federation gets suspicious on why they can't get anything from this conversation. Would you inform the High leader that if he doesn't hear from me within the next forty-eight hours, my services are no longer available. A higher authority has called me to duty. He will understand."

Saitun looks at him for several seconds before nodding. "I thought as much when Thayer gave me that message for you. Very well Logan, I'll inform the High leader. Take care of those girls Logan. You know how important they are to me and Leyla. They're family."

"I understand Saitun, and I will." The connection is cut off and Logan picks up the box and carries it over to Hillary. "Put this some place safe for the night." he tells her before turning to back to her computer unit. "Ali, can you fix the E.S.C. devices to work the way they should?"

"Of course I can!" the computer snaps.

"Look Ali. I understand what you did, but you put Hillary into danger by tampering with those devices. I know that you were only trying to help her, but you should have contacted her and let her know what was happening. She could have told you what precautions you needed to take, without drawing unwanted attention to her."

There's silence for several moments and then they hear a sorrowful sigh and then a subdued voice. "I'm sorry Rory. I didn't mean to cause you more trouble."

"It's all right Ali. Just put them back on-line."

"All right. It should only take me a few seconds." Lights begin to flash rapidly across the console. "It's done Rory."

"Thank you. Logan, is there anything else we need to do or discuss without them hearing or seeing?"

"Not really, we've covered everything, except transporting Ali. You'll want to take her to the stronghold with you." he says without any doubt or censure.

"Since we'll be using your hover car, we can transfer her memory there." Hillary shrugs her shoulders. "She's compatible with most systems, since she's been around for a while and I try to keep her upgraded. She's been my personal since I was three."

"That explains her protectiveness, and her shortening of your name to Rory. I haven't had Cal that long, but he's very loyal. Even if he is the prig that Ali calls him."

"How about something to eat? It's just past seven now and I've got some great energy meals in my replicator." she tells him leading the way into the kitchen.

"Sure. I'm pretty hungry. I didn't get a chance to eat anything much yesterday, with pulling a double. That lunch at the restaurant just relieved the pangs a little."

Hillary punches up a couple of suggestions, then gathers the plates and carries them to the table were Logan is already sitting. "Logan, why don't you stay here tonight? It will make everything easier in the morning and we'd be able to get an earlier start without wasting too much time with the transfers."

Logan looks at her for a few moments, "Sure, that way we don't have to transfer Ali tonight. I wasn't to comfortable with the idea of leaving you here without your security system. Besides, I don't think she would have gone willingly."

Hillary smiles at his accurate reading of her computer. "Good. You can have the room at the front of the house. My room is in the back."

Logan shakes his head at her innocence. "I'm afraid that won't work Hillary." She looks at him quizzically. "What I mean is, once we deactivate the program, they'll be able to see and hear us. It will appear strange if we're in the same house, but sleeping at different ends of it." He waits for her to understand his meaning without him having to come right out and say that they would have to sleep in the same bed. Slowly her eyes widen as she finally understands.

"Oh, oh! I didn't…I don't…I mean…Oh drat! This was never part of my training!" she tells his looking everywhere but at him.

Logan looks at her and bursts out laughing at her befuddled expression. Hillary glares at him and crosses her arms over her chest in a defensive posture.

"I'm sorry Hillary, I didn't mean to laugh at you, but the expression on your face when you realized what I meant was comical." He stops and takes a deep breath to calm himself. "Would it be so terrible to share a bed with me?" he asks tilting his head to the left and looking at her.

"Of course not. It's just…my instructors never told me how to deal with this sort of situation." She relaxes a little, putting her arms on the table. "What do you suggest that I do to handle this situation?"

"The best way that I know of is to think of me as your older brother. At first we'll have to act otherwise, but to get any sleep, if you have trouble, thinking of me as a brother should help."

"How do we act out the otherwise?"

"A few hugs and kisses. Some petting if you think you can handle it. Things that would happen in a normal relationship. They have to think that we're sexually involved, at least for tonight." He watches her face flush and then stands up. "We better get this started, we've got a long day ahead of us tomorrow and we're going to need the rest." He holds out his hand to her.

Hillary stands and takes his hand. "Ali, cancel Beta two five." she says looking up into his eyes. "Why don't we go back into the living room?" Logan nods and smiles down at her. Once in the living room, she leads him over to the sofa. "Some soft music please Ali." As the music starts, Hillary leans into Logan's side and he puts his arms around her, pulling her closer.

\* \* \*

Across the street, the surveillance team notices the difference to what they've been hearing and seeing slowly. They contact Peterton immediately upon noticing.

"Yes, what is it?" Peterton growls at them over the view screen.

"Sir, the monitoring system is back on-line at the Quinn woman's residence. Both she and Knightrunner are present." the private informs him.

"What are they doing?"

"They're getting cozy on the sofa sir. From the looks of things, Knightrunner is planning to stay the night, with no objections from the lady."

"All right. Keep tabs on them and let me know if anything unusual happens again. Peterton out."

"Unusual how? They're not going anywhere. Not tonight anyway." the second private snorts.

"Yeah and I don't want to have to listen to them getting hot and heavy with each other while I'm stuck here with you, and not my girl. I just hope they don't plan to leave any lights on, or we're both going to be in some serious pain."

Logan shifts his position and Hillary looks up at him. His eyes go from hers to her mouth and back again. Slowly he lowers his mouth to hers. As his lips touch hers, Hillary closes her eyes and leans more into him. She knew that this was only a show for those watching, but she had never felt the things she was feeling with Logan. For a moment she wishes that it could all be real for both of them.

After a few minutes, neither of them is acting any longer. Logan pulls away from her mouth and looks into her eyes. Without a word he picks her up and carries her into the front bedroom.

Over the next few hours, the two privates across the street get highly agitated with each passing minute with what they are seeing and hearing. By the time their replacements come to relieve them, they give the barest of reports, before going to find their own personal release. Both of them pray long and hard that they will never have to go through that situation again. Neither of them would wish that kind of punishment on their worst enemy.

# Chapter VI

Early the next morning, after transferring Ali to Logan's hover car, Hillary opens the door to her own car. "Give me a call when your ready to move."

"I will. Be careful." Logan bends down and lightly kisses her on the lips. "See you soon." Once she's inside, he closes her car door and goes back to his own.

He takes off and heads to the area where he plans to pick up the girls. He checks the time constantly. When he arrives, he sets his scramblers and prepares to land at the edge of the park the girls would be walking through on their way to school.

"Ali, you have a physical description of the girls. Please scan the area for them while I contact Hillary."

"All right Logan."

Logan punches in Hillary's car phone. "We're at the park now. The girls should be coming through shortly. Keep your phone on, once I have them, give us ten minutes to get to the rest area and then go ahead to the house."

"Okay Logan. Just remember to be careful."

"They're coming now Logan. There's a hover-camera following them about ten feet behind and five feet above them. It has laser capabilities and is fully charged Logan."

"As soon as they're close enough, disable it. Laser first, then the camera. If the camera goes out first, the laser will automatically fire at their last position and then three feet further."

He watches as the girls come closer, holding his breath, knowing that they had to time this perfectly. He opens the car door. "Now Ali!" As soon as the camera starts lowering to the ground Logan gets out of the car and calls to the girls. "Davena, Dessa, Merri, come on, get into the car." The girls stop and look at him and then back at the camera. "Quickly before the guards can come!"

Dessa grabs her sisters and runs to him. "What about Cassie, Logan? She's still at home and there are guards all over the place." she says as they jump into the car and Logan takes off.

"Don't worry. I have a friend at the house who's going to get Cassie. She'll be with us soon enough." He picks up his hand phone. "Hillary, be careful. According to Dessa there may be more guards then we figured on."

"I heard Logan, I'll be ready. If nothing else I'll see you on the other side." The connection is broken and Logan frowns in concern for both Hillary and Cassie's safety.

A few minutes later they reach the rest area. Logan stops the car and climbs out, signaling for the girls to stay put. Three minutes later he hears Cassie's mental shout of fear and disbelief.

"NO! LOGAN!"

Suddenly Cassandra and Hillary are there. Cassie is kneeling on the ground with a very still Hillary in her arms. Logan steps forward and kneels down beside them. "Cassie, what happened?" he demands reaching out to Hillary.

"They shot her Logan. She handed me the box and while I was putting the ring on, they shot her in the back." she tells him tears running down her cheeks. Slowly Hillary opens her eyes.

"Logan. They know. Erik was there. You have to get them out of here." she starts to cough.

"We will, as soon as we get you into the car."

"No Logan. Don't worry about me. There's nothing anyone can do for me now. Ali, gamma seta kappa nu upsilon."

"But what about me Rory?" They all hear what sounds like sniffles and fright coming from the car's computer unit.

"I give you to Cassandra Blackwood. Show her the same loyalty and love that you have shown me all these years Ali. She is a good person." She closes her eyes and then opens them again to look up at Logan. With what little strength she has left she reaches up to touch his cheek. "Logan, Baj nie kou wavi Maji oni."

"Your wish come true also my Maji sister." Logan looks into her eyes and accepts her thoughts and memories as his own. "Gentle journey little sister." He closes his eyes for a second and then opens them again. "Now Ali."

Within moments, Hillary's body disappears and Logan helps Cassie up and into the car, where her sisters wait quietly. Without speaking, Logan takes off and heads east away from the city. After several minutes he talks to Ali. "What was her last command to you? I know that she wanted you to send her somewhere."

"It was to send her body to her family near the sea. They will give her a special burial there."

He picks up on the sadness coming from the unit. "How much Manchon blood did she have?"

"Her great grandmother on her father's side was full blooded Majichonie. Her grandmother on her mother's side was also full blooded. What she said to you was told to all the children on both sides of the family for generations."

"Thank you for telling me Ali."

For the next hour, they travel in silence wishing peace to the one that had given her life for one of them, given it for someone she hadn't even known before that day. Logan cuts cross country and then heads west. He's glad to know that he was able to give Hillary some unforgettable pleasure the night before.

"Where are we going Logan?" Merri asks from the back-seat where she's huddled between Davena and Dessa.

"To the mountains. Thayer has a stronghold there and he asked me to take you there until things calm down." he tells her looking over his shoulder at the three girls. "We'll be perfectly safe there. Everything we could need for the next six months is all ready there."

"Will Uncle Saitun be there too?"

Logan is a little shocked by this question and looks over at Cassie sitting beside him in the front seat.

"We all believed as Leyla did that Saitun was safe and alive somewhere." she shrugs her shoulders and looks away.

"No Merri, he won't be there. At least not for a while anyway. It's too dangerous for him on Earth right now. Maybe in a few months he'll be able to join us."

Dessa leans forward. "You mean that we're going to be stuck up in the mountains for months?! What about Dad and the boys? That jerk Peterton is going to take our disappearance out on them!" she practically shouts hitting the back of the front seat with her small fist.

"I don't think that they will Dessa." Cassie puts in turning to her sister and taking her hand. "There was too much publicity when they were taken. The Galactic Press is keeping in touch with Dad every day. If they should lose that contact, it would bring in the Federation for sure." she tries to reassure her volatile sibling. "The President doesn't want that to happen."

Dessa sits back and Davena puts her arm around her twin and Merri to comfort them. Dessa and Davena look at each other. Logan, watching with his peripheral vision, sees Davena nod and Dessa shake her head even though neither has said a word out loud. He had thought that they could use telepathy but he hadn't been sure until now. Though he should have known from conversations with Leyla.

Testing the ring-links, Logan begins talking to Cassie. He starts out gently so as not to startle or frighten her.

'Cassie?' He waits until she turns her head to look at him. 'Davena and Dessa can communicate telepathically can't they?'

Cassandra looks back at her sisters and then back at him. 'Yes, we all can to some degree. We're all twins, only my twin died when we were six. She drowned before mother or father could save her. Leyla has been teaching us how to strengthen our abilities. Though I'm a little weaker then the others, we can all share our thoughts with each other, not just our twins. Leyla said that it would help to strengthen our bonds to each other as well. We can all path to each other easily now. It helps just in case…' she looks away from him unable to finish her thought.

'In case something like this should happen to you.'

She looks back at him. 'Yes. We all have a problem with distance, except for Merri and Colt. Though they're the youngest, their abilities are a lot stronger then the rest of us put together. Leyla's been teaching them how to better control their abilities. She says that the rest of us will get stronger in time. The only reason we haven't is because we've been hiding our abilities for so long.'

Logan nods watching the road. There is total silence in the car for a while until Ali interrupts it.

"Logan, Cal wishes to speak to you. He sounds quite urgent."

"Put him through Ali."

"I don't have much time sir. Several of Mr. Peterton's special forces team are attempting to gain entry to the house. I've already transported your belongings to the stronghold. Is there anything else that you wish for me to do sir?"

"Keep them out as long as you can to give yourself time to down load everything into the stronghold mainframe. You have the access code. As soon as you're done, rig your console to self-destruct the minute they try to gain access and then get the last of your memory out."

"Affirmative sir. I'm sorry about Ms. Quinn."

"Thank you Cal. I'll see you in about three hours." The line goes quiet. "Ali, program the nutro for five health energy bars please."

Within moments the bars appear and Cassie hands one to Logan and then one to each of the girls. They eat in silence and then several minutes later Merri sits forward and taps Cassie on the shoulder, her face extremely pale.

"Cassie, Colt's sick."

Cassandra turns to face her. "Are you sure sweetie? He isn't just not feeling well?"

Merri shakes her head and sniffles, feeling her twins pain. "No Cassie, he's really sick this time. There's a strange voice inside of him. We're really scared Cassie. It's trying to get to us, to hurt us!"

"Logan! Stop the car quickly!"

The car swerves to the side of the road and stops immediately. "Cassie what is it? What's the matter?"

"Someone is using Colt as a link to find Merri and to get to us."

"But how? Surely…"

"I told you, distance is no problem for them. If someone were to get control of one of them, its possible that they could control the other as well. Their minds are linked that strongly."

"All right let me see what I can do. Merri climb out and we'll see if we can help Colt." They step out of the car, and Logan lifts Merri to the hood of the car. "Now Merri, I want you to open your mind to me. Let me see, feel, and hear what you do. If I can, I'll help you and Colt."

Merri nods and looks into his eyes. Logan immediately feels the power of the youngest Blackwoods minds. Once he makes contact he follows Merri's link path back to Colt. The boy has been trying very hard to block a very strong mind toucher. Not only is he mind sick, but it is also starting to affect his physical body as well. Because of Colt's efforts, the mind toucher can't feel Logan's presence, and Logan quickly uses the link to assess the damage done to the boy's mind and body. After his assessment he strengthens Colt's block and retreats. When he pulls out of Merri's mind he blinks several times to bring his surroundings back into focus, and turns to face Cassie.

"Merri's right. Colt is extremely ill. There's a strong mind toucher with him and he's taking no precautions to protect the boy from his probing. For Colt to completely block him out, it's beginning to affect his bodily functions severally."

"Is there anything that you can do?"

"Maybe, if Merri's strong enough." He turns back to Merri and looks at her closely. "Have you and Colt ever teleported Merri?"

"Yes, we both can. Colt's better at it then I am though."

"Okay, good. What we're going to do is teleport Colt here to us. It's farther then either of you has ever gone, but with my help it will work. All you have to do Merri, is act as the link between Colt and me. I'll do the actual porting. You'll feel some extra energy flowing through you when we're done, but don't be frightened by it, Colt will feel it too. All right?" Merri looks at Cassandra and then back at him before nodding. "Let's set you over here, so that when Colt appears he won't bump into anything."

He lifts her off of the car and they move back about five feet. Cassandra and the other two girls follow and wait for Logan to tell them what they can do to help.

"Cassie, you stand behind Merri and a little to her left. Davena, you stand to Merri's right, but a little back. Dessa, you stand about three feet to Davena's right in the same position. After Colt appears, both of them are most likely going to collapse, so you'll have to catch them."

They all move into position with Logan standing in front of Merri. Once he's sure that they're all in the right positions, he looks into Merri's eyes and once again travels the link pathway to Colt. Once there he gently tells Colt what is going to happen and not to be afraid.

'With the mind toucher linked the way he is, we have to get him to release you first, or he'll be pulled with you. Count down from five very slowly and then lower your block. You'll feel a surge of power when I send out some kinetic energy to dislodge him from your mind. As soon as he's gone, I'll teleport you to us. You'll be a little disoriented when you get here but your sisters will help you.' he assures him. 'Okay, now begin counting down from five. Say it out loud as you do so that his external hearing will pick it up and help to distract him. I'll count with you. Five…four…three…two…one."

Logan sends a strong kinetic jolt through Merri and Colt and into the mind of the mind toucher. He also swiftly touches the other man's mind before swiftly teleporting Colt to them. As soon as Colt appears, Logan leaves Merri's mind and both children collapse. Cassandra catches Merri while Davena and Dessa grab onto Colt. Logan goes down on one knee, with one hand balancing him on the ground.

Cassandra and the girls take Merri and Colt back to the car and get them settled and then Cassandra returns to Logan's side. "Logan, are you all right?" She watches as he slowly nods, but when he still doesn't stand, she kneels down beside him. "Are you sure you're all right? You look a little pale." she pushes the hair away from his forehead and eyes.

Logan catches her hand and holds it tightly. "I'll be fine in a minute. I just need to catch my breath and redirect my energy. How are the kids? Are they both all right?" He asks in concern taking a couple more deep breaths and looking up at her.

"They're fine. Davena and Dessa are with them. They seem to be in a deep restorative sleep."

Logan nods and allows her to help him to stand. When he sways, she steadies him. Logan puts both hands on her shoulders and looks into her eyes. They stand there for several seconds before he releases her and steps away. "We had better get going. It's getting late and they'll be sending patrols out looking for us soon. Besides, if we wait too long the road to the stronghold may give you a good scare."

They walk back to the car and climb in neither of them saying anything. Logan looks back at the children and gently touches Merri and then Colt. They are comforting each other as well as receiving comfort from Davena and Dessa.

"They'll be fine by the time we reach the stronghold. Right now they're comforting each other and absorbing the extra kinetic energy I sent through them." He turns back around and starts the car. After about a half an hour, Logan feels Cassie's gently touch in his mind.

'Will they be harmed in any way by the extra energy?'

'No, of course not. If there had been any danger to them I never would have done it. The extra energy will help them, heal them. On my world most of our people have healing talents. Most of the energy that I send out is to heal not harm. The energy I gave them will heal them where they need it most.'

'I know that you wouldn't deliberately hurt them Logan. I just needed to be sure that there would be no unexpected harm done.' she tries to undo the damage her thoughtless words had caused. 'So the energy will heal Colt physically, while it heals Merri mentally?'

'If those are the types of healing that they need.'

"How long before we reach the stronghold?"

Logan checks his chronometer. "We should be there in about an hour and a half, two at the most. I'm going to go in at a different location, and catch a path further up the mountain. It will help to hide us from their scanners and allow me to activate the stronghold's defenses that much sooner."

Cassandra nods and looks back to check on the children once again. They are all asleep, and she breathes a little easier now, knowing that they are safe and secure with Logan to look after them. She faces front again and closes her eyes, thinking about the first time that she and Logan had first dated and how uncomfortable she had felt around him.

* * *

"Come on Cassie. You haven't been out since Joey went deep space exploring. Besides, if you don't come Logan won't either and Thayer says that he really needs the break right now."

Cassie finishes putting her bread dough into loaf pans and then turns to face Leyla. "You know that I don't like going out with anyone connected with the Security Council. Besides, I have to be here when the kids get home from school. Dad, Mark, and Daniel don't plan on being back until around supper time."

Leyla puts her hands on her hips and glares at her friend. "You know that I wouldn't ask you to go out with someone that I didn't trust. Besides, Dad trust him, and he grow up with Thayer. If Dad thought that he was dangerous I wouldn't be caught anywhere near him myself."

"Yes, I know all of that." Cassie admits looking at her and then away again. "It's just that…well I guess that my biggest problem is that I feel attracted to him. It makes me feel as though I'm being disloyal to Joey."

"Why? The two of you never signed a betrothal agreement. You've never even slept with him. Besides, how do you know that he's not seeing someone on his ship? I can't see Joey going long without a female companion."

Cassie shakes her head and turns back to her bread. "You really know how to cheer me up don't you?" She puts a damp cloth over the loaves. "Yes, he's probably seeing someone, and yes, he's probably sleeping with her too. I just…"

Leyla walks over to her and puts an arm around her shoulders. "I didn't say it to hurt you Cassie, you know that. I love you like you were my own sister. You're just afraid to let go, that's all. You've gotten comfortable with your relationship with Joey."

Cassie nods her agreement. she had felt comfortable with her relationship with Joey. They had dated for the past two years, and he had never forced the issue of them sleeping together. Oh she knew that he was sleeping with other girls, but she also knew that he was careful not to do it with anyone that they both knew.

"You don't have to go out with Logan all the time Cassie. Just once in a while when you both need someone to be around." Leyla encourages her. "He would never do anything to make you uncomfortable."

Cassie sighs. "Okay, I'll go with you. But if he tries anything funny…" She lifts her fist in a threatening gesture.

Leyla laughs and gives her shoulders a gentle squeeze before heading for the door. "Good. They should be here in about a half an hour. We'll go to Caulder Park for a picnic." she gives a wave and then leaves before Cassie can change her mind.

Cassie shakes her head and goes back to preparing her bread for baking. Thirty minutes later there's a knock on the back door. She looks up and smiles, waving Thayer Starhawk inside. "Hi Thayer. I'll be ready in a moment. I just have to butter these loaves and put them in the solar oven."

Thayer walks in and leans against the counter. "Leyla tells me you're a little uneasy about being around Logan. There's nothing to worry about from him Cassie, I promise you." He snitches one of the cookies from the platter on the counter beside him.

"Hey! Leave those alone. They're for the kids after school." she grabs the platter and sets it on the counter by the refrigerator. "I know he's your friend and all Thayer. I just feel strange about being around him. Mostly because of his connection with the Security Council. I've seen what they do Thayer, and I don't want them getting that close to my family."

Walking over to her, Thayer puts his hands on her shoulders and gently turns her to face him and look him in the eye. "Logan's not like that Cassie. If he were do you really believe that I would let him anywhere near Leyla, let alone you and the girls? Do you think that Saitun would? We've both known him for a long time Cassie, he's on our side no matter what his job. We both trust him with Leyla's life and safety."

She can see the truth of his words in his eyes and decides that she can do no less than to give his friend a chance. Like Leyla had told her earlier, she didn't have to go out with him all the time. "Okay. But like I told Leyla, he tries anything funny and I'll lay him out flat." she mock glares up at him.

"I get the point Cassie, and I'll make sure that he gets it as well. Now, are you ready to go?"

"Sure, just let me get my wrist-phone. Dad said that he would call me if they were going to be late."

They leave and go over to the Katmen home where Leyla and Logan are waiting. After reintroducing the couple to each other, they head for the park in Logan's hover car.

As the hours pass, Cassandra begins to relax around Logan and slowly begins to build a trust in him. Over the next several months, they meet together with Thayer and Leyla, and occasionally just the two of them meet to spend some time alone together.

After Saitun's disappearance they didn't see much of each other, and since Leyla and Thayer had disappeared, they hadn't seen each other at all. She had been hurt and confused by his seeming desertion of her when she had needed him the most.

\* \* \*

Logan looks over at Cassandra as his mind picks up on her thoughts without his having to probe. He looks into the back seat and notices that the kids are still asleep.

'Cassie?'

'Yes.'

'Did you really believe that I had just abandoned you? Did it really bother you that I stopped coming by to see you?' She turns her head quickly to look at him. 'You were sending.' he explains, not wanting her to think that he had deliberately been looking into her mind.

Realizing that he was telling the truth, she relaxes back against the seat. 'Sorry. Guess I'll have to watch my thoughts or take off the ring.' She blushes and Logan watches her twist the ring around on her finger.

'Please don't do that.' he requests softly. 'You still haven't answered my question. Did you really believe that I would abandon you?'

She turns her head to look at him. 'Yes, for a while I did. Then I realized that you were probably staying away to try and keep them from taking too much of an interest in us. It made it a little easier to deal with what was happening to us.'

'A lot of good it did. It would have been better if I had kept coming and let them know about our relationship. They most likely would have ordered me to keep an eye on your family and report anything unusual. It might have kept them from taking your father and brothers.'

'Maybe, but if they thought that you weren't getting the information that they wanted, or thought that you were more involved then you lead them to believe, they would have still arrested my father and brothers. They might even have arrested you.'

'True.' He had to agree that Peterton and the President would have become suspicious of him when there was nothing new to report. 'I never stopped worrying about you Cassie. Even if Thayer hadn't ordered me to get you and the girls out, I was working on a plan to do just that. I just didn't want to make a move until I was absolutely sure that there was no other way. No way would I have let those mean touch you.'

Cassie blushes again and looks out the window at their surroundings. "How much longer?"

"About another twenty minutes. I've already activated the defenses around the stronghold."

"Should I wake up the kids?" she asks turning to check on them.

"Sure, it would be good for them to see the defenses."

Cassie reaches back and lightly shakes Dessa awake. "Wake up the others, we're almost there. Logan wants you all to see the defenses."

Colt and Merri are still extremely weary but awake enough to see what is happening with the strongholds defenses. As they pass certain points, warriors in strange costumes appear from behind trees and boulders. They all have a fierce look about them. The girls gasp in fright, and Logan hears a soft 'WOW' from Colt.

"Are they real Logan or just holograms?" Colt asks looking at a very tall and fierce looking warrior standing in front of them. He couldn't tell if the man was real or not.

"A little of both Colt. Most of them are real though. They're a part of the Starhawk clan, or close friends and family to Thayer. A mixture of Cherokee, Sioux, and Apache bloodlines. They came together to ensure that the Native American way of life didn't die out. Over the centuries they've become stronger and more intone with mother Earth. No one knows for sure just how many there are, and we plan to keep it that way." he tells them stopping the car near the man that Colt has been watching closely.

The warrior walks over to the car and squats down to look inside. "Welcome Knightrunner. All is ready for you."

"Thank you Nightstorm. How many of our people will be staying?"

"Thirty of our warriors and their families. About a hundred and fifty all together. I see that you have brought a young warrior with you. Good. Our men will teach him, while the women teach the females."

"Me too." Merri tells him fiercely glaring at Nightstorm, looking him directly in the eye. "Colt and I stay together."

Nightstorm raises a brow at her fierceness and gently probes her, causing her to gasp and her eyes to widen. When she leans into the boy, Nightstorm is rudely shoved back and knocked to the ground.

"Don't ever do that again mister!" Colt warns him in a voice that the others had never heard from him before. He watches the man more carefully as he approaches the car once more.

"Colt! Calm down!" Cassie tells him sharply turning to her brother fearing that he might lose control.

"He probed us Cassie! He didn't ask, he just did it!" Colt tells her continuing to glare at the man who dared to touch his sister's mind without her permission.

"He is right Miss Blackwood. I apologize to you both for my intrusion. I did not mean to offend or frighten your sister."

Merri touches Colt's arm and he turns to look at his twin. 'He didn't mean any harm Colt.'

'That doesn't make it right Merri. Leyla always said that if someone doesn't ask first, then its wrong and could be dangerous.'

'I know that Colt, but he's part of Thayer's family and Logan knows him. I think you should apologize to him for pushing him over.'

'No.' Colt's expression turns stubborn.

'Yes Colt. He's already apologized for what he did. Now it's your turn. If you don't do it, I will.'

They stare at each other for several seconds before Colt releases a frustrated sigh. He knew that she was right and that she would do it too just to embarrass him. "All right! Just stop nagging at me." he says out loud and turns to face Nightstorm. "I'm sorry for knocking you over."

"It is all right. You were only protecting your family from what you saw as a threat, which is as it should be." Nightstorm commends him and then a slow grin spreads across his face. "Your sister may join in your training if that is truly her wish." He looks back at Logan. "We've noticed several Renegade Patrol ships in the area over the past few weeks. It is one of the reasons most of the others have already left. The ones that are staying are the ones with the closest blood ties to the Starhawk, and who have the strongest abilities."

"Do the others have a safe place to go to?"

"Yes. We have people in the desert to the southwest who will shelter them until it is safe for them to return."

"Good. I'm going to take Cassie and the children up to the lodge and get them settled in. I'll meet with you and the others at the sweat-lodge in two hours."

Nightstorm nods and stands up. Waving to those in the forest around them, he slowly fades into the trees and is lost to sight. Cassie and the kids look all around them, trying to see where he had gone to, but can see no sign of him. All they can see are shadows.

"That was too weird." Dessa says to no one in-particular.

"Scary." her twin puts in with a small shudder.

"Cool." comes from Colt and Merri.

Cassie and Logan look at each other and start laughing. Logan puts the car into gear and drives the rest of the way to the stronghold.

"That pretty much covers it descriptively." Cassie says then turns to Logan. "What did he mean when he said that their women would teach us females?"

Logan looks over at her and then back to the path they were traveling on. It wasn't meant for vehicles and so he had to drive carefully.

"They'll teach you how to defend yourselves and how to survive in the wilderness. This area is pretty much the same as it was nearly a thousand years ago. It's one of the few places that man hasn't reached out and destroyed. We have computers and replicators, but most of what we use and eat, we make or grow ourselves."

He pulls into the stronghold through the gates and hears the kids oohing and awing. Except for one two story building, the stronghold is setup to resemble a traditional Native American stronghold, with wigwams, teepees, and long-houses.

"The stone house is where the computer system is stored. There are rooms for living, but mostly everyone lives in the other homes." He explains as they get out of the car. "Cassie, you and the girls can stay in the house until you get used to everything. Colt can stay with me in my wigwam. It will help him and Merri to get use to a more natural separation."

"NO! We have to stay together!" Merri cries out, clinging to her twin's arm tightly. Terror runs through her at the thought of being away from him again.

Colt pulls free and wraps his arm around her, pulling her head into his shoulder. "Shh Merri, it's all right. We'll stay together. I think what he means is for when we get older. Not like it was when the E.S.C. took me away. We'll still be able to see each other and be together." he assures her hugging her close.

"That's right Colt." Logan agrees angry with himself for frightening the child. "Merri, as you get older, there will be times when you don't want Colt to know something, or when he doesn't want you to. You both need to learn how to block such thoughts from each other. If you can learn to do that, it will some day help to protect you both from something like what happened today. You have to learn how to sever your natural link to each other at the first sign of danger to the other. Or if you don't feel comfortable in severing it, making it so deep and so hidden that not even the strongest empath can find it."

"But we've been apart for so long already Logan." Tears begin to flow down Merri's cheeks and Colt looks beseechingly at Logan not knowing what to do to comfort his twin.

"Can't we wait for a couple of days before we do this Logan? We need to be together right now. I understand what you mean, but Merri needs time to get used to the idea and to heal from before. Until I was taken away, we'd never been physically apart before, not like we were."

Logan looks at both of them and then at Cassie who nods her agreement with what Colt had said. He would have to talk with her about it when they could find time alone. "Okay, we'll give you both a week, and start teaching you how to deal with such separations. We'll get you all settled into the house." He turns back to the car. "Ali, transfer yourself to the system located at one-two-seven right."

"All right Logan. Is that to be Cassandra's room?"

"Yes it is."

They all go into the house following Logan and looking around. He shows them the rooms downstairs, before taking them upstairs and showing them their rooms. He points to the room he would be using until Colt could move into his wigwam with him. It was going to take great care to heal the damage done to Merri by the forced separation from her twin.

After meeting everyone at the stronghold, the Blackwoods settle in and begin their new life of isolation away from the rest of the world. They all wonder about their father and brothers still in the hands of the President, and what is happening to them. They each say a prayer that Leyla and Thayer can find a way to stop the President before it is too late for their loved ones and others like them.

# Chapter VII

The day has finally arrived for Leyla to be awakened from her cryogenic sleep. Stephen Seven sets the controls and then goes to prepare the ship's temperature to a comfortable level for when she leaves the stasis tube. After making sure that everything is ready, he returns to the stasis chamber to check on the revival progress.

"How is she doing Aeneka?"

"Pretty good Stephen. Her body temperature is returning to normal and her heart rate and blood pressure are fine. She should be able to leave the tube in another hour."

"Good, everything else is ready for her. Sarah's been hounding me for the past week, trying to get everything perfect. Any more perfect and Leyla would think that she had awakened on the wrong ship."

"What's wrong with wanting everything perfect?" Sarah snaps at him. "Just because you don't mind everything covered in dust doesn't mean that Leyla would appreciate it. Besides, things have to be as germ free as possible when she leaves the tube."

"I know that you over stimulated excuse for a companion. But what you keep forgetting is that we're in space and that there is no dust. Not only that, but with both Leyla and Thayer in stasis, there are no germs of any kind to be transmitted."

Aeneka starts to laugh while trying to interrupt them.

"Why you no good piece off a garb…"

"That's enough! Both of you! There is absolutely no way that Leyla could possibly think that she was on the wrong ship the way you two are carrying on. Now stop it this instant, before I shut you both off for the next twenty-four hours."

There is immediate quiet from both of the computer units. They had both found out shortly after Leyla and Thayer went into stasis, that Aeneka could control all of the ships functions quite well, including their own.

"We'll be in communications range of Calidon within the next thirty-two to thirty-six hours Aeneka. We'll be in their deep space sensor range in about eighteen hours and thirty-seven minutes." Sarah informs her in a more subdued voice.

"Good. Thank you Sarah. When we reach the sensors, send a long range message informing them of our arrival time and inform them that we will contact them again visually once we're within the proper range to do so." Aeneka cuts off Sarah's audio link to the stasis chamber and turns her monitor to look at Stephen. "For the next three hours, I want you to make sure that Leyla consumes no less then thirty-five hundred calories per hour Stephen. We need to build her metabolism up as quickly and safely as possible. Her link with Thayer is now so strong that we will just make it to Calidon in time for them to be lifemated officially, before it happens on its own. Leyla's Manchon blood is now strong enough that her entire system has all but changed."

"But you said that everything was going back to normal." he reminds her not understanding.

"Everything is back to normal, for someone of her mixed bloodline. Over the next week, her metabolism will be extremely erratic, that's way we must build it up quickly in these first three hours. We have to counter the effects that may occur later on."

"What about Thayer? Is there anything special that we have to do for him?"

"No, there's nothing that we need to do for him right now, he's fine. All that remains of his mind-block is the natural shield before any lifemating. I've already explained to them both that until the official lifemating ceremony, there can be no physical joining. Neither of them was to pleased to hear that. Therefore, the less time that they spend alone together, the better. That's why I helped with our travel time."

"How much time do we have?"

"We'll revive Thayer in about forty-eight hours. We should be orbiting Calidon thirty-six hours after that. By the time he fully recovers, they'll have only about twelve hours to control their urge to mate. It won't be easy for them, but I have to believe that they can do it. Thayer will also have to control his urge to protect his mate. Until he has full control, he could very easily hurt someone unintentionally, or possibly even kill them."

Leyla finally sits up in her tube and Stephen walks over to help her out. When she first steps out of the tube, there is some disorientation, but it quickly passes and she looks up at Stephen and smiles.

"Hi there Stephen. Long time no see." She says to him before suddenly collapsing into his arms.

"Aeneka! What's happened?"

"Adrenaline rush. When she looked up at you she realized that everything had worked out. She'll be fine after a little rest. Take her to her room, I have to calm Thayer. When she passed out, she did so completely, and now he's beginning to panic."

Stephen carries Leyla out of the chamber while Aeneka tries to calm Thayer down.

'She's fine Thayer. Remember all the times she said that it didn't feel quite real? Well she finally realized that it was and her mind just shut itself down completely to cope with it. Give her a few minutes and she'll tell you herself that she's fine.'

'But why was our link broken?'

'It wasn't broken, it was blocked. Reach out to her and you'll feel what I mean.' she waits for him to do just that.

'Okay, I believe you. How long before I can get out of this damn tube?'

'You still have two days Thayer.'

'I want to be with her Aeneka!'

'I know that you do Thayer, that's why the extra time. You need to start controlling your urge to mate with her. As I explained before, you can't join with her again until the ceremony on Calidon. You have to be before the High Priest, you have to be willing to wait. To do so will show the people your respect for the Calidonian bloodline and your willingness to join our two people together once again as it should be.'

'All right Aeneka, but you had better make sure that the ceremony is carried out quickly after we arrive on Calidon.'

'I promise to do my best Thayer. I have no wish to see either of you suffer that kind of pain any longer than necessary.'

\* \* \*

For the next several hours Leyla eats everything that Stephen puts in front of her and goes over all she will have to say once they are in communications range of Calidon. She would have to establish herself right away as the rightful heir to the throne, and Thayer's right to be there. Now that they are closer to Calidon, Leyla feels a strong animosity reaching out to her. Though it is not strong yet, she knows that once the reach the planet, it will be quite easy to identify the source.

Trying to shield some feelings from Thayer was proving quite difficult and dangerous. Each time she did it, Thayer would fight the induced sleep of stasis. Several times since she had awakened, it had been necessary to mind numb him so that his mind could relax. She hoped that they would have to do it again any time soon. His last episode of frustration had manifested itself in a physical mind assault on Stephen, when she had become angry with him for not telling her about a small probe that he had noticed, but which her mother and Sarah had missed. Thayer's attack had sent the android sailing across the room and slamming against the bulkhead. By the time she and her mother had recovered and figured out what had happened, Stephen had collapsed and lost power. They had both quickly worked to numb Thayer's mind, and then Leyla had reactivated Stephen to be sure that he hadn't sustained any permanent damage.

It was now thirty-seven hours since she had awakened from stasis and it was time for her to officially open communications with Calidon.

\* \* \*

"This is the Royal Flagship FIRESTAR. We require immediate clearance to the planet and to land at the palace landing port." There is silence before Leyla receives a reply.

"You must verify your identity please." the young woman on the monitor informs her.

"I am the Princess Leyla Aeneka, daughter of Princess Aeneka Latona of the House Chaukcee." Again Leyla waits for a reply. When none is immediately forth coming, she demands strongly, "I insist that you get me the High Councilor Trocon Damori immediately. If I do not hear from him within the next five minutes I will invoke Terrema banor onta within ten." She turns off the monitor and turns her chair to face her mother who is now setup on the console in the bridge.

"If that doesn't get you results, then nothing will."

"True, but I don't want to do something that drastic mother."

"They may give you no other choice sweetheart. Your grandfather set it up so that the people would know that you had his support and blessings."

"But how can I get their support, when I'm threatening them with the lose of all memory and free thought? They haven't even seen me yet makes it even worse. This unknown person is threatening them just to get permission to land on the planet."

"Sweetheart, they don't know what the threat is, only that someone in our family has the power to change their lives and plans to use it if necessary. The true threat is not knowing what exactly will change in their lives, not you yourself."

Just then the monitor buzzes and Leyla turns back to it and turns it on again. "Yes?"

"High Councilor Damori will speak with you now."

Leyla sits a little straighter as Trocon appears on her monitor.

"Greetings Princess Leyla. I apologize for the difficulties you have encountered."

"That is all right Trocon. I am just as sorry that I had to resort to a threat to speak with you."

"Don't let it trouble you Princess. We've recently had a little trouble lately with unauthorized ships in the area. They have some of our codes and are using them to get to the Liman moon. With the disappearances happening there, everyone is edgy."

Leyla turns slightly towards her mother's monitor and sees her nod.

"Trocon, I need you to clear us through the outer defenses, and meet us at the palace landing site. I want only you and my grandfather's most trusted personal guards present. Do you understand what I'm saying Trocon?" She sees the stunned look on his face and then it goes curiously blank.

"I understand your Highness." Leyla notices the stiffness in his voice. "You must realize that Lord Mandraik will insist on being present upon your arrival."

"Yes I do realize this Trocon, but I do not wish him there."

"You spoke in the plural, 'us'. Who is it that comes with you Princess?"

Leyla looks once again to her mother. Aeneka looks at her for several moments before nodding.

"I bring back my mother's essence as proclaimed by Calidon law. Also with me is Thayer Starhawk, Manchon warrior and the one who is to be my lifemate."

"This will not sit well with many on the council. Mandraik has assured them that should you return to your true home, you would be joined to one of our own." He watches her face and sees her shock and her anger. Suddenly he finds himself shoved across the communications room, and hears Leyla's terrified shout.

'Thayer, NO!'

His momentum is stopped just before his body can be impaled by a metal protrusion in the far wall. Picking himself up from the floor, Trocon dusts himself off and slowly walks back to the viewer and carefully sits back down.

"Trocon, are you all right?" Leyla asks anxiously.

"Yes Leyla, I'm fine. But what..?"

"I'm sorry Trocon. I forgot to shield my emotions from Thayer. He naturally took out his own anger out on you."

"But how could he reach me from where you are? You are still at least two days from Calidon. And if he was the aggressor, how or who stopped me from being impaled?"

"I stopped you. We'll explain everything to you when we arrive Trocon. Please try to keep Mandraik away from the landing site. Bring

High Priest Metros with you. We will have to arrange a quick lifemating. We can't afford to wait for the people's approval of Thayer as my lifemate. Besides the fact that our bonding is nearly complete, Thayer needs the lifemating so that I can help him to better control his abilities until we know their full extent, and what if any assistance I'll have to give him."

Trocon shakes his head at the power the two of them had, but he nods his agreement. "It will be as you say Leyla. You must prepare yourself and your mate for the anger and animosity that will come from such a quick joining."

"I will. Thank you Trocon, and I'm sorry for what happened. We'll see you soon."

After turning of the viewer, Leyla turns to her mother shaken at what had very nearly happened. "We're going to have to bring him out of stasis sooner then you planned mother. It's too dangerous to leave him like he is now." she says shakily.

"Yes, I believe you're right. We'll have to use extreme caution though. His powers are a lot stronger then I first suspected. He needs to see you physically to control his anger. The downside to that will be the urge you will both have to mate. It will be a lot stronger than it was before you went into stasis."

"So what are we going to do? If he calls to me I have to go to him mother." she tells her shaking her head in dejection, not knowing how they were going to do it.

"I know you will sweetheart. That's why I've had Stephen working on a special para collar for Thayer. It will help you both until we reach Calidon."

"But what of the physical urging? Even with the collar, our bodies will still call to each other." Leyla stands up and begins pacing around the room.

"I've though of that too sweetheart. Sarah has managed to have the med-unit come up with a strong suppressive for Thayer and a weaker one for you. Stephen will also stay at his maximum strength until we reach Calidon."

"How long will the suppressant last?"

"Approximately sixty hours from the time of injection. That will give you about twelve hours on the planet without worry. The effects will wear off gradually after that to give you both a chance to get control of your emotions on your own, but you have to help to control yourselves while under the drugs influence."

"Okay, we'll have Stephen administer the injections and put the collar on Thayer before he comes out of stasis. I'll explain everything to Thayer so that Stephen doesn't have any problems with him."

"All right dear. Make sure that you get some rest before you meet with him after he comes out of stasis. You will both have to plan how you will act if Mandraik insists on being there when you arrive."

"Okay. I'll see you in a few hours then." Leyla touches her mother and then leaves the room. She slowly makes her way to the stasis chamber. Upon entering, she notices that Stephen has already assembled the necessary items. She nods to him and then walks over to Thayer's tube.

'I need to talk with you about something Thayer.'

'If it's about what happened with Trocon, I'm sorry.'

'No, its not that, but you almost killed him Thayer. You have to better control your anger and protectiveness of me. Right now you're letting my emotions dictate yours. I can help, but the main strength has to come from within yourself.'

'I know that Love. I promise to try harder to control myself. Now, what did you want to talk to me about?'

She leans against the stasis tube and runs her hand over it. 'Mother has suggested a…para collar…for when we bring you out of stasis. It will help you to regain some control over your emotions and it will help somewhat to suppress some of your urge to mate.'

'That doesn't sound too good, but all right.'

'We're bringing you out of stasis early so that we can have some time to plan how to deal with Mandraik. The collar will be in place when you wake up.' She nods to Stephen. 'You won't be able to communicate telepathically with me until the collar is removed.' She nods once again to Stephen and he places the collar around Thayer's neck. Just before he activates it, Leyla tells Thayer about the injection.

'You'll also be given an injection to help suppress your body's urge to mate. It will wear off in sixty hours.'

'What?! Now just…' his thoughts are cut off as Stephen activates the collar when he sees Leyla winch, no doubt from a mental shout from Thayer.

"I'm sorry my love, but there's no other way." she says softly to herself before looking up at Stephen. "Give him the injection just before he regains consciousness." She looks down at Thayer and places her hand lightly on his forehead for a few seconds and then turns away.

Before she leaves the stasis chamber she allows Stephen to give her the injection. "I'll be in my cabin if you need me Stephen." she tells him quietly and then quickly walks from the room. Once on the other side of the door, she runs to her room, closes the door, and collapses on the bed.

She hated what they were being forced to do, but she knew that there was no other way to handle the situation. Before Stephen had given her the injection she had felt Thayer's body calling to hers, and he wasn't even completely out of stasis yet. There would have been no way that they could have made the last of their journey without mating. She could only hope that Thayer would forgive her for what she had done, and understand that there had been no other choice.

# Chapter VIII

Thayer sits down heavily on his bed with his head in his hands wondering how he was going to deal with his imposed impotence. It wasn't that he couldn't understand the reasons for it, he could. It was just that he hadn't been give the chance or the choice to see if he could control it on his own without the help of a drug.

Both Leyla and Aeneka had tried for the past hour to explain to him why they felt they had to do what they had done, but it hadn't made it any easier for him to accept. Now he was expected to sit with Leyla in the same room and plan out how they were going to deal with Mandraik, while knowing that he should be wanting his mate, but unable to do so on the most basic of levels.

There's a knock at the door and he growls at whoever it was to come in. Leyla slowly steps into the room and stops several feet away from him.

"You can't stay in here for the rest of the trip Thayer. We have to make some kind of plans on how to deal with Mandraik and his influence over the people." she tells him quietly as he sits there glowering at her.

"I know that!" he growls. "And I hadn't planned on staying in this damned room for the rest of the trip either." he finishes sharply.

"Fine, then stop sitting there growling and snapping at me like some dog with a bone and come into the lounge. Stephen's prepared a meal that will help you to further regain your strength."

Thayer gets up so quickly, that Leyla is startled into stepping back.

Her action causes Thayer's frown to deepen even further. Watching her, Thayer realizes that his anger is such that it frightens her more than it normally would. The para collar was preventing her from gauging its extent and direction. Taking a deep breath he calms himself and relaxes his body into a less aggressive stance.

"I'm sorry Love." He steps closer to her and when she doesn't retreat from him, he takes her into his arms and hugs her close. "It's not you that I'm angry with, but myself. If I had better control…"

"It's all right darling, I understand." She reaches up and kisses him lightly on the mouth. "Please believe that if there had been any other way…"

He rubs his chin against her hair. "I know. Right now my male pride is stung, that's all. Don't worry, I'll get over it." He holds her away from him and smiles down at her. "Come on, lets eat and start planning the destruction of that farden rat Mandraik."

They go to the lounge where Stephen serves them and then leaves them alone. For the first part of the meal, they sit in silence and slack their hunger. Though Leyla had taken in more calories then she normally did in a week, she was still very hungry.

"From the last communication I had with Trocon, Mandraik is insisting on being there when we land. There's not much Trocon can do to stop him, unless we were to land sooner than planned." Leyla tells him pouring them each some more wine.

"That's fine, I'd rather meet him right away so that I can see his face. Something tells me that if we don't we'll need our defenses up constantly. No, our best action would be to meet with him while we have Trocon and the guards with us. I can see him trying to sneak up on us unexpectedly." he says with a frown.

"What about Stephen? I think that I should keep him with me. Something tells me that I'm going to need him near for some reason."

"That sounds like a good idea. No doubt they won't allow us to stay in the same chambers until after the joining ceremony. I'd feel better if he was with you when I can't be."

Leyla smiles at him across the table, and reaches for his hand. "Even if we're not officially joined, we already have a mental bonding that will always keep us close to one another."

"True, but we can't use that bond too often until we know when Metros will officially join us." Thayer shakes his head and smiles ruefully at her. "I don't know if I can deal with him being in the chamber when we physically join. On Manchon the physical part of a lifemating is usually done in private."

"I know what you mean darling, and I feel the same way, but from what mother told us its necessary to insure the safety of both mates. Sometimes one mate is stronger and there's a chance of them going mad. The weaker of the two is the first to succumb and the stronger follows in anguish of his or her loss."

"That shouldn't happen unless they aren't true lifemates."

"True, but who can really tell if its a true lifemating or not? From what I can understand, there have been too many imperfect matches over the years and the High Priest is the only one that can stop the joining at the first sign of danger."

Thayer looks at their joined hands and then up into Leyla's eyes. "What's to stop Metros from stopping our joining and saying that we're not a good match?" He watches her face, seeing that this is something that she hadn't thought of before.

Leyla considers what he says and then shakes her head. "No, I can't see him doing that. He wants too much for there to be a union between Calidonians and the Majichonie. If anything, I think that he would try to aide in the joining." she watches Thayer's eyes bulge and his jay drop. "Only mentally Thayer!" she giggles and after a few seconds he chuckles.

"Okay, for now we play it by ear. But when the time comes he's going to have to trust us to know that we're meant to be lifemates. I'm not making love to you in front of an audience of even one."

She looks at him, seeing the stubborn set of his jaw and the determination in his eyes, and knows that nothing will sway him in this. "I'm sure that we can convince him, and if we can't then mother will." They share a smile and then Thayer pulls her up from the table to stand in front of him.

"I need to have a workout with Stephen. Knowing that I should be wanting you right at this moment is extremely frustrating. I'll meet you and your mother in the comm-center in a couple of hours to discuss our plans for Mandraik." He kisses her and steps back shaking his head. "I'll be glad when we finally complete our joining. Otherwise I'm going to be one massive bruise."

Leyla watches him leave and then walks over to the observation area and stares out the window. As she looks out, she thinks about the dream she had during her rest period. Once again she sees the young girl sitting in a corner of a small chamber crying. She looks up and looks around the room asking, "Who's there?" Leyla thinks only of soothing her and soon the child sighs and her body relaxes. Just before she falls asleep the girl murmurs, "Come soon Matima. Please come soon."

Thinking on the word she had spoken, Leyla goes to the comm-center to ask her mother it's meaning. As she enters the room Aeneka's monitor comes on.

"Thayer is really giving Stephen a workout today. I take it he's still upset about the injection."

"Not so much angry as frustrated." Leyla answers sitting down in front of her mother. "His mind knows that he should want me, but…" she shrugs her shoulders.

"Yes, well…I'm sure that he'll make up for it at your joining." Aeneka assures her smiling gently. "What's troubling you baby? You look lost and a little confused about something."

"I am a little. What does Matima mean?"

"It means second mother, or spirit mother. Where did you hear it? I know that it wasn't a part of your word lessons."

"During my rest period I had a dream, only, it wasn't a dream. I'm sure of that now." Leyla looks out the side portal, and without thought reaches out to touch her mother's box. "This young girl, about twelve or thirteen, appeared in a small chamber. She was crying and I felt her fear and pain. I think that she felt me near and her crying slowed and finally stopped. She looked around the room asking who was there, but she couldn't see me." She looks back at her mother. "All I could think about was soothing her and easing her pain. Just before she fell into a peaceful sleep she murmured, 'Come soon Matima.' and I said that I would even though I didn't know what the word meant."

Aeneka draws the images from her daughter's mind that she is openly projecting. Touching on her image center, she sees that Leyla was right in saying that it wasn't a dream. All the while she is checking, she soothes her daughter, just as Leyla had soothed the child. She senses Leyla's discomfort and guilt at not being there right now for the girl.

"It wasn't a dream honey. I think that the girl was calling out to you at the time you went to sleep. Her cry was strong enough and emotional enough that you projected your psi self to her." Aeneka watches as understanding comes to Leyla's face. "Whoever she is, she will be a very important part of yours and Thayer's lives. She also has very strong psychic abilities to be able to reach you this far from the planet."

"Do you have any idea who she might be mother? I feel that I must find her as soon as we reach Calidon. That she's in great danger from someone."

"From the clothes she was wearing, I'd say that she's a servant in the palace. You'll need to talk with Detra Priss, the Servant Keeper, about her."

Thayer walks in with a towel around his neck, his hair still damp from his recent workout with Stephen. Kissing Leyla on the forehead, he leans against the console next to Aeneka's monitor.

"So have you two worked out a plan for dealing with Mandraik?"

"Not really. Do you remember the young girl that I told you about before we went into stasis?" When he nods, she tells him about what happened during her rest period. "I want to have her join us as soon as we can. She's in danger from someone whose close to her right now, and I can feel that the danger is to her life."

"And she called you spirit mother?" When she nods Thayer looks past her in deep thought. "We'll have to make sure that Mandraik doesn't find out how important she is to us, otherwise he'll try to use her against us somehow."

"Thayer's right sweetheart. If Mandraik gets the slights suggestion that this girl is somehow of any importance, he will use her. You will both have to guard your thoughts around him until you have her safe with you." Leyla stands up and paces around the small room. "But how am I to get her to us without drawing his attention to her?"

"Arrange for the Keeper of the servants to bring you all the young girls between the ages of twelve and fifteen. Once you've looked them over pick one, and then change your mind. Do this a few times. Your last choice should be the girl."

"But what if she sees Leyla and recognizes her as the one to comfort her? She may very well panic if not picked right away." Thayer points out thinking of the girl's reaction should she think that Leyla does not recognize her as her daughter spirit.

"I'll have to channel my thoughts to her and let her know what is happening. We'll have to hope that she's strong enough to control herself and not broadcast her thoughts." Leyla says coming to a stop in front of him.

"What about Mandraik? We can't make a move against him until we have proof that he's the one behind the attempts on your life, or that he's the one supplying Earth with telepaths." He reminds her putting his arms around her waist and pulling her closer to him. "At least if he tries anything on Calidon, we'll know it immediately."

"Yes, but what if he doesn't? We may have to do something to force his hand. No matter what anyone else says, I believe that he's the one responsible for everything that's been going on."

"You don't have to convince me Love. I believe he's responsible too." he assures her giving her a quick kiss on the lips.

"Then we agree that if we don't find anything to connect him to what's been happening on Earth, we force his hand?" she asks innocently looking up at him.

"Only to a certain extent. If you do anything to place yourself in danger I will beat you every day for a week." he warns her with a very serious and stern look.

Leyla smiles up at him and gives him a kiss. "I'm shaking in my sandals."

Meaning what he says, Thayer gives her a sharp slap on her backside, to show her he meant business.

"Ouch! That hurt Thayer!"

"It was meant to. I mean it Leyla. You are not to take any chances with him on your own. Either Stephen or I will be with you at all times. If we're not, Trocon or the guards will be. Do I make myself clear?" He rubs the spot that he had just slapped and waits for her nod before kissing her deeply.

Aeneka waits a few moments and then clears her throat. "Okay you two, break it up. We still have to come up with something to prove that Mandraik is guilty." She waits until Leyla steps away from Thayer before continuing. "I agree with Thayer dear. Don't take any chances with Mandraik around Leyla. He can be a very vicious man when he's cornered or feels threatened or betrayed."

"All right, I won't do anything on my own. But I think not doing anything could be just as dangerous."

"We may not have to do anything anyway. If that probe that Stephen spotted while we were in stasis was from Earth, and if he's guilty, Mandraik will be contacted and he'll make a move against us without us having to lift a finger. He won't want it known of his part in what's happening on Earth with the council." Thayer tells her.

"But how long do we wait? I don't want to wait too long, something could happen to Cassie's father and brothers. I don't think I could deal with it if they were killed simply because they're our friends."

"They won't be. As long as the President thinks he can use them to get to us they're safe. Besides, if what I remember of Denral's connection to the Federation is right, then they'll be keeping a close eye on things to make sure that there are no unusual accidents concern him or the boys."

Leyla thinks this over and has to admit that it was a possibility. Denral Blackwood had worked for the Federation for years. Though his position wasn't very important, they knew him to be a loyal and honorable man. They wouldn't let an act of violence against him or his family go unpunished.

"Okay, we'll wait and see. But if something hasn't happened by the end of two weeks, we do something ourselves."

"Agreed."

"Mother?"

"Yes, all right. But you must be careful. I won't be with you long after you're crowned. I must release my knowledge soon."

"Couldn't that release of knowledge be dangerous to us?" Thayer asks realizing that when Aeneka released her essence, all that she knew would be shared with the whole planet.

"No. Personal knowledge will go only to close family members and friends. Everything that we have said and done on this ship is personal. Only you and Leyla, and the young girl, along with a few close friends will gain from that knowledge."

Thayer and Leyla stand in front of Aeneka for several seconds and then move to leave. "We'll see you in the morning mother. We should reach Calidon sometime late in the day. We'll contact Trocon when we're about four hours away." Leyla tells her not wanting to think about the time when her mother would leave her.

"That sounds fine dear. Have a good rest." she murmurs as her monitor goes dark.

They walk quietly to their cabins, but as soon as their near, Thayer takes Leyla's hand and pulls her towards his. "Even though I can't make love to you, I can still hold you in my arms while we sleep." He tells her looking into her eyes and waits for her agreement.

Nodding, she lets him lead her into the room where they undress each other before climbing into bed. They cuddle close and slowly slip into sleep. Just before he succumbs to slumber, Thayer pulls her closer and whispers, "I love you."

## Calidon That Night:

Salis Tahquar enters her small chamber and walks slowly to her bed. She cautiously sits down on the thin feather tick. Madame Priss was getting more and more heavy handed with her punishments. Today she had accidentally dropped a vase in the chamber they were preparing for the Heiress. Madame had turned three shades of purple before kinetically throwing her up against the wall face first. Before she could recover from the shock of it, she had felt the lash of Madame's side whip.

She had gotten thirty lashes for breaking an ugly vase. Her back, buttocks, and legs were still stinging even though she had gone to the healer and been treated after she had regained consciousness. The healer had not been happy to see her again so soon. It was the second day in a row that she had to heal her. The old woman had shaken her head and made that tsking sound she always made when she was disappointed.

"You needs be more careful Firepetal. Soon they will tire of their games and then what will happen to you?" she always said, though things never changed.

"I try grandmother, I really do. It seems though that even when I do nothing wrong, Madame strikes me. Yesterday I did nothing and she lashed me. I don't know what to do. I try to stay away from her but she always seems to find me and find fault."

"They worry because of the Heiress. She comes and they know that when she does, they will lose their powers once and for all."

"But it's not fair grandmother. None of the others suffer as I do. Though I would not wish this treatment on another. It is wrong for Madame to treat me thus. For the last moon and a half I have suffered even more then usual." Tears spring to her eyes and slowly flow down her cheeks.

"I know that you do child. Ever since Mandraik had your parents taken away, things have been bad for all of the servants, but more so for you I'm afraid."

"Why do they do it grandmother? I've always done my work and never complained, even when given extra work to do, I haven't said a word."

The healer finishes with her and pats her hand gently. "They fear you child. Don't ask me why, I can not tell you." she warns holding up her hand and standing. "Just know that one day they will pay for their cruelty to you. Now go, get some rest. The Heiress will be here soon and you must be at your best when you meet with her."

Salis had given her a hug and then come to her room. Now she slips out of her tunic and trousers and carefully lays down on her stomach. Soon the Heiress would come, and maybe her Matima would come with her.

Closing her eyes, Salis thinks of the beautiful woman that was coming and would be her second mother. She would love Salis and no one would ever be mean to her again. "Please Matima, please come soon." she cries softly into her pillow. "I do not think that I can take this any longer. Please come and take me away from here."

\* \* \*

Back on the FIRESTAR Leyla once again dreams of the young girl. This time she can see the reason for the child's tears and pain. There are angry red welts all up and down her back from her shoulders to her knees.

'Who did this to you child, and why?' she asks gently.

'Madame Priss, Matima. I dropped a vase in the chamber that we're preparing for the Heiress.' When there is no answer or another question, she hurries to explain about the vase. 'It was an accident Matima, it slipped out of my hands. I swear it did!'

'Hush little one, I believe you. Don't worry. I will be there tomorrow and you will join me soon after I arrive.' Leyla watches her smile a little, but soon decides that it is more of a grimace then a smile. 'Are you in much pain little one?'

'No Matima. The healer took most of it away. It just stings a little bit when I move.'

Leyla concentrates on taking even that little pain from the child. The chamber begins to glow with a soft white light and then that light centers on the girl, surrounding her seeping into her. Leyla watches as all signs of pain leave her small body.

'Thank you Matima. That feels a lot better.'

'It's all right little one. Know this, never again will I allow anyone to strike you. Sleep now little one. Tomorrow you will begin a new life.' She watches her fall into a painless sleep. Just before she leaves, she places a shield around the girl. The shield would protect her from any threat of violence whether physical or mental. 'Soon little one, soon you will know only the peace, love and safety that all children should know and have in their lives.'

Leyla wakes up and sits up in the bed. When she does, the lights come on. Not wanting to wake Thayer, she orders them to dim to a soft glow. "Sarah, how long would it take us to reach Calidon at warp nine?" she asks softly.

"We would reach the planet at about one in the afternoon."

"At our present speed, when would we arrive?"

"We will reach the planet at about eleven this evening at our present speed. Both of these projections are based on the condition that we do not have to deviate from our present course."

Leyla feels Thayer stir and sit up. She reaches for his hand never looking at him. "Go to warp nine and then inform Trocon of our new arrival time."

"Affirmative Leyla."

"What's the matter Love? I thought we were going to take our time. Why the sudden hurry to get there?"

She turns to face him heedless of the tears flowing unchecked down her cheeks. "I saw her again Thayer. They've beaten her so badly. Her whole back is covered with red welts from a lashing. A lashing, for accidentally dropping a stupid vase. I can't leave her to them for another whole day. She won't survive another beating like that."

Thayer pulls her into his arms and kisses her tears away. "Don't worry Love, we'll get there in time. Try and get some more sleep. We can't have you passing out in front of everyone just after we arrive." He lays back down and pulls her down with him.

"I don't think that I can. Oh Thayer, how could anyone beat a child like that? Children are so precious, they should be cuddled and pampered, not beaten to the point where they want to give up on life." she turns her face into his neck and cries for all the children that she knows have suffered at the hands of people like Detra Priss.

"Hush Love. Everything will be fine." he murmurs in her ear. He feels her body slowly relax as she cries herself to sleep. Very carefully, so as not to wake her back up, he sets her away from him and carefully gets up. Looking down at her, he pulls on a robe and goes to the comm-center to speak with Aeneka. As he enters the room he hears her and Sarah arguing.

"Damn your diodes Sarah! I don't care what Leyla told you! I'm telling you to go to light-speed and to do it now!" Aeneka yells.

"But that will put us on Calidon in less than three hours Aeneka. That's if we make it that far! It's too dangerous to pilot through this system at that speed! With the irregularities of the asteroids, we could crash right into one and not know it until it was too late!" Sarah yells back at her not bothering to worry about what she's doing.

"What in the name of the Great One is going on in here?" Thayer demands raising his voice slightly to get their attention.

"I am trying to get this misbegotten bucket of bolts to take us to light-speed. We need to get to Calidon immediately." Aeneka tells him turning her monitor so that she can see him.

"I thought that was why Leyla told her to go to warp nine? We'll get there early this afternoon." he says reasonably.

"That will be too late. We can't afford to wait that long Thayer. The girl that Leyla's been seeing is in great danger. If we don't reach her by dawn...she... will...die." she tells him.

"How do you...?"

"The palace healer sent me a message. Mandraik and Madame Priss plan to have the child killed at dawn." she watches as Thayer pales and his jaw drops.

"Sarah, do as Aeneka said and take us to light-speed."

"But Thayer..."

"Stop arguing about it and do it now Sarah!"

"All right, all right! Don't say I didn't warn you when we crash into an asteroid." Soon they can hear the hum of the engines preparing for the jump to light-speed, and then the quiet as they make the jump.

"I've sent for Stephen. He'll remove the collar and give you an injection that will counter act the first one."

"But we still don't know how long we'll have to wait before Leyla and I can be formally joined. Do you really think that we should take the chance?"

Aeneka smiles at him. "I believe that you can control yourself enough to last twenty-four to thirty more hours." The smile leaves her face. "You will both need all of your abilities and the full connection you already have for what is to happen this day."

Stephen walks into the room carrying a small tray with a gray tube and two syringes. He stops near Thayer and sets down the tube and the smaller syringe, holding the larger one, he steps closer to Thayer.

"You'll need to roll up your sleeve and sit down in the chair. Once you receive the injection you'll feel a slight dizziness for a few seconds."

"What's the other one for?"

"That one's for Leyla when she comes."

"What's for me when I come?" Leyla asks walking into the room and looking at all of them. "Why is everyone up so early?"

Stephen gives Thayer his injection while Aeneka explains. "Stephen is going to give you and Thayer an injection to counter act the suppressant that you were given earlier. We'll reach Calidon in less than three hours. I want your bond with each other as strong as it can be before we reach the planet."

Leyla turns to look at Thayer as he turns his head for Stephen to deactivate and remove the para collar. "But Sarah said that we wouldn't…"

"Something's come up and your mother has ordered Sarah to go to light- speed." Thayer tells her rubbing at his neck.

"But that's too dangerous in Calidon's star system. The asteroids will…"

"It's a necessary risk sweetheart. Salis is in great danger and…"

"Who's Salis, and what's she…?"

"The little girl, Leyla. The little girl is to be killed at dawn." Thayer tells her and then pushes her into the chair after Stephen gives her the injection. The dizziness hits her and she puts her head between her knees. Once it's passed she sits up again.

"How do you know this? I just told you that I saw her again." she asks eyeing him narrowly.

"I told him." Aeneka tells her drawing Leyla's attention from Thayer. "Do you remember the old healer that taught you?" Leyla nods.

"She contacted me at about the same time you were telling Sarah to change to warp nine. Mandraik fears the girl for some reason and wants her dead before you arrive."

Leyla's eyes widen as she realizes that she had also told Sarah to let Trocon know their new arrival time. "Sarah! Have you contacted Calidon yet?" she asks anxiously, hoping that she wasn't too late to stop her if she hadn't.

"No I haven't!" Sarah snaps. "I've been too busy, and I was just getting ready to. Why?!"

"Don't! We don't want them to know."

"Fine!" she snaps again thoroughly disgusted. "Though it won't matter a damn bit once we crash into some damn rock and die."

"Enough Sarah!" Stephen snaps angrily. "You carry your open opinion program too far. You will apologize for your rudeness and disrespect at once.!" He waits for a few moments and then says sharply. "NOW!"

"I'm sorry for my behavior Leyla, Aeneka. I meant no disrespect to either of you." she tells them in a strangely subdued voice.

Leyla and her mother look at each other in total shock. It was the first time they had ever heard or seen Stephen raise his voice in true anger to Sarah before, and they had never seen her comply to an order from another computer unit in such a way, especially Stephen.

"She will not act in such a manor again, will you Sarah?" he asks strongly.

"No Stephen."

"Now if you will all excuse us, we'll go to the control room and make sure that we don't hit any rocks." He turns and leaves the room while the others stand there staring after him.

"Wow! What in the world was that all about?" Thayer asks turning back to face Aeneka.

"I think that they have become…romantically inclined." she admits bemused by the idea.

"Oh mother, be serious." Leyla giggles at the idea, for the moment forgetting her anxiety. "They aren't programmed…"

"Who says?" Aeneka asks her daughter. "When was the last time you looked at either of their updated programs? Don't forget your father set them up so that they could add their own programs without assistance from a human. He wanted them to be able to adapt to any situation to be able to anticipate the actions of those around us."

With her mother's final remark, Leyla remembers the argument and why they are all up. "Mother, are you sure that this Salis is the same one? That she's not just someone else that needs our help?" she asks hoping that there had been a mistake.

"When she contacted me, the healer sent an image of the girl. Sweetheart, she is the same girl that you showed to me earlier." Aeneka watches the tears gather in her daughter's eyes. "The healer says that Salis is a part of the Tahquar family. Their family has served ours loyally for several generations. If Mandraik fears her, there must be something that she knows that he doesn't want you to find out about."

Leyla nods her understanding and then turns away to look out the portal. They had to reach her in time, she thinks to herself. There had to be something that she could do to protect Salis until they reached Calidon.

"Aeneka, what could she know that would cost her life? Surely even Mandraik wouldn't kill a child just because he thought she knew something?"

"Yes he would. The Tahquar family is known to have members that pick up on unconscious thoughts. If Mandraik was near the girl when he was not conscious of who she was and knew what thoughts had gone through his mind at the time, when he found out who she was her life would mean less than nothing to him. His only thought has always been for himself. Chances are, if we weren't on our way, Salis would have been safe for a little while longer."

Leyla listens to their conversation with half her attention, while trying to come up with some way to warn Salis of the danger she was in. She thinks about the times that Salis had come to her while she slept, and wonders if she can reach her the same way. Relaxing, Leyla concentrates on the last image she had, which was of Salis sleeping. Within seconds she is standing beside the bed. She looks down at the sleeping child and smiles gently. Taking a deep breath she focuses and sends her message.

'Little one, wake up.' she waits. Salis stirs, but doesn't wake. 'Salis, you must wake up.' again she waits. She notices her eyes fluttering and then open. 'Good girl, now sit up.'

Salis turns onto her side and slowly sits up rubbing at her eyes. 'Matima?'

'Yes little one, it's me. I want you to listens closely to what I have to tell you. Can you do that for me?' Leyla waits for her nod. 'Good. Now, I want you to get dressed and go carefully to Lord Damori. When you reach him, tell him that Leyla sent you to him for protection.'

'But Matima, it is not yet dawn. Should I not wait until then?' she asks innocently.

'No!' Leyla says sharply and then takes another deep breath to calm herself. 'No you must go to him NOW little one. Do as I say, it is very important.' Leyla watches the confusion in Salis' eyes, and then sees her reach for her tunic and trousers laying beside her.

After she's dressed, Salis stands up and looks around the room before going to the door and trying to open it. 'The door won't open Matima. Someone's locked it.'

'Hold your right hand out to it and touch it.' Leyla instructs her putting an invisible hand on Salis' right shoulder. 'Now, think of yourself walking through the door.'

'But I can't, it's made of metal.'

'Yes you can. Concentrate, picture it in your mind. Good, now walk through.'

Salis moves forward and Leyla moves with her. Once through Salis stops and looks back. 'Wow.'

Leyla scans the area and then squeezes Salis' shoulder. 'Go now little one. The way is clear to the upper floors. If anyone stops you, tell them that you were summoned by Lord Damori. I will see you very soon.' With one last squeeze to her shoulder, Leyla leaves her. Opening her eyes and taking a deep breath, she finds Thayer standing in front of her, a look of concern on his face.

"What happened? We've been calling your name for the past twenty minutes." He watches as her eyes lose their far away look. "We even tried to reach you telepathically, but we were both blocked out."

"I'm sorry Thayer. I need to sit down for a minute, then I'll explain."

He leads her over to the chair in front of Aeneka and helps her to sit down when she nearly misses the chair. They wait for her to tell them what had happened to her.

"I went to warn Salis." she says watching their faces. "She's on her way to Trocon right now. We need to contact him and let him know so that he doesn't send her away before she can tell him that I sent her."

Thayer sits down on the console next to Aeneka. "What about guards? They'll stop her before she can reach him."

"I made sure that she had a clear path to the upper floors. If anyone asks, she's to tell them that Trocon summoned her."

"I'll contact Trocon and let him know." Aeneka tells them and her monitor goes dark for several seconds before she reappears smiling. "She's there, she just arrived. Trocon will meet us when we land, and Salis will be with him under close guard."

"Good, I suggest that we prepare ourselves. It looks as though we'll be confronting Mandraik a lot sooner than we planned." Thayer says standing and taking Leyla's hand to pull her up next to him. "We need to build up our bond quickly and get our shields into place against him."

Leyla looks up at him and nods her agreement. "Yes, we'd better. We'll see you in about an hour or so mother." They leave the room and go to the lounge to start their re-bonding and to strengthen the bond between them even more.

# Chapter IX

After safely navigating to Calidon, Stephen goes to prepare himself as Leyla's personal bodyguard, leaving Leyla and Thayer to land the ship.

"This is the FIRESTAR, we will be landing in fifteen minutes. Please inform Lord Damori immediately."

"FIRESTAR, this is Selina Damori, Chief Communications officer. My father is already waiting for you. He has that special package safe with him also."

"Thank you Selina. FIRESTAR out." Leyla shuts off the monitor and turns to Thayer. "There was someone there with her that was very antagonistic towards me."

"Yes, I felt it too. We'll have to ask her who was with her and check whoever it was. We can't afford to let any malcontents wander around with that much hostility."

"All right, but let's let Trocon handle it. If Mandraik has caused the antagonism by suggesting that my interest is not for Calidon, we need to go slowly with how we deal with the people." She turns back to the controls as the altitude indicator begins to buzz, and quickly prepares the ship for landing.

"Okay, but be prepared to defend yourself if necessary. You can bet that there will be a few that he's brought around to his way of thinking."

Leyla nods and brings the ship down. After shutting down the engines, she stands up and they go into the comm-center to get Aeneka.

As they walk in, they notice that Aeneka has turned on the outer sensors.

"I don't see Mandraik out there, but no doubt he'll show up before we leave the platform. Get to Salis as quickly as you can. You need to start your bonding with her right away."

"I will mother. Sarah, does Stephen have your portable unit?"

"Yes he does Leyla. He's waiting for you at the outer hatch."

"Okay, let him know that we're on our way."

Leyla picks up the vid-diary and Aeneka turns off her monitor. Thayer leads the way to the hatch. They both stop to straighten their cloaks, and then Leyla nods for Stephen to open the hatch. When it opens, Stephen steps out taking a quick look around before turning back and indicating that it was safe. Leyla steps out holding Aeneka and Thayer is one step behind her. She looks around and then goes down the ramp followed closely by Thayer and Stephen. Once at the bottom, Thayer and Stephen stand on either side of her.

Trocon smiles and steps forward. Normally he would have embraced her in greeting, but Aeneka's unit prevents such a greeting. Instead he bows to them. "Welcome home Princess."

Leyla bows her head. "Thank you Trocon." she looks sideways at Thayer. "This is my lifemate, Thayer Robus Starhawk of Manchon." They had decided that this would be the best way to introduce him. After they shake hands, she introduces Stephen. "And this is Stephen Seven, my companion and personal bodyguard."

Stephen bows slightly, then turns to Leyla saying something in the gibberish that they use to communicate privately around others. She looks at him and then replies in the same language, before handing Aeneka over to him and turning back to Trocon.

"Since only I or Stephen can touch the essence box, he'll carry her."

Trocon nods and turns back to the guards and raises his hand. The guards part and at the center stands Salis with her head bowed. After they part, she looks up and sees Leyla.

"Matima!" she cries out and rushes forward. One of the guards tries to stop her, but his hand is flung aside by the protective shield that is around her, before he can touch her.

Leyla steps forward and bends down as Salis runs into her waiting arms, tears streaming down her cheeks. Leyla gathers her close and hugs her.

"Hush little one, hush now. Everything is fine, you're safe now." Leyla rocks her back and forth until she calms. She then straightens up and turns her to face Thayer. "This is Thayer, he's going to be my lifemate."

Thayer goes down on one knee beside them and smiles. "Welcome Salis." He gently caresses her cheek. "It will be a pleasure to have such a brave and beautiful daughter like you." He watches as she blushes and smiles shyly at him before hiding her face in Leyla's chest.

Leyla holds her closer and undercover of comforting her speaks only to her. 'Salis, we need to bond together so that no matter what, I will always know where you are and that you are safe. All right?'

Salis looks up and nods smiling. 'Yes Matima.'

They look deeply into each others eyes and begin sharing their memories and thoughts. They stand there for several minutes before breaking off their new link. Leyla smiles and hugs her close once again. 'No one will ever harm you again little one.' She looks over to Thayer and nods, signaling that the bond has been made, then she turns to Trocon.

"I think that it would be best if we were to continue any further discussions in my chambers, where we will have more privacy."

"Of course Leyla, this way." Trocon signals the guards to surround them and then leads the way from the platform.

As they walk towards the palace entrance, a man and woman rush out. The man slows his step, but the woman continues at a fast clip, her eyes focused on Salis. Before the guards can stop her, the woman rushes over to Salis. Leyla, having thought that no one would dare to bother Salis while in their company and with so many guards, had removed the protective shield. The woman grabs Salis' arm and tries to pull her from Leyla's side.

"You little..." The woman's voice is cut off and she releases Salis' arm to clutch at her throat unable to breath.

"You dare to attack someone in my presence without a word?"

Leyla asks in a deadly quiet voice keeping the pressure on the other woman's throat and slowly increasing the pressure until she falls to her knees. She releases the pressure only enough for her to breath and speak. Though she knows who she is, Leyla still asks. "Who are you? What are you doing here?"

Madame Priss coughs and slowly answers as loud as her sore throat will allow. "I am Detra Priss, Keeper of the servants." she coughs again. "This girl left her quarters without permission, and has been missing for the past few hours. I've been searching for her."

"How do you know that she's been missing? Did you bother to ask anyone where she might be?" Leyla snaps, turning to look at Salis who is huddled close to Thayer's side, holding tightly to his leg.

"I know, because I myself locked her in her room. When I went to check on her she was not there." When the pressure lessens enough, she stands up and straightens her dress. "I don't know how she got out of a locked room. It was still locked when I went to check, but she was not there. I plan to take her back and teach her to..." she takes a step towards Salis and Leyla raises her hand placing a barrier between them.

"If you value your life, you will not take another step towards my daughter." Leyla tells her watching the shock emerge on the other woman's face. "That's right, I said my daughter." Detra opens her mouth to say something but Leyla forestalls her. "I will hear no more from you. Trocon, have two guards escort...Miss Priss...to a holding cell until I send for her."

Trocon signals two guards, and they each take hold of one of her arms and drag her away. She screams at them to release her. Leyla watches as the guards take her inside and then turns to Thayer and Salis.

"Are you all right little one?"

Salis nods but doesn't release her hold on Thayer's leg. Leyla notices that she's not looking at her, but at the man who had come out with Detra Priss and then stopped while the woman came at them. She turns to face him and can feel the hatred radiating from him.

"Do you also wish to attack my daughter?" she asks, easily blocking his attempt to probe her.

"No, no Highness. I have no idea whatsoever what that was all about." Dacus denies quickly taking a step back from them. "I only came to greet you as is expected of one in my position your Highness."

Leyla raises a skeptical brow and watches him closely.

'Careful my love. I sense that he's dangerously close to the edge of his control right now.'

'I know, but given the chance...'

'Not now, not where Salis can see. At least until she's more confident with us. We need to get her away from his as quickly as possible.'

She nods slightly before addressing Mandraik. "You can greet us more formally in a couple of hours Mandraik. Right now I wish to go to my chambers and rest." she tells him, easily leaving out the title of his station and therefore denying him the show of respect normally due him.

"Of course your Highness." He nods stiffly aware of her insult. He can feel his hatred for this Earth witch growing stronger with each passing second. He turns his head slightly as he hears the Tahquar brat suck in a breath, and sends her a dark look to keep her silent, before stepping aside to let them pass.

"Lord Trocon will inform you when I am ready to receive visitors." Leyla inclines her head and moves forward.

Thayer picks Salis up to carry her past Mandraik. He too had heard her quick intake of air, and seen the look she was given. He also felt her fear of the man increase considerably. 'Don't worry little one. He can't hurt you any more.'

'But Matima...?'

'Your mother will be fine. She can take care of herself. Put your head on my shoulder and rest. You don't have to look at him. I'll carry you to the room and nothing will happen to you.' he assures her. He feels her relax and cuddle closer to him. Ignoring Mandraik, he walks past him without acknowledging him at all.

Dacus watches as Trocon leads them into the palace and curses Detra for her stupid and foolish actions. At least he didn't have to worry about the old cow giving anything away about his plans. The block that he had placed deep within her mind couldn't be broken by even the strongest of telepaths. Any attempt to get past it would cause permanent and irreparable brain damage. Walking slowly in behind them, he tries to figure out how he was going to get to the girl. He knows that she can do him and his plans great harm is not stopped. If only the Earthlings had come when they were originally scheduled, he would have already have taken care of the chit and wouldn't have to wonder what she was telling them.

* * *

Upon reaching the rooms that would be Leyla's, Trocon stations two of the guards outside the doors and then sends the rest to inform the Council of her arrival. With that done, he closes the door and follows the others into the sitting room.

"The guards will see to it that we aren't disturbed by the wrong people. Now, would someone care to explain to me exactly what that was that just occurred out on that platform." He asks looking to each of the people sitting down in front of him with his hands on his hips and a frown on his face.

Salis looks from Leyla to Thayer, unsure herself what was going on any more. All she knew was that for the past two months, Madame Priss and Lord Mandraik had been very cruel to her and it had only gotten worse as the days passed.

"As my mother told you when she linked with you earlier, we had reason to believe that Salis' life was in grave danger. Though we have no physical proof, we do have the word of someone well trusted. We believe that Mandraik and Priss, have conspired to murder her sometime in the dawn hours of this day." Leyla informs him. When she hears Salis' gasp of fright, she reaches out her hand to her and holds it tightly. "That was one of the reasons that I sent her to you before dawn."

Trocon finds it hard to believe that even the power hungry Mandraik would stoop to killing a small child. "Who told you of this plot against the girl?"

Just then Aeneka's monitor comes on and she is facing Trocon. She laughs as he jumps back a step and clutches the back of a chair. "What is the matter old friend? You look as though you are seeing a ghost."

"I am...I have...I mean..." He takes a deep breath and then takes a tentative step nearer for a closer look. "How can this be? You've been gone for over twenty years." he tells her image and watches her smile.

"Saitun came up with the idea after I explained the workings of our essence boxes. If for some reason I went before him, we wanted a way to communicate with each other. Since no one but Leyla can touch my box, it was easier to create this and give us a way to talk privately."

"But what of the android? He too touches you." he says looking up at Stephen after sitting down in the chair in front of her.

Leyla explains it to him. "Stephen was given a bio-skin made from my DNA. It will continuously regenerate until it is no longer needed. A biochemist friend of my father's came up with the process after father explained to her what they needed and why." She looks up at Stephen and smiles with affection. "Stephen has been carrying mother around since she entered the essence box. I was too small, and couldn't even lift it, even though it's not that big. Carrying it anywhere would have been impossible."

Aeneka interrupts them knowing that Leyla could talk about that time for hours. "Back to your original question. Old Rachel contacted me about Salis nearly four hours ago. She had touched Mandraik in passing and picked up on some impressions of Salis that gave her great concern. When she called on the inner sight, she saw Priss and Mandraik standing over Salis' still and lifeless body grinning and gloating about their success. She had just recently healed the child from a beating given by Priss." she tells him sorry that Salis had to her this.

Trocon continues to frown, but he no longer has any doubts. He knew that if Rachel felt that there was a danger to the child then it surely would have come to pass if Leyla hadn't intervened when she did. "And she was sure that they had planned to do it at dawn today?"

"Yes she was. They wanted it done before we arrived. That was when I made the decision to jump to light-speed. I knew we had no other choice."

There is a long silence as each of the adults think about what could have happened during the time they were going so fast. Though she doesn't quite understand what they're talking about. Salis realizes that whatever it was, it had been very dangerous, and that they had risked much to save her.

There is a knock at the door, and Stephen goes to answer it, only opening it enough to see who it is and to listen to them identify themselves. After a few seconds, he looks at Leyla and speaks to her in their special language.

"Yes, let her in Stephen. It's Selina." she tells Trocon.

Trocon stands and goes to greet his daughter as she enters the room. After giving her a hug, he leads her over to the others. "Princess Aeneka, Princess Leyla, may I present to you both my daughter Selina Trocona Elinda Damori. Selina, the princesses and Princess Leyla's lifemate Thayer Starhawk."

Selina bows slightly at the waist, her uniform not suitable for the formal curtsy expected from a woman. "Your Highnesses. Please forgive my intrusion and my rudeness." and she turns to her father. "There's been another illegal entry into Calidon space. When a patrol shuttle went to investigate, they were fired upon. The ship then changed course and quickly left."

Leyla stands and steps closer to them. "Was anyone injured?"

"No your Highness. There was minor damage to the shuttle but no one was hurt."

"Thank goodness." Leyla turns to Stephen and signals him forward. "Hand me Sarah's portable please." Stephen takes the unit out of his side pouch and hands it to her. "Sarah, have you been monitoring Calidon space as I suggested?"

"Yes I have Leyla. There were some fireworks up there a little while ago. I don't think that there was any major damage done though."

"Did you get any information on the unauthorized vessel?"

"Yes. The design was that of an older model freighter, Earth type. I'd have to say that it was maybe twenty or thirty years old with some modifications to the engines. Would you like me to run an identifications check on it?"

"Yes please. Do a deep search on the owner and check all avenues. See who's bought, sold, or leased it. Check for any connections no matter how vague, to either President Carrison or Dacus Mandraik."

"All right, but it may take me a while to check out everything." She warns her.

"That'll be fine Sarah. Do what you can and inform us of anything that you find." Leyla instructs and then switches the unit to automatic control and hands it back to Stephen. She then turns back to the others. "If there's any connection, Sarah will find it." She sits back down next to Salis when she notices that Trocon and Selina are still standing.

"How long do you think it will take her to gather the information your Highness?"

"Hopefully not too long Selina, and please, call me Leyla. I can't get into the title distinctions when I'm with friends and family."

Trocon watches as his daughter's jaw goes slack from shock. "You'll find my dear that our future Queen is very open in her opinions on the hierarchy."

"Yes, my daughter has the tendency to shock people just for the effect. She used to laugh at her teachers whenever they tried to teach her the correct forms of address, and she would constantly ask them why. There were times when her father and I thought that they were all going to pull their hair out if she didn't use the proper title, or asked them again why about something." Aeneka tells her with a laugh, remembering the first time Leyla had a lesson with Trocon and called him Mister Damori.

"True. I felt that way many times after a session with her." Trocon admits and then watches Leyla blush scarlet.

"You didn't really make fun of them did you Matima?" Salis asks never having heard of anyone doing such a thing.

"Every chance I got little one. Though it wasn't really a show of disrespect on my part. When I got older and learned the reasons for the distinctions, I realized that titles can be very important at times." Leyla tells her not wanting her to think that such behavior was acceptable, and pulls her into her embrace. "When you know your friends, it's not so important when you're in private what a person's title is. Even in public at times. A title is a sign of respect nothing more as far as I'm concerned. It generally shows that someone has worked very hard in their lives. While sometimes it's just something that has been handed down through a family. I've found though, that if you show everyone the same respect that you'd show a Lord or Lady, King or Queen, then you help them to respect not only themselves, but others as well."

Salis smiles up at her in understanding. She always tried to show everyone respect. Leyla kisses her forehead and she lays her head against her shoulder. She was very tired. After leaving her room, she had been afraid to go back to sleep.

As she raises her head and looks down at Salis, Leyla notices her trying to hide a yawn. "Why don't you go and lay down for awhile sweetie?" she suggests and sees the fear enter Salis' eyes once again as she shakes her head. "It's okay honey, we'll be right out here while you sleep. We don't plan to go anywhere without you, I promise. I'll even send Stephen in with you to watch over you while you sleep, and Thayer and I will check on you all the time."

Salis looks up at Stephen, and then looks at Leyla and Thayer. She wanted to lay down, but she was so afraid. She bites down on her lower lip before looking back at Leyla. It had been so long since anyone had really watched out for her, she didn't know what to do.

'I promise that I will be here when you wake up. If you get frightened, all you have to do is call out to me and I will be with you in moments.' Leyla assures her lightly caressing her cheek. "All right?"

Believing her, Salis gives her a small smile and nods. Leaning up she kisses her on the cheek and then turns to Thayer. When he opens his arms to her, she falls into them. She gives him a kiss on the cheek and he kisses the top of her head.

"Sleep well and safe little one." Thayer tells her and gives her one final hug.

Stephen steps to the side of the sofa and holds out his hand to her. Shyly she places her hand in his. "I'll stay right next to the bed the whole time you're sleeping Salis." he assures her leading her to the bedroom his sensors had detected when he entered the room. "How about I tell you a bedtime story? I used to tell your Matima some pretty good ones when she was a little girl." he tells her as they walk into the room and close the door.

\* \* \*

For the next two hours, Trocon and Selina go over everything that had happened since the deaths of Leyla's grandparents. They tell them of how the year before the Queen's death, there had seemed to be a rising number of conflicts arising all over for no apparent reason amongst the lower and middle classes. People had begun to disappear, and there was even the occasional unauthorized ship spotted in Calidon space.

"At first most of the people to disappear were from those classes. They were of fairly strong abilities and not known to go off without telling someone." Trocon informs them and then Selina continues.

"Then we noticed that the majority of the missing people were those that had opposed new laws that Lord Mandraik wished to have passed by the council. These people all opposed him openly. At first we didn't notice anything really unusual, but then after the Queen's death, the problems just seemed to increase. More reports started coming in about disappearances and it wasn't just the lower and middle classes any more. Stronger telepaths were missing, some from many of the great houses. When people from the penal moon started disappearing the King passed a law that all prisoners must be given a monitoring device, which was to be placed behind the left ear. I think he would have had one placed on everyone if he thought that the people would accept it. By then the disappearances on Calidon itself had pretty much stopped anyway.

"The monitoring devices worked well until just before the King's death. Suddenly all the signals would be lost, and then an hour or two later start up again. At first it was thought that there was a malfunction in the receiver, but after doing a physical count after each malfunction, and a name check, we noticed that approximately a hundred prisoners were missing and no one knew how. The King ordered a full scale investigation, but the investigator was to report only to him on his findings. We have no idea what his investigation turned up, because shortly after the King's death, the investigator was found murdered in the palace gardens and none of his information was recovered."

Throughout most of their report, Thayer has been pacing around the room, listening and cataloging everything in his mind. Now he stops and faces the others. "How many people would you say are missing all together? Both from Calidon and the penal moon."

"Roughly about three hundred, three-fifty." Trocon answers looking up at him with a slight frown. "Why do you ask?"

Thayer returns to his seat next to Leyla before explaining. "There have always been telepaths on Earth. No one really knows how many because they've always kept to themselves, afraid to mix with society and be labeled as freaks. About two years ago, a friend of mine informed me that a number of telepaths had been found and taken into custody. Just before Leyla and I left, my friend and I were investigating another influx of telepaths. In the past two years, there have been nearly four hundred telepaths reported in custody. None with valid identification, or any record that they even existed before the Earth Security Council got a hold of them. Too many appeared for it to just be a coincidence. I find it hard to believe that people that have stayed out of sight for so long, would suddenly pop up and allow themselves to be caught. Not to mention that most of them are adults with only a few being under the age of eighteen. I have no doubt whatsoever that your missing people are now on Earth and being used to infiltrate groups that are opposed to the President. I believe that they've been turned into what we term as mind touchers. Telepaths that go into other people's minds without their knowledge or consent and plant suggestions into their minds to get them to cooperate."

There is a stunned silence as everyone considers the ramifications of this new situation. They all knew how hard it was to turn a telepath, but once turned it was even harder to return them to their more passive states of nonviolence.

"But why would our people cooperate with such a thing? It makes no sense. We all agree to a nonviolent use of our abilities." Selina says to no one in particular standing and looking around at the others. "From what little you've told us, these mind touchers probably kill anyone that will not change their way of thinking. Even our worst criminals aren't in prison for murder."

Leyla looks up at her sadly. "What if they were given no other choice? What if their families had been threatened? Have any of the missing people's families suffered from death or maybe the loss of position or possessions?"

Trocon and Selina look at each other, neither of them had considered that possibility. Trocon shrugs his shoulders. "We don't know, but I'll have it checked into right away." He closes his eyes to show that he is communicating telepathically with someone. Within seconds his eyes open again and he looks at Leyla. "We should know by mid-afternoon if any of the families have suffered any type of loss, no matter how small it may seem."

There is a knock at the door and Selina turns to go and answer it after receiving a nod from Leyla to do so. Opening the door, she steps aside to allow Brockton Centori to enter.

'Good morning wife.' he says into her mind with a lifted brow. 'If I didn't know that the Princess had arrived, I would beat you for not waking me or preparing my morning meal.' with having said all of this to her privately, everyone wonders what had passed between them to make Selina blush. "I have a message for the Princess and your father." Selina glares at him and then turns to lead him over to the others.

With his wife's back to him, Brockton delivers a swift hard and loud swat to her backside for the glare she had given him.

"Ouch! Brock..." Selina yelps turning to face him again only to be cut off by him.

"Be glad that's all you got for that look you gave me woman." he tells her with a smile and a quick kiss to her parted lips. He leaves her standing there stunned by his show of affection in front of strangers, and the future Queen. Stepping around her he walks over to the sofa. "Leyla, I'm glad to see that you've arrived safely."

Leyla stands up and takes the hands extended to her, allowing him to kiss her cheeks. "Thank you Brock. Though I did have my doubts at times." Turning to Thayer she holds out her hand to him feeling his jealousy. "Thayer, I'd like you to meet Brockton Centori, my third cousin and Selina's bond mate. Brock, my lifemate, Thayer Robus Starhawk of Earth and Manchon."

All eyes widen in surprise at Leyla's disclosure of her relationship to Brockton. Such relationships weren't acknowledged openly. Both

Leyla and Brock laugh at the expressions on their faces. Aeneka shakes her head at them.

"All right you two, that's quite enough. I swear, if I didn't know better, I would swear that you were raised together since you have the same wicked sense of humor." They both just grin at each other before Brock kneels down in front of Aeneka's monitor.

"Greetings Aunt Neka. Welcome home." he says sending out his pleasure at seeing her again even if he can't touch her.

"Thank you Brockton." After he stands up and steps back to Selina's side Aeneka encourages him to state his business. "You'd best deliver your message Brockton. I feel that it is very important in light of what we have been discussing here."

"Of course." He stands at attention and says formally. "Princess Leyla, Lord Damori. The Royal Council requests your immediate appearance before them in the Council Chamber." He relaxes again and goes on more personally. "One of the council guards informed me that Lord Mandraik called all the other members together charging that the Princess wantonly attacked Madame Priss without provocation when she tried to retrieve a runaway servant."

"Without provocation!" Leyla exclaims. "The damn woman broke through the guards and grabbed my daughter. To me that was provocation in the extreme. She's lucky I didn't kill her." Now it is Brock who looks at her in surprised shock.

"Daughter? What daughter? You never said anything to me about..."

Just then they hear Salis' scream of fear and anguish coming from the bedroom. Not thinking about protocol, Leyla teleports into the room. Salis is sitting up in the bed holding tightly to Stephen when Leyla appears. As soon as she sees her, Salis launches herself into her arms and buries her head in Leyla's chest. Brockton enters the room with his stunner drawn.

"What is it? What's happened?" he asks looking around the room as he stops at Leyla's side.

Reacting instinctively, Stephen attacks Brock and pins him on the floor, quickly disarming him. Before he can knock him unconscious, Leyla calls out to him just as Thayer mentally blocks his punch.

"Stephen NO STOP! It's Brock, he's family." Leyla shouts to make herself heard over Selina's scream and the other loud voices in the room. "He's family Stephen. Remember? Captain of the Royal Guard." she tells him and repeats it in their special language.

Stephen looks at her, then at his fist stuck in mid air, then at the others gathered in the room before looking down at his prisoner and focusing on his face. When he releases his hold on Brock's shirt, Thayer releases his other hand. Standing, Stephen reaches down and offers Brock his hand. "I apologize Captain Centori." Brock takes the offered hand. "When I saw your weapon, my only response was to protect Leyla and the child. Nothing else registered." he admits with a frown. Nothing like that had ever happened to him before.

"It's all right Stephen. I understand. I'm glad Leyla has you to protect her." Brock tells him brushing off his uniform.

Through it all Salis' grip on Leyla has only tightened even more. Leyla looks down at her. "What's wrong little one? Did you have a bad dream?" Salis shakes her head and burrows her head deeper into Leyla's chest. Leyla looks up at Thayer concerned. 'Something is very wrong here Thayer. Even with all of us her, she is terrified to death.'

'Could someone have tried to do something to her mind?'

Leyla looks back down at Salis. 'Let us see little one. Let us see what has frightened you so badly.' She starts to shake her head, but stops and slowly lifts her head. Sighing reluctantly she nods.

Taking a deep breath, Salis slowly opens her mind to them. Leyla and Thayer watch as the images that had been sent to her while she slept, play through Salis' mind. They are images of a man and woman being beaten and abused, and finally their bodies dismembered while they are still alive.

"Oh dear God." Leyla closes her eyes and pushes the images from her mind. "Were those your parents little one?" she asks in a very shaky voice already knowing the answer, but needing Salis to confirm it.

Salis nods and then begins to cry softly. She had always known that her mother and father were dead, but to know how they died was too much for her to handle.

Thayer takes her from Leyla and holds her close. "Don't worry little one. We'll find the people responsible for this and they'll pay for what they did. I promise you, they'll pay." He tells her with a firm resolve. Not only would the ones that followed the orders to do such a thing pay, but so would the person that ordered it done.

Trocon and the others watch them closely, wondering what had been done to the child. They knew that it had to have been something extremely awful, from the paleness of Leyla and Thayer's faces.

"What's happened Leyla? What's upset her so badly?" Selina asks stepping forward to run a comforting hand down Salis' back.

"Let's go into the other room, I'd like my mother to hear this too, and I only want to have to say it once if possible." She leads the way back into the sitting room, staying close to Salis and Thayer. They all sit down, and Thayer keeps Salis on his lap with his arms wrapped around her for comfort.

"Someone sent images to Salis of her parents being beaten and totally abused. They showed them being stripped and her mother raped by several men. Then they showed them dismembered while they were still alive. It was a slow and cruel death." Leyla stops when Salis sobs deeply. She reaches over and gently runs her hand over Salis' hair. "I'm sorry baby. I promise, that's the last time you'll ever have to hear about it, and you will never have to remember it again." She touches her head again and reaches into her mind to erase the memory from her subconscious as well as her conscious mind.

Though he knows what the child has been put through must be dealt with, Trocon doesn't want Leyla to have any more difficulties with the council because of Mandraik's manipulations. "I hate to interrupt Leyla. I know how important this situation is, but we need to do some damage control with the council. We've kept them waiting for nearly an hour and no doubt Mandraik is using it to his advantage." he tells her quietly.

Leyla looks up at him and then back to Salis. The anger builds up inside of her to the point that she feel's like she's going to explode if she doesn't release it soon. She feels Thayer's eyes on her and looks over at him. His face reflects her anger, but he quickly covers it so as not to alarm Salis.

'I feel the same way love. Whoever did this will pay with their lives. But Trocon is right. We need to deal with Mandraik as soon as possible before he can influence the council any further.' They look deep into each others eyes before Leyla nods her agreement.

"All right Trocon, let's go." She says something to Stephen and then stands up. "Stephen is going to monitor our meeting with the council. He'll check to see if there are any red Alpha's present. If there are any, Thayer or I will deal with them immediately." She waits to see if he has any objections before continuing. "I will not tolerate this happening again. Everyone will know that I have claimed Salis as my daughter, and they will find out that anyone that attacks her for whatever reason, will be dealt with to the fullest extent of the law."

They all nod their agreement with her and stand up. Stephen picks up Aeneka to carry her to the Council Chamber. Thayer stands and sets Salis on her feet between him and Leyla. They each take one of her hands and stand close to her sides. She would not be allowed away from them at any time while they were in the Council Chamber.

As soon as they leave the chambers, Trocon's guards quickly surround them to ensure that no one gets past them again. They felt lucky that the Princess had not dismissed them from her presence immediately for what had taken place out on the platform. They would be more alert and not let anyone associated with Mandraik past them.

# Chapter X

As they approach the Council Chambers, the guards at the doors pull the big ornate doors open for them. The guards to the front of the group separate to let Leyla and the others pass, while still protecting their sides and backs.

The guards at the doors cross their spears as the group steps forward as a whole. "Only the Princess and Lord Damori may enter." one of the men states to Brockton.

"The Princess will enter with all of those present, or she will not enter at all." he tells the other man with a dark scowl. When Mandraik was dealt with Brockton would take care of the guards that had followed him so blindly. "The Council has no say in whom the Princess wishes to accompany her to these chambers. Now step aside or you'll have me to deal with and you won't like the outcome."

The two guards look at each other and then after several seconds of silent communications, they lift their spears and step aside. "You may enter Captain."

Brock leads the way into the chamber and stops a few feet past the doors. "The Princess Leyla Aeneka Latona of the House Chaukcee and her entourage my Lords and Ladies of the Royal High Council." he announces and then steps to the side.

Leyla, Salis, and Thayer lead the way to the center of the room followed closely by Stephen, Trocon, and Selina. Brockton nods to the door guards, signaling for them to close the doors.

Trocon steps forward and addresses his fellow council members.

"Ladies and Gentlemen, I present to you the Princess Leyla and her lifemate Thayer Robus Starhawk of Manchon."

All of the council members bow or curtsy in respect, except for Dacus Mandraik, who only slightly bows his head.

"It was requested that only you and the Princess attend this meeting Trocon." Mandraik states. They can all hear the sneer in his voice when mentioning Leyla's title. "Instead you bring with you a strange man claiming to be lifemate to our next Queen, the head of our communications, a machine man, and a runaway servant. You insult us with their presence."

Trocon opens his mouth to revival him for his uncouth and disrespectful statements, but is stopped by Leyla's hand on his shoulder.

"And you sir, insult me and my family." She states glaring at him then turns away from him to address the other council members. "All present here with me are part of my family by blood, marriage, and adoption." She looks once again at Dacus. "There is no servant in this group, and you would do well to remember that Lord Mandraik."

One of the council members clears his throat to get Leyla's attention. When she turns around, Leyla looks straight at the High Priest. "Yes Lord Metros?"

"We truly welcome you and your chosen Highness. May the Great One bless you and yours for all time."

"Thank you my Lord. Now people, I will say this only once and you will heed me well. Salis Tahquar is now and ever will be known as my daughter. If any harms her, they will pay and pay dearly." She watches their faces, and can sense only a little resentment, but no out right hatred. "Before coming here someone sent images to Salis while she slept. That person will pay with her life." Everyone in the room draws a breath at this announcement. Those with Leyla look at each other wondering what she was up to.

"Trocon, send for Miss Priss and have her brought here to me." Trocon nods and closes his eyes. When he opens them again he nods once more. "I was accused of attacking this woman without provocation. I tell you that I had just provocation and was in my rights to subdue her."

Seconds later the doors open and Detra Priss is dragged into the room kicking and screaming. "You can't do this to me! I did nothing. That Earth bitch can't call a servant her daughter just to save the little brat from punishment." Detra looks around and spots Leyla. Pulling herself free of the guards she springs forward towards Leyla. Before she can make contact with Leyla's protective shielding, she's flung back against a wall.

Leyla looks at Thayer with a small pout. "Why did you do that? I wanted to see her face when she ran into the shield."

"Reflex." he says with a shrug and then grins at her. Leyla grins back and then turns to the council.

"As you have all just witnessed, the provocation was justified both now and earlier. Even though the first time wasn't an attack against myself, it was still done in my presence as this attack was done in front of all of you. I feel that the woman is most definitely unbalanced or under the control of another."

The council all nod their agreement, and start whispering amongst themselves. Every now and then one of them would look at Mandraik and see the look of disgust on his face.

"This woman was responsible for the care and well being of all the servants. She abused that responsibility by abusing those under her care, which I understand to be mostly children. True, at one time Salis was a servant, but even then, as a Tahquar she was deserving of a position her name entitled her to. Instead she was treated lower than the lowest servant should ever be treated. I tell you now that Detra Priss and another conspired to kill Salis at dawn this very day before my arrival." she informs them, not mentioning how she knows this information. All conversation stops. Leyla notices Stephen stepping closer to her and slowly continues until he can tell her exactly who the red Alpha is.

(A red Alpha is someone with mental abilities that is suffering from mental madness. They become quite unstable, and their abilities increase with the fluctuation of their brain activity. During this stage, any and all weapons created become poisonous and extremely deadly.)

"This second person fears Salis for what he believes she knows about him. He fears her so much, that he was willing to kill a child to ensure his own safety."

Stephen starts to speak, but it's already too late. Leyla is already under attack and defending herself.

'Thayer, protect Salis! He'll go after her as soon as he thinks we're distracted.'

'What about you?'

'I'll be fine. He's strong but his mind is in conflict with his actions.'

An arc of light is flung at Salis while they talk, but Thayer easily deflects it, sending it spiraling to the ceiling where it can do no harm.

'You betray yourself Mandraik.'

'It doesn't matter now Earth bitch. Once you're dead, the throne will be mine. I am the strongest on this world.' He sends a thought dagger hurling towards her.

Leyla deftly blocks it and sends one of her own back at him. 'You can't hope to win against me Mandraik. The power of all Calidon flows within me.' she tells him as he quickly side steps her dagger just before it strikes.

'Never! You can no more call upon the power then that Earth trash you brought with you is Majichonie.' He sends two more daggers at her, which she easily stops and destroys.

'That's were your wrong Mandraik. Just as you were wrong about my father. You thought his origins were only of Earth, but they weren't. Anymore than they are Thayer's. My grandfather was from Manchon and had the abilities of the healers of that world in his blood.' she taunts him unmercifully, trying to make him make a mistake and is rewarded.

"Impossible! He never would have suffered from injuries when I attacked him all those years ago if he had any abilities to speak of." Mandraik growls in anger as he realizes what he had just spoken aloud for everyone to hear.

"You are wrong as usual Mandraik. The blood of Calidon and Manchon flow through my veins. With my parents blood joined, I am the FIRESTAR our people have prayed for." She dodges another onslaught of thought daggers. "I have the power of both worlds behind me, and you will pay for what you have done to our people."

With her threat, Mandraik loses all semblance of control and sends several bolts of lightening streaking towards Thayer and the others in the room, thinking that she could not block them all.

Thayer helps her to block them, but one of the bolts gets through and someone grunts at the impact. Hearing the grunt, Leyla reaches out her mind and learns that Trocon was hit and collapses to the floor. Mandraik grins at her in satisfaction as the other man falls to the ground.

"ENOUGH!" Leyla shouts, sending Mandraik crashing into the wall behind him. Before his unconscious body falls to the floor, Leyla turns and rushes to Trocon's side. Old Rachel is already there kneeling beside him and trying to tend to him.

"There's nothing that I can do for him Highness, except try to make him comfortable. The bolt that stuck him is doing something to his system that I can not stop. It's almost as if he had been poisoned."

Selina gasps and falls to her knees at her father's side and takes his hand in hers. She holds it tightly to her cheek as tears run down her cheeks.

"Rachel, could the FIRESTAR and STARHAWK transmutation work?" Leyla asks looking down at the man who was now the closest she had to a grandfather in her life.

"I'm not sure child. If you were completely lifemated, it might be possible, but since your not it could be dangerous to try." Rachel looks up at Thayer. "With him as your mate, I believe that it has a better chance of succeeding. The healing power is strong within him, just as it is within you. As long as you don't hold the forms too long, the risk should be minable."

"We have to at least try, if for no other reason then Mandraik would like to see Trocon die. When we succeed in healing him, he will know that he was wrong again, and that we were the reason that he failed."

"If you try this, your minds must be without hate or malice Leyla. To let those emotions enter will corrupt what you hope to do." Rachel warns her quietly.

While the two women talk, Thayer is looking at Rachel and remembering the old woman that had come to him in visions while he was growing up on Manchon. Her voice had the same inflections and her image was almost the same. He looks down at Trocon and then back at Rachel and Leyla.

"We can do it. With no hatred or malice to interfere." he assures her looking directly into her eyes. "Trocon will live at least another hundred years and be bonded to a very wise and powerful old woman."

Rachel looks up at him for several seconds before looking away and standing up. She ushers everyone several feet away, while Leyla and Thayer take their positions. Leyla standing at Trocon's head, and Thayer at his feet.

Once everyone is far enough away, Leyla and Thayer look into each others eyes and link their minds. They each imagine their name sake, and then send those images to the center point between them and directly over Trocon's prone body. Slowly and carefully the project themselves into the images.

As the others watch, the FIRESTAR appears and gains substance slowly, followed by the STARHAWK. The two join together, creating a powerful light that shines down on the unmoving body of Trocon. Slowly his body begins to float up and is soon surrounded by the pale red and blue light. Within seconds Trocon's body disappears between the two great fire-birds. When his body disappears, the others look to where Leyla and Thayer had been standing, only to discover that they are no longer there. All that is in their place is the clothes they were wearing. A collective gasp passes through the group at the total fusing of their human forms with those of the fire-birds.

"Where are they grandmother? Where did Matima go?" Salis asks in a quivering voice clinging tightly to Stephen's arm.

"They're right in front of us Firepetal." Rachel points to the great birds. "Your mother has become the FIRESTAR, and her mate the STARHAWK." she tells her with a gentle smile, and she watches as Salis' eyes widen and light with joy and understanding.

"They're the ones aren't they grandmother? The ones that will bring us all back into harmony like the ancient stories promised."

"Yes child, they're the ones. They will bring peace, harmony, and freedom back to those whose lives they touch. Not just to our people, but to everyone that has fallen out of harmony with the universe."

Just then, Trocon's body reappears and slowly floats back to the floor. Seconds later Leyla and Thayer reappear with their clothes back on. The FIRESTAR and STARHAWK separate and return to their human bodies. When Leyla and Thayer have mastered their other selves, the shift will be more spontaneous.

Rachel and Brockton rush forward to catch Leyla and Thayer before they can collapse. Salis stands next to Leyla holding her hand while looking from her to Thayer assuring herself that they were both safe. Rachel signals for drinks to be brought to them. Once she's sure that Leyla can stand on her own, she kneels down beside Trocon and quickly examines him. Selina and the others approach slowly and cautiously.

"Rachel?" Selina asks quietly, not voicing her hope or her fears for her father.

"He'll be fine Selina. The poison is gone from his body, and his injuries are completely healed. We'll just give him a few moments to bring himself out of the healing trance."

Selina notices the tears in the older woman's voice and in her eyes and lightly touches her on the shoulder. Rachel looks up and gives her a misty smile and a nod of recognition. Selina returns the gesture, letting Rachel know that she had no problems with the older woman's feelings towards her father.

Trocon finally begins to stir and tries to sit up. Rachel and Brockton carefully help him into a sitting position and Selina braces him at his back with her legs.

"What happened? Why is everyone standing over me, and why am I on the floor?"

"Take it easy you old trigoat." Rachel gently reprimands him placing a hand on his shoulder to keep him still a little longer. "You were struck by one of Dacus' bolts. It poisoned your system." She watches as the shock enters his face and quickly reassures him. "You're fine now. Leyla and Thayer were able to attain the transmutation and use their other selves to purge the poison from your body."

"How could they do that? They aren't yet fully lifemated." he reminds her with a frown.

"Our bond to each other is already strong enough that the lifemating is more or less just the religious ceremony now Trocon." Leyla tells him, kneeling at his side. There is a commotion on the other side of the room that draws their attention. The council men are trying to restrain Mandraik. "NO! Don't you fools see? She must be joined to a Calidonian. It's not right, we need to purify the bloodline. There must not be such an abomination allowed to rule us."

"Release him!" Leyla commands standing up and glaring at Mandraik. Brockton and Thayer help Trocon to stand and then steady him. Not giving himself away, Brockton summons the Queen's royal guards and has them take control over Mandraik.

"Lord Dacus Mandraik. You are hereby placed under arrest for high treason against the royal family and the attempted murder of Lord Trocon Damori. In three days time, you will stand trial before this council and the people of Calidon for these crimes. As of this moment forward, you will lose the use of all of your abilities to prevent you from doing further harm to anyone, including yourself." Leyla declares with a strong carrying voice. Lifting her hand towards him, she concentrates and a yellow light shoots from her fingers to strike Mandraik in the center of his forehead. "NO!" he shouts as he feels the pain of her strike, just before he goes unconscious.

"You four, carry him to the holding area. Two guards are to remain by his cell at all times. No one is allowed to visit with him." Brockton orders his men.

Mandraik is carried from the room and all eyes turn to Detra Priss who is still pinned to the wall. Through everything that has happened, Thayer's hold on her has not lessened. Seeing that they are all now looking at her, Detra begins shaking her head violently back and forth. "No, please. Please have mercy your Highness." she wails.

"Silence woman!" Trocon demands in disgust and turns to Leyla. "What do you want to do with her your Highness?"

Leyla looks at the woman for several seconds, before turning to Lord Metros. "My lord. I ask your permission to probe this woman for information that I believe she has regarding Mandraik's dealings over the years, and his possible involvement in the deaths of both my grandparents."

"Though I would normally have to refuse your request your Highness. Under the circumstances, I believe that there is justifiable cause. When and how would you like to go about it?" He asks. Not only is he the High Priest, he is also the protector of minds. Only with his permission can a person be legally probed without their consent.

"I wish to do it here and now my Lord. I will project all that I see and hear so that each of you can as well. There can be no doubt of either of their guilt in this." She looks around the room at everyone. "I swear on the oath of protection that I will not in any way harm her if it is at all possible."

Each of the council members look at each other and then at Detra, before looking at Kasmen and nodding their agreement.

"Detra Priss. Do you give your permission freely for this probe to be done?" Kasmen asks. She must be given the right to decide for herself.

She glares at him and then at Leyla, knowing that she really had no choice in the matter. The probe would happen either way. "I have nothing to hide my Lord. I freely admit to my hatred. Do your probe. I know nothing of Dacus Mandraik's guilt to the charges against him."

"You have freely given permission your Highness. By her giving her permission, Detra has given the oath of protection. If her mind should attack you, you are free to protect yourself by any means, except death."

Leyla nods and looks at Thayer. "Bring her down and have her kneel in front of me."

'Are you sure about this Love? The High Priest can do the probe.' He says hesitating a little.

'I'm sure. Don't worry, I'll be fine. My mental shields will protect me from any of her attempts to attack me.' she assures him with a smile.

Thayer nods and slowly brings Detra down from the wall, floating her towards Leyla. When she's three feet away, he lowers her to the ground and forces her to kneel. "Harm her in any way woman, and you will not live long enough to enjoy it."

Detra's eyes widen at his spoken threat. When there are no objections made to the outsider's words, she realizes that if he didn't kill her for causing the Princess harm, one of the others would. She promises herself that she would do nothing to harm the Princess. Though she hated her, she did not wish to die for that hate.

# Chapter XI

One of the council members brings Leyla a chair so that she can sit comfortably during the probing. After sitting, Leyla motions Stephen forward. A small table appears beside her.

"Please place her there Stephen." After setting Aeneka on the table, Stephen steps back. "Ladies and Gentlemen, what you are about to see can be explained to you later. Just remember that the image is a true one and not man made. She can see and hear everything. Only the box which contains her is man made." She watches them for several seconds and then looks down at her mother's monitor. "We're ready mother."

The monitor comes on and Aeneka's image appears on the screen. "Good morn to you all."

"By the Sacred One!" one of the women exclaims in fright before fainting. She is revived while the others stare at Aeneka's image.

"Aeneka Latona. The Great One bless and keep you." Kasmen prays in a soft voice.

Aeneka smiles and nods at him. "He always has and He always will Kasmen." He nods his understanding and returns her smile. He was happy to be able to see her image one last time.

"I will begin now. No one must touch either Miss Priss or myself during the probe. This is for your own safety as well as ours." Leyla warns them.

Everyone nods in agreement and returns to their seats around the council table at Kasmen's suggestion. "This may take awhile, and we should make ourselves as comfortable as possible."

Leyla waits until all is quiet and then closes her eyes. She concentrates on Detra's mind and projects herself inside. She focuses on following her memories back to the events that happened just before and lead up to her being placed under arrest.

\* \* \*

"I don't know how she got out of her chamber Dacus. The door was still sealed and locked. She doesn't have teleportation abilities yet, so someone had to have let her out."

"Who? You're the only one that's suppose to have the damned key! We've got to find her and get rid of her before the Earthlings get here."

They go their separate ways to look for her and then meet up again just before Leyla is expected to land and meet with Trocon.

"The bitch will be landing in less than fifteen minutes. My man in communications says that Trocon has a special package for her with him at the landing site. We need to get there quickly and make sure that its not the girl. If it is the girl, you had better do something to get her away from them." They arrive, but too late, and Detra is captured and taken away.

\* \* \*

Leyla stops there for a few minutes, and Stephen hands her a cool drink. She nods her thanks and takes a huge swallow before turning to the others and taking a deep breath. "As you can see, they didn't want Salis to meet with me, and searched for her frantically in the hopes of preventing us from seeing each other." She looks at Selina. "Who was with you when I contacted you about my new arrival time?"

"A junior officer." Selina closes her eyes and thinks back to early this morning. "It was a nephew of Mandraik's. I believe he's still on duty."

"Brockton, have the young man detained for questioning." she tells her cousin and watches as he closes his eyes. "Ladies and Gentlemen. I am having him detained because of his hostility towards me. It is almost as great as his uncle's." The council nods their understanding and agreement. Leyla turns back to Brock with a lifted brow.

"He's in custody and someone has taken over his station." This last is said to Selina so that she knows all the stations are being seen to. Selina nods her understanding and smiles gratefully at her mate.

"All right then, let's continue." Leyla briefly touches her mother and receives comfort and pride from her. Smiling at her mother, she reluctantly removes her hand and once more enters Detra's mind.

* * *

"You have to keep a close eye on the Tahquar brat. I just realized that it was her that passed me in the outer chamber just after our discussion of the last shipment." Mandraik says pacing around Detra's small office.

"Do you know what you were thinking about? What you had just thought about?"

"Of course I know. Why else do you think that I want her watched you stupid old cow!" he snarls at her. "I was thinking about my contacts on Terra. If anyone should find out that I've been selling... Well lets just say it wouldn't be good for either one of us."

"She won't talk to anyone. I'll make sure that she doesn't get close enough to anyone to talk. I'll work her so hard that she won't have the strength to even think."

"Make sure that she knows that if she talks she'll pay dearly for it." He tells her with an evil grin.

"Oh she'll know, even if I have to beat it into her." Detra assures him hollowly. "I'll pay back her family for all the embarrassment they caused me over the years."

"Just deal with it." Mandraik tells her as he leaves the room.

"Sure my bastard Lord. I always deal with it." she says quietly to herself.

* * *

"I'm sorry people, but I must stop for awhile or I am likely to forget my oath and kill her." Leyla tells them glaring hard at the woman in front of her. "I know of at least two occasions that this creature beat

Salis to the point that not even Rachel's healing could take away all of the pain she was in from the beatings."

Though normally a soft spoken man, when Kasmen speaks now, his voice is hard edged by what he has seen and heard so far. "We quite understand Princess. I suggest that we stop for a couple of hours and have the noon feast and a bit of a rest." He looks over to where Salis is sitting huddled in Thayer's lap crying softly. His voice softens. "I think that a certain young lady could use her mother's comfort right now."

Leyla looks over her shoulder and then quickly stands. "Thank you my Lord." she says and walks over to Salis and Thayer, kneeling down in front of them. "Hush my little one. It will all be over soon." she soothes running her hand over Salis' hair, then gently asking her, "Would you rather stay in my chambers with Stephen while we finish with this?"

"No I...I want to stay with you and Feineda." she tells her with a quivering voice.

Leyla smiles at the look of shock on Thayer's face as Salis calls him father. "Then you shall little one. Your Feineda will watch over you while I take care of this business." Standing, she turns to Brockton. "Captain Centori. Have this woman placed in a shielded room and fed until we are ready to continue."

Brock nods and bows, then signals the two guards that had brought her in to do as instructed. "Make sure that no one gets in to see her."

The men nod and station themselves to either side of the prisoner. Thayer releases her from her kneeling position and stands her up. Knowing that her legs won't support her for a while without assistance, he waits for the guards to take her arms before totally releasing his hold on her.

Once Detra is removed from the chamber, everyone stands and stretches to relieve stiff muscles. Each of the council members excuse themselves to go and freshen up before going for the noon meal. Stephen picks up Aeneka and then stands beside Brockton and Selina to wait.

"I think that we should discuss your lifemating at the feasting." Trocon suggests leaning slightly on Rachel's steadying arm. He is still weak from Mandraik's attack and it will take a while for him to fully recover. "The sooner we have that done with the better it will be for all concerned."

"I am in total agreement with Trocon. With all that we have already seen and heard, your joining may well be the only thing that will keep the planet at peace." Kasmen puts in. Shaking his head he adds, "Once it's known of Mandraik's treason and his attack on Trocon, there could very well be considerable trouble with the people."

"All right, we can discuss the ceremony over lunch, but no matter what, it will have to take place no later then tomorrow night." Thayer warns them looking deeply into Leyla's eyes. "The urging is getting stronger with each passing minute. Soon we will have to complete the lifemating with or without the benefit of the religious ceremony."

Leyla blushes and then glares at him, before turning away and taking Salis' hand. She heads for the door, saying over her shoulder without looking at any of them, "Let's get going then. I don't know about the rest of you, but I'm starving. I'd also like to get this thing with Priss over and done with as soon as possible."

The others smile at her blush and follow her from the room. As soon as they walk out the doors, they are surrounded by Leyla's, Trocon's, and Kasmen's guards.

"It feels strange to be surrounded by guards all the time. I don't know if I'm going to be able to deal with this on a regular basis." Leyla tells them looking around at all the guards they've acquired.

"Once we get this matter with Mandraik taken care of, you won't be needing so many here in the palace. Just myself and three others." Brockton assures her looking over all of his men. "The only time you'll need a larger escort will be when you leave the palace grounds. Then you'll have anywhere from one to three dozen men with you. Though there aren't any really dangerous people on Calidon..." he shrugs his shoulders when Leyla looks at him with a lift to her brow. "With a few exceptions that will soon be taken care of. The main danger would be the wild animals in the out laying areas that occasionally wander into the city."

"I for one would prefer to deal with a wild animal then with some men." Thayer states walking beside Leyla and Salis. "At least with an animal, they don't attack or plan an attack for no reason. They don't use deceit and aren't malicious. Men have the capacity for all of those and many more."

"This is true Highness, but in some cultures, if not all, it is a necessary evil." Kasmen says deliberately using the title and then watching for Thayer's reaction. He is not surprised when Thayer's expression becomes one of shock. "Soon you will join with the Princess. Just as she will be crowned our Queen, so you will be crowned our King. You will have to get used to the use of the title."

"I'd forgotten all about that." he says looking at Leyla. "It looks like we'll soon have a lot more to do then simply raising a family and taking care of each other."

"Yes, now we have an entire planet to care for and protect. I just hope we're both up to this." She says with a frown and shaking her head. She begins to wonder if coming here would be worth all the extra responsibilities they would now have.

"Don't worry sweetheart. You can handle it." Aeneka assures her. "You've been trained for this from the very beginning. You and Thayer will be a wonderful Queen and King. You both care for people no matter who and you don't let emotion rule you except when it comes to family. That's something very important, but also something you will have to be sure to control at all times."

They soon reach the main dining hall and one of the guards enters first to announce their arrival. "Lords and Ladies, our future Queen and King, her Royal Highness Princess Leyla Aeneka Latona of House Chaukcee and his Royal Highness Prince Thayer Robus Starhawk of Manchon."

The guards part and there in front of them is the Calidonian royal court with all its Lords and Ladies present. The men bow while the ladies curtsy. As they enter the hall, Trocon and Kasmen quickly introduce the higher Lords and their Ladies, before leading the way to the high table.

Selina and Brockton stop at the lower table to the right of the high table. Leyla stops and raises a brow at them. Brockton smiles at her and seats Selina.

'This is our proper place. When in public little cousin, we must conform to the status quo.' he informs her and is heard by all of their group except for the guards.

'You know how I feel about that Brock. Besides, you're family. As far as I'm concerned your proper place is up there with us.' Though no scowl appears on her face, they can all see it clearly in their minds.

'That may be true Highness, but he is right. Once you're Queen you can change his status as is your right. For now though, it is best that they remain here.' Kasmen points out reasonably.

Leyla feels a gentle tug on her cloak and looks down at Salis. "May I stay with them mother?" Salis asks softly, almost in a whisper. Leyla senses the uneasiness in Salis' and notices her eyes darting around the room. Just as she's about to give her permission, her mother interrupts. "Just as Brockton and Selina must take their proper place, so must you granddaughter. Your place is with your mother and father at the high table. I know that you are feeling uncomfortable with these people because you once served them. That no longer matters. I will deal with them, and I will make sure that none questions your right to be called a Princess of Calidon." She has Stephen turn so that she can looking at Trocon and Kasmen. "It is now time that I reveal my ultimate gift to all of you. It will help to dispel any trouble that Mandraik may have intended to take place here." After receiving their nods of agreement, she instructs Stephen to carry her to the front of the high table.

As soon as the room quiets down, Stephen holds Aeneka above his head and waits. Gasps are heard all around the room as people recognize the image on the screen before them. Once sure that she has everyone's attention, Aeneka addresses them.

"What all of you are seeing is my essence that was given a protective box many years ago by my parents, the former King and Queen. The image of me was a gift from my bondmate, Saitun Katmen of Manchon and Earth." She waits for a few seconds for them to absorb this new information before continuing. "What you will now see is a gift given to me by the Great One to be used but once."

Suddenly the box and monitor begin to glow, and a soft pink globe of light forms. Stephen releases it and steps away. The globe hovers there for a couple of moments, and then a human form appears out of the light. As the light dims and fades away, Aeneka Latona is left standing there once more in a physical form.

"For the next eighty-four hours, I will retain this form. After my daughter and her chosen one are formally lifemated and have been crowned, I will return to essence and then share my knowledge. My personal knowledge will go to eight people. Those eight are, my daughter and her mate, my granddaughter Salis Chandelle Aeneka Tahquar Starhawk, Brockton Antoine Centori who is my second cousin and his mate Selina, Lord Trocon Damori my adoptive uncle and a true friend, the healer Lady Rachel who has been my mentor, and lastly Lord Kasmen Metros, our High Priest and the one to which I owe my never ending faith in the Great One and who has always guided my heart and mind. To the people of Calidon will go my general knowledge with this warning. The knowledge you gain must be used only for the good of all. If it is used for any reason to hurt, harm, or destroy another for personal gain, that person or persons will lose all abilities. Not only what I give to you, but also those that you were born with. We were given a special gift, use it wisely." She watches the faces around her and registers the fear, anger, and disbelief coupled with an overlaying of awe. "Now, let us eat and celebrate the return of peace and harmony to our kind."

Leyla, who is still in shock at seeing her mother's physical body, has to be led forward to her seat at the high table so that the others in the room can return to their seats. Salis is placed to Leyla's left, between her and Thayer. After that everyone else takes their seats. For several minutes there is only whispered conversations, and then it returns to more normal levels as the people accept what they have just seen and heard.

Only after she's been served does Leyla come out of her shock and look to her right to where her mother is sitting beside her. Slowly she shakes her head still not believing what she is seeing.

'How is this possible? How can you be sitting here in a physical body? I know that your physical form no longer exists.'

'Do not question the Divine One's motives daughter. Only know that He makes it possible and be happy that we have this time together.'

'But why here, why now? Why couldn't you...?' her thoughts trail off before she finishes.

'Why couldn't I do it for your father?' Leyla nods and looks down at her plate. 'I can only do this once sweetheart. Your father knew it could and would happen, but we agreed that it should only be done when it was absolutely needed and then only for your protection.'

'But he should be here! He should be able to tell you good-bye in his own way.' she mentally cries knowing that her father was missing his one chance to see his mate again before she fully left them.

'Would you cause him more pain by his having to say good-bye a second and more painful time sweetheart?' Aeneka asks taking Leyla's hand that is sitting so close to her. 'This is to be our good-bye my darling. Yours and mine. I know that in your heart you have never really thought of me as dead. When the time comes you'll be able to handle it better then you would have as a child. Please don't spoil our time together with regrets for your father. Believe me, he would and does want it this way.'

'All right, I promise that I'll try mother.' she squeezes her mother's hand and then releases it to begin eating.

"Do you know what the best part about being physical again is?" Aeneka asks and Leyla shakes her head. "Being able to touch you again, not just your energy. I can even touch and be touched by others without having to fear my destruction."

Salis hears this and sits forward to look across Leyla. "Does that mean that I can touch you too?"

Aeneka leans forward. "Yes it does sweetheart." They smile at each other and then sit back.

While they are having their own private conversation, Thayer and Kasmen are discussing the lifemating ceremony.

"No, I have no problems with your ceremony, except for at the end. There is no way that I can accept someone watching us while we consummate our union. In this you must accept our word that we are true lifemates, and leave us to that part on our own."

Leyla hearing this looks over at him and then at Metros and smiles at his look of confusion. "I'm afraid that I'm to blame for his refusal to have you present at the last stage of the ceremony my Lord."

"How so?" Kasmen asks looking past Thayer to Leyla.

"Well...I...I told him about how you can either help or stop a joining. Whichever was necessary at the time." she admits blushing and looking down at her plate of food.

"I see. Well, I can tell you truthfully that if it had been necessary I would have stopped the ceremony no matter what. But after witnessing the transmutation that took place in the council chamber, I can see that there will be no problems with your joining. You will have your privacy for the final part of the ceremony Thayer. No one will witness your coupling."

Leyla giggles as Thayer flushes in embarrassment, and Aeneka laughs as well. "That's the same shade you turned when I saw..."

"Aeneka!" Thayer growls at her to keep her quiet.

Salis looks from one adult to the other wondering what is happening. "Mother, why is father turning red? Is he angry about something?"

"No little one, your father isn't angry, just embarrassed. Your grandmother caught him in a very revealing state on the ship."

"Leyla! Why don't you just tell them that she saw me in the all together? Even Salis can understand 'revealing state'." He growls at her in a louder voice then he had meant to. At that moment most conversation in the room had stopped so that his words were heard by all and his face gets even redder.

"I think that's what you just did dear." Aeneka tells him with a smile.

Thayer glares at her even harder and then turns his glare on everyone else in the room as he hears a few muffled laughs. He picks up his wine goblet and takes a large swallow while still glaring at them all.

"Do stop glaring at everyone Thayer. It is neither polite or very nice. Besides, who cares? No one else will see you that way again except for me." At this Kasmen clears his throat and lifts a brow. "Oh...I forgot about that. Ah... well...maybe just one more..."

"What are you talking about Leyla? What haven't you told me?" Thayer demands setting down the goblet.

"What she means Thayer, is that before your final joining, you have to be checked over for any deformities or unusual marks that may be passed onto your children." Kasmen informs him carefully.

"By the Great One, you must be kidding?" He looks from one to the other. "Either Leyla or Aeneka can tell you what you need to know."

"But neither of them are a true healer, and wouldn't know what they were looking for." Rachel puts in, though Aeneka had some idea. Thayer looks at her for the first time. He hadn't noticed her sitting on the other side of Trocon, until she spoke to him. She had been very quiet the entire time they were at the table.

"You mean you're going...?" Thayer stops and his jaw drops open. He had thought that it might be Kasmen who would have to check him over, not another woman.

"Yes, I am the one that does the examining." she confirms and then holds up her hand to stop any further objects and addresses Kasmen. "There is no need for me to examine him Kasmen. There is nothing wrong with his mind or body. He has no deformities. What marks he has on his body are from childhood accidents and adult disagreements."

Though he would like to ask her how she knows this, Kasmen knows better then to question any of Rachel's statements. He nods and turns back to Thayer. "The ceremony will take place at the third hour of the new moon."

Leyla and Aeneka nod in agreement of the time. Though he would like to question Rachel on how she knew these things about him, Thayer says nothing and nods his agreement for the time of the ceremony as well.

Soon the people start to pass by the high table to wish Leyla and Thayer all happiness and saying a formal greeting and farewell to Aeneka. As the last of the Lords and Ladies leave the dining hall, Brockton and Selina join the others at the high table.

"It looks like I get to greet you properly after all Aunt Neka." and he steps forward as Aeneka stands and walks around the table and into his open arms. They hug and kiss and then Brockton holds her at arms length. "It's strange knowing that technically your older than me, but physically at this moment, I'm six years older than you." he says and pulls her back in his arms glad to be given this chance.

"I know what you mean Brock." She hugs him tightly and then releases him and steps back to look at Leyla. "It's even stranger for me. My baby girl is now taller than me and is only physically four years younger." She smiles at Leyla who comes around to join them and stopping beside her mother. "But I wouldn't give up this time with her for anything or anyone in the known universe." she says looking into Leyla's eyes willing her to believe that.

"Neither would I mother." Leyla assures her hugging her close while tears run down her cheeks. "Neither would I." They hold each other close and let their tears flow freely. As they finally separate, Aeneka feels a gentle tug on her dress, and looks down at Salis.

"Can I give you a hug too now?" Though she's thirteen, at this moment Salis sounds much younger. She was still getting use to the idea that she has a family again.

"Of course you can sweetheart." Going down on one knee, Aeneka opens her arms to her and Salis falls into them. "For what time I have with you, if you ever need a hug, all you have to do is ask me, and I'll be glad to give you one. All right?" Salis nods and hugs her even tighter.

"I'm glad that you're my Mistima, my grandmother." Salis tells her softly in her ear.

"And I'm glad that you're my Aloecha, my granddaughter." Aeneka whispers back. When she holds her a little away to look into her eyes, Salis opens her mind totally to her. Aeneka's eyes widen in shocked surprise and then pleasure at this gift shared that would normally only be given to Leyla and later to Thayer. As she receives the memories and thoughts Salis has gathered in her short life, Aeneka also sees that which Salis had withheld from Leyla concerning Mandraik. It was her attempt to try and protect her from what she knew was a dangerous man. After the bonding she hugs her again.

'You should have shared this information about Mandraik with your mother sweetheart. I can see and understand why you didn't. You wanted to protect her from his evil, didn't you?'

'Yes. He is a very evil man mistima. He wishes her dead very badly. I didn't want him to hurt her. Now that she's taken away his abilities, I can let her see and hear all of it.'

'Good girl. Wait until after she's done with Detra though. I have a feeling that what Detra knows and what you know will seal Mandraik's fate forever. It may also free someone that no one considered a prisoner.'

Salis nods and smiles. "I love you grandmother."

"As I love you granddaughter." They grin at each other and then Aeneka stands up. "Come, I think that we have some unfinished business to attend to before we can get to the more important business of celebrating a joining of lives and worlds."

Everyone agrees and then they head back to the council chambers, once again surrounded by guards. Though Thayer wishes that Leyla had taken the time to lay down and rest, he can understand her need to get this over and done with.

* * *

For the next two hours of probing, they have heard and seen Detra and Mandraik plot and plan the disappearance of most of the missing Calidonians. Though Mandraik mentions an outside contact several times, the name never enters Detra's mind.

Suddenly Leyla hits a strong mental block that is not one of Detra's making. "Someone's placed a very strong block in her mind." she tells the others before trying another probe. When she comes up against the block Detra cries out in pain and clutches at her head with both hands. Leyla quickly draws back releasing her. "If I continue to probe with the block still in place, it could kill her. I've never seen this type of block before." She tells the others in the room.

Aeneka steps forward and stands at Leyla's side. "Show me what you saw." Their eyes lock and Aeneka sees the block. It twists and turns and wraps around a large portion of Detra's mind. She pulls back and shakes her head. "Leyla's right. If she should enter the block wrong one of two things could happen. The worst would be that it would kill Detra very painfully and slowly, the least is that it would destroy all memory. Everything that makes her who she is."

"But who could have placed such a block? The only ones with the abilities to create such a block are in our family." Brockton points out in shock. "Leyla, you, and I are the only ones left of the House Chaukcee. Since you've only just returned it couldn't have been you, and I would never do such a thing to a person, for any reason."

Aeneka smiles at him gently. "I believe that I can speak for everyone here when I say, that we know that you did not do this thing." Everyone nods their agreement. "There is something that you seem to have forgotten about though, and that is the other side of our family." Leyla and Brockton look at her not fully understanding what she was talking about.

"House Draikmi." Kasmen says softly into the gathering silence and Aeneka nods.

"Which Dacus is also a member, though his ties are ten times removed. It also explains what happened with him earlier."

"Could that be why he said something about purifying Leyla's bloodline?" Selina suggests remembering Mandraik's words before Leyla had taken away his abilities and he had passed out.

"No. Dacus never planned to let Leyla live even if she had lifemated with a Calidonian." Aeneka tells them and then looks up sharply as she feels a familiar rage building. "Leyla, Thayer!"

Leyla catches her mother's warning and throws a shield around Mandraik and then one around Thayer. Standing she walks quickly over to where he is standing. "Thayer no! He can't protect himself from you now!"

Thayer glares at her and mentally pushes her back from him, his mind set on only one thing. Destroying the man that would have killed his mate for no reason at all.

"Don't try it my love. You may be bigger then I am physically, but I'm still mentally stronger than you are right now." To prove her point she forces him to his knees even as he fights her. She knew that he would not lightly forgive her humiliating him like this, but she had no other choice. "Remember, only when we have proof."

"But Aeneka..." he starts only for her to interrupt him.

"Proof Thayer. Not my mother's words. Proof of his guilt." she tells him and then re-enforces it mentally. 'We need proof for the people Thayer, or it will be murder in their eyes.'

Thayer shakes his head with a growl looking up at her, and then hears someone crying softly and looks around. Salis had left his side and was now standing with Aeneka, her head buried in the woman's chest, and Aeneka trying to comfort her.

"Damn!" he hisses and combs his fingers through his hair trying to regain control of himself. "Remove your shield Leyla." He waits and then looks back at her. 'Don't worry. He's safe for now. I need to explain this to our daughter. Now remove the damn shield.' and he nods towards Aeneka and Salis.

Leyla removes the shield from around him and allows him to stand, but she leaves the shield around Mandraik. She knew that it was likely that Thayer's temper may slip from his control again, and it was safer to keep Mandraik shielded then to trust her mate's control on his temper.

Thayer walks over to them and kneels down to Salis' level. He reaches out and gently touches her back and feels her flinch away from his touch. He cringes inside at the feelings her action gives him. The feeling is a lot worse then when Leyla had done the same thing when they were back on Earth and on the ship.

"It's all right baby, I'm not angry any more. I promise." he reassures her softly.

"You pushed her." Salis whispers accusingly. "She explained, and you pushed her away." She begins to cry a little harder and Thayer cringes again.

He looks up at Aeneka who just looks down at him not speaking and not helping him to get out of this mess he had made. He looks back at Salis. "I know honey, but that's all I did. I would never hurt your mother and she knows that. I would life-end myself before I would ever hurt her." He feels a hand on his shoulder and looks up at Leyla. He grimaces at her for what he has done and then smiles at her show of support. He places his hand over hers and then turns back to Salis. She still refuses to look at him. "Salis baby, please look at me." he pleads wishing that he could take back the last several minutes.

Feeling and hearing his sorrow and regret, Salis sniffles and then turns her head. When she does she sees him on his knees with her mother beside him, her hand on his shoulder.

"What he's telling you is the truth little one. It's the truth for both of us. I would take my own life rather than risk hurting him. We feel the same way about you sweetheart." Leyla says stepping more to Thayer's side. "His push was only because he knew that I was right, and he wished that I wasn't. When the shield went around him, his main concern was to protect me. Why would he try to protect me and then try to hurt me, just because I was protecting him?"

Salis looks at them both and wipes away her tears with one last sniffle. Though she didn't fully understand what she had just been told, she realizes that her actions had hurt her father. "I'm sorry." she tells him quietly.

"No baby, you did nothing wrong. Please don't apologize. Next time something happens though, don't turn away from me. Just yell at me. That usually works pretty good. If you have a hard time just ask your mother to teach you. She loves to yell at me. Ouch! She also loves to hit on me too!" he tells her sadly rubbing at the shoulder Leyla had just punched.

Salis giggles and the tension in the room dissolves. She steps forward and hugs his neck tightly. "You're going to be a silly father."

"Thank you moppet, so are you." He kisses her cheek and hugs her close, before standing with her in his arms. "Let's finish this thing up one way or another."

"I'll take care of the block so that Leyla can finish the probe without endangering Detra's life or sanity. I know this type of block and I'll be able to leave a clear path for her to follow." Aeneka tells them.

Detra watches and listens and then tries to back away as Aeneka approaches her, but can't move because of the mental hold on her.

"NO! Stay away from me! I don't want you anywhere near me you essence phantom.!" Detra screams causing Aeneka to laugh at the description of herself. She had often heard tales about such beings, but could never picture one.

"The essence part is true enough, but not the phantom part. I'm am more essence embodied, since I have all the functions of a physical body." she reassures the other woman. "You have nothing to fear from me Detra Priss. All that I plan to do is to open the block so that nothing happens to you." she slowly steps closer. "Unless you would prefer that my daughter continues as she has been? You must realize though that you are taking a great risk with both your life and your mind to do so?"

"What does it matter? All that I had is lost to me now anyway." She shrugs her shoulders no longer caring what happened to her. "Why should I care if she kills me now or later? Either way she will kill me." Detra looks from Leyla to Aeneka. "Besides, some of what she's pulled out of my head doesn't even feel like a part of me. I can't explain how it got there, I don't remember a lot of it. But since it did come from my mind, there's no way to defend myself."

"No matter what you may think the Princess will do later, Aeneka will open a pathway." Kasmen tells her stepping forward. "If you are to die at all, would you not rather die with honor to your family, then because someone did something to your mind that would kill you without that honor?" He asks knowing that at one time family honor was the most important thing to her until a few years ago.

Detra looks up at Kasmen realizing that what he says is true. She has no doubt that Dacus was responsible for the mind block and that her death because of it would not bring back the honor to her or her family. Knowing that she has no other choice, Detra reluctantly nods her agreement.

Everyone waits and within seconds Aeneka looks up at them. "It's done. The whole block is gone. When I reaches the end of the path it ceased to be."

"Good, then let's get this finished. I need a rest after all that's already happened." Leyla says and resumes her seat trying to relax.

\* \* \*

"I was honorable to your father and his family until my twenty-fourth year Dacus." Detra tells him softly.

"Yes, and then you showed your disloyalty to us by going into the service of the King and Queen." Dacus snarls at her.

"It wasn't disloyal of me to leave your father's house. He dishonored me and then refused my request to care for you myself after your birth. He wouldn't even let me see or touch you. He beat me when I tried. Why should I have remained with a man who did that and was so cruel as to take a newborn babe from his mother just minutes after his birth?" She stares at him, trying to make him understand how she had felt. "If I had taken care of you myself then maybe you wouldn't be the mean, cruel man that you are today."

"Some mother you would have made. You couldn't even stand up to one old man." he snaps at her not caring or wondering about anything she had to say or the pain she had felt at his loss. "No doubt with you to care for me I would have become just another servant instead of holding the position I now do in the hierarchy."

"At least the King and Queen would have treated you as decently as they've treated me. In fact they have treated you with more decency than you deserve, considering all the trouble you've caused over the years. What they have shown you is more than your father or his family ever showed me, and I never caused them any trouble."

"None of this matters except in case you refuse to help me. If you do, then I will be forced to inform the King and Queen of how you abandoned a newborn babe to the cruelties of a sadistic old man and his crazy mate." He warns her cruelly, watching as she flinches and smiling just as cruelly. "How long do you think that the Queen would want such a woman in her service?"

With each cruel word he speaks, Detra sinks deeper and deeper into a depressive state knowing that he was right. The Queen would not tolerate a woman that could leave a child to such a fate. She would dismiss her immediately. Children were to be protected at any and all cost. They were never left to the cruelties of men, not even their own father's or their relations. It didn't matter that she was just a servant, she still had the responsibility of protecting her child. Hanging her head, Detra slowly nods her agreement to help him with his dealings with the Earth leader. She had no other choice, she had no place else that she could go.

Shortly after her agreement, Detra witnesses the murder of the Queen. "By the Great One Dacus! What have you done?!"

"Only what should have been done a long time ago. With her dead and the Princess Aeneka long since gone, there will be no other heirs to the throne through the House Chaukcee. When the King dies my family will take their rightful place on the throne through me. We will become the new ruling family of all Calidon."

"You're wrong. Princess Aeneka's daughter is the rightful heir of Calidon. If the King should die, she will come to take her rightful place as the next Queen. When she does that, you will be punished for all the evil that you have done." she tells him.

"Not if she dies before she even gets here." He smiles viciously at her across the desk. "Already things are being readied on Earth to take care of both her and her meddlesome father."

"Carrison's man Peterton has taken care of Saitun Katmen. Now all that is left to do is get rid of the girl. Soon I will have the throne and no one will be able to stop me."

"You'll never succeed. Look how many times you've already tried to kill her and failed. She will come and that will be the end of you and your evil ways."

Dacus backhands her, sending her sprawling across the floor. "I won't fail!" he screams down at her, all his hate reflected in his face. "With the King dead, she'll only have nine moons to claim the throne. She won't get that chance and I shall become King." He laughs crazily and then stomps from the room. Detra slowly picks herself up off the floor and sits in the nearest chair wondering what she had given birth to.

Shortly after that, the King dies in the same way as the Queen, with no one knowing how or why except Dacus and Detra. To insure his own safety, Dacus places a block and the strong suggestion into Detra's mind that she hates and loathes Leyla Katmen, and all of those that would be loyal to her. It would also insure her loyalty to him and help him to destroy Leyla if she should show up, and any who would threaten his chance at complete power over Calidon.

\* \* \*

Leyla releases Detra from the probe and then stands up shakily to look down at her as she weeps in grief, pain, and sorrow for what she had helped to do. 'Release her Thayer. We don't need to hold her any longer. She's not a threat to anyone any more.'

'I already have Love.' He walks over to her side and wraps an arm around her waist to steady her. "Are you all right?" Leyla nods and then looks at Salis as she joins them and takes her hand.

"It wasn't her fault was it mother? All those bad things she did to me and to the others. It wasn't really her doing them?"

"No sweetheart, it wasn't really her doing any of it. Her only fault was in caring for a son that didn't care for anyone but himself." she tells her putting an arm around Salis and hugging her close for several moments. She then looks up at the council.

"In light of what we have all just seen and heard, I release Detra Priss from all charges brought against her, and absolve her of any guilt brought on her by the manipulations of Dacus Mandraik."

The council all nod their agreement. None of them able to speak after what they had just witnessed. Before any of them can leave the room, Leyla turns back to Detra and addresses her gently.

"Detra Priss, you are hereby given back your position of Keeper of the servants. From this day forward, no one will recall any cruelties inflicted by you while you were under the control of Dacus Mandraik. He and he alone is responsible for those crimes." Leyla looks to her mother as she makes her next statement. "I will invoke the memory loss of everyone to the things you did under his control." After receiving a nod from her mother she turns back to Detra. "At his trial you will testify to all that you know of his actions, dealings and plans over the past several years. None of this will change who you truly are. Since no one knows of your relationship to him except for those present in this room, all memory of his being your son will be removed from your memory. After his sentencing, you will be free of any remorse or guilt that may occur when his sentence is carried out. You have suffered enough because of him, and you don't need to suffer any longer."

"Thank you Princess." Detra says bowing her head unable to look at her directly, before she stands. Before turning away she does look down at Salis. "I never would have hurt you if it hadn't been for Dacus. Your birth parents were good people and I loved them as if they were my own children. I always considered you as a granddaughter, and I am deeply sorry for what you were put through." she tells her with great sorrow not sure if the child could ever forgive her. "I will try to make up for their loss for the rest of my days."

Salis nods her head slightly in acknowledgment of her words and her sincerity. She was glad that they wouldn't remember anything of what she had done to her. When she was little she knew how loving Madame Priss had been to all the children, and hoped that she would be again.

Brockton signals to one of his men. "Escort her back to her chambers and then have one of the older servants see to her needs for the rest of the day. No one known to work with Mandraik is to be allowed anywhere near her. If anything happens to her, you will answer to me personally. Is this understood?"

"Yes Captain." The man salutes and then gently takes Detra's arm to lead her from the chamber.

After she is lead out, Trocon calls the meeting to an end and all of the council members file out. The only ones left in the room are Kasmen, Trocon, and Rachel. Brockton and Selina stand off to one side with Aeneka while Leyla and Thayer speak quietly with Salis.

They turn to face them seconds later. "Now that we know that Mandraik and Carrison have been dealing together in the slavery of a neutral people, we have the proof we need. All we have to do now is to get our people back as quickly and safely as we can. I'd rather not involve the Federation in this unless its absolutely necessary."

"Let's wait until after Mandraik's trial to discuss such plans sweetheart. We need to concentrate on something positive for awhile and right now you need to rest. We can start preparing for and celebrating your lifemating." Aeneka tells her stepping forward to hug

Leyla and Thayer and then taking Salis' hand and heading for the doors. "You can help me come up with a menu for the feast."

"Can I really grandmother?" Salis asks in awe and begins to skip along side her grandmother in an abundance of energy which causes Aeneka to laugh. "We can have lots of sweet treats grandmother. Cook is ever so good at making all kinds of treats." Everyone laughs and smiles at her enthusiastic endorsement of the palace cook.

"We can have some sweet treats, but we'll need some other foods as well my dear. I think we'll see if we can get cook to try a few Earth dishes as well."

Leyla and Thayer smile while the others grimace at the thought and look at each other. Brockton shrugs his shoulders and wraps an arm around Selina's waist.

"Why not? They might have something that we'd all like." he says and then grimaces, not believing that he had said such a thing, and everyone laughs.

# Chapter XII

Nightstorm leads Colt and Merri to a deep part of the forest surrounding the stronghold. Over the past several weeks, Nightstorm and the other warriors, along with Logan, have been teaching the twins the old skills of survival. Though both are good, both have certain areas that they are better at. Merri has more of a kinship with the forest and can use her abilities in tune with her surroundings. Colt does a little better at hunting and building shelters, and handles hand weapons with the ease of a man nearly three times his age and experience. There is no true competition between the two. They try to help each other to improve on the skills they lack, but never talk down to each other.

"This is where we separate young warriors." Nightstorm stops next to an ancient maple tree and looks at both of them. "We will all return to the stronghold from different directions and at different times. Colt, you will go first. In about an hour Merri will head out, and then I will."

"How long do we have to get back to the stronghold Nightstorm?" Colt asks looking around and trying to decide which way he would take.

"If you are good enough, you will make it back in plenty of time for the evening meal. If not, you should be back for the afternoon meal tomorrow." He smiles as Merri shakes her head. "But you both have done very well in your training, and I know that we will be eating together this night."

"Okay, and we can hunt along the way, right?"

"Colt, this is a test of time. If you stop to hunt, you'll never make it back in time for supper." Merri chides him knowing that if her brother stopped to hunt, he would have to clean and dress the kill before continuing.

"Who says? I've been practicing. Besides, unitsi waya needs some more rabbit pelts. She's making Cassie a dress for the new moon dance next week. I promised Cassie that if Mother Wolf didn't have enough that I would get more for her."

"All right. Just don't complain when you miss supper and breakfast." she giggles and jumps back when he takes a menacing step towards her.

"That's enough you two. Concentrate on what we're here for. Now Colt, pick your direction and remember that you can not use any established trails. You must make your own path."

"I remember Nightstorm." Colt looks at his sister again. "Good luck Merri. Remember, no berry picking along the way." he taunts smiling at her as she wrinkles her nose at him. He turns and runs into the trees to the far left of where they had just come before she can try and hit him.

Merri chews on her lower lip as she watches her twin disappear into the trees. Every time he goes off alone she worries about him. She can feel Nightstorm watching her, and then he places a hand on her shoulder.

"He will be fine Winter-flower. He has become more cautious since you've been at the stronghold. No one but you can sneak up on him now."

"I know all of that Nightstorm, but the dream happens in the woods. What if the girl I keep seeing is just a trap for him? What if she shows up today and he doesn't return? He's gotten better at blocking me in the past week or so." She tells him still looking of after her twin.

"Come, sit with me." He takes her hand and together they sit down at the base of the old tree. "Now, you tell me again about the dream."

"All right, but it hasn't changed." she tells him taking a deep breath. "Colt is in the woods hunting on the east side of the stronghold. Near the stream, he comes upon this girl, and she's about our age. He stops to talk to her and after a while forgets to watch and listen for danger. Suddenly from the sky comes a speeder and a man and woman step out.

That's all I see, except for Colt's surprise." She looks down at her hands which are shaking a little. "It's always the same Nightstorm. I don't feel any danger from the girl, but when Colt sees the man and woman, the surprise on his face has a hint of fear to it."

"I see. What did you feel about the couple? Did you feel that they were a real threat to Colt, or are you just going by his reaction to their sudden appearance?" He asks knowing that she must think through her vision and examine all that she has seen.

"Maybe it was just his reaction. I didn't really feel as though they would hurt him. It felt more like they were concerned about the girl." Merri admits after careful reflection on what she had seen and felt.

"Then I would say that they are more then likely friends, especially if they are that close to the stronghold. Wait and see if it comes again. When it does, focus on the girl and the couple. I think that if you can understand them, you'll understand the cause of Colt's fear."

Nodding, Merri looks off into the trees. Her biggest fear is that in some way, this new girl will draw Colt even further away from her. Though she knew that they couldn't always be as they were, it frightened her to know that she was losing a part of herself. Sighing, she stands up. "I'll do as you say Nightstorm. Though I haven't always liked it, you have given me some pretty good advice." She bends down and gives him a quick hug and kiss before straightening and turning to the opposite side of the path that Colt had taken. "Thank you." she calls out as she loops off into the trees like a gazelle.

Nightstorm shakes his head and laughs to himself. When they had first started the training, Merri had refused to take any advice from him that she thought was made to make things easier for her. Over the weeks, she had discovered that his advice didn't necessarily make things easier, but it did make her think about her actions and what affect those actions could have on everyone else in the stronghold. She had come a long way in the past several weeks and he was proud of her.

'They are on their way Knightrunner.'

'Good Nightstorm. Do you think that they will make it back here by tonight?'

'I am sure that Merri will. Colt I am not too sure about. He wants to hunt up some more rabbits for unitsi waya. I think that he talked her into making a winter vest for Merri after she has finished with her present project.' He tells him, not sure if the other man knew about the dress the old woman was making for his chosen.

'Yes, I remember him mentioning something about it to me a few days ago. He's been practicing as much as his lessons allow to skin and dress a rabbit while running. The last time he brought me one, it looked pretty good, it only had one or two minor nicks. Otherwise the pelt was in fine shape.'

'Then he might make it if he doesn't need too many. I'll be leaving here in about another half an hour.'

'All right Nightstorm. I know I don't have to tell you to check on them, but please do. That way I won't be lying to Cassie when I tell her that you are. Ali has their biorhythms, and will monitor them from here. If there's any critical changes in either of them I'll let you know.'

'Fine. I'll see you in about six hours then. They should be close enough to the stronghold by then for me to leave them on their own.'

Nightstorm relaxes against the tree and reaches out first to Colt and then to Merri, to check on their progress. He pulls back quickly, before either of them can sense his presence. Colt has already caught three rabbits for Mother Wolf, and Merri had a pouch full of wild blueberries as well as having both hands full of them. He waits a little longer and then stands up smiling. They both knew each other quite well, even though they were blocking each other out more and more. Going to the far left, he begins making a trail that should take him within a mile of where Colt should be in about another hour.

\* \* \*

Logan leans back from his desk and stretches his arms above his head and then relaxes again. Though he would rather be working outside right now, there were things in the office that needed to be taken care of first. He turns and looks out the side window, and laughs as he watches Dessa sneak up on her twin and dump a bucket of water over her head. Tossing the bucket aside, she takes off at a dead run fro the side entrance of the house. There's a knock on his office door, and he sighs and turns back towards his desk calling, "Come in."

Cassie opens the door and walks in with two cups of coffee. "I thought that you could probably use a break about now." she tells him walking over to the desk and handing him one of the cups.

"You're right I do, and I can really use the caffeine right now." He takes the cup and stands up. Taking her empty hand, he pulls her around the desk towards him. "Dessa just paid Davena back for the dunking she gave her in the river last week." he says nodding his head towards the window.

Just then they hear the girls go running and screaming through the house and up the stairs. Logan smiles and shakes his head before sipping at his coffee. "I don't see how your father has made it through the years raising four sets of twins."

"He's had a lot of patience, a lot of love, and a whole lot of understanding. It's good to see them acting normal again. After Dad and the boys were taken, it was hard for any of us to really act normal. They've all opened up a lot since we came here. I think it's because they finally feel safe from Carrison and his people." she says taking a sip of her coffee and then setting the cup down on the desk, not really wanting it. She had only brought it to help keep her hands busy.

Logan sets his cup down beside hers and pulls her up closer to him and takes her other hand. "What about you Cassie? Do you feel safer here too?" he asks looking into her eyes.

Cassie looks down at their joined hands for several seconds and then back up at him. "Very safe Logan."

Smiling, he pulls her into the cradle of his legs as he leans against the side of the desk. Releasing her hands, he wraps his arms around her waist pulling her closer still. Slowly he brings his mouth closer to hers. "I'm glad that you feel safe here Cassie." he whispers against her lips. "I always want you to feel safe with me." and he brings their lips together.

The kiss begins as a gentle exploration, then begins to heat up as Cassie runs her fingers through his hair. When she reaches the nape of his neck she clutches his hair tightly in her fist. Logan answers her urging by pulling her even closer and deepening the kiss while his hands roam up and down her back.

When he reaches her bottom, he kneads them bringing her closer into contact with his hardening manhood. Slowly he rotates her hips from side to side making himself groan.

Feeling his hardness against her, Cassie moans and pushes up against him even more. As she does this Logan brings one hand up between them and opens up her blouse so that he can reach her breasts. She pushes into his hand and slides against his groin causing him to groan again.

The office door locks, and the curtains close over the windows shutting them off from prying eyes. Once their sealed off, Logan takes off her blouse and then her bra. Giving her small pecking kisses, he works his way down to take a dusky nipple into his mouth and suckling gently.

Cassie gasps and holds his head to her breast with a moan. He kisses his way to the other breast and lavishes it's tip with the same treatment. After a minute of his tender ministrations, Cassie moves her hips back a little and reaches between them to cup his straining member. She runs her hand up and down it's length through his jeans, gauging how much he wanted her and then gently squeezing.

With another groan, Logan pushes himself into her hand. He nips at her nipple in punishment, causing her to cry out and try to pull away, before he soothes the injury with his tongue.

Suddenly their clothing feels to restrictive and they begin quickly undressing each other, kissing and caressing each newly exposed area. After removing all their clothes, Logan picks Cassie up and turns around to settle her on the edge of the desk. He gently spreads her legs and steps between them. 'Wrap your legs around me sweetheart.' he encourages her.

Cassie looks into his eyes and lifts her legs and wraps them around him, locking her ankles together at his back. He steps forward and teases her with his tip. 'Logan, please!' she pleads trying to move forward and bring him into her.

'Soon baby, soon. Relax.' He positions himself at her entrance, taking a hold of her hips and slowly penetrates. When Cassie nips at his shoulder in frustration, he starts and plunges deeply into her. They both gasp and shudder.

'Oh God Logan!' she moans and tightens herself around him trying to hold him inside.

'Oh Cassie don't flex those muscles like that baby. If you keep that up this is going to be over long before either of us wants it to be.' He flexes his fingers on her hips until she relaxes her inner muscles.

Leaning his forehead against hers, Logan takes a deep breath and then begins moving inside of her going even deeper and stopping. After a few moments he begins moving slowly against her creating a building friction that will bring them the most pleasure. While he's moving inside of her, Cassie kisses him and caresses his back, running her nails gently down to his buttocks and squeezing tightly.

Their movements increase, and Logan plunges into her harder and faster. When he feels her tightening around him he slows to keep her on the edge of release. Suddenly he drives into her harder and harder rotating his hips with each inward movement. When she begins to shake with her release, he lifts her from the desk and plunges into her once, twice, and then loses himself to his own release, still pumping into her. He holds her close until his legs begin to shake and then leans her back against the desk so that he doesn't drop her.

Cassie cries out with her release and clutches him tightly to her even as he lifts her from the desk and plunges into her. When his release comes, she goes off again with the feel of his seed flowing into her.

They stay locked together for several minutes, Logan with his head against her shoulder and her caressing his hair. With a slow deep breath, he kisses her neck and shoulder before slowly raising his head. Cassie reluctantly lowers her legs as he straightens up. As he starts to withdraw, her muscles automatically tighten around him to keep him inside her warmth.

"I wish that we could stay like this for the rest of the day." he tells her slowly pulling out. As he does he feels a wrenching deep within himself at their loss of closeness. He gives her one last deep kiss and then levitates her clothes up and into her arms as he steps back from temptation. "We'll have more time for us tonight, while everyone else is celebrating Colt and Merri's success."

Cassie pulls on her slacks and blouse, but stuffs her bra and panties into one of her front pockets. She looks at him as she buttons her blouse. "So, you really think that they'll pass this last test?" she asks watching him pull up his jeans and then his shirt.

"I know that they'll pass. They've both done really good with their lessons, and Nightstorm believes that if they can meet this last challenge the other warriors will have no problem giving them the title of warrior. They should have no problems protecting themselves or others from now on as far as Nightstorm is concerned."

Though she hadn't always agreed with Nightstorm, Cassie had to admit that both Colt and Merri seemed more focused now then ever before. "There's no way they can be seriously hurt during this is there Logan? I know that there are going to be traps and snares setup to try and trip them up."

"Not if they follow their training, and don't let themselves become distracted from their purpose. Merri will most likely be the first one back, she's more in tune with nature and more likely to spot the traps. Colt shouldn't be too far behind her, maybe an hour or two. He'll have to be more on the alert because he's hunting." He straightens his collar, his eyes moving over her in a caress and catching sight of the slight bulge in her slacks pocket. He steps forward and pulls her into his arms once more. "I do hope that you plan on putting those extra pieces of clothing back on before I see you again, or I won't be held responsible for my actions in public." He caresses her breast and then cups her womanhood. With one last kiss and a groan, he steps away from temptation.

"You'd better go and check on Davena and Dessa to make sure that they haven't killed each other."

"It is awful quiet in here." Cassie says with a frown.

"I have some things that I need to check into before lunch. I'll meet all of you out by the cook fire before serving time."

"Okay, but don't be late this time or it might be you the girls kill instead of each other." she warns caressing his cheek and turning to the door.

After she leaves, closing the door behind her, Logan turns to his computer. "Cal, any news on the older Blackwood males?"

"Not really Logan. Though the last report I tapped into mentions something about one of them being ill."

"Check it again and find out who it is and what type of illness. Have Ali stand by as a distraction in case your detected."

"You know she's not going to like that Logan. She gets more and more like the Katmen's Sarah unit all the time."

Logan laughs. Cal and Sarah had gotten into an argument every time they had to speak to each other. "No one told you to share your information about Sarah with her Cal." he reminds the computer.

"I know. It was my own fault for mentioning the likeness in the first place and then explaining what I meant. I'll tell her that you want her to do it. Maybe then I can save my receptors from more of her complaints about menial tasks."

"You do that Cal and let me know as soon as you find out anything." He stands up shaking his head as he leaves the office. He couldn't really complain about how Ali teased Cal. She loved to pick on him about his accent, but at least she had gotten him to loosen up on his formality with Logan. With a quick look at his watch, he decides to go upstairs and take a shower before lunch.

Thirty minutes later he walks out to the compound to join the others for lunch. He waves to two of the warriors just entering the stronghold. He meets them at the eating area clasping each others right forearm in greeting. "Running Elk, how did the setting of the traps go?" he asks of the older warrior.

"Good Knightrunner. They will not find them too easily. It will take great skill to miss all of them."

"Winter-flower will not be able to say that she was treated unfairly. We put a few extra traps and snares in her path." says Little Bear who is a couple of years older than Colt and Merri, but a warrior in the true sense of the word.

"So, you think you've found a way to escape her sharp tongue do you?" Little Bear nods with a self satisfied smile on his face. "Well, don't be surprised if she still complains because she had more hazards to get through then her brother." Logan tells him and then chuckles as the smile leaves the young man's face and his shoulders slump. "Don't worry. If she gets through them all, her complaints won't be so strong." He pats the young man on the shoulder and gives him a gentle push over to where the others are waiting for them.

Cassie steps up to them as they come closer and Logan puts his arm around her shoulders bringing her closer still. Running Elk nods his approval and Little Bear grins causing Cassie to blush.

"Everything's ready gentlemen. Have a seat while Davena and Dessa serve everyone."

"But Cassie..." Dessa whines.

"No buts Dessa. You two are responsible for the mess that Morningstar slipped in and hurt her ankle. Its only right that you two do her jobs for her until she can do them for herself again without any pain."

Dessa turns to her twin, and Cassie can tell that they are arguing mentally over what happened and why they were in this mess. She lets them go for a few seconds and then interrupts them. "That's enough girls. You are both responsible, now get started. I'm sure that the men are all very hungry and they shouldn't have to wait to be served." The girls move off and start dishing up the stew and handing it out without another word.

"So Morningstar hurt her ankle. I hope that it's not too bad?" Logan asks in concern seating Cassie and then sitting down beside her.

"No, it's just a slight sprain. It should be better by tomorrow." She assures him in a whisper as Davena walks by, then louder. "I felt that the girls needed to learn that in a small community like this, their little tiffs don't always just affect them. That some times other's can be hurt by what they do or don't do."

Logan nods and then thanks Davena for his bowl of stew. "That's a good idea. Do you think that it will do any good though? I know how stubborn your siblings can be."

"For the most part. Davena already feels sorry. I think that Dessa does too, but is too angry with herself right now to admit it to anyone, even herself. Especially since she was the one to dump the water and left it where someone could slip. By tonight she'll be running herself ragged to make it up to Morningstar."

"Okay. It sounds like you have everything under control." He looks at her side ways and leans towards her a little to whisper. "Are you fully dressed under there?" He asks remembering how she had left his office an hour ago.

Cassie blushes and looks around them to make sure that no one was listening to their conversation. "Keep your voice down!" she hisses. "And to answer your question, yes, everything is in its proper place thank you."

Logan laughs at her blush and then leans closer to kiss her on the cheek. "Too bad. I was hoping to..." he whispers something seductive in her ear that causes her to turn even redder.

Cassie gives him a mental shove and knocks him off of his stool. "Behave yourself Logan Knightrunner." she huffs and turns away while he gets up and dusts the dirt off the seat of his pants.

Quiet snickers can be heard all around the table as Logan rights his stool and sits down with a silly grin on his face and a blush of his own.

\* \* \*

After lunch Cassie goes up to her room to ask Ali about how Merri and Colt are doing.

"As far as I can tell they're both doing fine Cassie. I'm fairly certain that Colt has come across several of the traps and snares, but only one surprised him."

"Can you tell if he was hurt?" Cassie asks anxiously.

"Probably only his pride. All his rhythms remain at normal rates. Merri its harder to tell. Her rhythms stay steady all the time. I think she may have only come across one of the traps or snares, but I can't be sure."

"That's good."

"Yes, but doesn't she have to come close to them so that she can tell the others about what and where they all are?"

"Partly. If she can sense them without actually getting to close to them, she'll do even better. That would mean that her sense of danger and a trap is very acute and that she's paying attention to her surroundings."

"Okay, I under...Wait! Something's wrong! I'm picking up extreme fear and anxiety from Merri."

'Logan!' Cassie mentally shouts to him without really realizing she's done it. Within moments he appears at her side.

"What's wrong?" he asks taking hold of her arm.

"Merri's in danger." Cassie cries clutching at him.

"Hold on honey." Logan closes his eyes. 'Nightstorm, find Merri. Something's wrong.'

'I'm on my way to her now Knightrunner.'

Logan opens his eyes and gathers Cassie close. "Nightstorm is on his way to her right now Cassie. Relax honey, she'll be fine." They stand together and wait for Nightstorm to contact Logan.

"Her rhythms are returning to normal Cassie, but they're still elevated." Ali says quietly just as Logan closes his eyes again.

'I've got her Logan.'

'Good. Is she all right? What happened?'

'A large force of Rebel Patrol ships. Colt's porting to us.' There are a few

moments of silence. 'He's here now. We're all going to port to the stronghold

together. Warn the others to prepare for a possible attack.'

'It's already taken care of.'

'It will take us a few minutes to get back. Merri's to shaken to attempt the distance right now, and I don't want to try and port her myself.'

'I understand Nightstorm. Go slow and be safe.'

He opens his eyes and looks down at Cassie tightening his hold on her. "Merri's spotted a large force of R.P. ships." Cassie gasps and tries to pull away from him. "Colt and Nightstorm are with her and they're going to port back here, but it will take them a few minutes because of Merri's state of mind and the distance they have to travel."

"Oh God Logan. Will they make it back in time?"

"Nightstorm will get them back here safely. Come on, we need to help the others prepare for a possible attack on the stronghold."

He takes her hand, quickly pulling her out of the room and running down through the house. When they reach the outside the others are already hard at work preparing the compound. Anything that might be used to start a fire is put undercover or covered with a fire resistant liquid.

Dessa and Davena are helping to gather the younger children and take them into the underground shelter. As they go, the older children gather supplies to take with them. Food, clothes, blankets, and plenty of water.

"Cassie, go and help the girls while I help the men and older boys prepare the rest of the stronghold." Logan says kissing her quickly on the mouth before giving her a little push towards the other woman.

'Be careful Logan.' she calls out to him as he rushes to join the men.

A few minutes later Nightstorm, Merri, and Colt appear just inside the stronghold gates. Cassie sees them and runs over to them and pulls Merri into her arms.

"Are you all right?"

"I'm fine Cassie. I feel like such a fool, but there was just so many of them that I got scared and couldn't think what to do."

"You did the right thing Merri." Nightstorm assures her. "You hid yourself and stayed very still."

"Cassie, why don't you take her over to the shelter so that she can..."

"No wait! There's something that I have to tell you!" Merri interrupts pulling away from her sister. "They know that there's a stronghold up here and they're looking for it."

"How do you know this Winter-flower?" Nightstorm asks with a frown.

"I heard one of them thinking about it." she says and then bites her lip and concentrates. "No not thinking it, telling it. Who ever it was, they knew that I was there and they were warning me."

"You didn't think of the stronghold did you? If you could pick up on his thoughts, he could have picked up on yours. For all we know they could already be on their way here." Colt scowls at his twin.

"I haven't thought of our location since we got here. Besides, I would have blocked any probe if there had been one, which there wasn't. Not even a seeking probe." she says glaring at him.

"There's something troubling you though Winter-flower. What is it?" Nightstorm asks watching the different expressions crossing over her face.

Merri looks at him and then at Colt and Cassie. "The thoughts were familiar to me and yet they weren't." she says biting at her lip again, unsure of how to explain it.

"How so Merri? How were they familiar?" Cassie asks putting an arm around her shoulders again.

"I don't know Cassie. It was a feeling of family. You know Nightstorm, it was like blood calling to blood." she says looking at him and he nods his understanding. "It was like that, only there was something different about it. Something that wasn't really right."

"Not right in what way?" Logan asks her.

"It was like there were two minds. One was very familiar, but the other one wasn't."

"Merri, I want you to open your mind to me." Logan tells her stepping closer and looking into her eyes. She opens her mind to him, letting him see, hear, and feel all that she had. After a few moments their minds separate and Logan blinks. "She's right. Whoever is with the patrol, he's a member of your family. He's being controlled by a mind toucher. Whoever it is, they knew that Merri was there close by and blocked his controller for the few seconds he needed to warn her." Logan tells everyone and then turns to Cassie.

"Take her over to Davena and Dessa and have them give her something to eat."

Cassie nods and takes Merri's hand and leads her towards the shelter where the others are waiting anxiously. As they walk away Cassie can feel Logan in her mind.

'Leave her with the girls and then meet me and Nightstorm at the east gate.'

'Why, what's the matter?'

'Nothing. I may have a way to get your relative away from the patrol. I'll need your help as well as Nightstorm's for it to work though.'

'What can I do Logan?' she asks while telling Davena to get Merri something to eat and listens while she instructs Dessa to get a bath ready for Merri and some clean clothes to wear.

'I didn't think that you had noticed. Lately your abilities have gotten a lot stronger. If I'm not mistaken, your almost as strong as Merri and Colt.'

Cassie looks up and around at him. 'Are you sure Logan?'

'Look down at your hand Cassie. Are you wearing your ring?' he asks her and she can hear the smile in his voice.

She looks down at her hand before answering slowly. 'No, I haven't worn it for the past two weeks.' Logan waits for her to make the connection and after a few seconds she does. 'We've been communicating without the ring!'

'Not only that, but you've been doing things yourself that before you needed my help with.'

'Okay. I still don't see how I can help you, but I'll be with you in a minute.' She turns back to her sisters. "Merri, when you're done with your meal and bath, please help the others with the smaller children. Davena and Dessa, you help Mother Wolf block the thoughts of whoever can't do it by themselves." She turns to leave and go and join Logan and Nightstorm, but Merri stops her with a hand on her arm.

"But Cassie, I want..." Merri starts to say that she wants to help the men, but Cassie stops her.

"You can stay and help with the children Merri. Their safety is more important than your being a warrior right now." Cassie tells her more sharply than she had meant to and sighs as she sees her youngest sister's expression. "Darling, I know that being a warrior is very important to you. But if the R.P. should make it into the stronghold, your one of the strongest telepaths we have. The men will try to stop them before they get this far, but if some get through someone has to protect the children. Be a warrior by protecting them."

Merri looks down at her feet feeling ashamed by her behavior. She wanted to be a warrior, but she wasn't acting like one right now. She knew that Cassie was right. Slowly she nods her agreement to stay and protect the children.

"Good girl. Now, Logan needs me for something. Listen to Mother Wolf and do as she says. I'll be back as soon as I can." Assured that Merri would remain with the children, she rushes to the east gate where Logan and Nightstorm are waiting for her.

"What happened?" Logan asks as they leave through the gate and it closes behind them and is locked.

"Merri wanted to go and help the men. I explained to her that it was more important that she use her skills and abilities to help protect the children." she tells them as she walks between them.

"You should not have had to remind her of such a thing Cassandra." Nightstorm says with a frown. "I will have to remind her of her duties as a warrior woman."

"Don't be too hard on her Nightstorm. I think that she's still feeling really ashamed of how she reacted when she saw the patrol."

"Will she be all right?" Logan looks down at her agreeing with her general assessment of her sister's emotions.

"She'll be fine." She looks around them. "Where are we going?" She asks not knowing the landscape on this side of the stronghold.

"There is an old abandoned stronghold several miles from here that we use for special training's" Nightstorm informs her. "We will teleport there in a few minutes and try to guide the patrol there. They are already close to it."

"Once we get them there, we'll free your brother from the mind toucher and then teleport back to this one." Logan lifts a branch out of her way.

"Then you know that it's one of the boys?" she questions stopping to look up at him.

"Yes, but not which one. The thoughts were those of a young person." Logan doesn't say anything more not wanting to tell her about her father. He takes her hand and continues walking, hoping that will be the end of it.

"There's something else. Something that you're not telling me." He ignores her and keeps walking until she tugs on his hand pulling him to a stop. "Logan, what aren't you telling me?" she demands turning him to face her.

Logan sighs and then turns his head slightly to look at Nightstorm. "You go on ahead and we'll catch up in a few minutes." He nods in the direction they are headed. Nightstorm frowns, but continues on. After a few seconds Logan turns back to Cassie and puts his hands on her shoulders. "I didn't want to say anything until we had gotten your brother and I could talk to him." He sighs and gently tightens his grip on her shoulders. "Honey, your father's had a heart attack."

She stares at him for several seconds and then shakes her head and tries to pull away from his hold on her. When he doesn't release her she finally stops and bites her lip to keep from crying out her agony.

"Honey, he's fine. From what Cal was able to get, it was a mild attack and he's recovering quickly. Peterton will make sure that nothing happens to him. Remember, they don't want the Federation to start an investigation."

"What will we do Logan? God, when will this nightmare ever end?" she asks looking up into the sky.

"Soon baby, it will end soon. I promise that it won't be much longer and you'll have your whole family back together again." He hugs her close for a while and then takes her hand and leads her to where Nightstorm is waiting for them.

"Let's get going. After we get Cassie's brother and take care of the patrol, I want to get back and send a message to Saitun Katmen. Maybe he can do something about getting the other two Blackwoods released."

Nightstorm nods and steps to the other side of Cassie. Together he and Logan teleport them to their destination. After arriving, Nightstorm looks around for a safe place for Cassie to hide when its time to get her brother. It had to be accessible to only Logan and himself if at all possible.

'I've found a place Logan. Come to the southeast corner of the old granary.'

Logan takes Cassie's hand once again and leads her over to the granary. Once at the southeast corner, they stop and look around for Nightstorm.

"Over here." he calls to them from a deep recess in the back wall. Cassie leads the way into the small room.

"This is perfect Nightstorm. With those two side areas at the front of the bin, we can make sure that no one but Cassie's brother comes inside."

"Yes, and I will create a mental blind until the right person is nearby."

"What am I suppose to do?" Cassie asks in bewilderment.

"You my love will call them to us. While Nightstorm and I wait outside,
you'll be in here. As soon as we see how many there are, we'll each stand in one of those side areas and wait. When you feel your brother close by and are sure that there's no physical form close enough to stop him, you tell me and I'll deal with the mind toucher."

"What if there's someone close to him? What will we do then? I don't want to hurt anyone if it can be avoided Logan."

"Do not worry Cassie, no one will be hurt." Nightstorm assures her. "I will knockout anyone within twenty feet of him. Once he's inside with us, no one will be able to sense him or us because we will no longer be here."

"Okay Cassie, start calling." Logan orders gently and kisses her cheek, then he steps back so that she can concentrate on what she's doing. "Just say something that will lead them here. If nothing else think as if you're really talking with them and expecting an answer."

For the next fifteen minutes Cassie calls out to her brothers Mark and Daniel. She tells them how much she and the children had missed them, and how much Merri and Colt had improved in the group they were now living with.

Just when she's about to give up, Logan and Nightstorm step into the building. Cassie notices a shimmering at the entrance and concentrates even harder on her brother.

'Daniel, where are you?' she now knows which one it is. 'I can feel you're close by. Please Danny, answer me.' she waits and then suddenly she can hear him.

'Cassie? Where are you?'

'Here Danny! We're in here!' Smiling she looks at Logan and nods.

'Is there anyone with him Cassie? We can't take a chance at probing." Logan asks reminding her of why they're there and who they're up against.

Cassie reaches out to feel around her brother. She can only sense two people near him. She quickly calculates how close and what position. 'There are two people near him Nightstorm. One about three feet to his right. I think that it's the mind toucher. The other one is about ten feet behind him and to the left.' she tells them starting forward only to be stopped.

'No, stay there Cassie. As soon as he's in, come up and we'll leave. Keep in mental touch with him to make the portation easier.' Logan warns her and then looks across to Nightstorm and nods. 'On the count of three, you call to Daniel, I'll block the mind toucher, and Nightstorm will knock them out. Ready?' He looks at her and Cassie bites her lip before nodding. 'One...two...three, now!'

Within seconds Daniel Blackwood is coming through the doorway and Cassie is running forward. Moments later they disappear and reappear in the center of the Starhawk stronghold. Logan pushes his wrist-comm and gives Cal his orders. "Cal activate Alpha one delta protection section B."

"Done Logan." Cal responds immediately. "I take it that means that your plan was a success?"

"It was Cal. Let me know the minute all of the patrol is asleep and we'll send Gray-wolf and the others to deal with them." Logan tells him watching as Cassie and the others hug and welcome their brother.

"Right Logan."

Suddenly Logan and all of the Starhawk clan fall to their knees clutching at their heads. Cassie and her family look on in stunned shock, not knowing what was happening. After about three minutes, Logan and the others get back on their feet. Each of them has a huge grin on their faces and the women are crying in joy.

"Logan, what is it? What just happened?"

"Nothing. Everything." He says picking Cassie up and kissing her, while swinging her around. He sets her back on her feet and smiles at the rest of the Blackwoods standing around them. "We've just heard from Thayer." he watches the shock on their faces and smiles. "Thayer and Leyla are now lifemated and they'll be returning to Earth soon. They will soon take care of the President and the E.S.C. We'll soon be able to go back to our own homes."

A loud cheer goes up and they all begin putting the stronghold back to normal. They begin making plans for a celebration. They would be celebrating Daniel's rescue and the return of Thayer's abilities. While they are working, they all realize that soon peace would return to the Earth and with it, a normal and better way of life for everyone.

# Chapter XIII

Early the next day on Calidon, Thayer and Leyla are meeting with the High Council about their return to Earth.

"Ladies and Gentlemen, please!" Leyla begs loudly holding up her hands to still any further protests. "We are not planning to remain on Earth, but we do need to return. There are people there who are counting on us to help them. Not only the people of Earth, but our own people as well."

"Your Highness, is it wise to return there though? After all they don't know about Mandraik's capture, and will still try to capture or kill you." The Minister of the Interior points out.

'He's right cousin. You will be taking a big risk going back there.' Brock comments telepathically for her thoughts alone.

Leyla frowns at him and then looks at the Minister of the Interior. "My Lord, both my husband and I realize the danger that still threatens us. We will not be returning alone however." Everyone quiets down to listen. "Thayer and I have discussed this and have agreed to take all of the royal guards, plus two squads of the army."

Once again someone is in doubt of the decision Leyla and Thayer have made without consulting any of them.

"Do you think that such a show of force will really be necessary Highness? Would not just the royal guards be enough to influence them into cooperating with you?" The Minister of Defense asks knowing that the royal guard alone was made up of two hundred men and women. With two full squads of the army added to that, the numbers would be up to at least twelve hundred men and women.

"Yes Lord Curtseys, such a force is necessary. Not only for the benefit of Earth's leaders, but also for our own people. Don't forget that more than half of our people that are on Earth are criminals. Criminals my Lord that have been influenced by people that have no regard for human life whatsoever."

"People, what she's telling you is true. The extra squads are to insure that the Calidonians on Earth do not cause any unnecessary problems for us. They will be gathered up and taken back to our ships and detained." Thayer tells them looking around the chamber. "Besides the guards and the army squads, Lord Trocon, Captain Centori, and Selina will also be accompanying us."

Everyone nods their agreement to this slowly, and then one of the lesser council women asks, "Who will rule in your stead Highness? Lord Trocon would normally be the choice, but since he is going with you...?"

Leyla turns to look at the High Priest. "We all feel that the best choice to guide you in our place is Lord Metros and Lady Rachel. Together we feel that they will govern the people the way we would. They will also begin preparing the people for the return of family and friends who may have been changed greatly by their experiences on Earth." Leyla steps a little closer to Kasmen and talks softly for only him to hear. "Will you accept this position my Lord. I could trust no others but you and Rachel for the well being of our people."

Kasmen looks around the chamber at the others, and his gaze stops as he comes to Aeneka. 'What do you think of their plans Princess?'

'Their plans are sound Kasmen. I believe that all will go well with what they need to do. Leyla means what she says about not trusting anyone else with the safety and well being of the people of Calidon. She doesn't yet know the others well enough to give them such trust.'

"What does the Lady Rachel have to say about your request?" he asks turning back to Leyla.

"She has agreed to do it my Lord High Priest Metros." she tells him showing her great respect for him by using his full title.

"Then I too will agree. If that old she-cat can handle it, then so can I." he says with a grin as Trocon frowns at him.

"Good. Brockton, after Thayer and I have been crowned, choose those in the army with the strongest mental abilities, and those strongest in hand to hand combat."

Brock nods. "How many ships are you planning to take? With that many warriors we will need at least two ships. But with the returning Calidonians, we will need at least two more for everyone to travel comfortably."

"Do we have that many ships available?" Thayer asks frowning slightly.

"Yes. They're older models, but give us a week, two at the most and we'll have them running as well as the Royal Flagship."

"Fine, have the work started immediately. Work around the clock if necessary to get them ready in the shortest amount of time." Thayer tells him and then exchanges a smile of relief with Leyla that everything was proceeding so well.

"Now, tomorrow we will begin Dacus Mandraik's trial." Leyla reminds them returning to her seat. "It will be held in the great audience chamber so that as many people as is possible can observe. Both high and low born will be allowed to attend. Brockton and his men will be stationed around the chamber. Any trouble makers are to be removed and detained immediately for questioning." Leyla looks at her cousin and receives his nod of understanding.

"Anyone wishing to add to the charges will be allowed to speak. Rachel will be on hand to assist Lord Metros in verifying the truth of all statements." Kasmen nods as some of the others begin to murmur amongst themselves. "The rest of you will be expected to watch the people and gauge their reactions to what they see and hear. Before sentencing, you will come to Thayer and myself and let us know what type of punishment the majority feel he should be made to suffer for his crimes. There will be three punishments that must be considered. Death, total and permanent memory loss and banishment, or permanent memory loss and reprogramming. Though for myself and my family, I would sentence him to immediate death, you ladies and gentlemen will be the people's voice. I will trust your word in what the people wish done." Leyla sits back and watches the reactions to her declaration cross their faces.

'I don't think that you should have given them such a responsibility sweetheart.' Aeneka says watching her daughter.

'It will give me a chance to see who on the council truly has the interest and welfare for the people in their hearts.'

'And what if they say memory loss and reprogramming when the people really want his death? Once he's been reprogrammed you can not legally put him to death for any of his crimes.'

Leyla looks at her mother and then over at Thayer, wanting to see what he had to say.

'She's right my love. Both legally and morally, it would be wrong to take his life after reprogramming. He would be a totally different person, with no idea of his former life.' He takes her hand and squeezes it gently. 'We need a way to sentence him that will be truly the people's choice.'

'I can see your points. All right, let's speak to Trocon and Kasmen after the meeting and see what they can suggest.'

Giving her hand one more squeeze, Thayer releases her and stands up. "I think that we have discussed everything for now ladies and gentlemen. We will see you at the coronation ceremony." Everyone rises to live. "Lords Damori and Metros a moment more if you please."

Trocon and Kasmen look at each other before resuming their seats. The other council members file out and Brockton signals the inner guards out of the room. Once the room has been secured, Thayer takes his seat and nods to Leyla.

"Gentlemen, my mother has pointed out to me that my decision to let the council voice the people's choice for Mandraik's fate may have a flaw." Leyla says looking down at the table and then back up again. "Tell me truthfully, do you think that they would try to keep him alive even if the people wanted his death?"

Trocon frowns and looks at Kasmen with a raised brow. Kasmen was the one to answer such a question. He knew better what the others where likely to do in this situation.

"I have no doubt whatsoever that the older members will do as the people wish Leyla." He rubs his chin considering. "It's more difficult to say with the younger ones. The majority of them have sided with Dacus one more then one occasion since the deaths of your grandparents. Though I could not tell you if it was because they believed him or because he had some kind of control over them. At this point though, even with all that they have learned about him, I would not totally trust them to abide by the people's wishes."

Leyla bites her lip wishing that she had asked them about it before making her announcement. Sitting straighter and looking directly at them both, she asks, "What would you suggest that we do to rectify my mistake in judgment? It is quite obvious to me that I have made one."

"I feel that the best thing for us to do is to have Kasmen announce at the start of the trial that Mandraik's punishment will be decided by the people. The choices given will be fine." Trocon tells her assuredly. "Without his abilities, I doubt very much that Mandraik would be able to influence anyone off planet should they choose banishment even without the memory loss. I don't think we'd have to worry about him either way."

"Then after he makes his announcement, all Leyla and I should have to do is nod our agreement without Leyla verbally going back on what she told them here today, and possibly causing ill feelings?" Thayer says looking at each man.

"Yes. This will let the younger council members know that you trust his judgment enough to allow him to change such a decision without consulting you. It should also keep the trouble with them to a minimum."

"Do you agree to this Kasmen?" Leyla asks looking at him.

"I see no problems with doing it that way."

"Okay then. We're done here. We had better get going. The coronation is to take place in about four hours, and I still have to get Salis ready." Leyla stands up and then looks over at her mother. "Plus I have a special good-bye that I must prepare myself for." They share a sad smile, both wishing that it was not necessary. They leave the chamber with their arms wrapped around each other, the men following behind.

\* \* \*

Leyla and Aeneka help Salis with her dress and makeup. "You're going to look just beautiful sweetheart." Leyla tells her daughter while adjusting hair pins. "All of the young ladies will want to know just how you did it."

"This feels so strange. I've never had clothes like these before. Do I have to wear these shoes? Can't I wear my sandals? These are tight on my toes." Salis tells them wiggling her toes in the new shoes.

"I'm afraid you do dear, they go with your dress." Aeneka tells her as she straightens the bow on the back of her dress. "You won't have to wear them more then a few hours."

"Good, I hate wearing shoes." she huffs.

Leyla and Aeneka laugh at her expression, and then Leyla goes over to the mirror to touch up her makeup while her mother watches.

"Though you take after your father, at times you remind me so much of myself darling. I wish…" Aeneka shakes her head and wipes away a tear before it can fall.

"I know mother. I wish that you could stay with us longer too." Leyla tells her turning around and hugging her.

Salis watches them for a few seconds and then leaves the room quietly. In the sitting room, she sees Stephen talking to the little box called Sarah.

"I know that you don't know the system Sarah, but Leyla says that we'll be taking the larger flagship. So transfer over there and stop complaining." Stephen orders.

"But there's plenty of room here Stephen." Sarah has a whine in her voice.

"Sarah, listen to me. There will be at least thirty guards traveling with just Leyla, Thayer, and Salis. I'm not sure how many Lord Trocon plans to take with him, but it will probably be at least another twelve. The flagship is large enough to carry seventy-five people comfortably, plus any servants that may come along."

"All right, but you had better be ready to help if I have any problems with that monster." she tells him petulantly.

"I will. I have to go now. They should be just about ready to leave for the coronation soon."

"Leave the box on so that I can monitor and record the ceremony for Saitun and the others."

"Okay. I have to go now." He puts the box back onto his belt and turns to face Salis. "Well little Princess. Are you ready for your parents coronation?"

"I guess so." she shrugs and walks over to him. "Stephen...how? How did grandmother die?" she asks biting her lower lip.

Stephen watches her closely, registering her sadness and a slight agitation. He sits down and pats the cushion next to him. Once she's seated beside him, he goes through his memory until he comes to that day. "Just after your mother's fifth birthday, your grandmother became ill. Some form of bacteria entered her system and slowly began to age her. The healers on Earth could not figure out what it was or find a cure. Technically she was not considered dead when she transferred her essence to the box. I think she did that so the bacteria could not enter her brain and do damage."

"So she wasn't physically dead when she entered her essence form?" Salis asks beginning to think about something that her birth parents had speculated on for a long time.

"No, and her physical body lived on for three days after the transfer." Stephen watches her and sees unusual light enter her eyes. If he didn't know any better, at that moment he would have sworn that she really was Leyla's daughter. She had the same look in her eyes that Leyla got when she thought of something that might get her into trouble. "What's going through your head little Princess?"

Salis shakes her head and looks up at Stephen. "Nothing Stephen, nothing at all. Would you tell mother that I'll be right back?" she asks jumping to her feet and hurrying to the door. "There's something that I have to check on." and she runs out the door.

Stephen is so surprised by her sudden move, that he doesn't react until the door closes behind her. Just then Leyla and Aeneka come out of the bedroom.

"Stephen, where's Salis? I thought she was out here with you?" Leyla asks looking around the room and then back at Stephen.

"She was. She said to tell you that she'd be right back, that she had something she had to check on."

The door to the hall opens and Thayer enters with Brockton and Selina. "Leyla, where is Salis going in such a hurry? She practically knocked us over in the hall." Thayer asks walking over to his mate.

"I don't know Thayer. Stephen says she said that she had something to check on." They all look at Stephen.

"Why didn't you go with her Stephen?" Thayer asks him.

"I didn't realize that she was leaving the chamber until the door had closed behind her." he tells them sheepishly.

Leyla looks at the door and then at the others, and Aeneka starts laughing, causing her daughter to frown at her.

"I'm sorry dear. But the look on Stephen's face reminded me of when you use to do the same thing to him."

When Leyla turns to the door, Brockton catches her look and steps in front of her to put a hand on her shoulder. "Don't worry cousin, Krander is following her. She'll come to no harm."

Leyla looks up at him and then smiles a little. "Thank you Brock. With Mandraik's people still loose, I wouldn't put it past them to try to use her to try and get us to let him go."

"We still have a half an hour before we have to leave for the coronation hall." Selina points out with a smile. "Why don't we sit down and have a drink while we wait for her to get back?"

"Good idea. Thayer, Leyla, what would you like?" Brock asks walking over to the refreshment tray and lifting a decanter of juice.

\* \* \*

Salis sits on the edge of her chair in Rachel's chambers, talking with her and Lord Metros. "Could we make a clone of grandmother for her essence to return to?" she asks for the second time. "My parents thought that it might be possible if the essence left the physical body before it was time, before it stopped functioning."

Kasmen looks at Rachel and shrugs his shoulders. "I don't know. It might be possible if it truly wasn't her time to go. What do you think Rachel? Would a cloned body work?"

Rachel looks down at her hands. She knew what Salis was talking about, her parents had discussed it with her several times. They could just never figure out when such a thing would be permissible. "It's possible, but it would take a great deal of energy." she tells them and looks up at Salis. "We would have to make the clone body age at an accelerated rate, so that it would be at the proper age, and then slow the process so that it would age normally. If it were done wrong, the body could be destroyed or disfigured and Aeneka's essence lost."

"But if we do it right, it could work?" Salis says excitedly, knowing that they could do it.

"Yes Firepetal, it could work." she tells her and then takes her hand. "But your grandmother would have to agree to this. It must be her decision to begin her life again after so long."

"Not only is it her decision, but that of the Great One as well. If He wishes her to return to Him, there is nothing that any of us could do to prevent that." Kasmen adds reminding both Salis and Rachel of the One that has the final say in all matters of life and death.

"Would you pray to Him my Lord? Ask Him if its all right for us to do this? I just want to give mother and grandmother the time they need. Grandmother didn't get the chance to live like she was suppose to, and I don't think that He meant it to be that way." Salis looks at him with pleading eyes.

Kasmen looks at her and smiles. "I will do my best little one." He pats her shoulder and stands up. "You had best return to your parent's chamber. The coronation begins in less then fifteen minutes." He nods to Rachel and then leaves them.

"Go ahead Firepetal. I will start the process, but you must get your grandmother's permission. Tell her to let me know of her decision as soon as possible."

Salis nods and then walks quietly from the room. As she steps through the door, one of her mother's guards steps to her side.

"You've worried your parents taking off like you did Princess." Krander tells her as they walk together.

"I didn't mean to Kran. I had to talk with grandmother Rachel and Lord Metros."

"They did not tell you what you wished to hear did they?" he guesses seeing her expression.

Salis shakes her head and begins walking a little quicker, not wanting to discuss it with anyone. When they reach the chamber, Krander opens the door for her and gives her a smile. "Things will work out for the best Princess. You're not alone any more." Salis looks up at him and nods. Once she enters the chamber, Krander closes the door and takes up his position just outside, relieving the guard that had taken his place while he followed Salis.

When she enters the room, Salis looks at all of the adults and then walks over to her parents and looks down at her feet. "I'm sorry if I worried you. I didn't mean to."

"It's all right little one, but next time, let Stephen accompany you all right?" Leyla places a finger under her chin to lift her face so that she is looking at her. Salis nods and shifts her eyes over to Aeneka.

"Grandmother, there is something that I wish to share with you."

Aeneka looks into her eyes and can see sadness, doubt, and confusion there. Slowly she nods her agreement.

Salis steps over to her and opens her mind. Their minds touch, and Aeneka can see and hear all that has gone through Salis' mind for the past forty hours. She sees the plans that she had made with Rachel and Kasmen, the hope that what she had remembered from her other life would bring happiness to her new family.

"Oh dear." Aeneka says quietly as their minds separate, and hugs Salis close as tears slowly run down her cheeks. The others watch them closely and wonder what could have passed between them, but remain silent. 'It was very sweet of you to think of something like that honey. But I don't know if it would be the right thing to do now.'

"But why? Everyone would be..." Aeneka places a finger over her lips.

'Darling, I've already lived my life. I've already said good-bye to my mate. What happiness could I bring him now that wouldn't cause him more pain if I should go before him once again?'

Salis looks down at her feet. 'I think that he would be happy just to have you back with him again. It wouldn't matter about the pain to come if he could have what was taken from you.'

Sighing, Aeneka looks at her daughter and son-in-law. To live out a normal life span, to see her grandchildren born, to hold them and see them grow, would be so wonderful. 'Let me think on it darling. I promise to let Rachel know my answer in plenty of time, should I decide to go through with your plans.'

Salis nods. "Okay grandmother."

They hug once more and then turn to the others. "We had better hurry to the coronation hall. We're running a little late." Aeneka tells them. When Leyla raises a brow at her, she says privately, 'Later sweetheart.'

Thayer holds out his arm to Leyla, and after a second she places her hand on it, still looking at her mother and daughter.

Brock and Selina lead the way out, followed by Salis and Aeneka, and then Thayer and Leyla. Stephen follows, closing the door behind them. As they move done the hall the guards fall into position around them.

# Chapter XIV

"Lords and Ladies, people of Calidon. We gather here today to acknowledge the heir to the throne of Calidon and her mate." Kasmen Metros announces for all to hear. "Last eve our Princess Leyla became lifemated to a Prince of Manchon." The crowd shouts their joy and Kasmen must hold up his hands for silence. "Thayer Robus Starhawk is now a Prince of Calidon. Today in your presence we will crown them as our new King and Queen." Another cheer interrupts him and he waits for the crowd to quiet down before he continues. "Princess Leyla, Prince Thayer, step forward and state your vows of leadership to and for the people, before the people."

Leyla and Thayer stand up from where they have been kneeling. Leyla places her trembling hand on Thayer's arm, and the proceed up the five steps to where Kasmen waits for them. Upon reaching his side, they turn to the people. Thayer is the first to speak his vows.

"I, Thayer Robus Starhawk, Prince of Manchon and Calidon, swear to you the people of Calidon, to protect you from all hostilities no matter where they may come from, to the best of my abilities. I hereby swear to hear all complaints and to judge them fairly, honestly, and without bias. By my blood I bring Manchon and Calidon together once again." Cheering follows this, causing Thayer and Leyla to share a smile. When the people are quiet again, Leyla speaks her vows.

"I, Princess Leyla Aeneka Latona, of the House Chaukcee, swear to you the people of Calidon, protection from all hostilities no matter where they may come from, to the best of my abilities. I hereby swear that all complaints will be heard and judged, fairly, honestly, and without bias. By my blood I bring Calidon and Manchon together as one." More cheering follows, but stops immediately when the High Priest brings out the ceremonial dagger.

Thayer holds out his right hand, Leyla her left. "With the mingling of your blood you are now one in mind, body, and soul." Kasmen intones placing an inch long cut in their forearms and then binds them together with a red and yellow silken cord. "By blood are you joined, by blood do you rule."

They kneel down in front of Kasmen and two squires bring forward the crowns. Kasmen nods to Aeneka who steps forward.

"As the Crowned Princess of Calidon of the House Chaukcee, child of my body and my love, I give to you the right to rule in my stead. I crown you Queen Leyla Aeneka of Calidon." She places the smaller crown on Leyla's head. She turns to Thayer. "As the Crowned Princess of Calidon of the House Chaukcee, I crown you King Thayer Starhawk of Calidon." She picks up the larger crown and places it carefully on Thayer's head and steps back, nodding to Kasmen.

"All rise." As one the people, Leyla and Thayer stand. Leyla and Thayer turn to face the people. "I give to you the new King and Queen of Calidon." Kasmen states removing the binding ribbon and stepping back. Shouts of 'Long live the Royal Family' can be heard from all corners of the coronation hall. Leyla and Thayer acknowledge these, than move back to the thrones. Once seated the people resume their seats. Aeneka leads Salis forward to stand beside Kasmen. There is murmuring throughout the hall. Many had heard of her change of status.

"The first decree of the King and Queen is to see their adopted daughter made a crowned Princess of Calidon." Kasmen informs the people as the murmuring gets louder. "From this moment on she will be known as the Crowned Princess Salis Chandelle Aeneka Starhawk." He nods to another squire who brings forward a small silver crown.

Aeneka picks up the crown and holds it over Salis' head. "As the Crowned Princess of Calidon of the House Chaukcee, hereby gift to you, the title and privilege of the Crown of Princess to the House

Chaukcee. Wear it in pride and wisdom." She places the crown on her head and then kisses each of her cheeks.

From somewhere in the crowd someone shouts, "Long live Princess Salis!" which causes Salis to blush bright red. Cheers follow as she turns to join her parents.

When everything quiets down the Lords and Ladies come forward to pledge their support to the new King and Queen. When they are done the rest of the people pledge their support and loyalty. After the last ones have given their pledges, Kasmen dismisses them all to the palace gardens for the feasting.

During the feast, Leyla and Thayer hear that several more of Mandraik's followers have been captured and are being detained for questioning.

"That's about fifty now. How many believed he should be king?" Leyla asks shaking her head.

"It's not really a matter of their believing that he should have been king, but the promises that he made to them." Trocon informs her quietly. "He offered a lot of them positions or possessions that they didn't have or deserve. Some he blackmailed into helping him. Those that were blackmailed or threatened will testify tomorrow at his trial."

"Then we shouldn't have any problems at the trial if we're lucky." Thayer puts in.

"True, and from what my people tell me, most of the planet would vote for his death for what he's put most of them through." Brock tells them from behind Leyla's right shoulder making her jump a little, since she hadn't felt him there.

"All right, then we'll go with Kasmen announcing that the people will decide his fate." Thayer says before taking a bite of the game-hen set before him.

Later, much to Brock's dismay, Leyla and Thayer decide to circulate through the crowd. It was fine at first, but then they separated from each other and the guards had a more difficult time of keeping them in sight.

After an hour Brock notices that Thayer and his guards are gone. Working his way through the crush of people, he finally makes it to Leyla's side. "Where is your husband?" he growls in her ear.

Leyla looks at him with a raised brow. "He went to see Rachel with mother and Salis. They should be back soon."

"Well I wish he would have let me know." he growls again and Leyla scowls at him.

"Brock, he's a grown man and perfectly capable of looking after himself. Besides, his guards went with him."

"That's another thing. Not one of them bothered to report to me either."

She looks at him and then excuses herself from the ladies she has been talking to who have been trying to hear their conversation. Taking Brock's arm, she pulls him off to the side. "Something else is bothering you cousin. What is it?"

Brock looks around and then signals her guards to surround them and to block anyone that tries to pass or probe. Assured that his orders will be carried out he turns back to Leyla. 'Nearly forty minutes ago, someone tried to get to Mandraik.'

Leyla gasps in shock. 'What happened?'

'The guards were knocked unconscious. Whoever tried, failed to either kill him or set him free. They obviously didn't know about the shield that you put around him. It kept him in the cell and whoever it was out.' He says with a grin.

Leyla nods and looks towards the palace. 'Have him moved, but don't tell anyone except for those guarding him where he's to be put. Not even Thayer or myself.'

'He has to be fed.' he reminds her.

'That can be done before he's moved. Do you have someone that can track whoever it was?'

'Only Krander, and he's with Salis. He won't leave her side until she's safely back in your private chambers.' Leyla raises a brow at this news, not sure if she wanted this guard so close to her daughter. 'Her birth mother was his godmother. Now that he's able to, he will protect her with his life. Before he wasn't allowed to get near her. If they were caught together…'

'If they were caught together Salis was punished for it. Okay, leave him with her.' Leyla looks around until she spots Stephen near by and signals for him to join them. Brock tells his men to let Stephen through.

"Yes Leyla?"

"Stephen, I want you to go with Brock's men to the cell holding Mandraik. Scan it and locate the Alpha pattern that was there forty minutes ago."

"I should not leave your side Leyla." he tells her impatiently reminding her of Thayer's orders to him.

"Brock will stay with me until you or Thayer return." When he still refuses to leave her, she speaks to him in their private language. "Now go."

Stephen turns without further argument and Brock has four of his men take him to the holding cell. He watches them leave and then turns back to Leyla. "He takes his job as your personal bodyguard very seriously."

"Yes, sometimes he takes it too seriously. Thayer doesn't help matters either." she grumbles watching until they disappear inside the palace. "Well, let's get back to circulating." she tells him with a smile, causing him to groan.

"Couldn't you just sit down and let them come to you?" he pleads.

"Oh come on Brock. You should know that people are more likely to let something slip out if they're approached first, instead of letting them do the approaching." She chastises him gently taking his arm. "Besides, I need to work off all that food I ate." and she drags him along behind her ignoring the guards' chuckling.

\* \* \*

After a while, Brock takes Leyla back to her chambers where Thayer and Salis are waiting for them in the sitting room. Thayer stands up and walks over to them.

"I'm glad you're both here, I need to discuss something with you." He takes Leyla's hand and leads her over to the sofa. After seating her, he turns to Brock. "Please sit down Brock." When the other man sits down in the chair across from the sofa, Thayer sits down between Leyla and Salis.

"Where's mother Thayer?" Leyla asks looking around the room

once more. They didn't have much time left and she didn't want to waste it.

"That's what I need to talk to you about." He feels Salis move closer to him and puts an arm around her shoulders for comfort and support. "Earlier, Aeneka approached me about helping with a project she and Rachel wanted to test before her time ran out."

"What project? She never mentioned anything to me about working on something."

"It was a last minute one. We should know the results in about an hour or so."

"But we only have about three hours left." she reminds him, standing and pacing around the room slightly agitated. "She knows how important this time is to me, to us." She turns around and looks at him. "You're blocking something from me Thayer. Something to do with my mother." she accuses.

Salis shivers and clasps her hands together tightly. 'Father, tell them. Mother is getting very upset and so is Brock.'

'I know sweetheart.' He places his hand over her clasped ones and squeezes gently. "Leyla, please sit down and relax and I'll tell you what's happening. Brock, please control your agitation, it's beginning to upset Salis."

Leyla moves back to the sofa and Brock takes several deep breaths to calm himself. After they've both relaxed, Thayer gives Salis a quick hug and then stands up to look down at them, drawing their attention to himself. "The project was to make a cloned body for Aeneka's essence to return to." Leyla gasps and Brock sits forward in his chair. "About two hours ago, I helped to age the clone to the right age for her to reenter. When the body was ready, Kasmen and I helped her to do the transfer. We should know soon if it worked or not."

"So what you're saying is that if it doesn't work, I don't even get the chance to say good-bye to her." Leyla says in a deceptively quiet voice, glaring up at him, not seeing the sudden pain and pallor of Salis' face. "That's right isn't it? If your little experiment fails, I lose my last few hours with my mother. I think that I could hate you for this Thayer Starhawk."

Thayer looks at Salis and then at Leyla and Brock. "Salis honey, go into the bedroom until I call you." He tells her quietly not taking his eyes from the other two. He senses her standing and looking at her mother, the tears flowing down her cheeks.

"I'm sorry mother! I didn't mean..." she cries before stopping and running to the bedroom and slamming the door shut behind her.

When Leyla starts to stand up puzzled by her reaction, Thayer gives her a mental push back onto the sofa. "No, stay put. Right now she needs to be alone, and you're the last one she needs to see at the moment." When Brock starts to object, Thayer turns to him. "Don't interfere, just sit there and listen." he warns the other man before he says or does anything more. He turns back to his mate. "Right now, more then before, Salis is feeling guilty. Your words have done a lot of damage Leyla." He sits down beside her and takes her hands in his. "The cloning idea was hers Leyla. She saw and felt how upset you and your mother were just before the coronation. She asked Stephen how Aeneka had died, and he told her everything he could. A memory of something her birth parents had discussed often came back to her, and she went to discuss it with Rachel and Kasmen. They told her that it might be possible, but that the final decision had to be your mother's."

"But why didn't she say anything to me? Why did mother keep it from me?" Leyla cries out softly in confused hurt.

"She didn't want to raise your hopes in case it doesn't work. She also didn't want you to blame Salis if that should happen." He squeezes her hands. "Sweetheart, all Salis wanted to do was to make you and your mother happy again and to give you more time together. Right now our daughter is in there blaming herself for everything that has ever happened and wishing that she had died from one of her beatings." He pulls her into his arms as she bites her lips and tears begin to fall down her cheeks. Kissing them away, he puts her a little away from him. "Love, you need to go in there and let her know that no matter what happens, you won't blame her."

Letting out a shaky breath, Leyla nods her head before pulling completely out of his arms. Standing she wipes away the last of her tears and straightens her dress. "I'll go and talk with her." Leaning down she kisses him gently. "Thank you."

The men both watch as she goes to the bedroom door and knocks softly. After a few seconds she opens the door and walks in, closing the door softly behind her. As soon as the door closes behind her, Thayer stands up and walks over to the refreshment tray. "I could really use a drink right now. How about you Brock?"

"Sure, I'll have a Blue Lemcho." Brock says standing and walking over to the tray to fix the drink himself. Once he has it he returns to his seat and takes a large sip. Setting the glass down he looks at Thayer. "Do you really believe that this cloning is going to work?"

Sitting back down on the sofa, Thayer takes a healthy swallow of his own drink. "If I hadn't believed that it would work, I never would have helped them." he says looking Brockton fully in the face. "I love Leyla beyond all things Brock. I feel as Salis does, that Leyla and Aeneka both need more physical time together. They were cheated out of that time when Leyla was still a small child, when she needed the physical presence of her mother. Even though she's an adult now, I still think they need time to make some happy memories. I just wish we could do this for others."

"What if it doesn't work? Leyla needed these last few hours with Neka just as much. If Neka was doing this for Leyla, she should have asked her how she felt about it. At least that way Leyla could have been with her now instead of waiting to see if she's going to have a physical mother or a fading memory of one." Brock points out calmly feeling for his cousin.

Thayer finishes off his drink and stands to go back to the tray. "I promised Aeneka that I wouldn't regret my decision to help her do this, and I won't. She's given up just as much as Leyla in making this decision Brock. But no matter what, no one has the right to take her choice away from her. Not even her own daughter." He says downing another drink quickly.

"You're right Thayer, and I'm sorry for the way I acted when you told me." Leyla tells him walking back into the room holding Salis' hand tightly in her own. "The time I've already had with mother will be enough if this doesn't work. It was time that I may not have otherwise had. If this does work, I will be forever grateful to my daughter and you for giving us this extra time together." She pulls Salis closer to her side and hugs her. "I want to go to Rachel's and wait."

Thayer walks over to them and puts both hands on her shoulders. Looking into her eyes he reminds her, "You know that there is a strong chance that this may not work."

"I know, but I...we, should be with her whatever happens." she tells him with a smile and looks from Salis to Brock, and back at Thayer. "It's only right that she be surrounded by her family whatever happens."

He continues to look into her eyes even as he speaks to Brock. "Contact Selina and Trocon, have them meet us at Rachel's in a few minutes. Kasmen is already there praying to the Great One to allow the transfer to work and to allow Aeneka to finish out her true life-span."

Brock nods and closes his eyes to contact the others. Within seconds he opens them again. "They'll meet us there." He tells them as he stands and leads the way to the door.

As they leave, Stephen meets them in the hall and gives Leyla his report in their special language while Brock's men give him a mental report. When they've heard everything, they look at each other.

'The child will have to be placed into wardship Leyla.'

'Yes, but who do we place him with that won't take out their anger and frustrations with his sire out on him?'

'Only you and Thayer can decide such a matter.'

'All right, let's wait until after the trial. After we know about my mother, I'll discuss it with him.' She turns back to Stephen. "We're going to Rachel's. I want you to wait outside with the guards until I call for you to come in."

"All right Leyla. Sarah finally has the information on the ship that you wanted her to check on." he tells them as they continue on to Rachel's chambers.

"Tell her that we'll be ready for her report in a few more hours."

Minutes later they meet up with Selina and Trocon outside of Rachel's chambers. After a brief knock they all enter to find Rachel waiting for them. "I knew that you would come before the hour was up."

"What's happening Rachel? How is she doing?" Leyla asks anxiously stepping closer to the old healer.

"Her vital signs are stronger and her brain activity has increased within the past ten minutes."

"Then it worked grandmother?" Salis asks quietly.

"From what I've seen and felt Firepetal, I would say that it has indeed worked." Rachel assures her and then looks at Thayer. "She needs a mental boost to waken fully."

"How much of a boost?" he asks stepping to the inner door.

"About a fourth of what you gave her earlier should be enough to do the job." Rachel follows him to the door and then turns to the others. "Give us a few minutes and then you can all come in." she assures them and walks into the other room and closes the door behind her.

Leyla watches the door close, wanting to go in, but forces herself to wait and turn to face the others when she hears them murmuring. She notices that Salis is standing off to the side away from the others, looking down at her feet. Knowing that Brock was filling in Selina and Trocon on what is happening, she walks over to her daughter.

"Are you all right little one?" Salis nods but refuses to look up. "You aren't still worried are you? You heard Rachel, it worked. All that has to be done now is to give her a little boost."

"I know. It's just that..." she looks up at Leyla. "Is it really right for us to do this mother? When I think about it, I wonder if we're not cheating."

"Oh sweetheart, don't think of it that way." Leyla hugs her close. "I think that this is what the Great One wants. Rachel taught me that He would give or take a memory that could keep someone in this life. If He wanted a sick person to be with Him, then nothing anyone did would make that person better. If He felt that they should stay, that they still had His work to do, then He would give the knowledge needed to save them so that they could finish what needed to be done." she tells her gently. "I believe that He gave you the knowledge that would give mother another chance to finish out her life. If He had wanted her to join Him then what you, your father, Rachel, and Kasmen did would not have worked." She kisses her on the forehead and hugs her again. "Now, don't worry any more. Everything will work out the way He has planned it to."

Though she still has some doubts, Salis looks up at her and gives her a small smile. "All right mother."

Selina walks over to them and smiles down at Salis. "How does it feel to give your mother such a special gift from the Great One?" she asks and then laughs as Salis blushes. "Must feel pretty good from the blush on your cheeks." she says as the men join them and Salis blushes even more as they all smile down at her.

The door to the inner chamber opens and Thayer signals for them to come in. Leyla and Salis enter first followed closely by the others. They all stop and stand around the bed.

"She will awaken in a minute. The only thing that we must be concerned about is memory loss. It is a possibility that can not be overlooked." Rachel tells them quietly. "But I do not really believe that it will be a problem for Aeneka. Her mind has always been strong and well disciplined, as has been her belief in the Great One's love."

All eyes go to the woman asleep in the bed. They watch closely as her lashes begin to flutter and her eyes slowly open. Though the body is different in age, the eyes and the thoughts reflected within them, remain just as strong and focused.

Leyla moves closer and reaches out to touch the aged hand gently. "Mother?" she questions while everyone holds their breath waiting for a favorable response.

"It...it worked?" Aeneka asks in a weak voice, having to force her vocal cords to do as she wishes.

Tears stream down Leyla's cheeks as she nods her head. "Yes mother, it worked."

Aeneka looks at all the faces around her and smiles through her own tears. She looks at her granddaughter and shakily holds out her hand. Salis steps forward and takes the hand into her own and holds it to her cheek.

"Thank you darling."

Salis falls to her knees and very carefully hugs her. "I love you grandmother." She sniffles and Aeneka pats her shoulder before closing her eyes and falling back to sleep.

Rachel steps forward and helps Salis to stand. "She needs to rest now. She will be able to get up in a few days, once her muscles strengthen enough to hold her body weight." she tells them indicating that they should all leave now.

Everyone understands and file out of the room. Once in the outer chamber, Rachel explains what will have to be done while Aeneka strengthens her control over her new body. "Though before the transfer, she had a type of physical body, it was still merely essence. She needs to relearn how to move and control her limbs again before she can move on her own." She leans against the wall and looks at Leyla. "I would like for Salis to stay here with her during this time. You and Thayer will be quite busy with Mandraik's trial, and I believe that the less time spends there, the better it will be for her. After her testimony, she won't need to be there for anything else."

Though she would like to argue with her about it, would like to stay with her mother, Leyla knows that what Rachel is saying is true. They could not afford to put off Mandraik's trial, and both she and Thayer needed to be there for however long the trial lasted. Rachel was also right about Salis. The less she saw of Mandraik, the sooner she would forget the things that had happened to her, and begin to heal.

"That will be fine Rachel. I'll leave Stephen here to help and to guard them both." She turns to Brock. "Would go and tell Stephen to come in please?" Brock nods and goes to the door.

Seconds later Stephen comes in and joins them. Leyla quickly explains to him what is happening and what his duties will be. "No one is to enter these chambers, especially the inner chamber, except for those present without Rachel's approval." she reinforces this in their private language.

"Understood Leyla." He hands her Sarah's box and then enters the inner chamber.

"Well, I think that we should all return to our own chambers and get some rest, and allow Rachel to get some as well. Hopefully this trial won't take too long." Thayer suggests before walking over to Salis and giving her a hug and kiss. "Good night sweetheart. If you should need anything, just contact us."

"I will father." she returns his hug and kisses his cheek.

"Make sure that you get enough rest honey. We'll stop by before the trial to check on you and your grandmother." Leyla hugs and kisses her.

"Okay mother."

Brock steps forward and goes down on one knee. "Krander will be right outside in the hall if you need him. He'll keep everyone out and help to watch over you."

"Thank you cousin Brock." she smiles at him and Brock ruffles her hair before giving her a kiss on the cheek.

"Get some sleep brat." He stands up and walks over to the door to wait for the others.

"I'll bring you a change of clothes in the morning, before I go on duty." Selina tells her kissing her cheek.

"Thank you Selina."

Kasmen and Trocon say a less emotional good night and then everyone leaves so that Rachel can get Salis ready for bed.

Salis turns to Rachel with a sigh. "Boy, I thought they'd never leave." They smile at each other and then start laughing.

"They are just concerned about you and Aeneka. We shouldn't laugh at them, though it was quite interesting to watch Kasmen and Trocon." Rachel smiles remembering the looks on the men's faces. Pushing herself from the wall, she straightens up. "Come Firepetal, let's get you a little something to eat and then it will be time for you to go to bed." and she leads the way back into the room where Aeneka is sleeping. "You can sleep on the side cot." She goes over to a small warming plate and dishes up a small bowl of stew. "After you finish this, go and wash up and then go to bed." She turns to look at Stephen. "Do you eat? Would you like some of this stew?"

"I do not eat in the way you mean. Though I can partake when it is needed to make others comfortable in my presence." Stephen explains.

"Then how do you...how do you keep your energy leave up?"

"When its necessary, I can plug into a regular power source and recharge. Usually I have my own power chamber that I can rest in for several hours and can build up a supply that will last for quite a while." He tells her.

"I see. Well, there is a power terminal over on the far wall. Feel free to use it if you need to." Rachel waves her hand in the general direction of the terminal as she heads out the door. "I'm going to bed now. Remember what I said Firepetal. Eat your stew and then go to bed. I'll see you in the morning."

"Good night Grandmother. Rest well." Salis calls as the door closes behind Rachel. She sits down on the cot and eats her stew while watching Aeneka sleep. Though she now agreed with what her mother had told her, she still wonders if what they had done was right. If it hadn't been for her birth parents, would she have been given the knowledge to have instigated this?

Finishing her stew, she takes the bowl to the sink and rinses it out. Going over to Aeneka, she gives her a kiss on the cheek and then climbs onto the cot. "Good night Stephen."

"Good night Salis." He turns off the overhead light and goes over to the power terminal. Though he still had power left from his last recharge on the ship, he had used a lot of power in his search for Mandraik's attacker, and he wants to replenish some of that loss. He did not want to be too low should he be needed for the protection of Leyla or the others.

# Chapter XV

After checking on Salis and Aeneka, Leyla and Thayer enter the great audience chamber to subdued murmuring. Once they're seated, Brock and ten guards bring in Dacus Mandraik. Angry voices can be heard as he's lead to the holding area where four guards will shield him from any attacks. After securing the prisoner, Brock walks over to the dais and stands to Leyla's left.

'I've placed my strongest shielders around him. Even you and Thayer would have a hard time getting through to him now.'

'Good, I think.' Thayer tells him on their private path.

Leyla just nods and smiles. She looks past Brock as Kasmen enters the chamber. He approaches the dais and bows to them. "Your Majesties."

"You may proceed Lord Metros." Thayer tells him loud enough for all to hear.

He bows again and then turns to the people. "We are here today to pass judgment upon former Lord Dacus Mandraik. You the people of Calidon will decide his fate." He pauses for a second to touch Leyla's mind, and he receives her mental nod for him to continue as they had planned. "You will have three choices in what should happen to him. Banishment, banishment with total memory loss, which will be forever, or death." During each choice there are murmurs, but when the death sentence is mentioned the voices grow louder. Kasmen holds up his hands for silence. "The charges against him are numerous. He is charged with treason against our former King and Queen, as well as for their deaths. He is also charged with the murders of Chandelle and Altain Tahquar, illegal transport of many Calidonians for the use as slaves, excessive abuse and the attempted murder of a child, illegal mind control and the placing of a mental block meant to kill, conspiring to take control of another planet, the attempted murder of Lord Trocon Damori, and finally the attempted murder of the Calidonian heir, her Majesty Leyla Aeneka Latona Starhawk."

Kasmen stops to take a few deep breaths and release them slowly, while watching as Brock's men control the crowd that has become more and more agitated. After order has been restored, he turns to Mandraik.

"Dacus Mandraik, what do you say to these charges brought against you?"

"I say that they are all lies. I am guilty of nothing except trying to protect Calidon from offworlders. Offworlders that the King and Queen allowed to come here almost thirty years ago. There has been no proof that the woman you have crowned is even of Calidonian blood. You have taken the word of a boxed image of our former Princess that could have been made by these offworlders to gain control of our people."

Outrage runs rampant throughout the hall at Mandraik's open disrespect and denial of the Queen. Leyla stands and holds up her hands for silence. As the crowd grows quiet she turns to Mandraik.

"You want absolute proof Dacus Mandraik, you shall have it! The people will see it and know you for the fool that you are.!" She unbuttons four of her gown's buttons and bares her right shoulder for all to see. On her shoulder is the bright red birth mark of a flaming star. "Here is your physical proof that I am who I say I am, of what I am. Have you more doubt? Shall I give you more proof then this?" There is complete and utter silence as the people stare at the mark and Dacus glares at her. "Well, would you care for more proof? I assure you that I am quite capable of demonstrating the validity of this mark once again."

"Majesty." Kasmen calls to her softly, drawing her attention to him. "He already knows who and what you are, and that you have the power of the FIRESTAR. He meant only to cause doubt in the minds of the people. You have dispelled that doubt by showing them the mark."

Taking a deep breath and buttoning up her gown, Leyla resumes her seat next to Thayer and nods to Kasmen. Returning her nod, he turns back to Mandraik and then to the people. "You will now hear the testimony of the accuser. Dacus Mandraik's accuser is Detra Priss. The charges of mind control are from his control of her over the past several years. The mind-block, the abuse and the attempted murder of a child are also from his control of Detra Priss. She has been forgiven for her unwilling role in all of these crimes as they were the result of that control."

Leyla and Thayer both hold their breaths hoping that the people will agree with their decision to forgive Detra her involvement. They watch as heads begin to nod and people talk amongst themselves. One of Brockton's men steps forward and bows.

"The people are in agreement that Detra Priss is not responsible for her actions while under Mandraik's control. None will hold what they are about to hear against her."

Both Leyla and Thayer nod their approval and relax. For the next three hours Detra reveals everything that she knows about the charges brought against Dacus, and tells of his dealings and plans for the people of Calidon. While she speaks the images that Leyla had seen in her mind, and which Stephen had recorded, are projected onto a large screen for the people to see.

When she finishes, two guards escort her from the hall and Kasmen stands and waits for the crowd to calm down. Several times during Detra's testimony, it had been necessary for Leyla and Thayer to assist him in mind calming them. Luckily that isn't necessary this time and they quiet as he holds up his hands.

"We will now stop to take our noon meal. When we return, anyone that has anything to add may do so." He lowers his hands and turns to Leyla and Thayer and bows. They stand and walk from the hall with Kasmen following close behind them.

As soon as the King and Queen leave the hall, the people start to discuss what they have seen and heard as they make their way out of the audience chamber. Most were not surprised by what they had learned, and were glad that Mandraik had finally been stopped.

* * *

After securing Mandraik in a well guarded cell, Brock heads to the dining hall. He receives messages from his men that had been stationed throughout the crowd. Before taking his seat next to Selina, he goes to the high table and stops behind Leyla and Thayer.

"Mandraik is secure with six of my best men."

"Good. Have you heard anything about the people's reaction yet?" Thayer asks sipping at his wine.

"According to my men there may not be any need for more testimony. The people would be willing to sentence Mandraik after the meal." He reports grimly.

"It appears to be the same here as well. We'll have to see. Kasmen will offer again to hear more testimony, but have your men ask around for a spokesman for the people's decision. I think that will be our best chance to prevent any deception on the part of any of the council that have sided with Mandraik in the past." Leyla tells him and then nods to the servant serving her to pour more wine.

"As you wish your Majesty." he bows and steps away, going to join Selina.

"How are things going Love?" she asks kissing his cheek.

"Fine. It looks like we'll be done with this mess soon after we go back." he informs her and watches her brow raise in question. "The people were more then willing to sentence him after hearing the charges without Detra's testimony against him. With what they saw and heard they are even more determined then they were before."

"What did they think of her part in all of it?"

"They agreed with Leyla and Thayer, that she should not be held responsible for what Mandraik forced her to do."

"That's good. Well she won't have to worry about thoughts of him once this is all over and done with."

They discuss the trip that will take place in a few days and how it will feel to leave Calidon for at least four months. All too soon its time to leave and Brock goes to get Mandraik from his cell.

"Any trouble?" Brock asks his lieutenant.

"Only a few people that wanted a closer look. We convinced them that it wasn't in their best interest to get too close."

"No one tried to force the issue?"

"Not after the men pulled out their stunners." the lieutenant tells him with a wide grin.

"All right then, let's get him out and head for the hall. We should be done with this in the next hour or so if the majority of the people have their way about it." Brock tells him stepping forward to unlock the cell door. As the cell door slides open, Brock is tackled and sent backwards into two of the guards and kept from falling. Before Mandraik can do more then jump to his feet from where he had fallen, the other four guards have put up a barrier to keep him in place. Though he tries, Mandraik can't move in any direction more then an inch.

Brock straightens up and lightly brushes off his uniform and straightening it. The other two guards do the same all the time glaring at Mandraik. Brock looks over his shoulder at the lieutenant.

"Put the chains on him." As the other man moves to do as ordered, Brock steps closer to Mandraik and stares deeply into his eyes. "That will be your one and only attempt at escape Mandraik. Though even if you did happen to escape, I doubt that you would have gotten very far." he tells him and smiles as the chains click into place. "A lot of people would like nothing better than to get their hands on you right now."

"My followers will free me Captain Centori." Dacus claims with great contempt for the other man. "When I am free, I shall take great pleasure in watching your slow and painful death."

"That's where we differ Mandraik. I will take no pleasure in your death, though it will be a quick one." Brock tells him in equal contempt, before signaling his men to start moving. "You have hurt too many people, including your followers, for any of them to want to help you escape your punishment." Leaving him with that thought, Brock moves to the front of the group and puts the other man from his mind.

When they finally enter the audience chamber, a hush encompasses the room. Everyone turns to glare at Mandraik as he is lead past them. Just before he walks from the crowd, a young woman steps forward and spits in his face. An older woman pulls her back and glares severely at Mandraik.

He returns her glare before the guards push him forward. While his men secure the prisoner, Brock approaches the dais to speak privately with Leyla and Thayer. "He attempted to escape when I opened his cell, so we put the chains on him. He still believes that his followers will set him free before sentencing can be carried out."

"We know that he has blackmailed a lot of people, including some of his followers. If we could only get him to admit that he had used them, maybe we wouldn't have to worry about their actions in the future." Leyla says quietly looking down at Mandraik.

Kasmen steps closer to join in the conversation. "That won't be necessary. The people have already made their decision and the ones with the loudest voices were those of his followers."

All three of the others turn to look at him. "Then no one else wishes to add anything to the charges?" Thayer asks.

"No, they feel that there is nothing more to add, and nothing will change their minds." Kasmen assures them. "We do need to inform the people that he no longer has any of his abilities though. It won't have any impact on their choice of punishment from what I have already heard. But it is a necessary legality."

"Call them to order then and proceed." Leyla tells him sitting back in her seat and beginning to prepare herself for what is to come. Kasmen nods and bows to them before stepping away and moving to the front of the dais and holding up his hands.

"Lords and Ladies, people of Calidon. It has been brought to our attention that you have decided that you need not hear any more against the accused. Is this true?"

A man of middle years steps forward and bows to Leyla and Thayer and then to Kasmen. "It is true Lord Metros. We need hear no more."

"What is your name sir?" Kasmen asks.

"I am Seabliss my Lord. The chief petitioner between our Lords and the rest of the populous."

"Very well Seabliss. What say the people of Calidon to the charges brought against Lord Dacus Mandraik?"

"The people of Calidon find Lord Mandraik guilty of all the charges brought up against him."

"Before we ask which punishment the people have decided upon, we must inform you that Lord Mandraik no longer has the use of any of his mental abilities. Will this change your decision on what is to happen to him?"

"NO!" The shout is heard from all corners of the chamber.

"No my Lord Metros, it will not change the peoples choice of punishment." Seabliss assures him.

"Then tell us what punishment the people have chosen this day."

"The choice of the people is death, my Lord Metros."

"Death to the traitor! Death to Mandraik!" the people begin to chant and Kasmen is unable to get them to quiet down.

Seeing his difficulty, Leyla and Thayer stand and send out thoughts of calm to the people, telling them to calm themselves so that the sentencing can be done. When the chamber is quiet once more they look to Seabliss.

"We thank you for your honesty in relaying the people's choice Seabliss. You may return to your place." Leyla nods to him and then turns to Kasmen. "Lord Metros, please continue."

"Yes your Majesty." He signals to Brock who in turn signals to the guards surrounding Mandraik. Dacus is brought forward struggling and cursing. When he is in front of Leyla and Thayer, the guards force him to his knees. Kasmen steps forward and looks down at him. "Dacus Mandraik, you have been sentenced to death. Do you wish to say anything before the sentence is carried out?"

"You may put me to death, but you won't stop me. Even in death I shall live on. My essence will spread throughout all of Calidon, and I will live on in each of you. Then you will see that I was right." He laughs and all the people begin looking at each other murmuring about not wanting any part of his essence, his memories. "You sniveling fools, there's nothing that you can do to stop it."

Thayer steps forward holding up his hands for quiet. When the people calm he looks down at Dacus. "You are wrong in thinking that Mandraik. When you pass from this life, your essence will go with you.

Your evil will not be allowed to touch anyone ever again. The FIRESTAR and the STARHAWK will see to that."

Mandraik begins struggling against his bonds trying to stand, but is kept down by the guards and the chains. "You can't do that!!" Mandraik screams at him.

"We can and we will do it Mandraik. This is no threat but a promise." Leyla tells him stepping to Thayer's side. "All your life you have cared for no one but yourself. Now no one here cares what you think any longer, no one wants any part of you left behind."

Brock nods to his men once more and they move to stand at the front of the hall to keep the people at a safe distance for what is about to happen.

"People of Calidon, your decision has been made and it is by mutual decision that the sentence be carried out at this time and in this place before all present." Kasmen informs them and then steps away from Leyla and Thayer to a safe distance. He was not quite sure what was going to happen, but he knew that it would not be good to be too close.

The guards holding Mandraik wait until Leyla and Thayer move into place on either side of Mandraik before releasing him and moving away. Leyla stands to one side and Thayer on the other. They allow Mandraik to stand, but then mentally hold him in place. Looking into each others eyes, they link minds and project their namesakes. Within seconds their physical bodies disappear and their other selves rise slowly. Once they are in position above Mandraik a black void, so dark that no light can be seen in it or through it moves down towards Mandraik. He begins to scream, but the sound is absorbed by the void as it moves over him, consuming him and all that he is. After a few moments the void disappears and no sign of Mandraik is left behind.

Seconds later Leyla and Thayer return to their physical bodies and take a deep breath. Looking at each other, they quietly sigh at what they had done, before turning to face the people. When they do, they see the shock, awe, and even some fear on the faces of the people.

"No longer will Dacus Mandraik be a part of our lives, or the history of Calidon. From this day forward, his name will not be spoken on this planet. After discovering the degree of involvement of his followers, and the reasons for their involvement, all memory of Dacus Mandraik will be wiped from their minds to prevent further corruption." Thayer informs the people calmly trying not to let their fear affect him. Moving to Leyla's side, he takes her hand and walks with her back to the dais and sits down.

Kasmen steps forward once more after checking their mental condition. He had noticed small reactions to the fear the people had shown. "This trial is now at an end. Please remember the King's decree and never again mention the name of Dacus Mandraik. You may go."

The people bow as one to Leyla and Thayer, then start to file out of the hall. As they go they murmur about what had happened, and all agree that to forget the evil that had been a part of their lives for so long was the best for everyone. There was nothing to be gained by letting it affect their lives any longer than it already had. None of them wanted to put the King and Queen through such an experience again. They had all seen their reaction when they returned to their human forms, and what they had seen had frightened them, they knew that it had been necessary.

Thayer and Leyla wait until all the people have left before following Brock and Kasmen out. They stop by Rachel's to check on Salis and Aeneka, before continuing on to their chambers. Kasmen and Brock walk with them and then excuse themselves after seeing them to their chamber.

Entering the outer chamber, Leyla collapses onto the sofa, while Thayer goes over to fix them each a drink. He joins her and hands her drink to her before sitting down.

"I hope that we never have to do that type of transfer ever again. Such darkness is frightening even to me." Thayer tells her shaking his head and taking a swallow of his drink.

"Yes, I know what you mean, but in some instances such a thing is necessary. We couldn't let Mandraik's evil touch anyone's life anymore." Leyla tells him placing a hand on his arm. "Darling, I know that what we had to do bothered you, and not just because of the darkness. It bothered me too. We're healers, not destroyers of life, but sometimes there just isn't any other way to handle such evil. What we did, we did for the sake of not only Calidon or ourselves, but for all the people out there that Mandraik's evil would have touched."

"You're right love." he squeezes her hand where it sets on his arm and then brings it to his lips for a quick kiss. "With any luck, there won't be another instance when we have to do that again."

"I hope that we don't either." she agrees and then stands up. "There's something important that we need to discuss though that has to do with Mandraik." She walks over to the table where a vase of fresh flowers has been placed and lifts one out. "Last night, Brock and I discovered that Mandraik has a small son."

Thayer finishes off his drink and sets the glass down on the table. "What about the child's mother?"

Leyla turns to look at him. "She committed suicide after her attempt to kill Mandraik in his cell yesterday afternoon failed." she looks down at the flower in her hand. "From the note that she left we know that Mandraik planned to sell the boy to someone off planet, and to sell her to one of the nomadic tribes."

Thayer shakes his head and stands up. "How could anyone be so cruel as to want to sell their own child? Do we know who she or her family is?"

"She was the daughter of a middle Lord. From what Brock has been able to find out, the father was offered land for her by Dacus. He promised to marry her if the family supported him at court and with the council. He also agreed that on the day of the marriage, he would give them more land and a better title, along with more power after the vows were spoken." Walking over to him, she stops in front of him and rests her head against his chest.

"Three days before the wedding Dacus raped her. When taken before the council, he contended that she gave herself to him willingly enough, and convinced them that her maidenhead was already gone. He had made his offer for a virginal bride. Because Dacus was believed, the family was humiliated and had to return the land they were given along with half of their own holdings for embarrassing Mandraik. After that her family turned away from her. My grandmother took her in and gave her a position in the orphanage.

When her pregnancy began to show, they brought her to the palace to assist in the nursery."

"So, he followed in his father's footsteps, but instead of a servant, he used and abused a Lord's daughter." Thayer says in disgust hugging her to him. "What's to be done about the child now? I doubt that the girl's parents would take the boy." When she pulls away, he picks up his glass and goes to fix himself another drink.

"I don't think that they would either. Because of the standing of both his parents, he becomes a royal ward. We have to decide who to place him with. It will have to be someone that will not take out their anger and frustrations out on him because of who is father was."

Sipping at his drink, Thayer walks back over to her. "Who would that be. Just about everyone on the planet has a great deal of anger towards Mandraik and might do that, though I don't really see it happening."

"I know, but it's still a possibility. That's why I want to ask Brock and Selina to take his wardship and possibly adopt him. No matter that Mandraik was his father, Kohanta is still a blood relative. They would be able to give him the love he needs and hopefully break any influence that his father may have had on him."

"That sounds fine to me, but aren't the ones that are given wardship suppose to be of the same class distinction as the parents of the child?"

"Yes, and Brock and Selina already qualify in that respect. Selina because she's Trocon's daughter, and Brock because he's a cousin to the royal family." she points out. "Trocon will be taking over Mandraik's position and I want to offer Brock Trocon's as our High Councilor. If we explain to the council that his advice to us has been extremely useful, I think that they will agree to his taking the position. When it comes right down to it, I would feel better having him to advise us then any of the others at this point. Besides that, I think that he's waited long enough for a higher position."

"I would rather he be our chief advisor as well. We can discuss it with Trocon and Brock tomorrow." He assures her setting down his glass before pulling her into his arms. "For now, I want to forget about everyone else for a while and concentrate on just the two of us." Before she can say anything, he kisses her deeply while running his hands up and down her back. Leyla wraps her arms around his neck and moves closer, rubbing her body against his.

Never releasing her mouth, Thayer lifts her into his arms and carries her into their bedroom. Slowly he lets her slide down his body when they reach the bed. Releasing her mouth, he steps back a little and kinetically removes her clothes. With a smiling gasp, Leyla does the same for him and then they come together once again, then tumble onto the bed. They kiss and stroke each other slowly and tenderly, coming together in slow stages that increases their desire with each passing moment. They draw their pleasure out for as long as possible, then suddenly at the last moment they metamorphose into their other selves as they come together. For several minutes the two great birds mate in mid air, and then return to their human forms. They stay together for several more minutes as their climax continues to run through them. Once it finally stops, Thayer collapses against Leyla weak from their experience.

After a few moments, Thayer carefully pulls from her and lies down beside her. When their breathing returns to normal, he goes up on one arm to look down at her. "It happened this time, didn't it?" he gently runs his hand over her stomach.

Smiling up at him, Leyla places her hand over his and holds it more firmly against her. "Yes, it happened this time." With her other hand she brings his mouth down to hers.

Kissing her deeply for several seconds, he pulls back a little to look into her eyes. "How do you feel about it? I know that you wanted to wait a while before we started our family..."

"I don't mind darling." Running their joined hands over her stomach she smiles up at him again. "We've already started our family with Salis. Besides, the Great One is showing us that things will be fine for us. I'm glad that it's happened now. It means that our bond is even stronger then it was before and will only get stronger as it grows and strengthens as our child grows and strengthens within me."

Laying back down, Thayer pulls her into his embrace. Together they lay quietly and think of their children and their future together. It was looking brighter and brighter as each day, each hour, each minute passed. Before neither had dared to dream of such happiness as they were now experiencing.

"We need to go and spend some time with Salis and Mother." Leyla kisses him and then sits up, climbing from their bed. "From the way mother was moving around Rachel's rooms, I think she'll be up and around very soon. Rachel seems to think that she may even be able to move into her own rooms tomorrow." she tells him walking over to her clothes chest and pulling out a pale blue caftan and pulling it over her head.

Getting up and going over to his own chest for fresh clothes, Thayer looks over his shoulder at her. "Do you want her to return to Earth with us when we go?"

Leyla frowns slightly as she brushes out her hair. "I'd like nothing more then to keep her all to myself, but Dad needs her more than I do. Yes, I want her to return with us. Even though it will be a shock to him, Dad really needs her with him right now. Before he left, I felt as though he were pulling away from me. He needs her to bring him back into himself."

Buttoning his shirt, Thayer walks over to stand behind her and puts his hands on her shoulders. "All right, we'll take her with us, but we need to check with Rachel to make sure that it will be safe for her to travel. I don't want to take any chances with her health at this point."

"Then we'll talk to Rachel before mentioning it to mother. I don't know about you, but I don't want to tell mother that she can't go if she decides that she is going." and Leyla gives a little shudder at the thought of what her mother would have to say about that.

They leave their chamber and quietly discuss the baby that they had just conceived. They decide to wait until everything is settled back on Earth before telling anyone but Salis about the baby.

# Chapter XVI

Over the next several days, preparations are made for the journey to Earth. The ships are made ready to accommodate the large force that would be going with Leyla and Thayer, plus the three hundred or more that would be coming back to Calidon with them on their return.

Sarah and Stephen go over star charts looking for the quickest possible way to Earth using hypersonic and light-speeds. They knew from the reports that Thayer has gotten from Logan, that they needed to get back to Earth within two weeks of their takeoff date, which was scheduled to take place in two days time.

"If we take them through the Orpheus system and then through Cygnus and Aquila, we should get there in a week and a half." Sarah shows him the route on the view screen, highlighting how they would go.

"We would have to get the passage codes from the Federation to go through those systems Sarah. Leyla doesn't want to have to bring them into this unless its absolutely necessary. How would she explain to them the fact that she is taking four ships filled with soldiers from a neutral world, to a world known for its aggressiveness? They would want a very good explanation for not only that, but for the reason a neutral world would even need such people when they had signed a non-aggressive pact with the Federation nearly thirty years ago through her own father."

"Why should she have to tell them anything about the people on any of the ships? For all they know, we could be showing them the political atmosphere on Earth. Or she could just tell them that we are going to Earth to escort a large number of Calidonians home." she explains reasonably. "Because most of that is a lie Sarah, and you know that she will not lie to them and dishonor Saitun's name. It is a show of force and there is no other way to explain it." he tells her walking around the control room thinking about the situation and how to help Leyla without creating any problems for her.

"I could always use the special codes that Saitun gave me to get us through. The Federation wouldn't realize that they had been used for a military type force until we'd been on Earth for a few days at least."

He stops his pacing to turn and face her monitor system. "They would know as soon as one of their agents informed them of our landing."

"Yes, but if Leyla could send Saitun a message as to what we were doing, he could waylay them from interfering too soon."

"All right, say that Saitun agrees to such a plan. He would be jeopardizing his commission with the Federation for illegal use of their codes. Not to mention the huge fine that Calidon would incur, and have to pay not only to the Federation, but to the people of Aquila and Panthera who's systems we would be traveling through."

"What is the big deal about why the warriors are going anyway? The Federation wants Earth brought under control as soon as possible anyway, and that's just what we're going to do. I think that she should go ahead and just tell them the truth and get it over with." Sarah huffs. "Calidon would be within their rights to retrieve their people from a situation that is detrimental to their society and beliefs. Federation law gives them that right. What Carrison and the Security Council are forcing these people to do goes against all of their beliefs and is causing them undue pain and suffering. If the Federation can't see..."

"All right, all right! Don't blow your circuits over it! I'll let Leyla and Thayer know about everything that we've discussed, and we'll see what they want to do. After all the final decision is theirs anyway." he reminds her gently. "I'll be back in a few hours to let you know what they decide to do." He turns to leave shaking his head.

"All right." He leaves the control room. "I had the technicians turn one of the smaller storage units into a private room for you. You can use it to recharge, and to get away from all the humans when you want." She tells him shyly as he walks through the ship.

"Does that include getting away from you and your nagging as well?" he asks innocently and then laughs as Sarah screeches at him and closes the ships outer door swiftly almost catching him as he steps off the ship.

* * *

"So that's the best we've found. The only other course would take us nearly four weeks, possibly as much as five." Stephen informs Leyla and Thayer in their sitting room. True to his word, he had told them everything that he and Sarah had discussed.

"All right Stephen, thank you. Why don't you go and finish programming the wrist linguist. We'll let you know what we decide shortly." She dismisses him and Stephen goes to the small work area that he had made out of a pantry in the small kitchen area of the private chamber. "So what do we do Thayer? Do we tell them the truth or lie for all we're worth and hope that they don't interfere?" Leyla asks pacing around the room.

"I think that we should contact Saitun and see what he thinks we should do. He has a right to decide his fate with the Federation. Who knows, he may even have a plan of his own." He steps in front of her to stop her pacing and places his hands on her shoulders. "Don't worry we'll find a way. We just need to think everything through carefully, and make sure that nothing unexpected happens."

She looks up into his eyes and then slowly nods her agreement. "All right, but let him know why we need to get there as quickly as possible. I want him to know that we wouldn't be considering using his codes if it wasn't absolutely necessary."

Thayer kisses her. "I'm sure that he would know that Love." Releasing her, he goes to lay down on the sofa. Once he's comfortable he closes his eyes and concentrates on reaching Saitun Katmen.

Leyla watches him closely as he goes deeper and deeper in to a trance like stake. When she hears Salis and her mother enter the room through the outer door, she turns to them and holds a finger to her lips to signal that they need to keep quiet.

'He's trying to contact father.' she tells her mother. 'Sarah and Stephen found a way to Earth that will take a week and a half. The only trouble is that two of the star systems are designated as Federation protected. We can't get through them without authorization codes.'

'Which systems?' Aeneka asks moving closer to her daughter. Since the cloning, Aeneka has felt a stronger emotional bond to her daughter than she ever thought was possible. The need to be closer seemed to increase each time they were in the same room together no matter how long they've been apart.

'Cygnus and Aquila. I'm not too familiar with them, but I think that they took a the nonviolence oath a long time ago. Long before father came to Calidon.'

Aeneka frowns slightly trying to remember anything she had heard of those systems. 'I remember. Both of those systems agreed to trade with the Federation as long as the Federation promised that their star systems would not be used as a go between for aggressive forces.'

'Do you think if we talked to their leaders and explained why we need to go through their systems with our warriors, they would let us go through without breaking their trade agreement with the Federation?'

'It's possible, since they know that Calidon is not a violent or aggressive world either. They would have learned this through their contacts with the Federation, and no doubt have been keeping up on our dealings over the years. It may even help us in the long run.'

Just then Thayer sits up and runs his hands through his hair. He smiles when he sees Salis and Aeneka. "Good afternoon ladies. I hope you enjoyed your stroll in the gardens."

Salis sits down beside him and hugs his arm to her. "We did daddy. Grandmother showed me the place where she first met grandfather." She laughs and looks over at her mother and Aeneka. "Did you know that when they first met, grandfather scared her so bad that she tossed him into the big fountain?" She giggles and Aeneka blushes.

Leyla smiles at her mother's blush, remembering when she had heard the story and her mother had blushed then too. She then becomes serious once again as she faces Thayer. "What did father have to say?"

"He says that unless we want the Federation to dictate our actions in the future, we'll have to find another way. He also said that if we were to use his codes, not only would he lose his commission, but he could also spend time in one of their penal colonies as well."

"Now what? There's no way the Federation will let us have the codes, and we don't have time to go the other way." Leyla says in frustration and begins pacing around the room again.

"Why don't you just do like you suggested before and contact them yourself? Explain everything to them, don't leave anything out. I believe that they will give their consent and there will be nothing that the Federation can do about it."

"Contact who? Get who's consent? What are you talking about Aeneka?" Thayer asks in confusion looking from her to his mate and back again.

"If we contact the leaders of the systems we need to go through, and explain what's been happening, our reasons for wanting to use their systems, I'm sure that they would give us safe passage." she explains.

"I just wish that we knew more about them." Leyla tells them stopping in front of one of the armchairs and flopping down in it.

"Why don't you ask Sarah?" Salis asks looking at each of the adults. "She knows a lot about planets and things. Maybe she knows about these ones too."

All three look at her and Thayer gives her a hug. "Out of the mouth's of babes." he says to no one in particular. Leyla pushes the call button for Stephen and within a few seconds he enters the sitting room.

"Yes Leyla?"

"Stephen, have Sarah relay all the information she has on the people of the two systems we need to go through into your memory please."

Nodding Stephen closes his eyes. Recently he had installed an internal communication link that allows him and Sarah to communicate privately almost as Leyla and the others do. After a few minutes his eyes open.

"Both systems are inhabited by people that are psi capable, though they are not totally human. In the Cygnus system are the Pantherians, part human, part cat. When they were first approached by the Federation, it was to enlist their men to train Federation troops to move quietly during a ground fight. After a couple of years, they decided that there was too much aggression in the hearts and minds of the Federation, and called their warriors back home." he states as if reading from a report. "The Aquilians are part human, part bird. They are totally non- aggressive, and refuse all contact with any species that participates in or condones slavery of any kind. Both are looking for allies to help them combat the growing aggression surrounding their systems, since the Federation is not doing it as was promised."

"Do you know who the leaders of these worlds are? What their names and distinctions are?" Thayer asks.

"The leaders of Panthera are Baylynx and his mate Leonessa, they are the high King and Queen of their world. Faucon and Jamia are the high King and Queen of Aquila."

"So how do we contact them? Telepathically or through the communications center? Since we're not familiar with their brain patterns, contact telepathically could be difficult and dangerous for us as well as them if we aren't compatible." Thayer asks him with a frown.

"I would suggest that your first contact be by way of the comm-center." Stephen puts in. "It would establish a base of trust that you could lose by entering their minds without their prior knowledge or consent."

"He's right darling. I'll contact Selina and have her start trying to reach them. Though with the distance between us I don't know if the center has enough energy to make it." Looking up at the ceiling, Leyla sets her mind to contacting Selina. Seconds later she blushes and looks down quickly. "Ah, she'll get in touch with us in a little while."

"What's the matter mother?" Salis asks puzzled by Leyla's facial expression.

"From the looks of that blush, I'd say she interrupted something very personal between Selina and Brock." Thayer tells her and then laughs as Leyla glares at him.

"No doubt you've never interrupted anyone when they were...in that situation?" she asks still glaring at him.

"Not since I was about ten years old and interrupted my parents." He admits with a blush of his own at the memory. "After having my backside warmed, I learned to send out a probe before making full contact."

"Well now that we've got that settled, I don't know about the rest of you, but I could use a cool drink." Aeneka changes the subject and moves over to the refreshment tray. She knew that Leyla's mistake was not entirely her own fault. Neither Saitun or herself had ever taught her to send out a seeking probe before making contact.

"If you don't need me any longer Leyla? I'll go and finish the wrist linguist. I've almost completed the programming and it will be ready soon for duplication."

"Yes, go ahead Stephen, and thank Sarah for the information." Leyla dismisses him.

Thayer joins Aeneka at the tray and pours drinks for the rest of them. He hands them out and then sits on the arm of the sofa. "I think that we should think about some form of payment to offer the Pantherians and Aquilians if they don't have something in mind when we speak with them." he suggests taking a sip of his juice.

"But what could we offer? From what I can understand, they keep to themselves, isolated from other species so that they don't have to worry about corruptive influences." Leyla points out.

"What do we have that would benefit either of them? If they're anything like Calidon and Manchon, they're pretty self sufficient." Aeneka puts in. She sits down next to Salis on the sofa and looks down at her drink trying to think of something that they could offer.

"Couldn't we give them information?" Salis asks softly. The adults look at her. "I mean...we could tell them things that they would need to know and may not find out themselves. Like if someone was planning something against them or something. If they don't have contact with anyone except for the Federation, how do they know that what they're being told is the truth? Grandfather would know and could tell us if something wasn't right."

"She has something there. We all know that the Federation doesn't always deal truthfully with the more passive systems. They think that because we don't believe in war that we're ignorant in other areas." Thayer stands and begins pacing the room. "With Aquila and Panthera, we could form a telepathic alliance that could keep tabs on the systems within their range." He's interrupted by a knock at the outer door.

Salis jumps up and runs to answer it. Selina and Brock enter the room and once again Leyla blushes. Thayer laughs and she glares at him, before walking over to Selina. "Thank you for coming." 'I am so sorry about earlier.'

'Its all right Leyla. I think that Brock was more embarrassed then either one of us.' Selina reassures her. "What can I do for you?"

"Is there enough power in the comm-center generators to reach the Pantherian and Aquilian systems in a short amount of time?" Leyla asks her walking over to stand beside Thayer.

"Well, at full power and with connecting relays we can transmit for about forty minutes." Selina tells her walking further into the room and smiling at Salis and Aeneka. "But it would all depend on how many relays we would have to use, and if we would have to wait any length of time."

"Is there any way to do it without using the relays?" Thayer asks thinking that anyone could tap into the communication through one of the relays.

Selina sits down on the love seat next to Brock, and thinks about it for a few minutes before shaking her head. "I can't think of any other way. We don't have enough power to do a direct link to their systems. As it is, we will be draining power from other power sites on Calidon."

Leyla frowns in confusion. "Then how did I receive all of my lessons over the years? Those took place for two to three hours at a time."

"That was done by a special collective sweetheart." Aeneka explains. She hands Selina and then Brock a glass of juice. "Your teachers and grandparents gathered together and added their energy to send the lessons. It was done that way so that the power units wouldn't be drained too much if there was an emergency."

"Couldn't we use a collective as a power source now?"

"I don't think so Thayer. It's just as draining on the people and we'd have to take the time to get everyone into the perfect mind sync."

"How long?"

"Longer then we have." Leyla says beginning to pace. After several seconds, she stops and faces the others. "What if Thayer and I act as the additional power source? We have the energy needed, and we're already in perfect sync with each other."

"True, but one of you would be needed to communicate with their leaders. It would only be natural for the leaders of Calidon to make the contact." Brock points out setting down his glass and looking at his cousin.

"He's right love. One of us would have to discuss things and I can't see either of us being able to hold both forms at the same time." Thayer points out quietly.

"What about Trocon? He's the High Chancellor, he has the authority to act on our behalf." Leyla asks but Aeneka shakes her head in the negative.

"It has to be a member of the royal family. Someone they could trust in, someone that would have nothing to gain by lying to them." She stops and looks at Salis and then at the others. "Salis can be the speaker. She's your daughter, and her word would be trusted. A child would have no reason to lie to them about such a serious matter."

Salis looks at her grandmother in surprise and pales slightly. "But I don't know how...I mean...I don't know what to say...how to explain." She stammers looking at her parents.

"We can implant all the information that you would need sweetheart." Leyla assures her walking over to her and kneeling down in front of her and taking her hands. "We'll place everything that you need to know into your memory and then when you speak to them you can use your own words. Your grandmother and Stephen will be with you for support, and so will Brock and Selina. I know that what we're asking you to do is frightening sweetheart, but it's also very important. Remember the holograms that we showed you? Well those people need us right away. They're part of our family too. You'll be helping them as much as your father and I are."

"Grandmother will stay with me the whole time?" she asks looking at Aeneka.

"The whole time sweetie. I'll introduce you and explain about your parents. All you have to do is tell them your parents wishes." Aeneka assures her.

Salis looks back at Leyla and then over to where Thayer is standing. "This would be my first official Princess duty wouldn't it?" she asks with a small smile.

"Yes it would Salis." Thayer returns her smile and Leyla squeezes her hands gently.

"Okay, I can do it." she tells them sitting a little straighter. Proud that she could do something to help. "Good girl." Leyla pats her on the leg and then stands up and turns to Brock. "We'll need the main comm room secure. No one but those in this chamber are to be anywhere near that room, except for maybe Trocon and Kasmen. Selina, please go and prepare for the transmission. There won't be any need for a scrambler to be used. We should be able to handle that as well." Selina and Brock are already standing, and nod before leaving quickly to get everything ready. "Mother, would you go and explain to Stephen what we'll be doing while we prepare Salis?"

"Of course dear." Aeneka leaves the room and Leyla pulls Salis to her feet gently.

Thayer walks over to stand beside them. "Now Salis, you'll feel a bit of pressure behind your eyes as we give you the information. Just relax and it will make it a little easier for you to accept the information. Ready?" He asks running a hand over her hair. Salis takes a deep breath and then nods.

Slowly they start to feed Salis the information that she will need. As she becomes accustomed to the transfer they gradually increase the speed, always being careful not to hurt her. After almost ten minutes, they stop and gently pull back from her mind.

Salis sags a little and Leyla wraps an arm around her waist to help her stand upright. Several seconds pass before she is able to stand on her own and she pulls slightly away from her mother.

"Are you all right honey?" Leyla asks in concern looking into her eyes.

"Yes. That was so weird, and it felt strange."

Aeneka and Stephen enter the room. Stephen is carrying a small wristband and walks over to Salis and places it on her right wrist. "If they speak in any language that is unknown to you this device will translate it for you and translate your speech for them."

"Thank you Stephen." She smiles up at him after looking over the translator.

"We had better go now. Selina and Brock are ready for us." Leyla takes her hand and they leave the chamber followed by the others.

As soon as they leave the chambers, the guards surround them. Two in the front, one on each side towards the middle, and finally two at the rear of the little group.

Stephen grumbles about wasting good men, when he was perfectly capable of protecting the royal family himself. Everyone laughs and teases him about not wanting to admit that he didn't have to worry about Leyla's safety any more.

"Don't worry Stephen, I won't shut you off. Besides, you're in charge of Salis now. That ought to keep you fairly busy for a couple of years anyway." Leyla reassures him.

When they reach the comm-center, the guards wait outside, while they enter. Selina quickly explains the power and circuitry used in the center.

"Is it possible to contact both Panthera and Aquila at the same time?" Thayer asks wanting to reduce the time he and Leyla would have to stay transformed.

"It should be, since they're in the same quadrant. We'll try and establish contact with Aquila first, since they are the farthest from us. Then we can pull in Panthera." Selina says making some quick calculations.

"Okay then. Give us about three minutes after we transform to establish our link with the unit before you start sending." Leyla suggests before stepping off to one side where she and Thayer will be far enough away from the others.

* * *

"Those are my parent's plans and offer Majesties. Our people need to be home with their families. They need to be at peace and to know that the evil is gone. That their families are now safe and will suffer no more harm."

There is a long silence from both the leaders of Panthera and Aquila. Salis watches them and then looks over her shoulder at Aeneka. 'Do you think that they'll agree grandmother?'

'I believe that they will little one.'

Salis looks back at the view screen feeling deep within her that Leyla is beginning to weaken. "Majesties, please forgive me for rushing you, but my parents need to rest soon. If you would like to think on it some..." She lets her voice trail off as they all face her once more.

"There is no need for Baylynx and I to think any longer on it Princess Salis. We grant you safe passage to and from Earth through Pantherian space." Leonessa says with a soft purring voice.

"Jamia and I also will give you safe passage to and from Earth. An alliance between our planets and people is a very good idea don't you agree Baylynx?"

"Yes Faucon, it is. We both know how the non-psi can twist things so much in their own minds that it is hard for even them to find the truth in their own heads." Baylynx growls.

"Very well. On behalf of my parents, and our people, I thank you all. My parents will contact you from our ship when we're in range. May the Great One bless and guide you all."

The others give the same farewell and then Selina cuts the transmission. A few minutes later Leyla and Thayer return to their human forms. Suddenly Leyla collapses, and Thayer barely catches her before she hits the floor. Slowly he lowers them both to sit down on the floor.

"Mother!", "Leyla!" Salis and Aeneka cry out as she collapses and rush to her side.

"It's all right, I'm fine. Just a little tired." she assures them smiling weakly. "Just give me a minute to catch my breath." She leans back against Thayer with a sigh.

"Selina, would you get her something to drink please?" Thayer asks anxiously.

"Sure Thayer. I know just what she needs." Selina hurries over to the dispenser and orders a high energy revitalizer for both of them. She hands one to each of them. "This should help to raise your energy levels back to normal or close to it."

"Thanks." Thayer says as they both drink slowly. When they're finished they both feel a little stronger, and Leyla is able to sit up on her own.

"Thank you Selina, I feel fine now. That drink did help a lot." Thayer stands up and helps her to her feet, steadying her when she sways slightly. Leyla turns to Salis. "You did wonderfully sweetheart. I'm so proud of you. You even said some things that were strictly your own." She hugs her and kisses her cheek.

"It wasn't as hard as I thought it was going to be. They were really nice, and Leonessa and Jamia are very beautiful and easy to talk to."

"Baylynx and Faucon weren't too hard on the eyes either." Selina says with a grin and then laughs as Brock growls at her and takes a menacing step forward.

"That's enough you two." Aeneka scolds. "I think that Leyla and Thayer need to get some rest now. The energy drinks will help, but what they really need is to get a couple of hours sleep." She tells them all and then heads for the door.

"Mother's right. I could use a nap right now. That was a little more draining then I thought it would be." Leyla admits stretching and then putting an arm around Salis. "You can tell us all about what you thought of the Pantherian and Aquilian leaders when we get up. All right?"

"Okay mother. Can I help Stephen with the linguist bands while you rest? I promise not to get in his way." She asks looking up at Stephen.

"It's fine with me Leyla. Sarah and I could continue explaining to her about Earth and your relationship with the Blackwood family."

"That sounds like a good idea Stephen. Just make sure that she's back in time to change for the evening meal." She kisses Salis again and then takes Thayer's arm after he gives her a kiss too. "We'll see you in a couple of hours sweetheart. Have fun."

They all separate as they leave the center. Two of the guards fall into step on either side of Aeneka as she goes to visit with Rachel. Krander joins Salis and Stephen, while the others go with Leyla and Thayer.

Leyla leans into Thayer once more and smiles to herself. Salis was dealing quite well with her new position, and the responsibilities that it had brought to her. She was beginning to come out of her shell and act more like a little girl should. Things were beginning to look a lot better for her immediate family. She just hoped that they would look just as good for her extended family as well.

# Chapter XVII

By the time Leyla and the others are ready to leave for Earth, all of Mandraik's people that have been captured, have had him wiped from their memories. It had been discovered that the only ones that hadn't been threatened or blackmailed into helping him, were those in his immediate family or people very close to them.

Mandraik's family believed that it was their time to rule the people of Calidon. They felt that the House Chaukcee had done nothing to improve the wealth of Calidon or its high ranking families. They felt that Calidon should have been an active member of the Federation all those years ago and then they could have used their abilities to take total control of the Federation.

The decision was made to mind wipe and reeducate these people who had decided that slavery and conquest was an acceptable way of life. Their lands and money were seized and divided up amongst the people that had suffered the most because of Dacus and his family's evils.

Kasmen and Rachel where already in control and would make sure that everything was made ready for their return with the missing Calidonians. "We will have everything set by the time you get back Leyla." Kasmen assures her once again. "The families understand that their people will be monitored before any of them will be allowed to join them. Some have even volunteered to help out if needed."

"That's good Kasmen, thank you. Rachel, will you have enough help for any wounded or unstable patients we may bring back?" Leyla asks turning to the older woman.

"There will be enough help. Healers from all over the planet will be here to assist where they are needed." She smiles at Leyla and Thayer. "There should be no need for the two of you to do more then any other."

At last its time to leave and Leyla and Thayer enter the ship waving farewell as they go. Stephen meets them in the entrance passageway.

"Salis and the others are with Aeneka in the control room. Sarah says the pilots can take off and pilot us through this system, but she's taking control of all the ships."

"How does she plan to do that? She's on...Oh no! She didn't!" Leyla squeaks.

"I'm afraid she did. I had no idea she had done it until this morning when I came to do the last check." Stephen shrugs his shoulders. "It might be better this way. At least we'd all get there at the same time."

Thayer looks from one to the other. "Would one of you mind telling me exactly what Sarah has done?"

Leyla looks up at him. "She had her portable duplicated and put a box in each of the ships. Now instead of one Sarah to contend with, we now have five."

"Great so we're looking at a possible mutiny if she gets out of hand on the other ships."

"That won't happen darling, I promise." Leyla assures him patting his arm. "I'll have a talk with her before she takes over any of the ships."

They take the turbo lift up to the control deck. As they enter the control room, they can hear Aeneka arguing with Sarah. "You don't have to tell them their jobs Sarah. They have been trained to pilot the ships, so let them get on with it."

"But I've modified the systems for better..."

"Sarah, your modifications won't make a difference to how they pilot the ships. They're for navigation and protection. Things that will be needed at hypersonic speeds."

Leyla steps forward. "Sarah, release control of the ships so that we can leave. When you're done doing that, transfer to the conference room." a couple of beeps can be heard and then the engines start. "Gentlemen and ladies, you may proceed. Contact the others and let them know that we're taking off now. Mother, we'll meet you and the others in the lounge in about fifteen minutes."

"Okay sweetheart. See you both in a little while."

Stephen leads the way to the conference room and steps aside for Leyla and Thayer to enter. "You better come in too Stephen. We may need you to help pursued her to do as she's ordered." Thayer tells him looking back at Stephen standing outside the door. Stephen enters the room and the door swishes closed behind him. They all face the monitor.

"Okay Sarah, why did you place portables of yourself on the other ships?" Leyla asks her quietly.

"It will make it easier when we make our speed jumps for me to control the ships, so that we all make the jumps at the same time." She explains. "If left to the humans..."

"If left to the humans, it would still get done. Sarah, you've already programmed the navigation systems for the route we're taking. It doesn't matter if we make the jumps at the same time, as long as we reach our destination." Thayer points out gently. "It's better that the men have control of their ships to feel in control. They know how to run them Sarah. They'll be with us through to the end, whether your piloting or they are."

"But I don't need to rest, and they do." she reminds them. "There aren't enough pilots to fly so that they can all get adequate rest."

"Then take over when the pilots need to rest, and give them back control when they're ready." Leyla tells her. "You'll have other functions to carry out as well. I'll make sure that you don't get bored."

"I still think that..." she gets no further as Stephen steps forward.

"Enough Sarah. Leyla and Thayer have told you what they want you to do, so do it and don't argue with them about it any longer. And if I catch you harassing the warriors or pilots, I will personally give your circuits an overhaul. Do you understand what I'm telling you?" he asks in a quiet but firm voice.

"Yes." she answers quietly.

"Good. Now check with the pilots on how far the ships are and how they are handling. Calculate when we will clear this star system."

Leyla and Thayer smile at each other and then Leyla looks to Stephen. "We're going to join the others in the lounge. Why don't you go and charge yourself up for a few hours, rest your memory circuits?"

Stephen nods and follows them from the room. When Leyla and Thayer head for the lifts, he heads back to the control room for one final check. He didn't completely trust Sarah to do as she was told.

As Leyla and Thayer walk into the lounge, they see Salis sitting at an instrument that looks like a harpsichord, playing a gentle song. They stand near the door, waiting and listening while she finishes playing, before walking further into the room.

"That was beautiful honey." Leyla smiles at her daughter as she claps along with the others.

"She reminds me of when your grandmother use to play." Aeneka smiles and wipes a few tears from her cheeks. "I don't think that I was ever as good as Salis, but mother always said that it didn't matter how good you played, as long as you tried and carried the songs in your heart."

"My father always said that we think less of our own abilities then others do." Thayer tells them as he goes to the dispenser to get Leyla and himself a drink. "I always thought my flute sounded like a sick cat whenever I played it."

Everyone laughs with him and then they each tell what they think of the instruments they've played and how they sounded. Trocon is the one to finally break the mood to discuss their plans for when they finally reach Earth. "Do you plan to confront this man, President Carrison right away, or wait until you've contacted your people at the stronghold?"

"I think that the best thing for us to do is to go straight to Carrison." Thayer says sitting forward. "Logan feels that Peterton may try to use our people to destroy the stronghold if he can't regain control of those already at the stronghold."

"How many are there?" Brock asks standing and moving over to the window portal.

"Five, two men and three women. The homing devices surgically implanted, were removed at the place they were captured to insure my family's safety. None of them wish to return to Peterton's control."

"Do they have any idea how many of our people feel the same?" Selina asks running her hand along the arm of her chair.

"As near as they can all figure, about three fourths of the people feel the same." he says looking at her.

"There's something else that we need to tell you, that we didn't want to reveal back on Calidon." Leyla says softly and waits until she has everyone's attention. "At least half of our people have been bred with Earth men and women."

Everyone gasps in shock and Brock spins away from the window. Selina puts her hands over her mouth, and Trocon falls back against his seat. Salis just sits there staring off into the distance.

"We're going to have to warn the warriors before we get to Earth." Brock warns them and walks closer. "Some of them have family members that were taken, and it will be a shock to them to find this out."

Thayer stands and walks over to Brock, placing a hand on his shoulder. "We'll tell them in a few days, but not right now. If you know which ones are involved, have them ready to meet with us. It would be best if we separate them from the others until they can accept this. We'll tell the others after that. I don't want to take any chances of tempers flaring or other emotions effecting everyone."

"What about the children from these unions?" Trocon asks looking to Leyla. "Our people will not give up their children. But keeping them may cause problems with their families on Calidon."

"I don't think that it will be a problem Trocon. Our people love their children too much to hold something like this against them." Aeneka points out reasonably. "The problem we may have is with the Earth parents. Some won't want to let them go. We need to find some type of compromise so that no one, least of all the children, are hurt by any of this."

"What if we brought the Earth parents back to Calidon with us? Or at least the ones that don't want to lose their children." Salis asks looking at Leyla and Thayer. "If they've been mated with our people, wouldn't that mean that they have some psi capabilities too?" She looks around at all of the adults. "From what I've learned from Sarah and Stephen this would be the President's way to get controllable Earth telepaths."

"That could be possible with Carrison, but I don't know about the other. What about our people's families back on Calidon? A lot of them have mates. How do they act when their mates return with another mate and children from those mates? How are these new mates going to live, going to be treated?" Leyla asks her daughter, wanting her to consider all aspects of the situation. She watches as Salis chews on her lower lip and looks down at the harpsichord.

"They could be the Langtoini, the second family!" she cries out excitedly. "Queen Latona once told me about it. A husband had been separated from his wife by a mind block of some kind, it had wiped out all memory of that wife. He mated with another and had two children with her before he regained his memory. He went to his first mate and explained about his second. They went before the King and Queen to ask that a law be made that would protect both mates and be fair. Each of the wives was given a house of her own. They were all charged with the care of any and all children. Also included in the law was the right of the second mate to become first mate to another. The children of the second mate could decide if they wished to live with the mother or father without any hurt feelings. The parents still share responsibilities and the family ties remain the same, but because of the new mate, they become separate." Salis finally finishes and Selina smiles at her.

"I understand what you're suggesting. Bring them all back and let Earth parents find new single mates on Calidon. That way they'll still be with their children."

"Yes! They're just as much victims as our own people are. Who knows, they may not even want to come to Calidon. It would give them a chance to start over, to get away from their enemies and any bad memories they may have."

"All right. We have an idea put before us. The seven of us must now decide if it is the best one for all those concerned." Leyla says looking to each of them. "On this journey we will advise our people on what decisions we have made that concern them and allow them to agree or disagree with those decisions. If someone disagrees, we will get their reasons for disagreeing, and see if they have any other suggestions. In all of this, we must all consider the ramifications to everyone for our actions. Now I think that we all need to think on what Salis has suggested, and meet again in thirty-six hours. That will give everyone time to consider everything very closely."

Everyone nods their agreement. Before they can begin discussing anything else, they are interrupted by the buzz of the ships communicator. Selina walks over to the unit to answer it. "Chief Damori here."

"Chief Damori, the cook wishes to let the King and Queen know that the noon repast will be ready in one hour."

"Thank you." she cuts the connection and turns back to the others. "I don't know about the rest of you, but I need to freshen up." She walks over to Brock and takes his hand. "Come on sweet. If you're real nice I'll let you scrub my back for me."

Salis looks at her puzzled. "How can he scrub your back Selina? The showers are sonic now." and looks to her parents and grandmother for an explanation.

Selina blushes as the others breakout in laughter. "You'll understand when you get older and find a mate little one." Brock tells her and pulls his wife into his arms. "We'll see you all at lunch." With that he pulls Selina from the room.

"I believe that I will have a small rest before the meal." Trocon tells them, standing and following Selina and Brock from the room.

"What about you Mother? Are you going to rest for the hour before lunch?"

"No, I think that I'll go over the files that Sarah has of your father's. I want to make sure that what I am remembering is right, that I haven't lost any or my memories." Aeneka says with a slight frown.

"Okay, we'll see you later at lunch then." Leyla gives her a hug and then watches her leave with a look of concern. Shaking her head slightly, she turns to Salis. "How would you like to practice your shielding before we go to lunch? Your father and I want you to be able to be able to protect yourself with as little effort as possible. I'd like it if it could become second nature for you."

"Could we really? That will be great." She agrees looking at the door. She shakes her head and then turns to her mother. "Can Stephen come and help?"

"That sounds like a good idea to me angel. He can act as your attacker, and test your shields." Thayer puts in and walks over to the comm to call Stephen.

"Wait Thayer. Stephen is recharging." Leyla reminds him. "Why don't we see if Krander would like to help out? I'm sure that he would enjoy helping with your lessons." she watches Salis' eyes brighten.

"Could he? Can I ask him?"

"Sure honey." Thayer signals her to come over to the communicator. He shows her how to use it and then steps back and allows her to work it for herself.

Salis pushes the button and then calls up Krander. "Yes Princess?" Krander answers questioningly.

"Would you like to help me with my shielding lesson before lunch?"

"I would like to very much Princess. Will it be all right with your parents for me to help you though?"

"Yes, mother suggested it. She thought that you would enjoy helping."

"I would enjoy it. Where shall I meet you for this lesson Princess?"

Salis looks at Leyla and Thayer. 'Tell him to meet us at the exercise room in a few minutes.' Thayer tells her.

"Meet us in the exercise room in a few minutes Krander."

"As you wish Princess."

Salis cuts the connection and turns to her parents. "Krander won't get hurt during the lesson will he?"

"No sweetheart, he won't get hurt. We'll practice a mild shielding. One that will keep him back a few feet from you." Leyla assures her. "At the most, he will receive a few bumps and bruises, and possibly a shock or two, but nothing that will really harm him. Besides, if I remember my lessons correctly, all warriors were required to help in the shielding practice of each other. He should know what to expect."

Salis nods and they leave the lounge. Walking through the corridors, Leyla and Thayer explain to her how to strengthen her shields just enough to keep Krander out of reach without hurting him.

They meet up with Krander outside the exercise room. "Thank you for helping out like this Krander. The shield that we plan for Salis to use against you will only be powerful enough to keep you a few feet away from her." Leyla explains as they enter the room. "You may end up with a few bruises and shocks before this session is over with, but nothing too painful."

"It wouldn't matter even if they were your Majesty. As long as the Princess is able to defend herself in some way, the pain would be well worth it."

They begin the lesson, and at first Salis' shield isn't quite strong enough to keep him away. Soon she discovers the right strength, and creates a decent barrier. By the time they stop for lunch, she is able to keep Krander four feet away from her for several minutes before losing her concentration. Though this frustrates her, Leyla and Thayer assure her that with time she will improve.

"That was perfect sweetheart. Once Stephen is fully recharged, we'll practice for a more aggressive attack and stronger defenses." Leyla gives her a hug at the end and then turns to face Krander. "I thank you again for helping out Krander. If you like, you can go to the sickbay and have the med-tech take care of those bruises for you."

"Thank you your Majesty, but that won't be necessary. I will be honored to show the others the bruises of our Princess' training." He smiles at them with a slight grimace. "If you will excuse me now, I'll go and get cleaned up before the meal." Thayer and Leyla nod their agreement and then follow him from the room.

At lunch they discuss with Salis the things that she did wrong and how she could improve on them. When the others are told of her success, they praise and encourage her to keep at it, assuring her that she will do better.

\* \* \*

When Sarah takes control of the ships, Thayer has Brock gather together all the warriors that have family on Earth. All together there are a hundred and sixty-five warriors with family that had been taken. Leyla carefully explains to them what they may find on Earth in regards to their family members and friends, and the solution they had come up with for dealing with the situation. They explain about the emotional attachments that may have developed and now be involved. They ask everyone to consider their decision and how it will affect those besides themselves.

They are given a few days to think this over, and then they come back with the decision to accept the Earth mates and any children that may be involved. They all agree that the Langtoini law would be fair to all those concerned. All they cared about was getting their loved ones back.

# Chapter XVIII

When they are finally in range of Panthera, Leyla and Thayer contact Baylynx and Leonessa.

"We really do appreciate your allowing us to travel through your system like this. If you hadn't, we would have reached out people and friends too late to keep them from hurting each other unnecessarily."

"We are glad that we can help you." Leonessa informs them. "We understand from your daughter that you are capable of telepathy over long distances of space and time."

"Yes, Thayer can communicate at great distances all by himself. I can only do about half his distance without his help, unless its with someone that I have already touched minds with. He can also reach anyone with Manchon blood, and with our lifemating it is easier to reach Calidonians as well."

"Will you be able to communicate with us and the Aquilians?" Baylynx asks Thayer.

"As long as you're all receptive to it, I don't see any problems. What stage of Alpha are you? It would be safer to know so that we don't use to much power when we touch your minds."

"Leonessa and I are both fours. Our son Lynx is a three, and the strongest on Panthera. Our council is made up of sixes and sevens. Except for our son, we are the highest on Panthera right now. Though one of our seers says that sometime within the next fifteen or twenty years, we will have alpha twos and possibly some ones."

"Then I should be able to communicate with both of you and your alpha six councilors. At our last testing both Leyla and I registered as alpha ones."

"What about your daughter?" Leonessa asks politely.

"Salis is an alpha four right now, but we feel that by the time she comes of age she will be an alpha two possibly even a one." Leyla tells the other woman with a proud smile. "She repressed a lot of her abilities, but her strength is growing steadily stronger with each passing day."

"If you have time on your return, we would be delighted to have you and your warriors stop here for a rest after your campaign."

"That would be nice Leonessa, thank you."

"If you need any other help while you're on Earth, just contact us, and we will do what we can." Baylynx tells them just before they end their transmission.

"We will Baylynx. The Great One bless and guide you." Thayer says in farewell.

They have almost the same conversation with Faucon and Jamia when the reach Aquila. They find out that Faucon and Jamia are also alpha fours. They agree to stay open to Leyla and Thayer and suggest that they along with Baylynx and Leonessa meet together as soon as possible after Leyla and Thayer finish on Earth to discuss their alliance.

"I'll contact my family about it. I have no doubt that they will agree to the alliance as well." Thayer tells them. "We'll contact you when we're through on Earth. You can either meet us on Panthera, or we can pick you up on our way back through since we plan to stop there."

"We'll meet you there. Jamia has relatives there that she wishes to visit any way. It will give us an excuse to stay a little longer."

"You mean your two people mate with each other?" Leyla asks with some surprise.

"Yes, though it hasn't happened very often. It started a couple of hundred years ago when several Pantherians came to Aquila after some major loss." Jamia tells her. "All the couples are lifemates, so we know that it is meant to be. Some of our elders are still not quite as sure as the rest of us, but they do nothing to interfere with the matches."

"That sounds promising. I wish them all the blessings of the Great One." Leyla tells them.

"Who knows, maybe all of our people will find their lifemates on one of our worlds." Faucon suggests out loud what they are all now thinking.

"It would definitely strengthen our alliance if that were to happen." Thayer points out. "When we return we can discuss how to unify our people with the least amount of stress on anyone."

"We'll bring it up to Baylynx and Leonessa when we get to Panthera. Good journey and may the Great One guide and protect you even as He blesses you."

\* \* \*

As they near Earth's system, the ships drop from hypersonic down to light-speed. For the final part of the journey, Sarah has control of the ships to insure that they do not deviate from their course the least little bit.

"Earth's sensors will pick us up soon Leyla. What do you want me to do?" Sarah asks as Leyla walks onto the bridge.

"Contact Earth Defense and give them the code that we got from Mandraik's nephew. That should get us to the planet without any trouble."

Sarah sends the code and then waits for a reply. "They want to know the reason for so many ships."

"Tell them that all of the ships are filled with cargo from Calidon for President Carrison. The contents of which are for his eyes only, with no exceptions."

Sarah relays the message and again waits for them to reply. The navigation monitor shows the course that they are to take to Earth. Leyla studies the course and punches up its location on the monitor. "Sarah, tell them that we're under orders to meet with Carrison before making delivery of the cargo."

"They're not going to like that Leyla."

"I know, but that's what I want you to tell them. If they give you any trouble, tell them that if we don't meet with him, we have orders to leave."

Once again Sarah sends the message. "Stand by for course correction." A new course comes onto the monitor and Leyla studies it before punching up the location and giving her agreement.

"Now tell them that the other ships will go to the original vector." She tells her and then mentally calls to Thayer and the others to meet her in the conference room.

"Carrison will meet you at the landing site. As far as they know, you are acting on Mandraik's orders."

"Good, let's keep it that way. Thank you Sarah. Put all the ships on yellow alert and inform the warriors to be ready at all times in case of an attack. I don't want Carrison's people getting the jump on us." With that she turns and leaves the bridge, making her way to the conference room. She is the first to arrive and goes to stand near the window to wait for the others.

Thayer, Salis, and Aeneka come in a few minutes later, and a few minutes after that Trocon, Selina, and finally Brock arrive. Leyla remains facing the window for several more seconds before turning to face the others.

"Phase two is completed. The other ships will proceed to the place where our people are normally taken when they first come to Earth. We'll meet with Carrison at the landing site outside his compound." She walks slowly over to the table. "To make our reception easier, Sarah has told them that we are under Mandraik's orders, as I requested." She turns to Brock. "How many of the royal guard are capable of teleportation?"

"Most of them are capable of long distance, about thirty-five can do short distances, and about twenty can't teleport at all."

"Would the ones that can go short distances be able to carry those that can't port?"

"It might be possible, but I don't think we should take the chance."

"Couldn't we just use the thirty-five, leave the twenty here on the ship to protect it, and send the others out to collect our people that are in this area?" Selina suggests.

"We'll have to. I don't want to risk anyone being taken. The others will move out as soon as Thayer sends word for them to do so. They'll get the records from the prison camp and begin collecting our people."

"How do you plan to handle Carrison and his man Peterton? As soon as you step off this ship they'll know who you are and there's going to be trouble." Brock points out with a frown of concern. "I think that besides the thirty-five, we need at least another twenty-five. With the twenty staying on the ship that will leave a hundred and twenty to secure this area." He drums his fingers on the table top. "With Trocon's guards, there will be ninety guards to protect you if necessary."

"What if some of our people are with Carrison when we arrive? No doubt he will have the strongest ones close at hand." Trocon reminds them. "How do you plan to handle them?"

"I'll neutralize their abilities and Leyla will teleport them to the holding area Stephen installed in the aft cargo bay. If it becomes necessary, we'll surround Carrison and Peterton." Thayer explains. "Brock, I want you to neutralize any weapons they may have. We won't make a move on them except for taking our people. Wait for a signal from me or Leyla before doing anything else."

"Father, why don't we just take them prisoner until we have all our people back?" Salis asks in some confusion. Since they were going to be so close to the people responsible, it seemed like the thing they should do.

Aeneka signals to Thayer that she would answer her granddaughters question, and Thayer nods his agreement.

"We couldn't do that sweetheart. According to Federation law, any act of aggression toward a world leader is considered an act of war. We have to be careful how we proceed, or the Federation will step in and it will become very difficult and dangerous for our people, both here and on Calidon. Carrison has to be even more careful then we do. He can't afford to have the Federation become involved at any cost. So what we need to do is to try and make him try something against us that will validate our taking action that won't draw the Federation in too soon. That's why we need to get to our people. If he has them do anything, there wouldn't be anything that we could legally do against him. It would be considered a civil dispute amongst a separate people."

"Then once our people are secure, we try to trap him into doing something the Federation would consider an act of war against us. But wouldn't they wonder why we didn't just leave after we got our people back?"

"Not really honey. Both your father and I have ties to Earth that can not be disputed by the Federation." Leyla tells her confidently.

"So unless they try to physically assault one of us, the men are to do nothing." Brock states with a deep frown not liking what he is hearing.

"They can monitor Carrison and his people and be ready to act when it's necessary." Thayer tells him. "Besides, there are others that need our help and may end up paying a heavy price if we should fail. We won't take any chances with their lives."

"What about your people at the stronghold? Won't they need some assistance as well?" Trocon asks.

"Not just yet. But everyone is to be ready to go to their aide if Peterton decides to attack. Though many have psi abilities, none of them are above a five. Though Logan Knightrunner is an alpha four, his abilities are somewhat limited."

"Cassie is a five, though she hasn't yet realized her full potential. Daniel is somewhere between a six and a five. Davena and Dessa are both five's. The two youngest, Colt and Merri are the strongest. The last time I tested them they registered as alpha threes, but together they have the power of an alpha one. By the time they have matured they'll most likely be a two or even a one on their own." Leyla informs them. "But none of them are capable of using their abilities longer then a couple of hours while under attack."

"Logan knows when we'll be arriving and has told everyone. If they need us, they'll call."

"Okay, when we disembark Trocon, Selina and I will go out first with Trocon's ten guards. Trocon will announce, you, Leyla and Salis. There will be twenty guards that will come out with you. Thirty guards will go out before any of us, and another thirty will come out after you." Brock tells them and then looks at Aeneka. "Are you sure that you want to stay with the ship Neka?"

"Yes, I'm sure Brock. Sarah and I plan to monitor the Federation transmissions missions and keep track of what they're doing. If it looks like they're moving in I'll contact you." she assures them.

"We'll leave Stephen here with you. Though I trust the guards to protect you, I'd rather he stays close to you. I just don't want to take the chance of anything happening to you." Leyla looks lovingly at her mother.

"You know that he's not going to be happy about this." Aeneka points out. "He had a hard enough time while we were on Calidon, letting you out of his sight. There he didn't really know what danger you were in. Here he does know the people and what danger they hold for you."

"Then I'll have to call up his main function program before he was programmed to be my bodyguard. I don't really believe that I'll have to do that though. Stephen cares about you just as much as he does me. Besides, I've already programmed him to make sure that you get safely to father if anything should happen to me and Thayer."

"Okay, everyone is covered. How are we going to handle Carrison?" Selina asks. "Do you have a set plan of action or do we take it by ear?"

"After telling him that we're here to collect our people, we'll see how he reacts. My guess is that he'll deny any knowledge of them even being here, then try to get us to take over where Mandraik left off." Thayer tells her going to get a pitcher of water and several glasses. "He'll even try to deny the attempts on Leyla's life, possibly even blame them on someone else."

When he sets down the tray, Salis pours out the water and passes everyone a glass. He smiles at her before continuing. "We'll be housed in the VIP guest house while we're with him. All the rooms have monitoring devices. The guards are to take care of those before any of us enter the rooms. None of us is to go anywhere alone." He looks over at Salis. "You young lady will stay with your mother and I at all times, understand?" Salis nods her head quickly.

"Brock, you'll need to have at least two guards with you if you go anywhere. You're the High Councilor now, so the danger to you is now greater than if you were only the Captain of the royal guard." Leyla tells her cousin when she sees him ready to deny the danger to himself.

* * *

Three hours later Sarah lands the ship. While they wait for Carrison to arrive, Thayer and Brock review with the warriors what is expected of them. They go over it several times until they are sure that all of them understand that any one of them could be used to start a war.

"Thayer, Carrison and Peterton have just arrived."

"Thank you Sarah. Tell Leyla and the others that we'll meet them near the entrance passage." He turns back to the warriors. "Take your positions and remember what we've said." The men leave the large meeting area and take their assigned positions.

Brock shakes Thayer's hand and goes to join his wife and Trocon. When the doors open, the first thirty warriors step out. They line themselves up on either side of the ramp and five out from the end.

Once they're in place, Trocon and four of his guards are the first to emerge. A few moments later Brock and Selina follow with the other six of Trocon's guards that would be accompanying them. They all stop at the third guard from the ramp. Trocon steps forward a few more steps and looks at Carrison and Peterton.

"Gentlemen, I am Trocon Damori, High Chancellor of Calidon. Behind me is Lord Brockton Centori, the High Councilor, and his mate Lady Selina." He watches their faces to see what type of reaction there is to his title. Peterton shows his shock, while Carrison does not. "I know present to you the Royal family of Calidon. Her Royal Majesty, Queen Leyla Aeneka Starhawk, His Royal Majesty, King Thayer Robus Starhawk, and Her Royal Highness, Princess Salis Chandelle Starhawk."

The guards stand straighter while Trocon, Selina, and Brock turn slightly towards the ship. Leyla and Thayer step out and then Salis steps between them. Trocon watches out of the corner of his eye as the President and Peterton stiffen.

Slowly the royal family approaches the end of the ramp with their guards. Leyla and Thayer reach out and find their people amongst Carrison's. Thayer neutralizes their abilities and Leyla teleports them to the holding area. As they pass Brock, Thayer nods to him that their people were now safe and secure on the ship.

'How many?'

'Ten. Three women, and seven men.'

They stop beside Trocon and the guards at the front step to the side. Thayer and Leyla look at Carrison. One of Carrison's men steps forward and whispers to him that their Calidonian mind touchers have disappeared.

"Our people have been returned to where they belong President Carrison. We have come here to secure the release of our people." Thayer states watching as Carrison glares at them.

"I don't know what people you're talking about, but I do know that you and that woman are wanted for crimes of treason against the Earth's government." He lifts a hand signaling for his soldiers to move. They step forward and draw their weapons. Moving to surround Leyla and Thayer and take them captive.

The royal guards quickly surround the royal family. The soldiers weapons disappear from their hands and they suddenly stop, looking at each other. Carrison looks around him looking for the reason they've stopped. Noticing that their weapons are gone, he signals them back. Once they move away from the royal family, the guards shift so that Leyla and Thayer are once again looking at Carrison.

"We have come here peacefully and will not provoke an attack, but we will defend ourselves if necessary gentlemen. At this time we only wish to talk with you." Leyla tells them speaking for the first time. "If you should make such a move against us again, I promise that more then just your weapons will disappear. We will also contact the Federation about your actions and file a formal protest."

Peterton leans into the President and whispers in his ear. "We have to be careful here sir. Since they're here and they used Mandraik's personal code to get through, its possible that they know everything. Another thing, I can't see Starhawk ruling a planet like Calidon without planning to use it some how. All the records that we have on him indicate that he's always on the look out for making easy money. We may be able to convince him to take over Mandraik's position with us if we're careful."

Carrison looks at him for a moment and then nods slightly in agreement. "Please forgive my hasty actions. My second in command has just informed me of my mistake and that a thorough investigation is being held. You and your people are welcome."

"And what of our people that you have in your custody?" Thayer asks with a slight frown having heard what Peterton had really said.

"You will have to give us some time to check into the matter. Like I said, I don't know what people you mean, but since you say that some of my staff are your people, we'll check all new arrivals."

Thayer nods his agreement. "Fair enough. Some of our guard will also check into it. With your permission of course." While Carrison is answering him, Thayer speaks privately with Brock. 'Tell the guards to be careful. No doubt someone will try to stop them from finding anything.'

"That will be fine your Majesty." Carrison says with a tight smile. "We'll send some of our men to assist them. See to it that our special investigative group gives them all the help that they need Mr. Peterton." Carrison says looking at the other man long and hard.

"Yes sir, Mr. President."

"Now if you and your party will follow us, we'll show you to our guest quarters." Carrison starts to turn when he notices their guards falling into place around them. "I'm sorry, but we don't have room for your guards. They'll have to wait in your ship."

"I'm afraid that isn't possible Mr. President. When we are away from Calidon and our ship, at least thirty of our guards must stay with us at all times." Thayer tells him seeing the frustration going through both men. "We'll divide those thirty between us. Ten will stay with me and my family, another ten will stay with Lord Damori, and the last ten will stay with Lord Centori and his wife. I'm sure that you have quarters that will suffice."

"Uhm, yes, of course. Besides the bedrooms the suites have a sitting room. We can arrange to have cots delivered to your rooms for them. Now if you'll follow us." Carrison says turning away frustrated that he was unable to separate them from their guards.

Thayer nods while Brock signals the other sixty men to return to the ship. 'Stay prepared to move at a moments notice.' The guards separate and the ones staying with the royal family stand fifteen on either side of them. The others wait until they move off before returning to the ship.

Aeneka watches them leave on the monitor. "Sarah, keep monitoring them at all times. The tracking devices they have can't be blocked or jammed by anything they have here."

"I have their signals now Aeneka. All of them are strong and continuous." Sarah informs her.

"Stephen, did you change the frequencies on all of the devices?"

"Yes Aeneka. There's no way that the Federation can detect them unless they know Sarah's frequency. Since only the family knows it, and Saitun would never give it up freely to anyone, that's not very likely."

"Thank you Stephen. Please check with the lieutenant that everyone understands exactly what they are to do." She waits until he leaves before contacting Leyla. 'Leyla, what's happening now?'

'We're almost to the guest house mother. There are about fifty of Carrison's soldiers surrounding us, but no one has tried anything yet.'

'Well, just make sure that everyone stays alert. Sarah is tracking you and the signal is strong and clear.'

'Okay mother. Tell Stephen to go over the area with the men again to make sure that they know it as well as they know the royal palace. I don't want any of them getting lost out there, especially the women.'

'I will sweetheart. Give Salis a hug and a kiss for me.'

\* \* \*

"This will be Lord Centori's rooms, and Lord Damori's are just down the hall." Peterton shows them the rooms. "Your Majesties will be on the floor above. We have a suite there that has two bedrooms, instead of the one like these."

Salis tightens her hands on both of her parents in fear. 'No! They plan to try something with us away from the others. Something to do with a gas.'

"We would prefer to have a room on this floor with the others Mr. Peterton." Leyla tells him causing him to frown in annoyance. "A cot for our daughter will be just fine. She sleeps in our bedchamber anyway."

"Yes, of course." He signals to one of the aides and tells him to have a portable bed brought down for the Princess. "We can give her something a little more comfortable than a cot to sleep on." He smiles at Salis, who only stares back at him. Peterton clears his throat and leads them to a room located between Trocon's and Brock's.

Thayer thanks him as six of the guards enter the room and neutralize all of the surveillance equipment. He then allows Leyla and Salis to enter only when he receives the all clear. He stands at the door with the other four guards and turns back to Peterton as the man clears his throat again.

"The President would be honored if you and the others would join him for the evening meal. Drinks will be at seven-thirty and the meal will be served at eight."

"Very well. Tell him that we will join him." Thayer nods slightly and then turns his back on the other man and enters the room followed by the guards who shut the door in his face.

Leyla meets him at the door. "There were four cameras and ten listening devices throughout the suite. Trocon and Brock reported the same in their rooms as well."

"Carrison wants us to have supper with him. I told Peterton that we would."

"I don't like them or this place. I wish that I could have stayed on the ship with grandmother and Stephen. There's a feeling of sadness and death in this place." Salis tells them in a soft voice.

Krander steps closer to her side and sends her calming images of happy things. Salis takes a deep breath and then releases it slowly, then smiles up at him gratefully. Leyla walks over to her.

"Hopefully we won't be here long sweetheart. I can feel the sadness too." She places a hand on Salis' shoulder and rubs it gently. "Why don't you go and lay down for awhile? Your father and I will discuss our next move."

"Okay, I am kind of tired. Can Krander come in with me?"

"Sure he can sweetheart, if it will make you feel more comfortable." Leyla nods to Krander and he leads Salis into the bedroom. After the door closes Leyla turns back to Thayer. Not wanting the guards to hear her she speaks to him mind to mind. 'I'm beginning to think that we should have left her on the ship with mother and Stephen myself.'

'Maybe, but I think that this will strengthen her. We have to give her a chance to control her fears before they begin controlling her. Krander will help her as he just did until she no longer needs his help.'

"So what do we do about Carrison? No doubt he's sitting in his office right now trying to figure out how to get at us, or how to control us. He's probably having a fit about not seeing and hearing what's going on in these suites." Leyla says going to the replicator and ordering a pitcher of apple juice. Before pouring it, she analyzes it to make sure that there are no drugs mixed in with it.

"At least they haven't messed with the replicator." she says turning to the guards present and warning them. "No one is to eat or drink anything from here without analyzing it first."

They all nod and take the glass she hands each of them. Suddenly they all look up as they hear a mental scream. Leyla and Thayer look at each other as Salis runs into the room. "Selina." They all say in unison.

Leyla teleports them all to Brock and Selina's suite. When they arrive, Selina is on the floor with Brock's head in her lap, tears running down her cheeks. Leyla steps over to her and kneels down. "What happened?" She asks quietly reaching out to touch Brock's forehead.

"I don't know Leyla. He was fine a few minutes ago when he got a drink from the replicator. All of a sudden he just collapsed." she looks up at Leyla. "His essence is fading, I can feel it. Can you...?" her voice fades.

Leyla looks from Selina to Brock and then up at Thayer who sadly shakes his head. Tears form in her eyes and she looks back at Selina. "I'm sorry Selina. There's..."

"No!" Salis cries out and runs forward, falling down on the other side of Selina and places her right hand on his forehead and her left over his heart. She closes her eyes and lifts her head. All watch as a healing blue light surrounds her and moves through her hands to touch Brock. His body raises up a few inches and arches a little before convulsing three times and then lowering back to the floor.

The healing light slowly returns to Salis and she lowers her head while her hands fall away. Her chin touches her chest as she takes several shallow breaths. Selina looks from Brock to Salis and back again. Brock's lashes flutter and then open and he looks up at Selina with a smile.

"Are we having fun yet?" he asks shakily while tears of joy run down Selina's cheeks unchecked.

"Yes, every minute." she tells him.

Slowly Salis raises her head and Leyla notices that her eyes seem dull and dazed. She stands up and walks around Selina to help her to her feet.

"We'll take Salis back to our room to rest while your guards help Brock into bed. Don't let anyone eat or drink anything else from the replicator without an analyzes."

Salis stands up and leans heavily into her mother. Leyla looks to Thayer, and he walks over to them and picks Salis up. Just then Leyla notices Trocon standing off to the side. "Make sure that your people do the same." He nods and then looks down at his daughter and son-in-law. As Thayer carries Salis past him, Trocon reaches out and lightly caresses her cheek.

"Thank you for what you did Princess." Salis only smiles slightly before closing her eyes. Thayer continues out the door with four of the guards. Before following them, Leyla tells Trocon and Selina of the evening meal with Carrison.

"If Brock doesn't feel up to it, we'll cancel and meet with Carrison in the morning."

"I think that he'll be fine in a few hours. We'll give him an energy boost when he wakes up."

"Okay. Drinks are to be served at seven-thirty, the meal at eight. If he doesn't wish to attend, don't force him."

"Of course not. We'll let you know when he wakes up." Trocon watches her leave and then turns back to his daughter and holding out his arms to her. Selina runs into them and buries her face in his neck. They give and receive comfort from each other while the guards give them some privacy. After a few minutes they go to sit with Brock.

"Salis has grown stronger. With Brock's healing I think that she may now be an alpha three."

"I hope so father. While we're here we're going to need all the power we have to counter Carrison's attacks, especially if they are as sneaky as Brock's poisoning was."

"Well, it can only be hoped that we don't come so close to losing someone again." Trocon says looking at Brock's sleeping form. "So far of what we've seen, I don't believe that there is any way to deal honorably with the President. He's as power mad as Dacus ever was. We're going to have to be even more careful of hidden traps."

Selina nods and wipes a cool cloth over Brock's face. Even though they weren't lifemated, if Brock had died, she would have followed him into the next life. She would be glad when they left this place and the mad man that lived here.

# Chapter XIX

"What do you mean the suite monitors aren't working?" Carrison demands glaring at Peterton.

"There's nothing coming from them sir. I figure that when their guards entered the suites, they disabled all of the monitors and microphones some how." Peterton says frowning at this latest disturbance to their plans. "We do know that something happened in Centori's suite, though we're not sure how they entered the room, Starhawk came out carrying the child and the Katmen woman followed them a few minutes later."

"They're capable of teleportation you fool. As for the monitors, have our people get them back on line. I want to know what's going on in those rooms, what they're planning."

Peterton nods and turns to leave just as someone knocks at the door. Carrison calls for them to enter and Erik Ritage enters the room.

"Sir, we've tried all the probes, but none of them have been able to penetrate their ships defensive shields."

"Has anyone left the ships?"

"Not that we've detected sir. We've placed movement sensors around all of the ships. If anyone tries to leave or go aboard we'll know about it."

"Have all the prisoners moved to the old base until I've found out exactly what Starhawk is up to."

"Yes sir. What about Knightrunner sir? Do you want us to attack the stronghold he's in? We're sure that the only psi's he has with him, that he can trust, are the Blackwoods. I doubt if any of them are strong enough to hold off a full scale attack from all sides, at least not for very long."

"Mr. President, I suggest that we wait on an attack. It's possible that Starhawk could help us get past their defenses if we can get him to come over to our side. After all he is friends with both Knightrunner and the Blackwoods." Peterton puts in.

"I don't agree Peterton. I don't believe that Starhawk will turn on the Katmen woman's people. They've gotten too close." Carrison looks back at Ritage. "Gather your men. I'll contact you within the next thirty-six hours on when to attack."

Ritage nods and leaves the room signaling his two guards outside the door to follow. He then orders, "Get the men together. We move on Knightrunner in less then thirty hours."

After entering his office, Ritage calls the prison camp and tells them to start moving the prisoners. "If anyone tries to stop you, shoot to kill." After the call he leaves the offices and goes to the guest house to check on his men there before leaving the compound.

\* \* \*

Aeneka and Stephen enter the bridge as Sarah puts the ships on red alert. "What's happened Sarah? Why have you ordered a red alert?" Aeneka asks with a frown at the noise the alarms are making.

"I monitored a call to the prison camp from the office building. They're moving the prisoners and were given orders to shoot to kill anyone trying to stop them."

"I'll contact Leyla and Thayer. Stephen, have the guards prepare to move in case they're needed." 'Leyla, Thayer, we have a situation.'

In their suite Leyla and Thayer look at each other. 'What is it mother?'

'Sarah just monitored a call to the prison camp. They're moving our people from the camp with orders to shoot to kill anyone attempting to stop them.'

'Have the guards prepare to move.' Thayer tells her and signals to one of the guards. "Go ask Krander to come here please."

'Mother, have the strongest psi's on the other ships put a shield around the camp. Tell them that Thayer and I will be there shortly.'

'All right dear.'

Krander enters the room and stands at attention. "You wanted to see me Majesty?"

"Yes Krander. Leyla and I have to return to the ship. You are to stay here with Salis at all times. Don't let her out of your sight. You are not to leave this room for any reason or to let anyone enter. Our people will teleport into the room. Do you understand me in this?"

"Yes Majesty. She won't leave my sight for a second."

"Good. Return to her now. Hopefully we'll have returned before she wakes up."

Krander returns to the bedroom as Leyla turns back to Thayer. "I've told Selina and Trocon what's happened. They'll keep a close watch for any signs of danger while we're gone."

"Okay, let's go." They teleport out of the suite, and moments later appear on the flagship right in front of Stephen. Leyla speaks to him quickly and he steps forward. All three disappear and reappear on one of the other ships. Stephen goes to the weapons room and sets the ship's disrupter cannons to fire on the communications tower.

"Has anyone attempted to leave yet?" Leyla asks as they walk into the war room where the strongest psi's are linked to create the barrier.

"No Majesty. They're still gathering the people and don't know of the barrier yet."

"Is there any one area that they are gathering in?" Thayer asks studying the hologram stationed above the table.

"They seem to be gathering at the center building."

"There's a lot of fear and anxiety running through all of the prisoners. More than just our people are here. There are also Earth men and women and many children. They all share our people's fears."

Thayer reaches out and touches the minds of a few of the Earth people. "We're going to have to go and get them. If we try to take our people without the others, we're going to cause a lot more fear and anxiety. It will also make our people that much harder to control."

Leyla nods her agreement. "You're right. Sarah?"

"Yes Leyla."

"Tell all of the guards to prepare to disembark as quickly as possible. They are to only stun Carrison's men and to approach our people with extreme caution."

"They're ready now Leyla."

"Thank you Sarah. Tell Stephen to wait ninety seconds, and then destroy the tower."

"All of the people are together now Majesties." the link spokesman tells them. They hear the explosion as Stephen blows up the communications tower.

The ships doors open and the guards rush out quickly, dealing with Carrison's men. Those capable of teleportation do so directly to where the prisoners are. Within minutes the camp is secure and Leyla and Thayer leave the ship followed closely by Stephen.

"Stephen, go to the records computer and find out where the rest of our people are." Thayer orders as they stop in front of the mixed group of prisoners. Brock's replacement steps forward and salutes.

"All monitoring systems have been neutralized your Majesty."

"Thank you Captain." Thayer nods his dismissal and the other man takes up a position a few feet away.

Leyla steps up onto a stool and gets everyone's attention before explaining what is happening. She tells the Calidonians of Mandraik's death and their families safety.

"As for the rest of you, since you have been mated with our people, and have children with them, you must decide now what you wish to do." She looks at each of them slowly. "Even though some of our people already have mates back on Calidon, you are welcome to go with them and have a place there. You will stay with your children without fear of them being taken from you. Those of you that wish to remain on Earth will be helped to deal with what has happened to you, and to get you back together with your families if possible."

"We know that some of you women have been away from your families for several years, and going back to them will be impossible." Thayer says compassionately. "For those, there is a place here on Earth where you can go to live without fear of recriminations for what you have been through. The people will accept you and make you welcome. You will become a part of their families. I promise that you will not be left alone to deal with this."

"We need to know which of you wish to go to Calidon and which of you wishes to stay. No one will think badly of you for not going with your children, but I must warn you that the children will go. My mate and I can not allow any of our people to remain on Earth right now. When it's more settled, they may return if that is their wish, or you can come and visit them when you feel more comfortable." Leyla stops to gauge their reactions and then mentally tells her people to take their children and separate themselves from the others. "I have asked our people to remove themselves and their children from you so that you can make your decision. I am not trying to be cruel. If you wish to go, return to their side."

Slowly some of the women go to their chosen mates and cling to them and their children. The men are more reluctant, but their affection for the women are just as strong. Of the two hundred and fifty Calidonians, approximately one hundred and seventy-five have been joined by their Earth mates. Of the Calidonians standing alone, most are women. Only twenty-eight men are left alone holding their children close. They do nothing to force the women to join them.

Leyla and Thayer watch as one of the Earth women struggles to overcome her fears. Knowing that they must hurry, Thayer signals for the guards to start leading the group to the ships. They have gone only about twenty feet when the woman cries out and runs to her mate and infant child. She flings herself onto her mate's arm and clutches their child close to her breast. Thayer signals again for the group to be lead out.

Stephen enters after the group leaves and goes to where Leyla and Thayer are standing. "According to the records, there are only ninety others still alive. Approximately forty-five died from being tortured or were killed trying to escape. Sarah is locating the ninety now."

"Thank you Stephen. Why don't you..."

"There's something more that you should know Leyla." he

interrupts her. "Those ninety are from the penal moon and they were considered the most dangerous to Calidon."

"Dangerous by whose standard? Mandraik's?"

"No, your grandfather's." he tells her softly. Leyla nods her understanding before quickly looking away.

"We need to get the others out of here and get back." Thayer reminds her putting his hand on her shoulder, not sure what Stephen had said to her to upset her this way. "Peterton will send someone to check on the loss of communications soon."

"Yes...you're right. Stephen, find a transport for these people and program it to take them to the stronghold. Put one of the new scramblers in and one of Sarah's boxes, so that she'll be in control. Stay here and separate the mate's of our people on the flagship, and then send them and their families there. No one is to use their abilities. Sarah is to use the ships transporters to send everyone, including you."

"We'll go ahead and use the transport that they were going to use to move them."

Leyla nods her agreement and then turns to the others. "You're going to be taken to safety shortly. Please do your best to help the people that we are sending you to. Until Carrison and Peterton are taken care of, we are all in danger from them. If you wish to remain free, you have to help us to help you." She nods to the guards that will stay with them until their ship is ready, then takes Thayer's hand and walks with him back to the ship.

Once on the ship, Thayer tells the barrier holders what to do once they're gone and then follows Leyla onto the bridge. "Sarah, when the people are on the transport and secure, put a sleep gas through the entire ship. I don't want any of them to panic before Logan has them secure at the stronghold."

"All right Thayer. How long do you want them to sleep?" Sarah asks as she runs through the transports supply file to find the right gas.

"For at least ten hours. No doubt they can use the rest."

"Consider it already done."

Leyla and Thayer teleport back to the flagship and tell Aeneka what to expect before teleporting back to their suite. As they appear, Salis jumps up from her seat and rushes over to them. "Is everyone safe?" she asks anxiously.

Leyla hugs her tightly and closes her eyes. "They're fine little one. Most of the Earth mates have decided to go to Calidon."

"I'm so glad." Salis returns her hug. "That man Peterton called wanting to speak to you and father. Krander told him that you couldn't be interrupted." she giggles and looks over at Krander and then back at her parents. "When he asked why not, Krander told him to take three guesses and that the first two didn't count. Peterton turned really red and had a disgusted look on his face."

Thayer laughs and pats Krander's shoulder. "You handled him just right young man." Krander blushes at the praise and everyone laughs softly. One of the other guards brings Leyla and Thayer a drink.

"We've tested the replicator on different foods and drinks Majesties." he tells them as he hands them each a glass. "Any alcoholic beverage is laced with a poison, as well as some of the foods. The juices are fine, but it appears that the rest of the foods may contain a sleeper drug."

"Have you informed the others?" Thayer asks taking a sip of his drink.

"Yes Majesty. We've also been able to neutralize all of the poisons and sleep inducers, except for the one ingested by Lord Centori."

"Very well, thank you." Thayer nods to him and then turns back to the others. "We'll have to be extra careful at the meal this evening." He looks to Krander. "I want you to analyze everything that is set before us. Not only the food and drink, but the dishes we're to use as well, even the napkins." Krander nods his understanding. "Pick someone from each of Brock and Trocon's guards to do the same."

"As you say Majesty." Krander agrees and then closes his eyes, this is to indicate that he is talking telepathically to someone.

"I think that we should start getting ready." Leyla tells him and looks at the chair where Salis had been sitting. Clothing for the three of them suddenly appears. "Why don't you go first while I get some things for the others to wear?" she suggests to Thayer. "While Salis and I are getting ready, you can go and talk with the others."

"Sounds good. It will be nice to have a normal shower instead of a dual one." he kisses Leyla and Salis before gathering his clothes and going into their private bath.

After sending the others a change of clothes, Leyla leads Salis over to the love seat, where they sit down together. The guards move away to give them some privacy. "How are you feeling sweetheart?" Leyla asks noticing that Salis still looks tired.

"Fine. I don't remember too much about what happened in Brock and Selina's room though. Every once in a while I feel a lot of energy flowing through me. It's like..." Just then one of the surges goes through her and Leyla notices a white light going all around Salis and her body stiffening. The light slowly fades, but she can still see it in Salis' eyes as her body relaxes once more. "It's like my whole being is changing every time it happens." she finishes softly looking at her mother with fear plainly showing in her eyes.

Leyla smiles reassuringly at her and takes her small hand in her own, squeezing it gently. "It's nothing to be afraid of sweetheart, it's only your body changing. It would seem that you are becoming more my daughter then I had ever hoped possible." Leyla says with wonder in her own eyes at such a thing happening.

"I don't understand mother." Salis looks at her in bewilderment.

"I'm not sure that I do either sweetheart. I'll discuss it with your father, grandmother, and Trocon. Until then, try not to worry. It's nothing that you have to fear."

Thayer comes out a few minutes later and Leyla sends Salis in to take her shower, telling her that she would be in shortly. Once Salis disappears into the other room, Thayer sits down beside Leyla and raises a brow.

She tells him about the surges Salis was having. "I think that she may be one of the elite. If she is, we'll have to keep a close eye on her. If her surges are anything like mine were, she's liable to unconsciously teleport to just about anywhere. We'll have to stay in constant mind contact with her as well. Her surges are mild right now, but they could become stronger at any time and port her before she realizes its happening."

"I agree Love. We'll have to find some way to direct where she might port to." Thayer says understanding the danger Salis could be placed in.

"The most likely places for her to port to would come from her subconscious. If we could plant strong enough images of the ships, or even the stronghold into her subconscious, I'm sure that she would go to one of them."

"Then that's what we'll do. You can plant the images of the ships, and I'll give her images of the stronghold."

Leyla nods and stands up. "I'll start while we're getting dressed, then you can do yours before we leave for dinner. Why don't you go ahead and check on Brock and let them know of our success with the recovery?"

"Okay." He stands up and kisses her. "I'll meet you in Brock's suite when your ready." He signals to three of the guards and they leave the suite.

Leyla goes into the bedroom and lays out Salis and her clothes before going to take her shower. She teases Salis about taking so long, but as she takes her shower she worries about the surges. She hopes that they stay mild until they were far away from Carrison and his people. She didn't want to take any unnecessary chances with Salis' safety. There was always the possibility that fear could trigger an unusually strong surge.

They needed to finish up here and get to the safety of the stronghold as soon as possible. She was sure that was the only way to insure that nothing happened to Salis at this time when she was most vulnerable.

# Chapter XX

"I'm afraid that we've found nothing on any of your people as of yet. We've checked all the records, and except for the people that you took when you arrived, no other Calidonians are shown to be anywhere on Earth." The President tells them as they sit down for drinks.

"I find that hard to believe Mr. President, considering that those ten came at different times, with at least fifty other Calidonians." Thayer challenges. "We have records that show no less then four hundred of our people were sent to you and Mr. Peterton. Money was exchanged between you and our former High Chancellor several times."

"That's impossible. I admit that we've had dealings with offworlders, but I don't recall anyone from Calidon. Do you?" the President asks Peterton as he sits down.

"No I don't. I remember some Alterians though. Strange creatures Alterians. If it wasn't for their bluish-green skin, you'd almost swear that they were from Earth."

"We're going to send out our other ships to scan the planet." Leyla informs them sipping the drink that Krander has handed her. "We have special equipment that will locate our people."

"I'm afraid that I can't allow you to do that." Carrison says frowning at her. "For our people to see your ships, could cause a worldwide panic." "Not if you make a public announcement that explains what our ships will be doing. We would appear with you to waylay any fears." Leyla offers knowing that he would continue to refuse.

Just then Erik Ritage enters the room and walks over to the

President. As he whispers to the President, Thayer communicates with Leyla and the others.

'Be prepared to teleport back to the ship at the first sign of trouble.'

'I don't know if I have the strength to make it.' Brock informs him.

'Leyla and I will help anyone not strong enough.'

Carrison stands up. "I'm afraid that you'll have to excuse me for a while. There's something that I need to check into. I'll leave Mr. Ritage here to keep you company. Peterton, come with me."

They leave, and Ritage gets himself a drink, then sits down near Thayer. "So, you're the King of a planet now Starhawk? Must be nice to better your station so greatly without lifting a finger." Erik says sarcastically swallowing down half of his drink.

Brock starts to stand up, but stops when Thayer shakes his head slightly. "Considering that you know absolutely nothing about me, that's a very judgmental statement to make. For your information, on my home world of Manchon, I am a Prince of the royal family. So my now being King is no great change for me." Thayer tells him with a smile of contempt, seeing the shock come and go on the other man's face.

"True, if that's the truth that is. The same can't be said of you though can it your Highness?" Ritage says contemptuously to Leyla. "You were born and raised right here on Earth."

"I may have been born and raised here Mr. Ritage, but my mother was the Crowned Princess of Calidon. I received special training while I was growing up for the time when I would become Queen."

Once again Ritage is shock to find out something that his intelligence people hadn't known, or told him about. He takes another large swallow of his drink and turns his malicious eyes on Salis. "What about this one? I've heard that you're claiming her as your daughter. Since neither of you are old enough, and you haven't know each other that long, I wonder who she really is?" he says leering at Salis and then glaring up at the guard that steps in front of her blocking his view.

Krander glares back at him, but doesn't move from his position in front of Salis. He would not let this garbage eater sully Salis with his filth.

Thayer stands up and puts out his hand for Leyla to take. "I think that its time we returned to our suites. When the President returns, if he returns, give him our apologies. I will not put my family and friends through any more of your vulgarities and innuendoes."

Leyla takes his hand and stands. Ignoring Ritage, she steps around him and leads Salis from the room with the others following closely behind. They each glare at Ritage as they pass him, and he salutes each of them with his glass.

After they've all gone, Ritage fixes himself another drink and downs it before laughing and leaving the room to join the President.

After they all go to their separate suites, the others teleport to Leyla and Thayer's to discuss what was happening and make plans for how they would protect themselves.

"Something's going on. I expected them to at least question us on the disappearance. They didn't even bring up the destruction of the tower." Trocon says pacing around the room.

"They're probably waiting for us to admit that we took our people so that they can act against us." Brock puts in.

"Are any of our people still where Carrison can get to them?" Trocon asks stopping near Leyla.

"No. As far as we can tell, they're all on the other side of the planet. They're in the desert region, which makes mechanical teleporting almost impossible. They would have to fly over to find them and then fly back." Leyla informs him.

"Is there any way for us to get there and back without their knowing?" Selina asks holding onto one of Brock's hands. Though he was doing a lot better since his poisoning, he was still pale and tired looking.

"If we had cloaking devices other then the ones we do, it would be possible. Right now, both Earth and the Federation could pick us up." Thayer tells them.

"What about a human cloak? We could easily block the sensors and radar's." Brock suggests.

"It would take a lot of mind power to do something like that Brock.

Thayer and I need to stay here to keep Carrison and Peterton busy." Leyla reminds her cousin.

"We could use the strongest alpha's in the guards." Selina says picking up on Brock's thinking. "I think that we have at least forty-five that are five's and six's. Would that be enough?"

"Yes, we could split them into three groups. The first fifteen going in, the second coming out, and the third as relief. That way we wouldn't exhaust them all at once." Brock smiles at his wife.

"What if they're scattered throughout the region? They would have to cloak and recloak too many times for it to be totally effective." Leyla points out reasonably.

"What about sending them a message to meet in a certain area?" Salis asks looking at her father. "Tell them that we're here to take them all back home?"

"It's a good idea honey, but I don't think that it would work. The ones still missing are the ones placed on the penal moon by the late King. He considered them a danger to Calidon, they were to spend the rest of their lives there with no possibility of ever leaving. I can't see them willingly going back to that."

"Why not tell them they're to be used in the takeover of Earth?" Brock suggests looking around at the others. "Anyone that helps will be given a position in the new government. That should get their attention and get them to the area that we want."

"That would work if we had someone convincing to communicate with them." Leyla says thinking about it. "I think that we should use one of the other prisoners. One that came with them. That person would help to validate the offer."

"We can try it." Thayer says slowly. "Contact your mother and have her get Stephen to check the ones on our ship to see if any of them arrived with any of the ninety."

Leyla nods and closes her eyes. The vid-phone buzzes and Thayer signals the others out of the room before answering it. "Yes."

"Mr. Starhawk, I thought that I should see if everything was all right with you and the others since you left before I could return, and the meal could be served." Carrison says with false concern, not bothering to use Thayer's proper title.

"Everything is fine Mr. Carrison. But your man Ritage has the manners of a churl. He was very insulting and offensive to myself and my family. I suggest that if you plan to have any more dealings with us, you keep him away from us from now on." Thayer tells him pointedly.

"Do I hear a threat in your words Mr. Starhawk?"

"No Mr. Carrison. What you hear is a promise that we will not tolerate such a thing again."

"I see. Very well, I'll see what I can do about keeping him away from you from now on."

"Thank you. If you will excuse me, my wife is getting ready to serve us something to eat. We'll talk with you in the morning." Thayer ends the call and turns around. Selina and the others come back into the room.

"Do you think that it was wise to threaten him Thayer? He may do something unexpected." Selina points out sitting down near Leyla.

"I don't think he'll try anything yet Selina. He's not sure yet if he can get me to take over for Mandraik or not. Until he is, we should be all right." He looks at Leyla. "Any luck?"

"Stephen says that only one of the people on our ship had any contact with the ones we're looking for. Both her and her mates refuse to have any contact with them at all." she signals to one of the guards for drinks to be served. "There is a man on one of the other ships that will help though. He was with the largest group and knows which ones we should contact."

"All right, tell Aeneka to have Stephen meet me on the bridge. We'll teleport to the ship the man is on and start making the contacts. While I'm gone, why don't you try and find Denral and Mark? They're most likely being held in the east building of the compound."

"Should I go ahead and port them to the ship?"

"Not unless you're sure that it won't endanger Denral. He's still healing and we don't want to shock him too greatly right now."

"How long do you think it will take to contact the minimum number of the ninety?"

"Hopefully no more then an hour. We'll contact as many of them as we can in that time. Hopefully enough of them will be together at each contact that it won't take too long."

Leyla nods and Thayer ports out of their suite and to the ship. "Why don't the rest of you go and get something to eat and some rest." Leyla suggests looking around at the others. "If anything comes up, I'll contact you right away, otherwise we'll meet in the morning."

Trocon nods and stands up. "That sounds like a good idea to me."

"Yes it does. I think that Brock needs to get some more rest. He's still looking a little pale to me." Selina says looking at her mate with concern.

"I'm fine my love. Though I could use something to eat. I wish we didn't have to use these replicators though." he says with a frown. The others all understand his reluctance. They have all had their own doubts as well since his poisoning.

"Why don't I contact the ship's cook and have him prepare something for us? I can port it to you in your rooms when it's ready. I could go for some Calidonian foods and drinks right now myself." Leyla says and receives nods from everyone. She contacts the ship's cook and tells him what they need. "Everything will be ready in about twenty minutes. I'll send it to you as soon as its ready." They nod and then port to their rooms.

"Krander, have the guards switch with those outside and get a report on any activity that's taken place."

"Yes your Majesty." Krander goes over to the others while Leyla speaks quietly with Salis.

"I'm going to go and lay down while I do my search for my friends honey. Your grandmother will contact you as soon as the food is ready. When she does let me know. All right?"

"Okay mother. Is there anything else that you want me to do?"

"If anyone calls, ignore it." Leyla tells her and then goes into the bedroom and closes the door behind her. Taking off her dress, she slips into her robe before laying down on the bed. Closing her eyes she carefully concentrates on Mark, feeling that it would be safer to contact him first rather then Denral. After several minutes she finally locates him. Because she has touched his mind before, she can easily detect the mind toucher that has been controlling him. She quickly checks the rest of the area, and then deals with the mind toucher. Sending a mental charge, she neutralizes his contact with Mark and puts him into a deep sleep that will keep him out for several hours.

With that taken care of she touches Mark's mind more firmly. 'Mark, Mark Blackwood. Mark, it's Leyla, wake up.' she watches as his lashes flutter. 'Mark, you must wake up now!' she practically shouts in his mind.

His mind responds immediately. 'Leyla! You're safe, they didn't catch you.'

'No, and I'm fine. I'm on Earth now. Don't move and don't open your eyes.' she warns him knowing that there is a camera monitoring him.

'It's not safe for you here. Carrison...'

'We know all about Carrison. Don't worry Thayer is with me. How is your father doing?'

'He's fine. He's still weak, but he'll make it.' he assures her.

'Do you know where he is?'

'The floor above me. There are two mind touchers assigned to him. I don't know why, since he's not that strong a telepath.' It's then that it dawns on him about his own mind toucher. Before he can warn her, Leyla reassures him.

'I've taken care of him. Give me a couple of minutes to locate your father, and I deal with his mind touchers as well. In three minutes, contact him and let him know that I'll contact him.'

Not waiting for him to say anything more she pulls away and goes to the floor above. She locates Denral, then locates the mind touchers that are in contact with his mind. The first one is very easy to knock out, but the second takes a little more energy. After making sure that no others have been alerted, she returns to Denral's cell. 'Denral.'

'Leyla, it's true. You're back. What of your father?'

'He's safe Uncle. How are you doing?'

'I've been better. I wish I knew how Cassie and the others were doing. Daniel disappeared about three weeks ago. They won't tell us what happened to him.'

'He's safe Uncle, and so are the others. Logan Knightrunner has them all safe up in the mountains.' she assures him noticing that he was becoming agitated. 'I want to port you and Mark to our ship where you'll be safe. There's no way that Carrison and his men can get to you there. Do you feel up to it?'

'Anything would be better than staying in this cell another minute.'

'All right, I'll make the preparations and have you both out of there in the next five minutes. There's one more thing. An older woman will meet you on the ship. I don't want her appearance to shock you so I'll warn you now that it's my mother you'll be seeing and talking to.'

'How can that be? She's been dead...'

'She'll explain everything to you. I must go now. Before I port you, I'll neutralize all the monitors in the area. Be ready.' She opens her eyes and sits up to see Salis standing beside the bed and nods at her.

"I've already told the others that you'd be sending them their food soon." Salis says handing her a glass of juice and stepping back. When she had first entered the room, she hadn't been sure what she was supposed to do, so she just stood still and waited for her mother to sense her presence in the room with her instead of touching her or talking to her.

"Thank you sweetheart." Leyla stands up and goes into the other room. After sending the food to the others, she contacts her mother and tells her to prepare for Denral and Mark. While Salis and Krander pass out the food, she ports Denral and Mark to the ship's medical center.

"How long before they notice that your friends are missing mother?"

"Not long. I neutralized their monitors so that they wouldn't see exactly how they escaped. As soon as they discover that its not a malfunction the alarms will go off and they'll start searching for them." Leyla sits down at the table. "I need to contact your father." she closes her eyes again and contacts Thayer. 'How much longer Thayer?'

'About another twenty minutes. What's wrong?'

'Nothing yet, but there could be trouble soon. I ported Denral and Mark to the ship. Their escape will be discovered soon.'

'Okay, I'll finish this up quickly. Tell the guards to keep everyone out no matter what until I get back. If they have to, have them put up a shield to block off the hallway at all entry points.'

'All right, see you soon.'

"Is father almost done?" Salis asks setting down her glass of ganza milk.

"Yes, he'll be back soon." she looks for Krander and signals for him. "Krander, Thayer wants the outer guards to keep everyone from this area. If they feel its necessary, they are to block the hall at all entrance points with mental shields until he returns."

"I'll tell them Majesty." He quickly goes to the door. He returns a few minutes later. "They're prepared Majesty. If they sense more then three people approaching, the shields will be put in place immediately."

"Very good Krander, thank you. Go and finish your meal."

"How did they escape?! What about the mind touchers assigned to them?" Carrison demands of Peterton. "Why didn't they sound the alarm?"

"We don't know sir. We haven't been able to rouse them." Peterton informs him. "None of our mind touchers can get any information from their minds. None of the hall or room monitors picked up anything either. There were a few minutes of static, but nothing to cover an escape. It appeared to be a malfunction."

"Starhawk is behind this, I know it. Ritage, I want you to take a dozen men up there and search their rooms. If you find them, arrest the lot of them immediately." Carrison orders.

Peterton waits until the other man leaves before addressing the President. "Do you really believe that Starhawk would be stupid enough to take them to his rooms? I would think that he would take them to the ship."

"Under normal circumstances I would think the same, but I think that he would want to see them and talk with them to find out what they knew as soon as possible." Carrison tells him drumming his fingers against his desk. "We'll have to wait and see what Ritage turns up and take it from there if he doesn't find them." He just hoped that they could get control of all of them before the Federation could interfere.

# Chapter XXI

Thayer arrives back at the suite just as one of the outer guards informs Leyla that a dozen men are headed to their area. He walks over to instruct the guard. "Warn Trocon and Brock. Tell them to prepare for a room search. They are to do nothing to provoke the searchers."

The guard nods and leaves the room. Five minutes later a guard knocks and opens the door. Before he can speak, Erik Ritage pushes past him and into the room.

"Nobody move, everyone stay where you are. Some prisoners have escaped and all rooms will be searched." Salis moves closer to Leyla and Ritage snarls at her. "I said to stay put." He steps forward to grab her, but is stopped by her shield. He tries again and is stopped again, but this time receives a shock of warning.

"I suggest that you not try that again Ritage. A shield surrounds each of us at any violent intent against our persons." Thayer informs him with a growl. "Now, get on with your search and then leave. We'd like to get some rest."

Ritage glares at him and then at Salis, before nodding to his men. They search the rooms thoroughly, then shake their heads when they find no traces of the prisoners. Ritage frowns in frustration and then nods the men out of the room. "We're going to check the other rooms. If we find the prisoners in either of them, you will all be arrested for aiding political prisoners."

"Since we have no idea what you're talking about, we have nothing to worry about do we?" Leyla tells him sweetly.

"We'll see your Majesty." Ritage sneers at her. Pushing past the guards he leads his men to Brock's suite. After checking Trocon's rooms and finding nothing, they quickly leave the floor and then the building.

Brock and Trocon come to Leyla and Thayer's room shortly after Leyla sends Salis to bed. They discuss what actions they should take now.

"I think that we should go to your stronghold tonight before they decide to attack." Brock points out. "No offense to you cousin, Thayer, but the people so far are not very trustworthy."

"No offense taken Brock. All the people aren't like the ones you've met here. But I do think that you're right about going to the stronghold. I'm getting tired of Ritage staring at Salis." Leyla states with great irritation. "At least we know that her shield is more automatic now."

"How do we know that he will even attack? He doesn't want the Federation involved any more then we do right now. He may try and wait us out." Trocon puts in.

"We know that he's planning an attack, and if we're all around, all the better for us. I suggest that we wait until after the meeting tomorrow." Thayer says looking at each of them.

They all agree to wait and then Trocon and Brock return to their rooms. Thayer puts all the guards on alert for the night, with two watching at each door. Relief was to be given every two hours.

That done, Leyla and Thayer enter their bedroom. While Thayer steps into the bathroom to change, Leyla covers Salis and lightly touches her mind to be sure that she is having a peaceful sleep. She had worried that Ritage's attack may have distressed her. Assured that she was sleeping peacefully, Leyla climbs into bed.

Thayer enters the room shortly after she climbs into bed. Before going to sleep, they discuss all that had happened and what could still happen. Thayer contacts Saitun about returning, only to find out that he was already on his way and that he would meet them at the stronghold in less then twenty-four hours.

\* \* \*

Early the next morning they all prepare for their meeting with the President. Leyla is worried about Salis. Since waking, she has had several surges and each was stronger then the last and they were coming more often then she would like.

"I'm worried about her Thayer. We should send her back to the ship now, before the meeting."

"We know where she's likely to port Leyla, and I think that she should be there. If she does teleport, it may be a surprise that we need. I do believe that we need to send back at least half of the guards though. It will be safer to teleport twenty-one, rather then thirty-six."

Still concerned for their daughter, Leyla nods her agreement. They contact the others about Thayer's plan, and it is agreed that each of them would send five of their guards back to the ship.

The President's escort arrives and leads the way to the meeting hall. When they reach the turning point, Thayer signals the guards that would be returning to the ship. Once they're on their way, he nods for the escort to continue, without bothering to explain. Leyla notices that several soldiers are following the guards back to the ship and warns them.

As they walk, Salis sees several people wearing silver wristbands with small antennas. Before she can ask her parents about them, a young girl drops something that she's carrying and a soldier steps towards her pushing a button on his belt. The girl grabs her wrist and cries out in pain. The soldier stops beside her and says something to her which causes her to shake her head. He pushes the button again before speaking once more. This time the girl nods and hangs her head. Salis looks away, knowing what the wristbands are for and what the guard had said. The bands were used for punishment and control and they caused the wearer extreme pain.

Sensing her daughter's distress Leyla tries to comfort her. 'The pain only lasts for a few seconds sweetheart.'

'But to give pain for an accident? Why are people so cruel, especially to children?'

'I don't know honey. For some I think it's to make them feel big and important. Don't worry, we'll help her and the others after we've dealt with Carrison.'

Salis nods and looks back at the girl. The soldier now has her pinned up against a tree with his hand down her blouse. The girls' eyes meet and Salis senses the other girl's shame at what is happening to her. Wanting to help, Salis gives the girl's mind a gentle shock that knocks her out. Before total darkness takes her, she mentally thanks Salis.

Leyla and Salis smile as the soldier is forced to catch the girl before she falls to the ground. 'Your compassion has saved her from further public humiliation. I'm very proud of you sweetheart.'

'She won't wake up until tomorrow, and she won't remember what he tried to do to her.'

Minutes later they enter the meeting hall and are shown to a conference room. They notice four soldiers standing around, so Leyla and Thayer quickly probe the other rooms and find fifty more waiting. Thayer warns the others to stay close to him and Leyla no matter what happens.

Upon entering the conference room, their guards form a semi circle around the royal party, protecting their backs. Thayer leads them to the table at which Carrison and Peterton are seated.

"Please sit down your Majesties." Carrison indicates the grouping of chairs. "I'm afraid that we won't be able to meet with you for very long. It would seem as though we have had several unexplained prison escapes since your arrival. The latest one being in this very compound last night." he says looking at each of them.

"Yes, so Ritage said when he barged into our rooms last night." Thayer informs him stiffly making no move to sit down. "You are lucky that we came at all. Since you had already agreed to keep him away from us, and then sent him to our rooms. We're not inclined to trust your word at this point in time."

"I'm sorry that you feel that way, but there was no other way since that is his job here." Carrison informs him just as stiffly. "As for this meeting, it was brought to my attention this morning that men from your ships are responsible for the destruction of a communications tower at the prison camp where they are sitting. I was also told that they are responsible for the escape of close to six hundred prisoners at that camp."

"I know nothing about any prisoners sir, only of a large number of our people that are eager to return home." Thayer informs him politely. "They were taken by force from their homes and placed on a ship that is owned by you for the express purpose of transporting slaves."

"You used our people to create mind touchers for you to control." Leyla frowns with distaste. "All of them are glad to be leaving. We will question them soon on how they were treated, and I'm sure that we will find that it was not very kindly."

Peterton glares at her while Carrison frowns. "I must insist that they be returned. They are dangerous to the government and..."

"They are Calidonian citizens taken against their will and forced to do things that go against their beliefs." Thayer states with some force cutting him off. "Should you try to take them, the Federation will be called in to settle the matter."

"There's no need for that." Peterton intercedes, losing his glare. "Return the Earth people and children that were taken with them and we'll consider the matter settled."

"That's no longer an option Mr. Peterton. They became citizens of Calidon the moment that they mated with our people and produced children. They now have refuge with their mates and will remain with them." Leyla informs him.

Carrison slams his hands down on the table and stands up glaring at her. "Then there's nothing more to discuss. Your group will be taken into custody...."

Suddenly an enormous energy surge flows through Salis as she becomes extremely frightened and she disappears. The light from the surge is so bright that it blinds them all temporarily. When it fades and their eyes have recovered, Thayer and the others discover that they are completely surrounded.

"I don't know what happened to the girl, but we'll find her soon enough." Carrison threatens and signals to the soldiers to take them.

Before any of the soldiers can move, Leyla and Thayer teleport their people to the safety of their ship. As soon as they arrive Leyla asks Sarah about Salis. "Is she on any of the ships?"

"No Leyla, she's not, and she seems to be out of my tracking range."

"Okay. Take the ships to ten miles off the stronghold, but first head in the opposite direction for about ten minutes, then turn on the scrambler and head for the stronghold."

"We're on our way now Leyla. Do you want me to use the cloak too?"

"Yes, but wait until just after you turn on the scrambler. We'll use it to further cover our trail."

Everyone goes to their cabins except for Leyla and Thayer. Leyla goes to the lounge, while Thayer goes to the bridge. Leyla looks out the window and reaches out to Salis. 'Can you hear me Salis?' she opens her mind completely and picks up on Salis' fear. 'Sweetheart, where are you?'

'I don't know mother. There are trees all around me and strange noises. I'm really scared mother.'

'I know sweetheart. Your father and I will be with you soon, I promise. Try and stay calm.'

'There's someone coming mother! I can feel them!'

Leyla can sense the terror running through Salis' mind and body, and fights her own fear for her daughter. 'All right honey, listen closely. Stand against a big tree and think of yourself as being a part of the tree. Blank out all thoughts and feelings. You know what Carrison's soldiers dress like, gently reach out and touch their mind. You'll know if its a friend or an enemy right away.'

'All right mother.'

"Sarah, how long before we reach our destination?"

"At least another twenty minutes Leyla."

"Can't we make it any sooner?"

"Not by much. We have to watch out for local air traffic since they can't see us."

"Do what you can please." she asks before leaving the lounge and going to her cabin to change her clothes. She walks in as Thayer finishes changing. "You heard."

"And saw. You handled it just fine love. She's not too far from the stronghold from what I could tell."

"What if whomever is approaching her is with Carrison? Will she be safe enough until we can reach her? I'm afraid that her fear may become too much for her to handle."

"She should be okay. How long before the ships reach the area?"

"About another eighteen minutes or so. Sarah will try for less, but she has to be careful of local traffic." Leyla begins pacing the room. "I want to port to her, but we could end up in the middle of Carrison's men."

"Sarah, how much longer?"

"Twelve minutes Thayer. I was able to speed up a little and take off a couple of minutes."

"Thank you." He looks at Leyla. "Change your clothes and then meet me in the vehicle hold." Not waiting for her response, he goes to find Stephen. He quickly explains what he has planned and gives the new codes that they would need to get the ships past the strongholds defenses. "Use the codes when you're five miles from the stronghold. They'll let you in, but keep anyone else out. Have Sarah scan the area around the stronghold for about fifteen miles. I want to know of anything unusual in the area."

"Are you taking any guards with you?"

"No, it will be better if we go in alone. If it is Carrison's men, we'll get Salis and port directly to the stronghold and meet you there."

They enter the vehicle hold and Stephen leads the way to an open speeder. The front and sides are protected by laser shielding, and the back has a small opening. "This is the fastest speeder that we have, and it's fully armed with side mounted stun cannons."

Leyla comes in and joins them. "Sarah says that we're about seven minutes away."

"Climb on." Thayer turns to Stephen. "Put everyone on alert. From now on we're on our guard." Stephen nods and steps back as Thayer gets on the speeder. Seconds later they disappear.

\* \* \*

"I know that you're there. I can feel your eyes on me." Colt Blackwood looks around him, trying to find the person staring at him. "You don't have to be afraid. I won't hurt you, I live near here."

Salis gently touches his mind again and finds only kindness and concern for her. She steps away from the tree and says a soft hello.

Colt jumps a little, he hadn't realized that she was so close. "Hi. I'm Colt. Are you lost?"

"Not really. My name is Salis. My father put this place in my memory in case I accidentally ported, so that I would be in a safe place until they could come for me."

"Why come here, why not your own home?" Colt asks in confusion. It made more sense for her to go home then to come to the mountains.

"We don't live on Earth." she tells him. "Sometimes I wish that I was still at home. The things that I've seen here since we came make me glad that we're not going to stay here. The President is an evil man, surrounded by other evil men."

"Not everyone on Earth is like him. We're hoping to get him out of the leadership really soon. Some friends of ours are trying really hard."

"My parents are trying too. There was a man that made my father really angry. He made my skin crawl whenever he looked at me or talked to me." Salis informs him.

"There's no one like that here." he assures her.

Just then a shadow passes over them and Colt spins around, pulling his knife and stepping in front of Salis to protect her. With the sun in his eyes he can only make out the shape of a tall man and a smaller one approaching them through the trees.

"Stop where you are!" Colt orders as they step closer. Though his voice is shaky and he's scared to death, he wouldn't let anything happen to Salis.

Peeking over his shoulder, Salis already senses who it is. "Father!" she cries out and rushes into Thayer's open arms.

"Are you all right little one?"

"Yes father, I'm fine. This is Colt. He's the one I felt when I was talking to mother." she tells him turning to face her new friend.

"You can put down the knife now Colt. No one's going to hurt Salis." Leyla says stepping closer so that Colt can see her clearly.

Salis looks from one to the other. "You know him mother?"

"Yes sweetheart. Colt's part of the family I told you about. Our families are very close and have been for years."

Colt looks at all three of them, unable to believe his eyes. "You're back. You're really here." he says in surprise. When Leyla nods, he rushes to her and hugs her tightly. "Thank the Great one. We didn't know if we would ever see you again."

"I'm glad to see you too." she tells him hugging him just as tightly.

"We need to get to the stronghold. The ships should be there in a few minutes." Thayer says leading the way back to the speeder and helping Salis inside. After Leyla enters, Colt climbs in last and watches the back as they head for the stronghold.

\* \* \*

"When Ali picked up on Colt's anxiety, I sent Cassie and the others to the shelter. They're on their way back up now." Logan tells Thayer and Leyla as he opens the door to the house and steps aside for Leyla and Salis to enter first.

"Has there been any trouble with the patrols?" Thayer asks leading the way into the large sitting room.

"Not much. They fly by every couple of days, but haven't tried anything yet."

"What about the people that we sent to you yesterday?" Leyla asks sitting on a love seat and hugging Salis close to her side.

"The men are a little hostile, and the women are fearful. Nightstorm doesn't think that there'll be a problem helping the women, but the men he's not too sure about."

"Have any of them given you any sign that we can't trust them if Carrison should attack?" Thayer wants to know. He would not risk his family.

"I wouldn't trust the twenty older ones. They've been under Carrison's control the longest and I'm not sure they could break their conditioning."

"Then we had better separate them from the others. If Carrison attacks we don't need to worry about trouble from within." Leyla states looking at her mate. Thayer nods, but before he can say anything more, Cassandra and the other Blackwood siblings rush into the room.

When Cassie sees Leyla she rushes forward to hug her. Leyla barely makes it to her feet before she is enveloped in the other woman's arms. "You're back. I thought that I would never see you again." she says crying and hugging Leyla tightly. Since the death of her twin, the two of them had become like sisters.

"Nothing could keep me away when I heard that you were in danger." Leyla assures her.

The other Blackwoods step forward to greet her and Thayer. Merri is the last to greet them. Leyla notices the direction of Merri's attention and brings Salis forward. Salis holds tightly onto her arm and stands partially hidden behind her, unsure of all these new people, and the love she can feel her mother has for them all.

"I'd like you all to meet our daughter Salis. Sweetheart, this is the Blackwood family. Cassie is the oldest and my closest and dearest friend. She's like a sister to me. Then there's Daniel, Davena, and Dessa. You've already met Colt." Each of them nods as they're introduced. "And this is Merri, she's Colt's twin."

The two girls look at each other and Salis finally breaks the silence between them. "Hello Merri." she says shyly. When Merri just stares at her, Salis bites her lower lip moving closer to Leyla's side and looking down at her feet.

"I dreamt about you." Merri states accusingly. Salis looks up at her startled. "Colt met you in the woods." Colt looks at his twin, not understanding her hostility towards Salis. Before he can question her about it, Nightstorm comes in.

"Your ships have arrived Starhawk."

"Thank you Nightstorm." They clasp arms in greeting and then Thayer turns to the others. "Our flagship has a surprise for you Blackwoods. Anyone care to see what it is?" The four younger ones rush from the room and out the front door.

"Salis honey, why don't you show them to the ship?" Thayer suggests and she nods before slowly joining the others.

The adults follow more slowly and Leyla smiles as she notices Logan putting his arm around Cassie's waist and her friend smiling up at him. As they near the great ship, Cassie and Daniel notice how quiet their younger siblings have gotten and look up. Both gasp as they see the cause, who is walking down the ramp.

"Da." Cassandra whispers as their father steps down and is surrounded by his younger children. Once he's done hugging and kissing each of them, Denral opens his arms to her, and Cassie rushes into them crying. They hold each other close as tears of joy run unchecked down their cheeks.

"You're alive Da, you're alive."

"Yes Cassandra Rose. Alive and getting better every second." He assures her. Of all of his children, Denral had worried most for his oldest when he had been taken. Without Leyla there to give her balance, he hadn't known if she could handle what was happening to them.

"Come inside and rest Da. Merri, run and ask Morning Star to fix some of her special healing tea and send it to the house." Cassie says remembering her father's illness. Merri rushes off not wanting to stay to close to Salis.

Just then Stephen, Aeneka and Krander step from the ship. Upon seeing Salis, Krander runs down the ramp. Seeing him, Salis cries out and flings herself into the young guards arms. Colt scowls deeply at this show of affection, not understanding why it bothered him to see them this way.

"I was worried to death about you Firepetal. Don't you ever do that to me again young lady." Krander tells her sternly completely forgetting about her new position. Someone laughs and Krander looks up to find Leyla and Thayer smiling at him. He blushes as he realizes what he had just told his Princess in front of her parents and he begins to stammer. "I mean...I..."

"Don't worry Krander, we understand. You have just as much right to worry about her as we do." Leyla tells him gently smiling even more.

Aeneka and Stephen join them and they all head to the house. As they walk Aeneka carefully looks Salis over. "Are you all right little one?"

"I'm fine grandmother. Colt kept me company until mother and father came, and I wasn't very afraid." She tells her and smiles over at Colt, only to frown when she finds him scowling at her.

While the Blackwoods are getting reacquainted, Logan and the others go into the office and close the door. "There's a large force of men to the northeast of us about ten or twelve miles. I haven't mentioned it to the others yet. I meant to tell you earlier."

"Twelve point five to be exact sir. There are three hundred men with blast cannons and sonic disrupters." Stephen informs him.

Logan nods, "From the data that Cal has, we figure that they came in small groups during the night."

"Carrison must have been planning a sneak attack the whole time we were there." Thayer says looking out the window and watching his Native American family go about their daily routines.

"Do you think that he'll take part, or stay clear of everything?" Leyla asks looking from Thayer to Logan.

"Both him and Peterton will stay well away from the fighting. My guess is that Erik Ritage will be the one leading the attack." Logan says with great contempt for the other man, and slams his fist onto the desk. He apologizes when the women jump a little at his show of anger.

"How soon before they attack?" Cassandra asks walking quietly into the room and going to stand beside Logan and wrapping her arm around his waist.

"What are you doing here? You should be..."

"I felt your anger and frustration." she tells him shrugging her shoulders.

"Soon. They'll want to attack before they think that we'll get here." Thayer tells her. He then explains what had happened that morning.

"But you're already here and if they attack..."

"Then they'll be attacking the royal family of Calidon and declaring war on Calidon itself." Aeneka finishes.

"And if we cloak the ships until the last minute, they won't know that we're already here until its too late." Leyla puts in and then speaks quickly to Stephen in their private language.

Stephen nods and looks out the window for a few seconds before looking back at her. "Sarah has all the ships cloaked and their shields are extended over the stronghold at maximum power."

"We should move the women, children, and the sick into the ships." Aeneka suggests to Thayer and Logan. "If any of the soldiers should happen to get inside, at least they'd all be safe."

"That sounds like a good idea. We should probably go ahead and take the ones you sent too, just to be on the safe side." Logan adds looking at Thayer for confirmation.

"Let's do it then, and get everyone moved. I want everyone ready when the time comes." Thayer says and leads the way out of the office. Everyone would help in the transfer. There would be no one left to be in harms way should the soldiers get past their primary defenses.

Thayer wished that he didn't have to put his father's people into such danger. He knew though that they would have it no other way. They protected their own, no matter the cost to themselves.

# Chapter XXII

Nightstorm and the other warriors go to check the progress of Ritage and his army. When they return, Nightstorm relays the information they had gathered. "They've split up, and it appears that they are planning to attack from all directions." He looks at the map of the stronghold and the surrounding area and points to each of the areas that a group was approaching from. "Right now they're all moving slowly because the land is too rough to travel quickly if you don't know it. It will take them at least an hour to get to a point where they can begin to pick up their pace. From that point, they should be here in about two hours."

"So we've got roughly three hours before they get here." Thayer looks at the map closely. "That should give us enough time to get ready for them. Which group is Ritage with?"

"He's with the group coming up through the river pass here." And Nightstorm points to the area.

"Are there any practice traps set up in any of the areas that they'll be coming through?"

"Yes. Each area has at least four pits, a dozen snares, and at least as many snap poles."

"Well that should help to thin them out a bit. Do we have any immobilizing pads?"

"Yes. I had Cal transport the half dozen crates that I had left. They're all singles, but there are twenty-five in each crate." Logan tells him.

"All right, let's get some guards and start placing them around the stronghold, about a hundred feet out from the ships."

For the next hour and a half they conceal one hundred and fifty immobilizing pads. Once they were activated, anyone stepping on one would be unable to move until the pads were deactivated. After everyone is clear of the pads, Thayer mentally activates them and joins the others inside the walls of the stronghold.

"Everything is set in here Thayer." Leyla tells him as he comes in. "The people we sent here are secure on one of the other ships. I had Sarah put all the males asleep to be sure that they didn't cause any trouble. They won't wake up until everything is settled here."

"Good. The areas out past the ships are ready too. The pads should cut down the number we'll have to deal with."

Brock ports himself in front of them. "Sarah says that Ritage will be here in less then an hour. She's also picked up several patrol speeders headed this way from the city. They'll get here shortly after Ritage."

"Damn. Carrison must have realized that we had headed here. Has there been any communication between Ritage and the speeders?"

"No. Sarah's been jamming their signals since we got here. Ritage doesn't know about them yet. With any luck he won't notice them until its too late. She is letting him communicate with his group here though. She didn't want to give our presence away."

"Good. Have her ready to contact the Federation at the first shot. Remind her to let a few shots through the shields so that there will be no doubt of the attack. She'll know which ones she can let through safely." Leyla tells him. He quickly nods and ports back to the ship.

Forty minutes later, Ritage and his men are spotted. The attack begins and Sarah allows five blaster bolts through before closing the shields. A few sheds and a hover car are destroyed by the bolts and large holes are made in the ground near the house.

"It's time we got rid of those blasters sweetheart." Thayer says as several bolts hit the shield. Leyla concentrates on the small blasters, while Thayer deals with the larger ones. Once the blasters are taken care of Leyla and Thayer laugh at the expressions on the men's faces as their blasters disappeared.

"They should be advancing on the pads now. Once they've thinned out a bit more we'll send out some of the guards to fight hand to hand." Thayer says. "We won't send out all of them at once though. We need to keep them engaged as long as possible, for the Federation to monitor the situation and see the damage done and the danger to the people."

"How long will that take?" Leyla asks with a slight frown.

"They should already be monitoring." Logan assures her. "I warned them that if they received any messages from this area, that they were to act without delay."

"How long will it take them to reach us?"

"Not long. There are three planet cruisers already in the area that have been keeping watch on Earth. They've been trained to act in just such a case. They'll should be here within two hours."

'Leyla, Sarah says that the speeders will be here in about thirty minutes.'

'Thank you Selina. Tell Stephen and Krander to have the guards ready to be ported out for hand to hand combat.'

'They'll be ready in five minutes Leyla.'

Leyla looks at the others. "Selina says that the speeders will be here in about thirty minutes."

"We'll have to be ready for them." Thayer says then cocks his head to the side and listens. "They've reached the immobilizing pads."

Leyla, Logan, and Nightstorm concentrate on the areas with the pads. They each search for Ritage among those caught on the pads. Logan is the first to spot him several feet in front of the pads and looking back at his trapped men. He growls low in his throat, which causes the others to follow his mind path to Ritage, just as he knocks him into a tree.

"No Logan!" Thayer blocks Logan so that he can no longer reach Ritage. "We'll deal with him later!"

Logan glares at Thayer, but then regains control of himself and nods. "I want him when this is over Thayer. He life-ended someone very special and he must pay for taking her life."

"Show me." Thayer orders him softly looking into his friend's eyes, waiting for Logan's assent before looking into his memories. He sees

Hillary Quinn as Logan had seen her the last twenty hours of her life. He sees the girl's own memories also in his mind and withdraws. "You can deal with him in whatever way you feel will avenge her death. I won't interfere, but it must wait until after the Federation has seen what is happening." Thayer tells him and Logan nods his agreement.

"The guards are ready Thayer. We need to port them into position. Ritage and his men are on the move again."

"Okay, you do half, and I'll do the other. If any go down, we'll port them back to the ship and replace them with someone else."

They begin porting the guards so that each one is in front of a soldier. By being ported in, the guards have the advantage of surprise for several seconds. When the soldiers recover from this shock, the fighting beings in earnest.

\* \* \*

The fighting has gone on for almost two hours when six Federation battle speeders appear. They hover over the fighting for several seconds, before someone speaks over a loudspeaker.

"Earth Security Forces. This is Federation Security, and you will stand down from your attack at once. Your President will shortly be taken into custody for this attack against the Calidonian royal family and their people." The voice insists.

The fighting stops and Leyla and Thayer teleport their guards back to the ships, and Ritage glares up at the battle speeders.

"You are mistaken. The royal family of Calidon is not here. The people in this stronghold are rebels and dangerous to Earth's security. You have no jurisdiction here." he yells up at them.

The gates to the stronghold open up, and Leyla, Thayer, and Logan step out, followed closely by Nightstorm. As soon as they stop, the ships are uncloaked.

"You are quite mistaken Mr. Ritage. We have been here since early this morning. We arrived shortly after President Carrison attempted to detain us in his compound." Thayer says in contempt. He looks up at the battle speeder. "As King of Calidon and a royal Prince of Manchon, I hereby claim blood-rite to this man Erik Ritage. He willfully and without cause shot and killed Hillary Quinn, a sister of Manchon." he waits for a reply to his demand.

"You have proof, or witnesses that this man committed this crime?"

"Yes. Logan Knightrunner and Cassandra Blackwood are witnesses to the crime. Both have memory of the deed being done. She was shot in the back while delivering a gift to Miss Blackwood from my wife." again he waits for a reply.

"I see. We know of Logan Knightrunner. Do you confirm this claim against Mr. Ritage Lieutenant Commander Knightrunner?"

"I confirm it Lieutenant." Logan says watching Ritage glare at him.

"Very well. By the Galactic Federation's agreement with your planets, you have the blood-rite your Majesty."

Thayer nods and Leyla ports four guards around Ritage. Once the guards have him secure, Thayer nods towards the stronghold. "Take him inside. Nightstorm will show you where to place him."

Leyla then quickly disarms and immobilized the soldiers so that they will not give the Federation men any trouble when they land to take them into custody. They would then be loaded onto the transports and taken back to the city.

\* \* \*

At the Presidential compound, Saitun Katmen carefully works his way quietly towards Carrison's office. He can hear the resistance to the Federation forces that had arrived a few minutes after he had entered the building. He was taking a big chance in seeking his revenge against Carrison, but if everything worked out, no one would ever know that he had been there.

Stunner in hand, he reaches Carrison's office, and slips inside undetected and quickly disables the rooms monitors. For several moments he watches as Tomas Carrison and Erik Peterton destroy the information that could be used against them.

Knowing that the Federation troops would soon be entering the building, Saitun raises his stunner and fires at Peterton. As he falls to the floor, Carrison spins around, searching the room. Saitun steps out of the shadows his gun trained on Carrison.

"Afternoon Tomas. Destroying evidence again I see."

"Katmen!" Carrison gasps in shock. "But you're dead. Peterton told me that..."

"Yes well, Peterton is unable to explain why and how I've returned from the dead." Saitun's smile holds no humor. "It's over Tomas. In more ways then one for you. Federation troops are all over this compound, and will soon be in this office."

Carrison moves slowly towards his desk hoping to get to his hand blaster. "They have no reason to attack us like this Saitun. We've done nothing to warrant such an action from the Federation."

"Haven't you?" Saitun asks knowing why the other man was trying to reach his desk. "Attempted murder of a future leader of a neutral planet isn't excuse enough for this assault?" Saitun asks knowing that the charge alone wouldn't constitute this type of assault. "No, you're right, that isn't enough for this type of attack. But then, attacking the entire royal family of Calidon is." he let's this sink in for a few seconds. "If that isn't enough, then there's the murder of the crowned royal Princess of that same family twenty-one years ago, that just might justify this assault. The statute of limitations doesn't run out on such a crime with the Federation you know."

His last statement stops Carrison as he finally reaches his desk. Carrison wonders how Saitun could possibly know of his part in Aeneka Katmen's death. He had made sure that the man that had helped him, followed soon after her. "That's absurd Saitun. I hadn't been anywhere near your wife when she took ill or when she finally died."

"True enough, you weren't, but the man you used had been. It's well known to the Federation that you used the man for certain work, and that he followed your direct orders. You made one fatal mistake though, and that was in not checking that there weren't any records of what he had done for you and when." Saitun watches as his statement causes Carrison another shock.

Carrison reaches for the hand blaster attached to the back of his chair. Before he can touch it, a sharp pain enters his head and he clutches it crying out in pain and collapsing into the chair.

"You won't be spending any time on some penal planet Tomas."

Saitun tells him walking closer to the desk. "You're going to die right here where you ordered the deaths of innocent people, and ruined so many lives. The shame and humiliation you caused countless women, and little girls. Most of all, for the death of my beloved Aeneka who never did anything to hurt anyone in her life. I don't need to know why you killed her anymore. All I needed to know was that you did it." Hearing men coming, Saitun slips back into the shadows. "Good-bye Tomas. May your time in hell cause you to suffer greatly for all you have done and all that you have taken from me and mine." Concentrating all of his mental energies on the other man's brain, Saitun drives it through his skull. The other man's eyes turn white as his brain is liquefied within.

Just before men enter the office, Saitun uses the last of his strength to port himself back to his ship that is hidden just outside the compound walls. He waits a couple of minutes to gain a little strength back and then leaves. As he lifts off, he hopes that when he reaches the stronghold, that he will find his family alive and safe. He wouldn't ever tell them about what he had done before he arrived. No one would ever know that he had deliberately used his abilities to end another's life. He just hoped that he could one day forget, and that the Great One would forgive him this sin, because he wasn't sure that he could ever forgive himself. He vows to the Great One that he would never again use his abilities in such a way again. Until he died, he would use his gifts to heal, never to take another life.

* * *

Saitun reaches the stronghold as the Federation troops are loading the last of Ritage's men into a prison transport. He goes to stand behind Thayer and Logan as they talk with the Captain of the patrol.

"No we do not want the Federation to handle these men." Thayer tells the Lieutenant. "If you check with the Federation Council, you will see that as of today, Calidon and Manchon hold the governing power of Earth."

"That may be your Majesty, but until we have confirmation, we have to keep them in our custody."

"Then you will have to do that here Lieutenant Saris." Saitun states stepping forward so that the other man can see him clearly. The Lieutenant salutes and stands straighter. "Relax man. Now, I suggest that you get one of your people to contact the G.F.O.P. council before trying to take those men off planet. I'm sure that you can find someplace suitable on the planet to secure for your use."

"Yes sir Captain Katmen sir." Saris turns to one of his privates and Thayer looks at Saitun.

'We weren't expecting you until tomorrow.'

'I was closer then I realized when I spoke to you.'

Thayer frowns, but before he can question him, the lieutenant turns back to them with a frown on his own face.

"We should hear from the council in a few hours." he tells them looking at Saitun. "At 1630, President Carrison was found dead in his office. From the preliminary examination, it appears that his brain was liquefied within his skull. Captain Katmen, I must ask where you were at 1630 this afternoon." he looks Saitun in the eye.

"I was outside the Presidential compound Lieutenant." Saitun tells him without hesitation.

"Lieutenant Saris, just where is this line of questioning going?" Thayer asks drawing the other man's attention from Saitun.

"The medics say that they can find no trace of a sonic device having been used your Majesty. There were no other telepaths in the area capable of causing such an injury." Saris explains and looks back at Saitun. "We'll need to see your flight logs for when you arrived and left the compound sir."

"Very well Lieutenant." Saitun raises his arm and speaks into his wrist unit. "S-two, transfer data from location files this date, from 1300 to 1900 hours, to the Federation cruiser at this location." he drops his arm and smiles slightly at the lieutenant. "You'll have all the information within a few moments. I'll tell you what those records will show. At 1320 I passed Saturn base ten, at 1520 I passed moon base one and stopped at Robinson space station to refuel. At 1547 I left the station and flew straight to where my former home was located, arriving at 1610. I hovered there for nine minutes and then flew to the compound, arriving at 1627, landing outside the compound. I was there for approximately six minutes watching Federation troops secure the compound. At 1632 I left the compound and came straight here, arriving at 1853, seven minutes ago." Saitun finishes and raises his eyebrows as if to say does that cover everything?.

"Thank you sir." Saris nods. His private returns and hands him a computer board. He looks at it and then hands it back dismissing the private. "Everything you've told me is on record sir, and is confirmed by your ships computer system. I'm sorry that I had to question you about this sir, but I had no other choice."

"I thought that it would confirm things for you. Now if you will excuse us Lieutenant. It's been a long time since I saw my daughter and I would like to do so with her husband present. Might I suggest that you take your prisoners to the Presidential compound until you hear from the council. Good evening Lieutenant Saris."

With that Saitun turns and begins walking towards the stronghold with Logan and Thayer on either side of him. They stop near his ship and Saitun punches in an order for S-two to scramble the cloaked listening devices that Saris had put in place around the stronghold and Calidonian ships. They continue into the stronghold and are met by Leyla.

They stop in front of each other and Saitun looks Leyla over before stepping forward and hugging her close. After a few minutes, he lets her go and steps back a little to really look at her.

"You look so much like your mother. I wish that she could be here to see us now."

Leyla smiles at him mysteriously, then looks to her left. Saitun follows her look and notices an older woman standing with Stephen Seven and a young girl of about twelve or thirteen. He looks back at Leyla and then back at the woman and stares at her for several moments before slowly walking towards her.

Aeneka stands as still as a statue, never taking her eyes from his face as he slowly approaches her and stops two feet from her. After a few more seconds she steps closer to him and slowly reaches up to touch his cheek softly. A familiar current of energy flows between them, causing

Aeneka to smile as, once more their minds are linked. 'It's really me my love.'

'How can this be? I helped you to place your essence in the box. I saw you within it.'

Aeneka turns a little and holds out her hand to Salis. Saitun watches as the girl takes her hand and steps up to stand in front of him. "Saitun, may I present to you our granddaughter, Salis Aeneka Chandelle Starhawk, crowned Princess of Calidon, and the one responsible for my return to the physical plain."

Saitun looks from one to the other and then kneels down in front of Salis. Taking her free hand in both of his, he kisses it and then places her fingers to his temple. "Welcome to my family little one, and thank you for the gift of my heart, which has been lost to me for so long." he tells her and opens his mind to her.

Salis blinks a couple of times and then takes Saitun's hand and places it to her own temple. She shares with him all that she was and all that she has become. Before he draws his hand away, she touches his mind once more and opens it further than it was before.

'What have you done to me little one?'

'I know that you and grandmother couldn't be lifemated before, and how sad it made both of you. If you want to you can be lifemated now.'

Saitun looks at her for several more seconds, then hugs her close to him. "Thank you little one. It is a gift that I will accept with pleasure." He releases her and stands to face Aeneka. This time he takes her into his arms and holds her tightly to him, kissing her temple.

Wanting to give them a little privacy, Salis goes to stand with parents and Logan. Leyla wraps her arms around her and smiles over her head at the couple once again able to touch and feel each other after nearly three decades.

After several moments, Saitun releases Aeneka, but keeps her close to his side as he faces his daughter and Thayer. "We have some serious matters to discuss over the next couple of hours. We need to have everything planned out when Saris hears from the council." he looks directly at Thayer. "When did you contact the Federation about gaining governing power of Earth?"

"Just before Leyla and I left Earth. I filed for the governorship under Manchon claims. Logan and I feel that a good number of the Earth's population has ties to Manchon, and possibly to Calidon as well. We have records for several families including your own, that show a blood tie. Since most of those ties are to upper Majichonie society, it makes the ties and the reason for our governorship more than justified."

"But will they accept the claim? We still don't have the signatures from the hundred families we need." Logan reminds him.

"We won't need them. We've got three hundred Calidonians to make our claim legal and binding. Even though they'll be returning to Calidon, over a hundred and seventy will be leaving extended family who are now considered Calidonians by marriage, and entitled to our protection." Leyla reminds them.

"Let's take this inside." Saitun says turning with Aeneka to go into the house. "We need to get everything down in writing so that there will be no doubt that we can prove our claim." He looks back at Leyla, "You'll need to get those people to sign that they want the Calidonian and Majichonie governments to protect their mates' families, as is their right."

"I'll have Sarah print up the proper forms and have them distributed." she agrees as they enter the house.

They go into the sitting room where Denral and Cassandra are waiting with Selina, Brock, and Trocon. Before sitting down Leyla suggests that Salis goes to stay with the younger Blackwoods. "You can tell them some more about Calidon."

Salis looks at her and bites her lower lip. 'But Merri doesn't like me mother. When she looks at me it's almost as if she hates me.' 'I'm sure that she doesn't hate you honey. I think that she's just not sure about you yet. Just try to be her friend, I'm sure that in time you two will be the best of friends.'

Salis shrugs her shoulders, but goes to find the young Blackwoods. She was sure that her mother was wrong, that for some reason Merri Blackwood hated her and didn't want her around. But she was willing to try to be her friend since it was so important to her new mother. At least Colt liked her. He had liked her right away. It still surprised her that he had been so willing to risk his life to protect her when her mother and father had shown up and they couldn't really see them. He had even gone so far as to put himself in front of her so that should there be an attack, they would have to go through him to get to her.

After checking the rest of the house, she goes outside to look for them. She finds Davena and Dessa helping an older woman prepare a meal and decides to help them.

\* \* \*

"We will need any records that you have on the Majichonie bloodlines that are on Earth, and where they can be located. If we can prove that they are spread out over the entire planet, and don't want to be moved, it will strengthen our claim even more." Saitun says looking from Thayer to Logan and back again.

"All my records were lost when they broke into my apartment." Thayer admits with a frown.

"Cal still has our original files in his memory, along with an updated file from the one you lost." Logan assures Thayer. "I've had him continue the search and update it as often as he can without it being traced back to us. We have close to four hundred names now and information enough on at least half of them."

"Can we send them a message through their personal computers?" Cassie asks thinking that they could use Cal, Ali, and Sarah to send out the messages. "Tell them that they can claim your protection and be guaranteed an easier way of life without having to pay for it with their children or unreasonable services."

"That could work if we could do it without the Federation finding out." Denral says nodding his head in the direction of the cruiser sitting outside the stronghold gates.

"I'm sure that Sarah and Cal could do it. Possibly Ali as well. They're all capable of blocking Federation signals." Logan agrees. "We can have them do several at once so as to hit as many as possible in the time we have. The three of them should be able to get at least a hundred and fifty or sixty done in time for our meeting with the lieutenant, and some kind of answer as well."

"Let's get them working on it then. We still need to figure out what laws will be used and how we'll enforce them." Saitun tells them. "We have to prove that the people of Earth won't be suffering under the new leadership. If we can't, they may dismiss our claim and take over the planet as an ungovernable."

"I think that we should use the laws that we have on Calidon and Manchon. They're broad enough that they won't restrict them any more then they do us." Thayer suggests. "In fact, it will give them more freedom then they've had in a very long time."

"Do we have a copy of Manchon's laws?" Leyla asks him.

"What about the law that prohibits anyone from leaving the planet Thayer? Unless Niccara has changed it, that wouldn't be one to include when we submit the laws to the Federation." Logan reminds him.

"It will be changed, so we'll just omit it when we submit our laws to them. We'll do the same with any other laws that will be changed in time. They don't know what our laws are, so there shouldn't be any problems." Thayer says to Logan and then looks over at Leyla and answers her question. "Cal will have Manchon's laws on file. When we came to Earth, we wrote them all down so that we would have a part of Manchon with us all the time. Though it wasn't really necessary, we had already memorized them long before we left Manchon. It made us feel closer to home."

"Let's have Sarah and Cal combine them and see what they can come up with." Aeneka puts in still holding onto Saitun's hand. "They can give us a good idea of what we have to work with. They can also weed through and take out any duplicate laws so that we don't repeat ourselves. When we get the alliance going, we can implement new laws that will be used by all that join the alliance."

Leyla and Logan instruct Sarah and Cal in what they want, and ask them to have it completed as soon as possible. There is a knock on the sitting room door, and Salis, Davena, and Dessa carry in the evening meal, bringing their conversation to an end for the time being. The girls set up the food on the long side table and then leave. Salis stops to give her parents and grandparents each a hug, before following Davena and Dessa back outside.

"Salis expresses her feelings very openly considering all that she's been through." Saitun says as he watches her leave the room. "I'm glad that you were able to help her and that you brought her into our family."

Leyla smiles at him as she fixes her plate. "I don't think either of us had any other choice. Before we ever reached Calidon I dreamed of Salis and she dreamed of me. Though I hate to say it, I think that everything that she went through was already planned. I wish there had been some other way for her to come into our family without having to lose her own."

Saitun stops filling his plate to look at her. "You dreamed of each other before you ever met?"

"Yeah, and even in the dreams Salis referred to me as her matima. It wasn't until we were closer to Calidon that I told mother about the dreams and she told me what matima meant. When she did, I just knew that Salis was meant to be my daughter." Leyla tells him and then takes her plate and goes to sit down. "While we were at the Presidential compound, she experienced energy surges like I did when I was her age. From the things she has done since they started, we're sure that she's an elite."

Saitun and the others finish filling their plates and then sit down. They talk while they eat, trying hard not to think about all that still had to be done to help the people of Earth. There was no telling how long it was going to take to heal the mental and physical abuses that had occurred over many years. The planet as a whole would have to be treated, not just those with psi abilities.

Once they finish eating, and after Leyla and Cassie see to the children, they finish their conversation about how to deal with the Federation. It is agreed that someone would have to take the physical governorship since Leyla and Thayer had to return to Calidon.

"I suggest that Saitun and Aeneka become the governors." Trocon says looking at the couple. "They represent both Manchon and Calidon, and both of them have dealt with the Federation before. I think that the Federation would also be less likely to try to pull anything over on Saitun since he knows how they operate."

Saitun and Aeneka look at each other. It would be a challenge, but one that they would welcome. Neither of them felt the need to leave Earth again, and Leyla no longer needed them to guide her. She had proven herself capable of handling the position she had been trained for.

"We'll do everything that we can to bring the people to the point where they can trust each other again. History will show that though we went through a lot to get there, we finally found a way to live in peace and harmony with each other and our world." Saitun says agreeing to his and Aeneka's taking the governorship. "It may take a while, but it will happen."

# Epilogue

All of the men that had been with Erik Ritage during the attack of the stronghold are taken into custody by the Federation troops, and removed from the site within a couple of hours. Before the Captain of the troops can leave, Thayer has him arrange a meeting with the local Federation representative to discuss Earth's future.

After establishing their legal claim to provide protection to the people of Earth, Leyla and Thayer begin helping the ones most abused by Carrison and his followers. Some of the women and girls that were taken are able to return to their families, but still others, who have no family left or can not bare to face them, are taken in by many of the different Native American tribes. They would help them to deal with all that has happened to them, and help them to relearn their value as human beings that are loved and cared for, and deserving of such.

The men that can be helped to overcome their sense of anger and guilt for what they were made to do, are given the chance to do whatever they feel is necessary for them to feel good about themselves once again. They will receive counseling and training to help them deal with the rest of society as normally as possible. When they are ready, they will be offered positions as protectors of Earth and her people.

The men that can not be helped, and that may be a danger to themselves as well as to others, would be removed. They would be placed on a world where they would have to fend for themselves and decide how they would live or die. Only a select few would know on what world these men would be placed to insure that no other race could use or manipulate them. They could not be allowed to endanger the lives of innocent people because of their refusal to be helped. As time passes they would be checked on, and be given the opportunity to return to society if they can show that they are capable of doing so for the benefit of all mankind.

The children that were held captive have their minds wiped clean of the horrors that they have been put through. Whenever possible, they are returned to their parents. If that isn't possible they are placed with couples that have lost a child, and who will give them the love and protection that they need. They are given memories that will allow them to grow up and lead normal lives without fear of what they went through in the past.

Erik Peterton is taken into custody for crimes against Earth and the Federation of Planets. The records taken from the President's office clarify that the charges of conspiracy and slavery against him are valid, and he is removed from Earth to stand trial before a Federation judicial system.

No evidence is found as to who or what had killed President Carrison. There were no energy traces man-made or psi, that could lead to the guilty party. Saitun is questioned twice more and then left alone when Thayer files a formal complaint. With no other leads the matter is finally dropped.

*  *  *

After dealing with Erik Ritage, Logan and Cassie leave for Manchon, where they will discuss with the Queen and her council the Telepathic Alliance that Leyla and Thayer feel is necessary to protect their people from further abuse. As soon as Earth is more settled, Leyla and Thayer plan to stop at Manchon to visit his mother and find out Manchon's position, before going on to Panthera to discuss the Alliance in more depth.

Saitun and Aeneka would stay on Earth until the Alliance is well established, and then hand over the governorship to someone else.

Until then, they will be the governors of Earth and help the people out of the blackness that Carrison had created.

The Blackwoods ready themselves to travel with Leyla and Thayer to Manchon where Cassie and Logan would be lifemated. Their lifemating would take place after the decision is made on whether or not the Majichonie would join the Alliance or not. Preparing to leave, Denral Blackwood feels a sense of going home that he doesn't fully understand. He also has the feeling that he will soon find something that was lost to him long before his birth.

Merri Blackwood is in constant conflict with her mind and body. She still does not understand why she fears Colt's growing relationship with Salis, or why she dislikes the other girl so much. Since they had met, Salis had tried to be her friend, but for some reason Merri's mind would not let her accept her kindness. She is so confused by her conflict, that she doesn't see that her nonacceptance is causing Salis pain, and that pain is slowly driving her twin away from her little by little.

Leyla's main thought through all of this is for her people, and what the Federation will think of the Alliance they are trying to put together. They all hope that the Federation will not see it as a threat, but as a way for the people with psi abilities to protect themselves from being used for personal gain or oppression of another living being that doesn't believe the same.

They would make sure that no one went through what the people of Earth and Calidon have been put through ever again. With the Great One's blessing, they would not have to use their gifts to make sure that didn't happen.